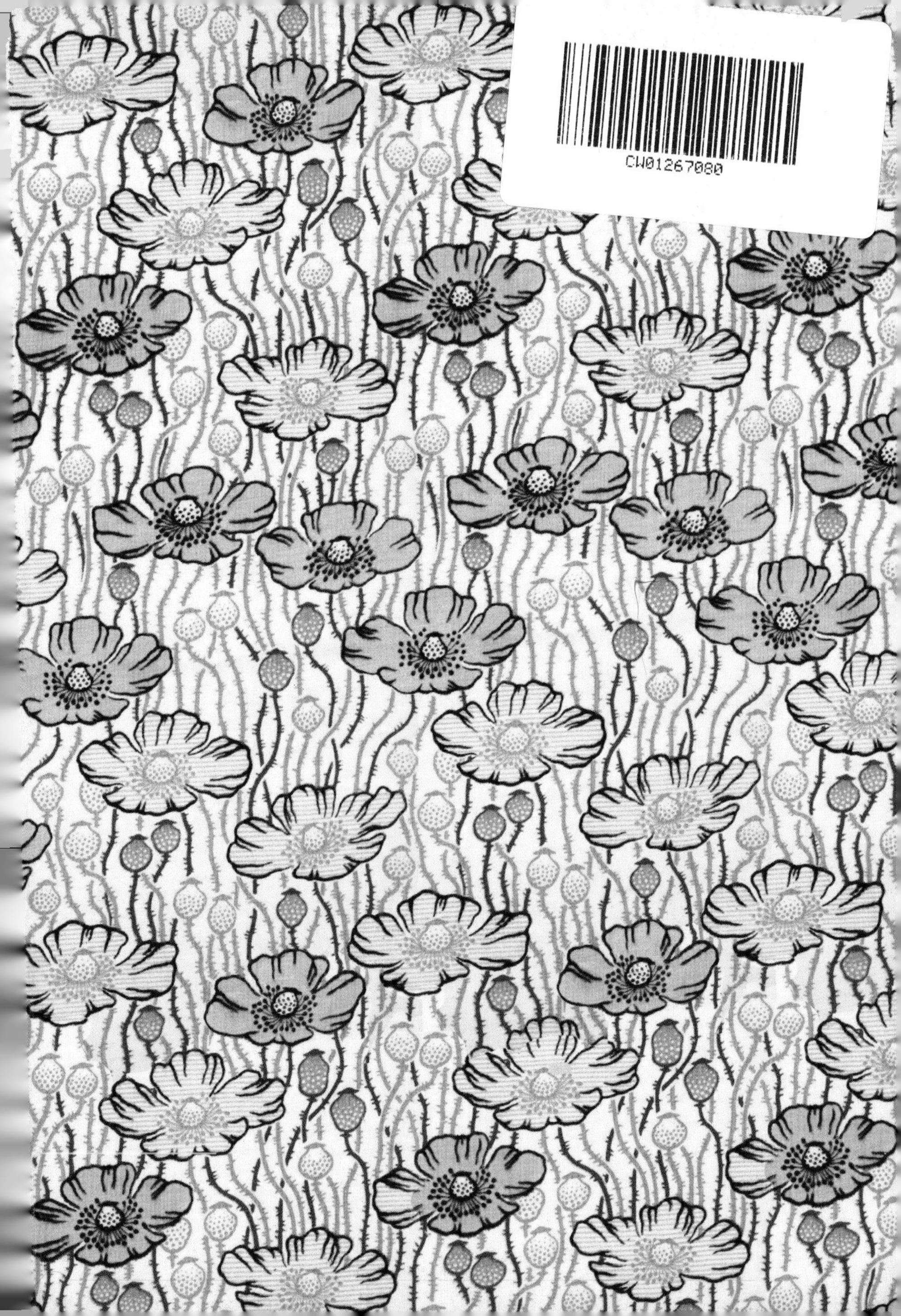

THE CALL

Persephone Book N° 129
Published by Persephone Books Ltd 2018

First published in 1924 by G Allen & Unwin

Preface © Elizabeth Day

Endpapers taken from 'Poppyland',
a duplex-printed cotton designed in 1904 and
manufactured for Liberty in 1912 © V & A

Typeset in ITC Baskerville by
Keystroke, Wolverhampton

Printed and bound in Germany by
GGP Media GmbH, Poessneck

978 191 0263 198

Persephone Books Ltd
59 Lamb's Conduit Street
London WC1N 3NB
020 7242 9292

www.persephonebooks.co.uk

THE CALL

by

EDITH AYRTON ZANGWILL

with a preface by

ELIZABETH DAY

PERSEPHONE BOOKS
LONDON

PREFACE

In 1920, while she was working on the novel that would be published four years later as *The Call*, Edith Ayrton Zangwill (1875-1945) wrote to her friend Nina Salaman that her central topic, women's suffrage, was 'too remote to be topical & too recent to be innocuous.'

When the book was published in 1924, six years had passed since the Representation of the People Act had enfranchised property-owning women over the age of 30 in England, Wales, Scotland and Ireland. Britain was still recovering from the ravages of World War I. The hard-fought battles of the suffragette years – the protest marches, the arrests, the hunger strikes, the militant action that involved everything from bricks through windows to cut telephone wires and setting cricket pavilions alight – were over.

So was Edith Zangwill correct in her assessment that the struggle for the women's vote was neither topical nor innocuous? I think she was being too hard on herself. For *The Call* is not just a novel about suffragettes. It is, rather, a study of what it means to be a woman caught between the competing and sometimes conflicting demands of career, love, family and political engagement. In this respect, its themes are timeless. It is a quintessentially modern novel, that just so happens to have been published in 1924.

Covering the years 1909-18, it tells the story of Ursula Winfield, a brilliant young woman seeking to make her mark on the male-dominated world of science, despite the fact that her gender denies her fellowship of the Chemical Society which admits only men. At the start of *The Call*, Ursula has not given much thought to the fact that women are also denied the vote. Her world, as she tells her mentor Vernon Smee, 'is divided up into animal, vegetable and mineral; not into men and women. The difference between the sexes seems to me so small in such a wonderful, complex universe. Why, I should never think of the subject, only suddenly, when I am quite happy with my experiments, I come crash into some absurd artificial sex barrier – as though my work wore petticoats!' When Professor Smee asks her if she is a suffragist, Ursula says she is not: 'I utterly and entirely disapprove of them. Their street rows and interruptions at public meetings are scandalous.'

Over the next 400 pages Edith Zangwill charts Ursula's gradual conversion to the Cause. She plots the trajectory of her radicalisation from distracted scholar to ardent suffragette with careful nuance, so that the reader comes to see – as Ursula does – that it is the only possible course of action for this engaged, intellectually able young woman.

To begin with she is caught between two worlds – the Edwardian gentility of parties, femininity and courtship on the one hand; the militancy and aggression of a fervently-held political cause on the other. She reacts only superficially, and views the suffragettes in the particular idiom of her social class and upbringing: unconsciously, she is aping the reactions of the male society in which she has been brought up. But one day (it is July 1909) a suffragist pamphlet is pressed into her hands, and from this point onwards Ursula applies her interrogatory mind to the issue.

Slowly she begins to make the Cause her own. And she is finally convinced when she finds herself in court, sitting in on the case of a prostitute and her young daughter 'of nine or ten' who has been sexually assaulted by a client. The leniency of the three-month sentence passed down by the magistrate, compared to a twelve-month sentence for a man who has stolen a pair of boots, horrifies her. She begins to see that the suffragettes were right: 'it was the law that was insane, or rather the lawmakers. . . . The suffragettes were right. There was some connection between such things and the Vote.'

It is after this incident that *The Call* really hits its stride as a suffragette novel. Edith Zangwill painstakingly recounts Ursula's first encounter with the 'Leader' at her headquarters; her reluctant agreement to be a speaker; the long train journeys she undertakes to spread the message; the effort required to muster up enough energy to speak to large gatherings of people; the dispiriting cold suppers offered by well-meaning local hosts; and the inability of her family and her lover to understand Ursula's new-found zealotry. Finally, in November 1910, she witnesses the police knocking down an elderly woman at a protest and 'nothing before had ever fired Ursula with such an irresistible passion for Women's

Suffrage, with such a burning faith in the value of militancy. The Cause, from being an intellectual desirability, suddenly became a religion. Militancy was no longer tactics; it was martyrdom.'

The struggle for the vote is only one of the many themes that run through the book. An equally crucial one is the struggle of a woman scientist to be treated as equal by contemporary male scientists. The details were closely based on the life of Edith Zangwill's stepmother Hertha Ayrton (1854-1923). (She was recently chosen as one of the ten most influential women in science by the Royal Society.) Sarah Marks – she gave herself the name Hertha – was born into a Jewish family living in Portsea. After the death of her father, a jeweller, she was sent to London to be educated and there was taken under the wing of the educator and artist Barbara Bodichon. Hertha spent some years supporting her family by teaching, and then applied to the newly-founded Girton College, Cambridge. She went up in 1876 to read mathematics, although physics was her main interest. At Girton she constructed a sphygmomanometer (pulse recorder) and founded the Girton fire brigade. After Cambridge, she went to William Ayrton's evening classes in electricity at Finsbury Technical College, published articles in various scientific periodicals on the subject of the 'hissing' of an electric arc (which she traced to the reaction of oxygen with carbon) and in 1899 presented a paper on the subject to the Institution of Electrical Engineers, and became its first female member – quite an accomplishment, given that the second woman was not admitted until 1958. In 1906, she was awarded the Royal

Society's Hughes Medal for her work on the electric arc. This time it took 102 years for another woman to win the same medal again.

Hertha's husband William Ayrton was a scientist working in the field of electricity – an 'electrician' in the parlance of the time – who was admirably supportive of his wife's work, indeed Hertha's biographer Evelyn Sharp commented that 'Will', as he was known, had 'an exceptional point of view about women':

> His belief in the right of women to equality of opportunity with men was as important in the husband of a woman like Hertha as it was then rare among men of science. From the first he recognised Hertha's unusual ability, and he never failed to encourage her in her scientific work. What was still more remarkable, while welcoming her co-operation if this happened to be of advantage to them both, he always insisted on her pursuing her own line of research whenever possible, and making her own experiments.

He had also supported his first wife, Matilda Chaplin Ayrton (1846-83). She had been a doctor, one of the 'Edinburgh seven' who, along with Sophia Jex-Blake, battled for the right for women to qualify (a right that was lost in 1873 and not gained for many years). Among other things she opened a school for midwives in Japan, where Will Ayrton had worked for several years, being known there as the founder of electrical engineering. Matilda died young of tuberculosis –

leaving an eight-year-old daughter, Edith or 'Edie' Chaplin Ayrton. Hertha and 'Will' Ayrton's courtship began in Finsbury and 'revolved around her critical proof-reading of his Practical Electricity' (ODNB). After their marriage in 1885 they lived in a four-storey terraced house at 41 Norfolk Square, Paddington (it has a Blue Plaque); here there was a laboratory where one imagines the young Edie frequently saw her stepmother dressed in precisely the sort of garb later worn by Ursula Winfield.

Hertha Ayrton's frustrations with the overwhelmingly male-dominated scientific sphere of her day (she was refused election to the Royal Society because she was a married woman) brought her into contact with the suffragettes. She wrote to *The Times*, asserting the right of her acquaintance, Marie Curie, to be regarded as the sole discoverer of radium after the newspaper assigned credit to her husband. Subsequently, she became one of the most generous financial backers of the Women's Social and Political Union, the leading militant organisation campaigning for women's suffrage from 1903-17. She also 'laundered' the WSPU's money through her personal bank account when it appeared the union's funds were about to be sequestered, and went on several suffragette marches.

Yet arguably her most significant role came during the operation of the notorious 'Cat and Mouse' Act of 1913, under which suffragette prisoners on hunger strike were released, only to be incarcerated again when they had sufficiently recovered. A few of the hunger strikers, including Emmeline Pankhurst, were cared for in Norfolk Square, which must have given Edie some of the material later deployed to great effect in *The Call*. However, not everything Ursula goes through is taken from Hertha Ayrton's life – she never went on hunger strike herself, for instance – but in choosing to make her protagonist a gifted young scientist, Edith Zangwill cleverly subverts traditional notions of 'male' and 'female' intelligence. Hertha had invented a device designed to dispel gas from the trenches: made of waterproof canvas and measuring three feet, six inches long, it was a hand-operated device that became know as the 'Ayrton fan'. Just like the fictional Ursula, Hertha was stymied by the authorities' obfuscation and incomprehension and it was adopted far later than she would have liked. But in the end, over 100,000 of them were used by British troops and the 'Ayrton fan' saved thousands of lives.

Thus, to Edie, growing up, it was clear that women could do whatever they set their minds to. She herself went to Bedford College, and published first short story, 'Jacky' in the *Pall Mall Gazette* in 1901. She later joined the WSPU alongside her stepmother and became politically active. And with both her mother and her stepmother being Jewish, it was not surprising that she fell in love with the essayist, playwright, poet and novelist Israel Zangwill (1864-1926): 'angular, tall, gaunt, and bespectacled, a powerful and epigrammatic speaker who attracted large audiences.' His novel *The Children of the Ghetto* (1892) 'with its powerful realistic depiction of ghetto life, established him as a spokesperson for Jewry within and outside the Jewish world' (ODNB) although he was to be best-known for his play *The Melting Pot* (1908). It was in 1895 that he met the twenty-year-old Edie, although it was not until 1903 that she 'leapt from one end of the alphabet to the other and became Mrs Zangwill' as a journalist noted wittily at the time.

All her novels were written after her marriage, very much with her husband's encouragement; and three children were born in 1906, 1910 and 1912. This was the year she helped her stepmother found the Jewish League for Woman Suffrage, of which Israel Zangwill was naturally a member: he spoke publicly in favour of women's suffrage, although he was hissed and jeered at for his efforts. Even before her marriage, through to the 1930s, Edith Zangwill 'took seriously all her roles as wife, mother and political activist, and in many ways saw them as mutually sustaining . . . she was active as a suffragette and pacifist, giving speeches and writing articles for the WSPU and other organisations, often uniting the causes of peace and women's rights. She served as treasurer of the Women's Peace Crusade and on the executive committee of the Women's International League for Peace and Freedom, and, as chair of the British Section of that group's Disarmament Committee' (Meri-Jane Rochelson in 'Edith Ayrton Zangwill and the Anti-Domestic Novel' 2007).

To the charge that WSPU members like Edith Zangwill were 'unwomanly' her husband Israel once replied memorably that: 'ladylike means are all very well if you are dealing with gentlemen; but you are dealing with politicians.' The concept of the ladylike, of womanliness, of how women should and shouldn't behave, as well as the depiction of the friendships and ties between women, are all key themes in *The Call*.

Even Ursula's mother has a teasing and affectionate camaraderie with her daughter, despite their being very different sorts of people: Mrs Hibbert is flirtatious and fluffy, desirous of male company, highly sociable and forever appearing at doorways 'with a swish of silken skirts'. Ursula, by contrast, wants nothing more than to be left to her own devices in her laboratory at home, conducting comparative studies of nitrogen in: 'a shapeless, blue-cotton overall and . . . dark goggles made still more disfiguring by side-flaps.' The real-life Hertha once abstractedly emerged from her laboratory at the top of the house and, taking no notice of some guests of Edie's, went round switching off lights while muttering to herself that 'the main fuse will go'. This is exactly the kind of thing Ursula would have done.

The strength of the mother and daughter's affection becomes clearer as the novel progresses, and Mrs Hibbert proves herself to be a person of hidden depths, but it is also the source of some of *The Call*'s lighter, more humorous moments. There is a wonderful scene when Ursula and her mother pay a social call on Professor Smee's wife, who has got the wrong end of the stick and mistakenly believes her husband nurtures an unrequited passion for Mrs Hibbert. There follows an entertaining series of miscommunications, culminating in Ursula's mother's compliment on the tea. '"I expect the secret of the tea lies in the making," she observed smilingly with the full intention of being ingratiating. "I wish you could show my people how you do it, Mrs Smee." "'Thank you, I have something better to do!" Poor Charlotte's voice trembled with rage. "Putting me on a level with her cook," she felt furiously.'

It is a rare writer who can combine such a lightness of touch with an ultimate seriousness of purpose, but Edith Zangwill moves easily between the two states, never once losing sight of the comic absurdity of life, even its darkest, most difficult moments. (In fact, by the end of the novel Mrs Smee and Mrs Hibbert have reconciled in an unexpectedly moving way.) Throughout *The Call* Edith Zangwill puts female solidarity, friendship and mutual respect on a footing equal to any kind of conventional romantic narrative arc between men and women. We see this again in the solace and strength Ursula is able to find from her suffragette colleagues, who work alongside her offering practical and emotional support. When she is incarcerated in Holloway, her sense of isolation is relieved by a group of suffragettes singing the 'Marseillaise' outside her cell. Later, she is transferred to another prison and goes on hunger strike. What follows is one of the most devastating parts of the book. Edith Zangwill is unsparing in her description of the mental and physical agonies involved. 'Her lips were like wood, and her tongue seemed to have grown too large for her mouth. She had a backache, too, as well as the headache which had got steadily worse. And she was so cold: most of the time, she was shivering.'

Including such a passage was a bold and memorable thing to do, for there are very few fictional accounts of hunger-striking militant feminists written at this period (although there is a searing one in Persephone Book No, 94, the 1911 *No Surrender* by Constance Maud) and this one hits the modern reader with startling force. As I write, one hundred years after the passing of the Representation of the People

Act, it is sometimes easy to think of the suffragettes as noble, untouchable symbols, belonging to historic iconography rather than the realm of flesh and blood. Edith Zangwill reminds us just how much these heroic women endured to change our society for the better.

Yet Ursula's work as a suffragette is not limited to militant action. It extends to the way in which she chooses to live her life. She defies the traditional marital set-up in order to pursue a cause she believes in, and also – crucially – she carries on working when time permits. This culminates after the outbreak of World War I, when she puts aside her suffragette activities and applies her brilliant mind to the terrible wounds and fatalities suffered by soldiers on the Western Front as a result of 'liquid fire'. The term was used several times in contemporary accounts of trench warfare and the most likely explanation is that the German army launched attacks using mustard gas and flamethrowers simultaneously, resulting in sheets of flame and clouds of obscuring black smoke. Ursula invents an extinguisher (the real-life Hertha had of course invented the 'Ayrton fan') that puts out 'the little artificial flares' she creates in her laboratory, and spends many fruitless months trying to get the War Office to pay attention to her potentially life-saving discovery. At every turn, she is stymied by administrative incompetence and institutional sexism. What she doesn't know is that her one-time mentor, Vernon Smee, is deliberately obstructing her in favour of promoting his own, inferior invention – a fine example of the irrepressible arrogance of his male ego, which is willing to put lives at risk in sulky pursuit of his own glory. Finally, an order is placed for five thousand 'Winfield extinguishers', but it comes a long fourteen months after Ursula alerted the authorities. 'I have lost all faith,' she writes to her fiancé Tony. 'However many they make, it will not bring back the men who have suffered and died, the men whom my extinguisher would have saved.'

One of the reasons the War Office would not countenance either Hertha Ayrton's real-life invention or Ursula's fictional one was that they could not imagine something invented *at home* could be useful in a war situation: a constant *leitmotif* of the book is the balancing of domesticity versus science, home versus laboratory, war versus the home front, men versus women. Why shouldn't women have the vote? Why should only men be sent to the trenches? Where is it written that men should be scientists in a lab and women be bored at home, forced to learn about 'domestic science' rather than science itself? Under the guise of a fictionalised biography of a woman scientist, Edith Zangwill demands answers from her readers; by allowing Ursula 'a lab of one's own' (the title of a 2018 book about women scientists) at home, she was subverting accepted concepts of propriety and acceptability.

Thus the ramifications and varieties of domesticity turn out to be an important theme in *The Call*. It was not for nothing that Edith Zangwill was the mother of three young children *and* wrote novels (six of them between 1904 and 1928): she well understood the difficulties of balancing the creative with domestic responsibilities, and indeed her extant diaries show that 'she remained ambivalent about the trappings of domesticity that accompanied early twentieth-century married life and that indeed took centre stage in her own diaries' (Mari-Jane Rochelson). This is why *The Call* begins with a detailed and enthralling description of the Hibbert house in Lowndes Square: in this book domestic details about running a house are, most unusually, given their due alongside Ursula's political actions, elegantly making the point that a woman's work behind closed doors is just as worthy of our attention as what goes on in the wider world. The novel gives a rare insight into a woman's domestic life in the first two decades of the 20th century.

This is why Charlotte Smee is in the novel: she symbolises the tedium and frustration endured by women who have no occupation. Brought up in a loving working-class family, by marrying an eminent scientist she has married 'up', but that leaves her with absolutely nothing to do – unless she had children, but alas she suffers five miscarriages. She lives comfortably in Clarendon Road in Notting Hill and her only occupation is conferring with the cook about her husband's meals and waiting in in case someone calls on her. She is nearly hysterical with boredom and would in fact have loved to do the cooking herself. But, as in Persephone Book No. 105 *Diary of a Provincial Lady* (1930) by EM Delafield, this was socially completely unacceptable. It would be another thirty years before a Clarendon Road housewife would consider doing her own cooking (out of wartime necessity, cf. *Housebound* by Winifred Peck, Persephone Book No. 72). And then of course thirty years further on, say by the 1980s, Clarendon Road would be so gentrified that the middle-class housewife would again be affluent enough to leave the cooking to someone else.

Charlotte Smee comes into her own during the First World War by being extremely efficient at running a canteen. But Edith Zangwill fails to answer the unspoken question – what on earth will Charlotte do with herself when she is forced to return to her old life in Clarendon Road? Edie did, however, address this question in her 1928 novel *The House* which explores the issue of home ownership, critiques the idle life of the 'lady of the house', and urges useful work as being vital to women's happiness. In addition, by making Ursula a scientist who could and would continue her career after the war, she is staking a claim to women's potential usefulness outside the home: 'With Ursula's wartime research, Edith Zangwill makes her most clearcut argument for women's contribution to the professions and articulates most emphatically the detrimental effects of shutting women out of public life after the war' (Stephanie J. Brown 'Too recent to be innocuous': An Interwar View of Women's Suffrage in Edith Zangwill's *The Call,* 2017).

Yet, in the end, the most important aspect of *The Call* is its feminism and its implicit and explicit exploration of feminism's varieties and facets. For this reason it is interesting to compare it with HG Wells's *Ann Veronica*, (1909), since this also features a young, female scientist who rebels against a patriarchal society. It, too, offers glimpses of the suffragettes, most notably in a chapter inspired by their attempt to storm Parliament in 1908. The Vernon Smee figure in this case is an older, married man called Mr Capes who is Ann Veronica's college tutor. But, unlike Mrs Smee, Mr Capes's wife is almost entirely absent from the narrative, and Ann Veronica makes no attempt to hide her desire to be made love to by this married man. Although Wells shows his protagonist chafing against the sexist *mores* of the time, Ann Veronica is shown to be disillusioned by suffragette militancy and chooses love, marriage and pregnancy over commitment to the cause, a very male view of a woman's preoccupations. (In 1914 Amber Reeves, one of Wells's lovers and in some respects a model for Ann Veronica, published her own version of a feminist novel, *A Lady and Her Husband,* Persephone Book No. 116; it is about a 'happily married' woman who realises that the young women working in her husband's chain of teashops are mistreated and tries to do something about it. It was her Cause.)

The title of *The Call* has several meanings – military, feminist, vocational, emotional – and they are all interlinked. 'I had to fight in the woman's Cause,' Ursula tells her fiancé when he returns from the Front. 'It seemed a sort of – call, and I nearly died for it. And you had to fight in the war, that was a call, too, and you nearly died for it. And now, I suppose, we are called to each other not to die, but to live.' It is a powerful reminder of the sacrifices made by generations of women so that we might gather the fruits of their harvest; so that we might live our life – and throw everything at it.

Elizabeth Day, London 2018

PUBLISHER'S TIMELINE

The Call begins in July **1909**: the heroine, Ursula, encounters suffragettes at Henley (p.51)

End of September: first reports of hunger strikes and then of forcible feeding (p.163)

December: a large Albert Hall suffragette meeting (p.166)

March **1910**: after attending a court case, Ursula sees 'the suffragettes were right' (p. 202)

May: death of the King (p. 206)

June 18th: Suffrage Procession (p. 222)

July: Conciliation Bill to give one million property-owning women the Vote passes first reading in the Commons (p. 237)

November 10th: Albert Hall meeting in support of the Conciliation Bill, and to challenge Asquith's procrastination (p. 244)

November 18th: Black Friday – march on parliament, women assaulted by police (p. 249)

April **1911**: census protest (p. 271)

June: Suffrage Coronation Procession (p. 272)

Autumn: Ursula has many speaking engagements at suffragette meetings

November: Manhood Suffrage Bill (p. 298) followed by organised window-breaking (p. 299)

March **1912**: major window-breaking demonstration in the West End (p. 300)

June **1913**: Ursula imprisoned (p. 307), then discharged under the Prisoners' Temporary Discharge for Ill-health ('Cat and Mouse') Act (p. 317)

Spring **1914**: Ursula back in prison and endures forcible-feeding (p. 321)

August: she is released after war is declared (p.327)

Autumn/winter: she convalesces

Spring **1915**: Ursula returns to her lab (p. 356); she works on ways of fighting liquid fire (p. 364)

June **1916**–September **1917**: she negotiates with the War Office about her invention (pp. 374–83)

June **1917**: Third reading of the Representation of the People Bill (including the women's enfranchisement clause) passes in the Commons (p. 385) – it subsequently becomes law in 1918

Winter **1917–18** *The Call* ends

THE CALL

TO ALL THOSE WHO FOUGHT FOR THE
FREEDOM OF WOMEN
THIS BOOK IS ADMIRINGLY AND AFFECTIONATELY
DEDICATED

CHAPTER ONE

Number 57 Lowndes Square was a typical West End house of the more fashionable sort, with its freshly painted front, its spotless steps, its shining brass door-furniture, its window boxes filled under a yearly contract and now displaying pink ivy-leaf geraniums and marguerites. It was the sort of house that inspired trust in tradespeople and caused the socialist to fulminate. Passing hansom cabmen raised inquiring whips to anyone who issued from it, and the secretaries of charitable societies coveted its drawing rooms for afternoon meetings. As the humbler caller drove up, she was discreetly thankful for her hired landau with man in livery half a crown extra, while the newly arriving servant felt with satisfaction that this was probably a 'good place' with not too much to do and plenty to waste.

The interior, as revealed by a fat-faced butler of concentrated respectability, was in exact harmony with the exterior. The hall was light and fairly wide without being spacious, and was fitted with the usual hall appurtenances. There was a large and handsome dining room containing a large and handsome mahogany table, a large and handsome sideboard, and a suite of handsome leather chairs. Behind this lay a smaller room known as the library, although no one ever read in it; indeed there were hardly any books. It served, however, as a useful cloakroom at dinner parties and receptions. Still further back was Colonel Hibbert's snuggery, a little room of epicurean armchairs and blank outlook. At one side was the writing table – again a figure of speech, for the gallant colonel never wrote anything but cheques. A portrait of Mrs Hibbert, a fair, pretty little woman with china blue eyes and fluffy hair, held the place of honour over the mantelpiece, while pictures of racehorses and one or two mess groups hung round the walls. In a corner stood a bag of golf clubs, while a cigar box, a silver lighter, and a stand of spirit decanters, with attendant siphon and glasses, were ranged on a little table conveniently to hand. Literature was represented by the *Field*, the *Sketch*, the *Sporting Times*, and *Country Life*. Indeed the whole room succinctly displayed the Colonel's three tastes in life – good living, sport, and his wife.

On the next floor Mrs Hibbert reigned supreme. Here was the large white and gold double drawing room with its so-called Louis Seize furniture, in which the blue ribbon of social distinction had been won, for royalty had honoured Mrs Hibbert's 'little parties,' as she termed her recurring annual crushes. The mistress of the house was still further revealed by her boudoir that opened off the half landing. Whatever might be the season, this room was bright and charming, if a trifle artificial, with its hothouse flowers, its Dresden china groups and its little tables laden with silver knick-knacks. There were a quantity of photographs about, chiefly of good-looking young men, but among them stood conspicuously one of condescending royalty, still more condescendingly autographed. This showed a gentleman already portly and middle-aged, although it was dated some ten years earlier, when in his irresponsible 'Welsh' days, the Hibbert circle saw much of 'the dear Prince'.

Above these reception-rooms – for the house agent's phrase most fittingly described them – naturally came the bedrooms. Colonel and Mrs Hibbert's spacious chamber was again exactly what would have been expected, from the lace bedspreads on the twin Sheraton bedsteads to the tortoise-shell backed brushes with gold monograms on the dressing table – silver toilet articles had become so impossibly common, Mrs Hibbert complained. The only point of divergence from the usual housing of the smart set was the fact of the matrimonial chamber being in the singular. With regard to the other bedrooms on this floor, they also were luxurious and characterless, and evidently but seldom used. The next storey was given over to the servants. From this point the wide staircase with its deep-pile Wilton carpet dwindled into a straight, narrow, felt-covered flight.

On the topmost landing, where the felt finally terminated, came the first unusual note. A door was ajar, and from the room within came a curious fizzling sound and a faint but still more curious odour. Some demented domestic appeared to be frying a late and unsavoury lunch in her bedroom. On pushing open the door, it was seen that the room was not a bedroom, neither was the girl standing there a domestic – no servant in that house would have condescended to a shapeless, blue-cotton overall and, still less, to hideous, dark goggles made still more disfiguring by side-flaps. A laboratory bench with its porcelain sink, gas taps and hooded fume cupboard proclaimed the nature of the apartment, but all was dominated for the moment by a hissing jet of flame that darted out between two small, dark objects held in metal clamps which stood on a table in front of the girl. This rushing flame was thrown into still greater prominence by the fact of the window blinds having been lowered, doubtless to keep out the hot glare of the July sun. Indeed, in consequence, a curious violet light was thrown on all the other objects around, the small sector-shaped metal boxes, the littered coils of thick black wire, the large dark case with metal knobs and little windows, and, most noticeably, on the girl's face and on her hands palely busied at the metal stands. She seemed to be adjusting screws, presumably to make the flaring jet of flame behave in a more subdued fashion.

Presently she was successful. The flame ceased to thrust itself out and played steadily upwards with a stable brilliancy, bathing the base of the upper of the two small, dark objects, which one now realised were electric light carbons, while the hissing sound became duller and more regular. The girl, though still wearing the concealing glasses, was better seen in this steadier light, and one could notice that she had brown, curling hair and good, well-marked features, but the light of the arc still tinged her skin with a bluish pallor. She had turned to a large frame of resistance coils standing some two feet high on the floor at her side, when suddenly the flame again rushed on with its former vehemence.

'Bother!' The ejaculation was energetic. At least this girl was human!

She straightened herself and began once more working at the screws in the metal holders. There was a knock at the door, and, without waiting for an answer, with a swish of silken skirts a little lady rustled in. She stopped short, giving a cry of horror and shielding her eyes with her hands. 'My dear Ursula! What an appalling light! What a smell!'

'All right, Mother.' The girl had already switched off the arc. Now she pulled off her spectacles, revealing rather beautiful dark eyes, and then went and drew up the window blinds. 'The sun was shining in so,' she explained. 'But the windows are all open; the smell will soon go off. What has brought you up, Mummy? It's months since you honoured my lab.'

'You know that you are only too glad not to have it honoured,' Mrs Hibbert laughed. The remark showed more sense than her rather fluffy prettiness would have suggested. 'Even now I have come in fear and trembling lest you should snap off my head. But don't you ever sit down like a Christian? Do give me a chair.'

Ursula obediently pulled forward a couple of the high laboratory stools, but although Mrs Hibbert perched herself on one, her tiny shoes with their Louis Seize heels and gold buckles dangling far off the ground, the girl herself did not use the other. As her mother said, she had got out of the habit of sitting. 'You needn't talk as though I were an ogre,' she now observed, referring to the earlier remark. 'When did I ever snap off your head?'

'Ah, but you don't know yet what I've come about. That smell hasn't gone yet. Are you sure the gas isn't escaping?' Mrs Hibbert eyed the Bunsen burner uneasily.

'Quite sure, Mum; but to satisfy you – ' Ursula struck a match.

'My dear, how dangerous!' Mrs Hibbert had blown it out with a little scream. 'And you call yourself scientific! Even I know that you don't look for gas escapes with lit matches. Why, when we first came to this house, one of the workmen did no end of damage like that; the servants' hall had to be papered all over again.'

'But there's no danger in looking for non-gas escapes with lit matches!' The girl laughed. 'It's all right, Mummy. The newsboys really won't be calling out "A horrible tragedy in Lowndes Square."' She struck another match.

'Well, it does seem to be all right.' Though reassured on this point, her daughter's movements had drawn Mrs Hibbert's attention to another cause for agitation. 'Ursula, what a dreadful state your hands are in! They're positively grimed!'

'Oh, it will all come off.' Ursula gave them a rub on a duster.

'Yes, but it spoils your skin. And you have got a great black mark on your cheek as well. Why can't you do your experimenting in gloves and a thick veil, as I have begged you again and again?'

'Oh, Mum, what a worry you are.' The words were good-natured, if disrespectful. 'What does it matter about my hands or my face either? It isn't as though I had a complexion to spoil. I can say with old Father William, "Now I am perfectly sure I have none, I do it again and again."'

'What nonsense!' The maternal pride was up in arms. 'Of course you are a brunette, but you would have a very nice complexion if you would only take the least care of it. Living in this horrible atmosphere with such a dreadful flaring light is enough to ruin anyone's skin – it's no wonder you are a little sallow. I thought it was like the infernal regions when I came in – with the added disadvantage of having to climb up to them. But when you get a colour, as you did the evening at the Colonial soirée, you really look quite beautiful; everyone said so. Didn't old Lord Spencer tell your stepfather that you were the handsomest girl present – a black pearl, he called you, and you know what a judge of women Lord Spencer is.'

'Well, I think it was fearful cheek. Anyway, the pearl isn't going to be cast before Lord Spencer! But I believe the Colonel made the whole thing up. Your august spouse would swear that black was white to please you, so he certainly wouldn't stick at calling my dingy-drab complexion pearl-like.' The girl had turned to her apparatus and was tentatively touching one of the carbons. 'No, you are the beauty of this family, Mammykin,' she rattled on with half attention, 'so don't try and shuffle out of it. Now if you were to stain *your* little lily hands, that would be a different matter.'

Mrs Hibbert gave a complacent glance at her tiny ringed fingers with their perfectly manicured pink nails. 'How can you be so ridiculous, Ursula?' she protested fondly. The mother and daughter seemed to be good friends, although they were so amazingly different; indeed the relation between them was more that of an indulgent, busy husband to a pretty, empty-headed wife. 'It is a comfort, though, that you can still be silly when you are so clever.'

'Now, Mother, Mother, to what does all this lead?' Ursula assumed an air of mock severity. 'Oh, I know your wiles, you wicked woman!' She had apparently concluded that her little carbon was cool enough to handle, for she now took it out of the metal clamp and held it up, studying it earnestly. As she did so, the sunlight falling on her face revealed the fact that her eyes were dark blue and not hazel as most people imagined. 'These are rotten carbons,' she murmured.

'Ursula, I do wish you would attend, after I have toiled up all these stairs to speak to you, instead of getting your hands worse than ever touching those dirty little sticks.' Mrs Hibbert's voice was aggrieved. 'You know I have often told you that it really is not right the way you shut yourself up here away from everyone. You might have a hump or a hare lip!'

The girl had obediently laid down her carbon; now she went and sat on the other stool in an attitude of exaggerated attention. 'Mother, Mother, is this the conduct of an honourable woman?' she asked jestingly, though with an undercurrent of irritation. 'Didn't you solemnly promise me that if I went to that Colonial function you would leave me in peace for the rest of the season? I have told you I must re-write the paper that I am going to read at the British Association in Plymouth at the beginning of September – that leaves me barely two months. If I go out, I am good for nothing the next day. I simply cannot spare the time.'

'Well, I think you are most disagreeable, and it is very hard on me.' Poor little Mrs Hibbert seemed on the verge of tears. 'All other girls are only too pleased to be taken out, and here you are nearly three-and-twenty and you have never been anywhere, and won't even be presented! Think how it affects me. I have to go about alone year after year without a soul to speak to. I might as well not have a daughter!'

'Poor little Mum, it is a shame.' Ursula could not help smiling at the picture of her popular parent wandering through society in forlorn silence, but all the same she gave the 'lily' hand a sympathetic squeeze. 'But, Mother, if I once started the social business, I'd have to go everywhere, or people would be offended. How could I do my work? And you have got the Colonel; you can't need both of us.'

Mrs Hibbert was not to be appeased. 'Your stepfather is quite different. Besides, it is not only that I want you with me, but people are talking about your never putting in an appearance. Of course they can't imagine that a girl can lock herself up in a hot, smelly attic all through the season for choice! I know that odious Mrs d'Arcy Jenkins is telling everyone that I keep you in the background so as not to give away my age. "It is so hard to believe that you really have a grown-up daughter, dear Mrs Hibbert, especially when we never see her," she said the other day with her hateful laugh.'

'Cat! Never mind, Mammykin, it's only because she is jealous of your figure. It was Mrs d'Arcy Jenkins, wasn't it, who sat near us at the Colonial soirée supper? – a surging woman with an irrepressible "tum". Why, if I did go out with you, she'd only say you dragged me about as a foil. And so I should be! You know, Mummy' – Ursula put her arm affectionately around her mother's shoulders – 'as I get older, you seem to get steadily younger. I live in hope of one day being asked after my lovely daughter.'

'Don't be so absurd.' In spite of the reproof, the mother's laugh sounded gratified. Ursula's suggestion of inversion was, of course, ridiculous, but Mrs Hibbert's slight figure and fair, unlined face did give her the appearance of another girl. Even were a certain staleness noticed in her neck and hands, a certain faintly-faded expression in her china blue eyes, no one would have credited her with being the mother of the tall, dark-browed Ursula. 'Oh, my dear, look!' the little lady now cried, jumping off the stool and holding out her arm with a tragic gesture. 'My poor sleeve is ruined – black with dirt! Why don't you have this room properly swept and dusted every morning?'

'I am so sorry, Mother.' Ursula apologetically came to the rescue. It was while she was on her knees, delicately flicking the injured sleeve with her handkerchief, that she at last heard the real reason for her mother's unusual visit. 'You know, Ursula, that I *never* ask you to do anything that interferes with your work,' Mrs Hibbert observed with aggrieved reminiscence. 'Why, I always want everybody to do exactly what pleases them best and not to consider me at all. You cannot say that I am selfish! But certainly I should have thought that a day on the river would have been the best thing in the world for your paper. It would freshen up your mind.'

'A whole day!' Ursula suppressed a groan. 'Do you want me particularly, Mother? Isn't the Colonel going?'

'No, that's it – so tiresome!' Mrs Hibbert's face brightened. She felt that she had gained her point. Indeed, she always did. 'Your stepfather has just got a horrid jury summons. Yes, I really believe those judges and people arrange it just in order to spite me, for why should they have picked out Thursday week more than any other day? And both the other times he has had to serve, it has been most inconvenient. There was the day of my first at home after we were married, you remember? – oh, no, you were at school – but it looked most marked for your stepfather not to be there. Well, about Henley – Thursday week is the first day, you know, and I have asked two young men – '

Ursula was laughing infectiously. It lit up her face, which was a trifle heavy in repose. 'So that is it,' she said. 'You want me to come to Henley to play gooseberry? Oh, you abandoned female! I don't know what matrons are coming to; they were very different in my young days. The modern mother is a terrible responsibility. All right, Mammykin, I'll chaperone your two young men – little soldier boys, I suppose?'

'Yes, Captain Talbot and Mr Cartwright.' Ursula's guess had not shown any particular perspicacity, for nearly all her mother's friends were in the army. Indeed, even in the first decade of this century, the military figured largely at the two extreme ends of the social scale, although they were almost unrepresented at the centre – the superior artisan looking upon a soldier in the family as a disgrace, while the professional man considered such a thing an impossible luxury. 'I introduced you to Captain Talbot that solitary time you have condescended to appear at one of my Wednesday evenings,' Mrs Hibbert now suggested.

'Oh, yes, I remember. A tall, heavy man, with an uneasy suspicion that his moustache might have dropped off since the last time he felt it. His stare of painful stupefaction when I told him I had never been to Ascot or the Oaks was quite pathetic. And when he heard that I worked at Chemistry, he just retained enough presence of mind to gasp out that "it must be deuced handy if anyone was ill, what?"'

'You are too critical, my dear. There is more in Captain Talbot than you think.' A touch of resentment was manifest in Mrs Hibbert's tone. She looked across at Ursula. 'How like you are to your poor father!'

The remark seemed almost involuntary. Indeed, there was a distinct pause before Mrs Hibbert added the orthodox sigh. The little lady had again perched herself on the high stool. She was thinking of the day when she had been seventeen, and Ursula's father had swept her into matrimony by the overwhelming force of his passion. People had warned her that Andrew Winfield was eccentric, but she had never imagined that he would be so tiresome and incomprehensible as he had proved himself. And then he was always aggrieved that she did not possess all sorts of ideal qualities with which he had chosen to endow her! Certainly he had been comparatively nice during the hateful months before and after Ursula's birth, but things had soon got just as bad again. Besides, they were poor, and she had always hated poverty. It was really a relief when Andrew had gone off to Australia; although it was like his silliness to work his way out before the mast, when he surely could have managed to borrow enough money for his passage. And to think of his blundering into a fortune when he got there, and then dying directly after. How well she remembered the will being read to her by the old family solicitor. 'It may come as a surprise to you to learn that you are a wealthy woman,' the lawyer had said. Moreover, apart from the ten thousand pounds which were Ursula's, the money was left to the widow unconditionally; so a couple of years later, when Mrs Winfield wished to change into Mrs Hibbert, she could feel that her personal income would remain pleasantly unaltered. Yes, she had really been very fond of poor, dear Andrew.

Mrs Hibbert had been silent as these old memories passed through her mind. Now, as she glanced at her jewelled watch, she gave a little scream. 'Good heavens, how late!' She jumped down from the stool. 'And I have got three at homes this afternoon, and then a dinner at Lady Tremoine's, and the Lonsdale House reception – oh no, that's been put off; the Duchess is ill or something, such a relief. Well, ta, ta, my dear. By the way,' she added suddenly as she reached the door, 'would you like to have any of your queer, scientific folk on Thursday week? There's that Smee man; he's youngish and not so impossible.'

'What?' During her mother's unusual meditation, Ursula had been fixing another carbon in the clamp, and she now looked up with rather a dazed expression. 'Oh, you mean ask Professor Smee to Henley? Yes, I might, though I don't suppose he could come. But I am almost sure to see him at the Chemical Society next week. I will talk to him about it then.'

'Very well. *Alors c'est fini*. Ta-ta.' Mrs Hibbert rustled out of the laboratory with which she was so little in keeping. With a happy sigh, her daughter again switched on the current. The hissing sound and faint, curious odour returned to the top floor of Number 57.

CHAPTER TWO

On Thursday evening, at a few minutes to eight, Ursula Winfield passed under the archway of Burlington House and through the Chemical Society's familiar doorway on the right. The inadequate entrance hall and stone staircase – the walls of which had not then blossomed from a dingy terracotta to their present verdant hues – were more than usually populous with a black-coated male throng, for Sir William Leveridge, the evening's lecturer, was admittedly the greatest living English chemist and physicist. When Ursula reached the meeting room on the first floor, she saw, to her dismay, that it already seemed full, save for the front bench reserved by tradition for past presidents. Here her friend, Professor Smee, was already seated; he was, indeed, the most recent past president, for his two years of office had only come to an end the previous March. He was talking to another man, but he caught sight of Ursula and nodded to her with a smile; it lit up his dark, good-featured face and made the forty-three years that *Who's Who* assigned to him still more surprising. Then, as he noticed that the girl was still standing by the door looking round for an empty place, he indicated one, not on the sacred bench, indeed, but next to it.

Ursula shook her head. Such a seat was not for her – a mere visitor. Fortunately, at this moment, she noticed that on one of the back cross-benches there seemed to be room, or rather two young men made it for her by politely crowding down. As Ursula thanked them, she reflected with some bitterness that these youths – for they were hardly more – might be Fellows of the Society, while she, as a woman, could never attain the position. It was only through Professor Smee's kindness in giving her the necessary introductions that she was able to come to the meetings at all. Yet her work was quite as good as that of any man – she was sure of it. And tonight's lecture, 'A Comparative Study of Nitrogen and the Rarer Gases,' dealt with her own particular subject. For the last two years she had been working on the extraction of nitrogen from the air; indeed, a paper on her experiments had quite recently been published by the Royal Society. It made the fact of her anomalous position tonight all the more galling.

From the privileges possessed by the young men sitting beside her, Ursula's mind turned to the young men themselves, a personal line of thought that was unusual in her. But a sudden picture of her mother's horror came before her were she to introduce her present companions into the Hibbert circle. Yes, to her mother these anaemic-looking young chemists in their 'reach-me-down' suits would seem hardly human, particularly if they were innocent of dress suits and shook hands with their gloves on. Indeed, physically, Ursula could not but admit that her two neighbours fell short of the Lowndes Square standard – literally short, for neither of them could have been more than five foot six. But mentally, she was sure, they were far in advance of it; besides, unlike her mother's friends, they had probably achieved the dignity of self-support. Yes, and if there was any justice in nature, it was these men who ought to have possessed the fine bodies and not the gilded guardsmen who made so poor a use of them. Any physique would be good enough for Captain Talbot's idle existence, in which even the chance of war seemed negligible.

There was a slight stir. The President, Professor Lyall Fleming, an extremely stout, suave personage, had come in. He was chairman, and so Sir William Leveridge was doubtless following. Ursula craned forward eagerly; the lantern that stood at the end of the bench rather blocked her view, and had been, indeed, the cause of the lack of congestion on this bench. She had never seen the great scientist; and chemistry not being a picture-postcard profession, even his photograph was unfamiliar to her. A little, shrunken, unimpressive old man, with a sparse white beard and a deprecating manner now ambled into the room. The dignity of his entrance was further diminished by a stumble at the step of the platform. Fortunately the chairman with his usual large, bland competence put out a saving hand, and then started forthwith on his introductory speech, which proved a model of sonorous tact.

Sir William Leveridge's great talents evidently did not include that of lecturing. For the paper, which he began to read in a quavering mumble, proved both incoherent and long-winded, while his experiments entirely failed to do anything that he expected of them. Ursula's familiarity with the subject enabled her to follow the rambling remarks and to extract their importance, but the attention of most of the audience was unequal to the strain. Suddenly her own name startled her attentive ear. No, it was a man – 'the valuable recent experiments of Mr – .' The name was certainly like Winfield. Who could he be? It was odd that she had never heard of his work. Old Leveridge was fumbling on the table amid his confusion of papers. Now he seemed to have found what he wanted, and, putting on his spectacles, he began in his vague, gentle way to read from a typewritten sheet. The colour flooded Ursula's face. Why it was *her* paper, her Royal Society paper. *She* was Mr Winfield! What an honour to be thus publicly mentioned by Leveridge – although he denied her sex. Ursula felt amused by the old man's unconscious effort to preserve science as a masculine monopoly.

After this little interlude, the lecture droned on as before. There were several false finishes rousing a hopeful applause, but each time the expectation of the wearied audience was disappointed. Sir William would smile and start on as before, his imperturbable and almost inaudible current of speech broken only now and then by an ineffective experiment. From where Ursula sat, the lecturer's notes could be seen unhidden by the apparatus in front, and so these vain hopes of an end were not raised. The thick pile of manuscript was, however, growing gradually lower. Page after page was turned, with an incredible slowness, but still it was turned. Presently the pile looked as though about half were read – then three-quarters –

only a few pages more – perhaps only three – two – this was the last. A distinct brightening came over the faces. The two young men next to Ursula were audibly jubilant. 'And now we will turn to another, and perhaps not less important aspect of the question, the commercial production of nitrogen.' Sir William drew from his pocket a fresh sheaf of closely scrawled pages.

In spite of Ursula's own interest, she could not but feel sorry for the audience. 'SOS,' she heard the young chemist sitting beside her ejaculate, while his companion sat staring with fallen jaw, a sullen image of despair. Again the indistinct monologue commenced. It might have been more bearable had the room been less sweltering and stuffy, but this was before the ventilation of the place had been taken in hand, and, on account of the noise, the double windows on Piccadilly had always to be rigorously shut. Ursula's neighbours had begun to debate in whispers whether escape was possible – the exit was tactlessly near to the platform; still there was a limit to human endurance, one of them observed. However, as all things come to an end, the lecture also, at last, found a conclusion. Leveridge began gathering together his scattered mass of paper amid a breathless pause. 'Don't clap, you fool, you'll set him off again,' one of the young men muttered anxiously. There was a distinct sigh of relief, preceding some polite applause, as the great scientist definitely sat down.

The chairman now announced that the meeting was open for discussion. No one seemed anxious to take advantage of the invitation. Instead, watches were consulted. After a moment or two Professor Smee got up. There was clapping and the watches were put back. When Vernon Smee spoke, people had a trick of staying to hear him. Indeed, the Professor's enemies said that his science consisted in a skilful verbal and literary presentation of other men's ideas. This was not quite fair; Smee had done some good, original work on radiography. It was a fact, however, that owing to the popular appeal of his subject, he had received far more general recognition than other and greater men whose work lay upon more recondite lines.

On this occasion Professor Smee evidently did not intend to make a regular speech. 'I am going to keep you for just two minutes,' he began reassuringly, 'for the subject of the lecture is quite out of my line, and we have been listening to a most exhaustive discourse' – Ursula smiled – 'from the greatest living authority on it.' Yet bold as it sounded, Professor Smee went on to say he was going to correct one of Sir William Leveridge's statements. Had they ever heard of the carter to whom another man said, 'That there's a nice horse o' yourn. What be his name?' 'His name?' the carter replied. 'Why, he be a she and his name be Betsy.' Now Sir William had spoken of a *Mr* Winfield's work. 'Like the carter,' Professor Smee announced with a smile, 'I say that this gentleman is a lady and his name is *Miss* Winfield. As Miss Winfield is here tonight, perhaps she will tell us something about her experiments.'

There was an interested stir. As only one woman was present that evening, Miss Winfield's identification was not difficult. It seemed to Ursula that everyone in the room was looking at her. Her heart began to thump. She felt sick. It was the first time that she had ever been called upon to speak in public. She stood up, thinking that she would just say it was too late for further discussion tonight. A burst of applause made any words impossible. The two men next to her were especially demonstrative; they were probably young enough to enjoy the proceeding as 'a lark'. Besides, Ursula was a fairly constant attendant at the meetings. The Fellows had got used to her presence and, with some exceptions, rather liked it.

The President looked annoyed and whispered something to the secretary whose seat was beside him. Both men extremely resented this unexpected development. A woman had never spoken at the Chemical Society before. It was too bad of Smee, Professor Fleming felt angrily, and just what might have been expected of him. Why, last year, during his term of presidency, he had tried to get the charter altered and ladies admitted as Fellows. Of course, one isolated speech from this girl was of no importance, but it would be brought forward as a precedent. Such a state of affairs would discredit the Society, reduce its meetings to frivolous social functions. The introduction of frivolity was the reason always advanced by Professor Fleming against the admission of women to masculine institutions. He was genuinely unconscious of any sex hostility that lay behind his argument. However, the step could not now be helped, though they must find some way to prevent its recurrence, he reflected. The tumultuous applause was stopping, so he gave a slight bow in Ursula's direction. 'Will you not come and speak from the platform, Miss Winfield,' he suggested, with the tone of courtly deference that he almost invariably used towards women.

Ursula made her way between the benches with some difficulty and stepped on to the low platform. Her chief reason for doing so was an almost unconscious instinct to get nearer the apparatus. If she had Sir William Leveridge's experiments at hand, it would be easier to describe her own. She soon found, to her surprise, that she was speaking quite coherently, although her voice was flat and seemed to belong to someone else. Remembering Sir William Leveridge's inaudibility she raised her tone, and then felt that she was shrieking like a peacock. However, the chief thing was to be heard, she told herself.

Presently she got more control over her vocal organs. As a matter of fact her voice was excellent, being both strong and musical, a gift of which she had hitherto been unconscious. To her delight she found that she was holding the audience. There were several bursts of clapping, and once, when she described rather happily some experimental tribulations, she was fairly stopped by laughter. Presently she felt that she had said enough, but she did not know in the least how to end. 'That's all,' she announced abruptly, and walked back to her seat.

There were a few questions and brief remarks, but Ursula's speech had really been the 'all'. As they went into the adjoining back room, where tea and 'light refreshments' of a rather stodgy character were spread on the long central table, Sir William Leveridge came up and spoke to her. He was most kind, not to say friendly. Ursula was surprised. She had always heard that the great scientist objected to the modern, emancipated woman. She would have been further surprised, and indeed incensed, had she known that her appearance rather than her work was the cause of the old man's almost affectionate interest. Sir William had an innocent *penchant* for pretty girls, a weakness he was rarely able to indulge, for usually he was closely dragooned by a stern middle-aged wife.

A few minutes later, as Ursula had left the building and was walking along Piccadilly, she again heard herself addressed. This time Professor Smee accosted her. 'Are you too toplofty over your triumph to speak to an old acquaintance, Miss Winfield?' he asked.

Ursula laughed. 'I don't know whether to be furiously angry or abjectly grateful,' she told him 'I think I am both. Seriously, it was very good of you to give me such an opening, although I was rather terrified at its suddenness.'

'There was no need for you to be terrified. How well you speak!' There was just the faintest shade of effort in Mr Smee's voice. Although he would never have confessed it, he had had a prick of jealousy at Ursula's success. 'Have you had much practice?'

'No, you have just sponsored my first effort. By the way, I didn't know that women were allowed to speak at the Society's meetings. I have never heard one.'

'Nor I. As far as I know, your maiden speech was a double first. The President is wild about it. You know how conservative Lyall Fleming is.'

'Then it was particularly good of you. Thank you.' She looked up with grateful eyes.

Vernon Smee was pleased. He was always susceptible to his environment, indeed he had a good deal more of the artistic than of the scientific temperament. Yes, he deserved Miss Winfield's approval, he felt; his action that evening had not been popular. The other men had not said much, but they evidently considered him a bit of a traitor – one of a beleaguered garrison who had helped the enemy to scale the wall. For his part he never could see why women should not be allowed to take up any work they wanted; if they were not able to do it, they would soon drop out. The fact that his own wife had no interest at all outside the domestic did not alter his point of view. Still, he would have to be more careful, he now told himself. His championship of women was doing him harm professionally. All his life Vernon Smee had been apt to do the fine thing on impulse and then regret it.

'I think you are very chivalrous,' Ursula said suddenly. 'That is the only chivalry women want nowadays, to be given equal opportunity.'

'You mean that the modern Andromeda is capable of tackling the dragon herself, if only Perseus will cut her bonds.' Miss Winfield was much more attractive than he had realised, Professor Smee was telling himself. Of course, he had always considered her a clever girl, indeed, almost a genius in her own line – and twenty-two years of poor Charlotte's conversation made him appreciate genius in a woman! But he had always thought that Miss Winfield erred in the opposite direction. She was altogether too intellectual, too impersonal. Her absorption in her work had seemed at times quite inhuman. But perhaps it was because he had only come across her at scientific gatherings. She might be different in private life. He glanced at the strong, clear-cut profile beside him. How handsome she was; he had never fully realised it. Her dress must be particularly becoming, or perhaps it was the flush that the evening's excitement had brought to her cheeks. 'I did not know that you were so interested in the woman question,' he said aloud.

'I am not.' Ursula gave a laugh. 'Indeed, I can't see that there is one. My world is divided up into animal, vegetable and mineral; not into men and women. The difference between the sexes seems to me so small in such a wonderful, complex universe. Why, I should never think of the subject, only suddenly, when I am quite happy with my experiments, I come crash into some absurd artificial sex barrier – as though my work wore petticoats!'

Professor Smee smiled. 'Of course, you are a suffragist?' he asked. The agitation was then at its height and no conversation could go on long without some reference to it.

To his surprise Miss Winfield hesitated. 'Of course, I am not an Anti,' she said doubtfully. 'But the question does not seem to me important. Have votes really been of much use to men? But though I am undecided about the suffrage' – her tone grew hard – 'I am quite decided about the suffragettes. I utterly and entirely disapprove of them. Their street rows and interruptions at public meetings are scandalous!'

'You are rather severe, Miss Winfield,' Professor Smee deprecated. 'Now I have a sneaking sympathy with the abused militants! Didn't men adopt much more violent measures when they were trying to get the Vote?'

'But women ought to have more sense! Besides, these "militants" make themselves so ridiculous. Why, everyone said it was on account of the suffragettes that the Chemical Society voted against altering its charter to admit women last year when you brought up the question.'

'But if it hadn't been for the suffragettes, it might never have occurred to me to bring up the question. But I forgot to tell you,' Professor Smee branched off suddenly, 'though I couldn't get that through, I believe we are going to have "women subscribers". You won't be able to vote, but you will have all the other privileges – and at a lower figure.'

'Well, that is only fair.' Ursula laughed. 'If we can't call the tune, we ought not to be charged as much for the piper! In any case, it will be the greatest boon. You can't think how troublesome it has been not having access to the library. And I shan't have to worry you for introductions for the meetings. That is another of Andromeda's bonds you will have cut. I don't know how to thank you enough.'

Vernon Smee was quite touched; the girl was really charming in her gratitude. So often one slaved and got no thanks at all. He was going on to say something of the sort, when Ursula spoke again. Was she not taking him out of his way, she suggested. Here they were at Hyde Park Corner. She herself meant to walk home; Lowndes Square was not far and it was such a lovely night. But he must not think it necessary to accompany her; she so often came home alone.

Professor Smee assured her that Lowndes Square was on his way, which was not wildly untrue. He lived at Clarendon Road, Notting Hill, or Notting Hill Gate, as his wife was always careful to call it. His further remark was absolutely veracious, that if Miss Winfield did not object he would like the walk with her after being cooped up all day at College. Far from objecting, Ursula was delighted, and told him so. She had just remembered that she wished to consult him. She was in a great hole, she explained. Some months ago she had sent in a paper to read next September at the British Association and they had accepted it. But now she was not satisfied; her later work in the laboratory had been giving such queer results. She wanted to carry out a whole new series of tests and then, probably, re-write the paper. Only these new experiments needed more power than she could get at home; besides, she must have an assistant, or, preferably, two. She meant to go and see the authorities at the Davy-Faraday laboratory tomorrow. Did Professor Smee think they would let her work there for a few weeks? And would she be able to start at once, or was there an endless lot of formality? Because time was pressing; she had less than two months for the whole job.

'Why not come as a special student and work at my College?' It was a sudden inspiration on the part of Professor Smee. 'I could give you a room at once and no formality. The vacation is beginning next week, then you will have the place all to yourself.' He was warming to the theme. 'One or two of the students will be staying on and they'd like to work with you. Besides, South Kensington is much nearer for you than Albemarle Street.'

So Ursula had again to thank him, and was so enthusiastic and softened that her companion really regretted reaching Lowndes Square. He was standing on the doorstep saying goodbye when an electric brougham glided up. The man beside the chauffeur jumped down and opened the carriage door. 'Oh, here are my mother and my stepfather,' Ursula exclaimed.

The Colonel emerged, followed by his wife, whom he carefully helped out. Mrs Hibbert was wearing a wrap of gorgeous Chinese embroidery – loot from Peking. 'Have you had a nice time, Mummy?' Ursula asked, as she and her companion went forward. 'You know Professor Smee?'

'Oh, yes. We met at the Royal Society soirée didn't we, Professor?' Mrs Hibbert shook hands and gave her rather vacant little laugh. 'I am always so alarmed at those scientific functions. I think I'll get electrocuted or something. But won't you come in, Professor Smee – for a few minutes at any rate?'

'Yes, have a whisky and soda,' the Colonel urged hospitably. 'You've been to a meeting, haven't you? Dry work those meetings, I should think, what?'

The invitation was accepted. Indeed, Vernon Smee was rather impressed. He had no idea that Miss Winfield's people lived in such style. He had never met Colonel Hibbert before and had only retained a vague impression of the introduction to the mother. He remembered just noticing that she looked exceedingly unmaternal.

'I think it is Miss Winfield who should have the whisky and soda,' he went on when they were all in the dining room and the butler was carrying round a tray with drinks. 'Your daughter's speech was the feature of the evening.'

'No, what? Did Ursula speak? Well done, old girl.' The Colonel's enthusiasm was amused but hearty. 'Wish we'd been there, Vi.' This was to his wife. 'Not that I'd have understood a word, what?'

'Oh, Ursula, did you really stand up and talk to them all? How could you do it? Isn't she wonderful and clever?' Mrs Hibbert turned to the visitor for acquiescence.

'Don't, Mother.' Ursula was rather embarrassed. 'Won't you take off your cloak? It's awfully hot in here.' The suggestion was merely to change the subject. 'Why, that's a new frock, isn't it? Oh, Mummy, what a creation!'

'Do you like it?' Mrs Hibbert stood up with girlish complacency. The gown was of chiffon tinted in sweet pea shades and embroidered with these flowers. As Worth's man had put it, 'It is *réussie*, Madame.'

The Colonel was gazing at his wife with fatuous admiration. Mr Smee was looking at her too, but more critically. Really, it was rather absurd for a woman of Mrs Hibbert's age to go on like this. She must be older even than Charlotte, although she did look so amazingly girlish. He turned his eyes to Ursula, who was standing beside her mother, a curious contrast in her plain tailor-made coat and skirt. Yes, for his part, he certainly admired the daughter more. He would like to see Miss Winfield in a beautiful evening gown like that. What had she worn at the soirée a few weeks ago? It could not have been anything very striking or he would have remembered it.

'Professor Smee is dreadfully bored. My poor little frock doesn't interest him. But you know it is all this silly girl's fault. You ought not to have begun about it, Ursula. By the way, are we going to have the pleasure of seeing you next Thursday, Professor Smee?'

'Oh, I quite forgot to ask him. Dear me, and now I am making matters worse – how rude I sound! I am chaperoning my mother to Henley, Professor Smee, and we wondered if you could spare the time to come too?'

Next Thursday – a week from today. And his vacation began on Wednesday! It just fitted in. Again Vernon Smee found himself accepting. He had always wanted to see Henley, although somehow the opportunity had never before come his way. He wondered if he ought to mention that he was married. Miss Winfield was evidently not aware of the fact. But Charlotte hated boating. Besides she would be so entirely out of her element in this set; it was bad enough with the ordinary scientific lot. Of course, though, he did not want to ignore Charlotte. He would tell Miss Winfield about her at Henley; or there might be an opportunity even sooner at College. 'When do you want to start your experiments in my laboratory, Miss Winfield?' he said aloud.

'Tomorrow. Would it be all right if I brought down my apparatus at about eleven? Professor Smee is going to let me work at his College for a time,' she explained to her parents. 'We haven't enough power here!'

'What d'you mean, not enough power?' the Colonel demanded testily. He felt that in some way the remark reflected on his position of domestic authority. Nor was he much assuaged when Professor Smee entered upon an elaborate technical explanation. 'Can't you tell the electric light people to send their man round?' he inquired. 'Considering what they run me into, by George, there oughtn't to be any trouble. Make 'em fix it up for you, Ursula, the "watts" or whatever you call 'em. Rum name – what?' The feeble joke quite restored the Colonel's good humour.

'I am afraid that would hardly be possible.' Professor Smee laughed a shade contemptuously. He was thinking what an old fool Miss Winfield's stepfather was. Indeed, the Professor was apt to be a little severe in his judgment of men, as opposed to women, which was perhaps the reason for his getting on less well with his own sex. 'Well, I must be going. Thank you so much for your hospitality.' Charlotte would be wondering what had happened to him, he felt uneasily.

As the door closed, Colonel Hibbert gave a snort. 'Bit of a bounder,' he observed tersely.

Ursula flushed. She was always slightly on the defensive at home. Not only did she resent this condemnation of her friend, but it also seemed an attack on science. 'Of course, no one can be a gentleman who isn't in the army, according to you,' she said bitterly. 'It is fortunate that all other people do not have the same definition of the word.'

The Colonel also grew red. He and Ursula were apt to have these passages at arms, although on the whole they were good friends. His stepdaughter was not at all the type of woman whom he admired, or even of whom he approved, but still he thought her a 'good fellow.' In their arguments he was always hopelessly beaten, for the vocabulary of the gallant Colonel was not much larger than that of an African savage. 'You're talking dashed nonsense,' he now stuttered.

'George, dear! 'Mrs Hibbert came to the rescue. 'George, you are very naughty and unkind, for you know that Professor Smee is a very great friend of Ursula's. But, Ursula, darling, he isn't quite – quite – is he now? Though I think he is very nice indeed, and not a bit "professory". He has the most beautiful eyelashes.'

'Eyelashes!' The Colonel laughed indulgently. 'That's all you women think about. Why ever did you ask the fellow to Henley, Vi?'

'Yes, I think, too, that Henley will be a great waste of Professor Smee's time,' Ursula interrupted angrily. 'Professor Smee has more important things to do. His work has made him known all over the world – that can't be said about most of your "officers and gentlemen"! Why, without men like Professor Smee, the army would be non-existent. You would be fighting with bows and arrows! It is a condescension on his part to go to a miserable regatta.'

'Well, he seemed glad enough to condescend,' the Colonel growled, not without truth. 'But I dare say Henley wasn't the attraction, what?' The witticism restored him to good humour.

'I shan't go to Henley.'

'Now, Ursula, darling, don't let us have all that again. I am so tired, and you promised me.' Mrs Hibbert turned to her husband. 'I can't think why you are making such a fuss about Professor Smee, especially when you know how extraordinarily sensible Ursula is. I assure you I felt thankful when I heard how poor Lady Fletcher's second daughter ran away with the coachman – '

Ursula, who was standing a little way off, in indignant silence, suddenly laughed. 'Yes, Mummy, there are compensations for having a daughter who shuts herself up in an attic all day; at least I shan't elope with the coachman! So old-fashioned, too. The poor girl might have found a chauffeur.'

'How absurd you are! How goes the enemy? I am so sleepy.' Mrs Hibbert tapped her lips with her closed fan to suppress a yawn. 'Oh, Ursula, I forgot to tell you, I have asked another man to Henley – a positive Adonis, my dear! We met him at the Mountjoys last year, and tonight he took me in to dinner. His mother was Lord Mountjoy's sister; Balestier is his name, Anthony Balestier. Oh, yes, and they said he was a Balliol scholar and all that sort of thing, so you will approve of him. But you would never think he was clever, he is too handsome!'

'Another beau to your string, Mother! Good night, you reprehensible person. Good night, Colonel.' Ursula started at a run up the many flights to her bedroom on the top floor.

CHAPTER THREE

When Ursula looked out of her bedroom window early on the Henley morning, she saw bright sunshine and a pale, cloudless sky. It gave promise of a day of English summer at its best, a best that is unbeatable. Well, she would try and dismiss all thought of the fixation of nitrogen from her thoughts, the girl told herself. It would be silly to fall between the two stools of work and play. Besides, her experiments at the College were going very satisfactorily. She felt much less driven for time, and altogether happier about her paper than when her mother had first broached the Henley idea. Banish the BA! Today she would frankly 'frivol', as her mother called it.

Moreover, the party today would be much more interesting than she had at first expected. There would be Professor Smee to talk to instead of the usual inane young officers. At College she naturally did not see very much of the Professor, still, the daily meeting during the last week had given her a sense of familiarity. Indeed, their acquaintance seemed suddenly to have ripened into friendship during their walk home from the Chemical Society together. She thought that on the whole she liked Professor Smee better than any man she knew.

And then there would be this Mr Balestier, of whom her mother had spoken. He, too, sounded rather interesting. Was he really such a beauteous being as her mother had pictured? If so, he was probably unendurable. For Ursula rightly considered that the young men in the Hibbert set were outrageously spoilt, especially those with any pretension to good looks. Certainly, in her mother's presence these youths were fairly humble, but then they were generally more or less adoring. It was their Sultan-like attitude towards girls that Ursula resented. She wondered if Mr Balestier shared the failing. He must, at least, be much cleverer than the others to have got a Balliol scholarship. But in a Henley crush, she reflected, a Balliol scholar might be of less use than the ordinary Lowndes Square young man. It was, perhaps, an occasion on which muscle was of more importance than mind. 'What price brawn versus brain?' as one of her mother's subalterns would have said.

The girl's unwonted holiday mood reflected itself in her toilette. Discarding her usual severe tailor-made style, she put on a new gown of embroidered white linen. 'My dear, how nice you look!' her mother exclaimed, as Ursula looked into the room during her parents' leisurely half past nine breakfast – the girl had her own at eight o'clock Later, when Vernon Smee saw her on the platform at Paddington, the same thought occurred to him, although he naturally did not, like Mrs Hibbert, express it. Yes, Miss Winfield was really beautiful, he felt. Something in him was always strangely stirred by beauty in a woman, although he had never quite made up his mind whether he ought to admit the sensation. Perhaps he cared so much because all his life he had been stinted in this respect. How he envied the men who had pretty daughters or a handsome – but, of course, he did not mean to reflect upon poor Charlotte. Indeed, he thought, he almost preferred his wife's middle-aged plainness to Mrs Hibbert's belated youth. The hostess looked a trifle tawdry, he thought, in her frilly dress with her pink chiffon parasol. Or, perhaps, it was only because she was standing next to her daughter. Ursula had no frills and no parasol – Ursula the triumphant. Vernon Smee went up to her.

There was an expression in his eyes as he shook hands that made Ursula lower hers. She hoped ruefully that Professor Smee was not going to be silly; she was still in ignorance of his being married. Once before an agreeable scientific friendship had been spoilt by the man falling in love with her. Not that she would mind it, indeed, admiration was rather pleasant, if only people would have the sense to keep it to themselves, and not worry her about it! For if there was one thing in the world about which she felt certain, it was her disinclination to get married. Her work was far too interesting. But here was someone else coming up; it must be Mr Balestier.

Yes, he was handsome, there was no doubt about it, although, perhaps, he hardly justified her mother's description of him as an Adonis. Still, his fair, crisp hair, his blue eyes, his well-cut features were pleasant to look upon, while his figure was altogether admirable. She noticed that Professor

Smee, who was standing nearby, had suddenly grown short. Why, Mr Balestier must be quite six foot two or three, although his excellent proportions kept one from realising it.

The airy badinage with which Mrs Hibbert was greeting the newcomer was now interrupted by Professor Smee suggesting that they ought to find their seats. It recalled her to a sense of her duties. 'Oh, you don't know my daughter.' She brought up the guest. 'Mr Balestier, Miss Winfield.'

Tony Balestier felt faintly surprised. It was not due to the fact of there being a grown-up daughter, for he unhesitatingly assigned some sort of step-relationship, which the difference in name seemed irrationally to corroborate. It did, however, strike him as curious that the two women should be of such utterly different types. Miss Winfield looked 'intense'; she was probably a bore. She would expect him to talk 'seriously' – as though he didn't get all the serious talk he wanted with other men. When a fellow wasn't working, he wanted to amuse himself; that was what your intellectual women never understood. Now, Mrs Hibbert was just the sort he liked, entertaining without being vulgar, pleasantly foolish without being a fool. How ripping she looked today, though to do the stepdaughter justice, Miss Winfield was quite as good-looking in her own style.

Captain Talbot and Mr Cartwright now appeared. They were both typical public school men, and could by no possibility have belonged to any country but our own. In their aggressively spotless flannels they positively shone with cleanliness. A move was at last made towards the train, one of the series of Henley specials, but the platform was so dense with the smartly-dressed, basket-bearing crowd, that it was quite difficult to move along it. Ursula found Professor Smee beside her. 'I always think you could tell the station by just seeing the people,' he commented. 'Flannels mean Paddington, broadcloth and heavy watch chains, Waterloo. At Euston there are tweeds and gun cases. Liverpool Street is stamped by bowlers and reach-me-downs.'

Ursula was amused. 'Yes, it is quite true, a complete scientific classification! I hadn't thought of it,' she agreed. 'And it is the only way in which one can tell a London station. Why are the names never put up?'

'We think it would be pandering unduly to the foreigner, I suppose.' The whole party had been wandering along the platform, looking in at each successive crowded carriage. They had first-class tickets, of course; but in a plutocratic mob this meant congestion rather than distinction. Clearly, it would be necessary to separate. Presently Professor Smee announced that here were two places. The others seemed to have disappeared, so Ursula jumped into the compartment. Then she looked blank. There was certainly one seat – indeed a polite man made it into a 'corner' by moving up himself – but the space seemed hardly sufficient to admit of two. However, the Professor did manage to niche himself in beside her. The close proximity made Ursula uncomfortable. Even as a child she had objected to human contact. It impinged upon her sense of freedom.

The stiffness of her expression was not lost on Professor Smee. With considerable tact he began to talk of her work. Ursula responded gratefully; indeed, in a few minutes she was quite oblivious both of herself and her cramped surroundings. Smee was amused; he was also vexed. For once Miss Winfield had been human, even feminine. Her embarrassment had struck him as rather charming. Now she had again become an intellectual abstraction, a scientific statue. The old story of Pygmalion and Galatea crossed his mind. Or the Sleeping Beauty – perhaps the idea was in essence the same. Was Miss Winfield not quite alive, not quite awake? It was the Prince's kiss in the fairy tale that broke the spell. How pleasant to be a Prince! But such imaginings were hardly suitable for a middle-aged married man. Not that he was really middle-aged, he reminded himself. Indeed, middle-age was merely a concomitant of marriage. As long as a man was single, he was considered young. He remembered that Miss Winfield did not know of his wife's existence; at least, he did not think she did. Perhaps this was the opportunity to tell her. They were practically alone, despite the crowded compartment. The other people were all engrossed in their papers or conversation. 'Don't let us talk shop,' he urged, as Ursula came to a pause. 'Today is a holiday. You don't know how rarely I get one! My wife and I lead such very humdrum lives.'

'Your wife!' Ursula's surprise was undisguised, but Vernon Smee could not detect the faintest trace of any other sentiment. He was conscious of a slight sense of pique, although he would not acknowledge it. He would have been still further piqued had he realised that Ursula's astonishment was succeeded by a profound relief. What a comfort, she was thinking! Now there could be no question of Professor Smee falling in love with her. She could just enjoy his friendship without any bothers. 'You must think me extraordinarily stupid,' she said aloud, 'but somehow it never occurred to me that there was a Mrs Smee. You look so very unmarried.'

'How does matrimony show itself?' Obviously the only thing to do was to continue the conversation in this light vein. 'Is a Benedick better dressed or worse? Does he wear his hair longer or shorter?'

'Oh, I can't explain, but there really is a difference. But I hope Mrs Smee did not think it rude of us not to have asked her today. Would she have cared to come?' The inquiry was unconcerned, for in the Hibbert set married people were extremely detachable. 'You must explain that the fault was yours.'

'Yes, I will. But my wife does not care for boating.' There was a pause. Vernon Smee was reflecting that if he wanted to see much of Miss Winfield, he ought to suggest her meeting Charlotte. And he did want to see a great deal of Miss Winfield; it was only today that he had realised how much he wanted it. Hang it all, why shouldn't he? He only proposed a friendship of the most platonic description. If he had been thinking of anything else, this girl was not the sort to have allowed it. Why, the idea of Miss Winfield flirting with a married man, or, indeed, with any man, almost made him laugh. It seemed to him ridiculous that under such circumstances his wife need be dragged into it at all. If only Charlotte had not been so unreasonable. For she and Miss Winfield would never hit it off together, he told himself gloomily. Indeed, Miss Winfield might despise Charlotte's hopelessly *borné* attitude so much as to be set against him too.

However, it could not be helped. 'I thought perhaps you would call on my wife one day, when you have time,' he suggested.

Ursula's face fell. If there was one thing in the social world that she disliked more than another it was calling. But Professor Smee's wife was in a different category from other people, if only because the Professor had been so kind. Still she really could not go just now with her BA paper on hand. She explained this to Professor Smee, and was relieved at his agreeing – almost with alacrity. 'After the British Association, I have promised Mother to go up North for a month; Colonel Hibbert has a place in Ayrshire, you know. But when I get back, I shall be very pleased to call on Mrs Smee.' Ursula blushed as she said it, for her blatant honesty rebelled even at a white lie. Still it might really be a pleasure, she reassured herself. Professor Smee's wife would not be like her mother's callers. 'Does Mrs Smee do any scientific work?'

'Oh dear, no. My wife objects to science even more than she does to boating!'

'But she must be interested in *your* work?' Ursula persisted. She felt it incredible that a woman could be married to Vernon Smee and not be interested.

'Not even in my work, I fear.' It occurred to Professor Smee that it must be rather pleasant to have a wife who was 'interested', a wife with whom one could really talk, instead of having to listen to a never-ending babble about maids and tradespeople. He did not consider whether he had ever made the least effort to arouse Charlotte's interest, or whether, on his side, he had shown any interest in her pursuits. 'My wife is very domestic,' he said. 'I fancy the kitchen department claims most of her attention.'

'I see.' Poor Professor Smee, how dreadful for him to be tied to an utterly brainless woman, Ursula was telling herself. She was really unaware that successful domesticity required brains as much as any other occupation.

The compassion in the girl's voice did not escape her companion. Instead of resenting it, Vernon Smee was beguiled into further confidence. 'I suppose it is hard on Mrs Smee, too,' he suggested with rather an unfair pretence of fairness. 'Naturally, as she knows nothing of science, she is a little apt to resent my devoting so much time to it. In the evenings, for instance, it is lonely for her – but how can I help it?'

'Of course, you can't help it. You must do your work.' Ursula checked her indignant outburst 'But surely Mrs Smee is proud of your position, the distinction you have gained,' she urged instead.

'I don't think the little distinction I have achieved makes much difference to her. Probably my wife hardly realises it. Indeed, I think she preferred it when I was quite unknown. I was only twenty-one when we were married, a boy – a young idiot, I dare say.' He laughed, but there had been an underlying bitterness in his tone.

'Don't.' Ursula felt as though she could not trust herself to say more. She was too angry, too sorry. What a dreadful, underbred woman this Mrs Smee must be. In her flattered sympathy she forgot that it might also be rather 'dreadful' and distinctly 'underbred' for a man thus to discuss his wife.

At Henley the party reunited and hurried down to the boats. These had already been ordered; Ursula was a little amused when she saw that they took the form of a canoe for two and a sculling boat. As she expected, her mother was soon sitting in the canoe, while Captain Talbot, with more alertness than his appearance suggested, had firmly grasped the paddle. 'So much better than having one great heavy boat,' Mrs Hibbert babbled pleasantly, as the party was getting embarked. 'And, of course, we will keep together and change about.'

'Well, there is certainly one link; we have got all the lunch!' Ursula's voice showed a slightly resentful amusement. Really, it was too bad of Mother! Chaperoning the older generation was no child's play! Here she would be left all by herself to entertain three men, two of them absolute strangers. What on earth should she say to them? As her mother knew very well, her small talk was small only in quantity. However, one thing would have been worse: if she herself had been manoeuvred into the canoe with one of the men – unless, indeed, that man had been Professor Smee. But he probably could not row.

As though to falsify Ursula's thoughts, Professor Smee volunteered to take an oar. The boat was the usual Thames double sculler, and as the Professor was considerably the oldest man present, politeness gave him stroke. At first all went fairly well, but as they reached the more crowded part of the river, Smee's incompetence declared itself. In spite of Jack Cartwright's efforts to follow the stroke's erratic time, the two pairs of sculls were constantly getting involved. 'Hope you folks can all swim?' the young sub asked presently with a cheerful grin. 'Wouldn't it be better, sir, in this jam, for one of us to take her alone? Shall I come forward, or will you keep on?'

'I will keep on.' Vernon Smee was rather breathless, but he was determined to show that he could do it. Of course it was years since he had rowed, but when he was a lad at the Science Schools he often used to go out on the Serpentine. And he could do it now if there was anyone to steer. Why had Balestier not put on the rudder? Then he noticed that none of the boats had one. But this constant shouting of 'Look out, sir,' 'Mind your oars, sir,' was maddening. If only people would be quiet, he could get on perfectly – Crack!

They had run into another boat and had snapped its rowlock. There were angry recriminations, the Professor's being naturally the angrier as he was to blame. Fortunately the pressure of other small craft drove the two disputants apart. Professor Smee still sculled on doggedly. They were certainly going better, he congratulated himself. Then he noticed that young Cartwright was steering with a paddle in the bows, while Balestier, in the stern, was vigorously pushing off any other boat that came critically close. 'I think that I've about done my share.' Vernon Smee laid down his sculls pettishly.

Balestier took his place. The Professor's annoyance only increased when he saw how much better the boat went. They were gliding in and out among the other craft in an almost magical way. Indeed, vexation and fatigue quite prevented his enjoying the scene as a whole, or even realising it. The one comfort was to notice that Cartwright was still using the paddle. It had not been, as he had imagined, a reflection on his incompetence.

Ursula was very silent. She was wishing that Professor Smee had not come. When he was so much more distinguished than these other men, how could he condescend to compete with them, to put himself on their level? Indeed, it had been considerably below their level! A man like Professor Smee should have rested on his oars in a literal sense and have left rowing to empty-headed boys. All he had done so far was to spoil everybody's pleasure. Henley could hardly be enjoyed as a target of disparaging shouts – not to mention the constant expectation she had had of finding herself in the river.

Now, however, this was over. Their course grew slower and slower as the boats grew denser, but it was entirely peaceful. Mr Balestier had shipped his sculls and was now also paddling – indeed, this was the only possible means of progression. It was wonderful how they got along at all, Ursula felt. The river seemed a solid mass of skiffs – you could have walked from shore to shore – and yet somehow their boat nosed out a little dark, watery path between. How extraordinarily bright it all was! Ursula had not been to Henley since she was quite a child, and so her impressions were undulled by custom. She had never seen such a light-coloured crowd, she reflected. Usually in a mass of people the faces show as little pale spots on a dark background. Here they were almost dark, or at any rate, swallowed up in the dazzling setting of bright cushions and parasols, white dresses and male flannels. The quiet trees and meadows on either bank gave relief in this kaleidoscopic picture. It was very beautiful, the English verdure. Ursula almost wished she could escape into it, away from the brilliant, moving, chattering scene. If only in some quiet reach she could have the bathe with which Professor Smee had threatened the whole party. How she would enjoy a good swim!

By most skilful manipulation, their boat had now been brought alongside one of the posts that marked the line of the course and not too far from the coveted finish. A race was just going to start. Professor Smee felt more and more out of it, as the other two men began an eager discussion as to crews and chances. Confound them, he thought with renewed irritation, they seemed to know all the men rowing and half the spectators. Even Ursula had impinged enough on her mother's circle to have a good many acquaintances in the fashionable Henley crowd. Indeed, Miss Winfield was rather sought after on her rare appearances, probably because they were so rare. She was something of a mystery, this handsome girl, who was also presumably an heiress, and who spent her life in the attics of her mother's house. There was a story going that at the last Hibbert at home, a figure in a blue overall, with grimy hands and face, had suddenly appeared on the stairs. Pushing past some startled guests, the apparition had switched off a few unnecessary lights, with a murmured, 'I've got a lot of current on too – the main fuse will go,' and then had as rapidly disappeared. If the anecdote were true, it testified to the courage of hostesses that they continued to ply Ursula with useless invitations. Even now a friendly summons to lunch was heard from a neighbouring houseboat. 'Do come,

Miss Winfield, and bring Mr Balestier and Mr Cartwright – oh, all your party,' the speaker added with a rather marked afterthought as she caught sight of the third male figure.

Ursula would have resented the unintentional slight to Professor Smee more, had he not so obviously resented it himself. Again it seemed unworthy. But, in any case, the invitation must naturally be declined. 'I am chaperoning Mother,' she explained. 'Have you seen her – in a canoe?'

'Me-and-'er-ing,' Jack Cartwright murmured. The vile pun was not even original.

But nothing had been seen of the errant canoe. Indeed, with the best intention it would have been impossible to keep two boats together in such a crowd. However, before they separated, Mrs Hibbert had arranged a definite rendezvous for lunch, and Ursula knew that she could count on finding her there. For, despite the mother's apparent fluffiness, she was really extremely practical, more so in many respects than the scientific daughter. As Ursula had wickedly hinted, a first-rate lunch would take precedence in her mother's mind over any man, however delightful. Indeed, little Mrs Hibbert's flirtations were too transparent to be serious. 'It is so tiresome of the dear boys to fall in love with me,' she used to complain to her husband. 'I always tell them that I can only be a mother to them.'

Any search for the 'meandering' canoe was, naturally, out of the question until this race was over. Indeed, had it been possible, Ursula doubted whether anything would have dragged Mr Balestier and Jack Cartwright from their post of vantage, for Eton was rowing in this heat – it was the Ladies'

Plate – and they were both Eton men. It now transpired that they had even been at school together. 'I knew you at once,' Cartwright said, 'though, of course, you wouldn't remember me. I was still in the Lower School when you went up to the 'Varsity.' Something of the former overpowering awe for a sixth form boy survived in his tone.

'Was Mr Balestier too grand in those days even to speak to you?' Ursula laughed. 'What a dreadful place Eton must be!'

Young Cartwright turned red. The solemn sanctity with which the public school man invests his school had been profaned. However, everyone knew that Miss Winfield was rather odd. 'Once Balestier spoke to me. He said he'd beat me if I made such a row again outside Upper School.'

'It was hardly an ingratiating way of opening an acquaintance,' Ursula suggested.

Tony Balestier looked amused. 'Boys are a set of young savages,' he said, with an unexpected open-mindedness. 'But I know your name quite well.' He turned to Jack Cartwright. 'Didn't you win the hurdles two years running? Yes, and I believe I saw you play for the Oppidans at the Wall. You were keeper of the Field, weren't you?'

The young sub blushed again, this time through embarrassed gratification. 'Bit o' luck, those hurdles,' he murmured modestly.

'Dear me, I had no idea we were entertaining such a hero!' The tinge of mockery in Ursula's voice was carried off by her smile.

Professor Smee had been sitting beside her in an almost sulky silence. Perhaps his irritation had made him undiscerning, for he took the girl's remark literally. 'I suppose it was because I went to a vulgar little grammar school and not to Eton that we were taught to work instead of play,' he now observed.

Ursula turned to him. She would not let herself be conscious of any bad taste. 'Where were you at school?' she asked.

'Oh, it was only a day school. I'm sure you've never even heard of the town; it's in the Staffordshire pottery district. They specialise in things like pudding basins.'

'But not in pudding heads!' Ursula smiled at him pleasantly. 'Did you come straight to London then from your little day school?'

'Yes, I got the Whitworth Scholarship at South Kensington. Otherwise, I suppose I should now be making pudding basins myself. I was quite astounded at winning it, for I had had no special coaching like most of the other competitors.'

'Rotter.' Jack Cartwright just managed to keep his expression of opinion to himself. 'Beastly bad form,' the young fellow was thinking. It was the severest censure in his vocabulary. Anyway, this Smee chap was making an ass of himself going on in this style when Balestier was every bit as big a pot in the intellectual line. Hadn't Balestier been head of the school and a Balliol scholar and all that sort of thing? But he didn't go bragging round like a rotten little board school kid!

A shot was heard; it meant the start of the race. Everyone gazed up the course. After what seemed a long time, but was really a very few minutes, a boat was seen rounding the bend. The cox was not in the Eton blue. But there was the nose of the second boat. It was barely a length behind. Yes, and it seemed to be creeping up. It *was* creeping up. Balestier and Cartwright began to shout – indeed, there was a roar of cheering. The two boats were almost level as they passed. 'Well rowed, indeed,' came from all sides. Before the boats disappeared round the bend, Eton was leading.

The finish at this point was almost a foregone conclusion. But by how much would they win? Presently the official tug came along. 'Eton two and three-quarter lengths' – there was a gasp of astonishment. No one had expected more than a length. '*Floreat Etona*,' Cartwright yelled. Both he and Tony Balestier looked as though they had come into a fortune.

Ursula had been caught up in the general enthusiasm, but now she felt a little contemptuous. How absurd it all was! Why did the Englishman take his sport – and nothing else – seriously? She remembered a Russian scientist she had known, who had been invited to some meet. 'What a great organisation!' he had said to her afterwards, laughing aloud in his amusement; 'and all for the capture of one so small an animal that my little boy of twelve could readily shoot it!' Ursula had stared for a moment in genuine horror; then she, too, had laughed. 'We call that vulpicide in England,' she explained. 'It is a great deal more reprehensible than killing all your relations.' And now again, she reflected, was not Henley 'so great an organisation' for 'so small' an end? What did it really matter which of the two boats was a few yards ahead?

Jack Cartwright had meanwhile been untying the painter and they were again moving. Keeping watch for her mother distracted Ursula's thoughts, but she saw no sign of her until the appointed lunch place had been reached. There was the little canoe already established in the best nook under the overhanging trees. 'Oh, there you are at last, you naughty people,' Mrs Hibbert called out gaily. 'I am absolutely starved! Wasn't it too lovely, those darling boys winning after all? I can't understand anyone not sending their sons to Eton – the blue is too sweet.'

It was while they were having lunch that a little craft passed, unlike any that they had seen before. It was carrying a large white notice stretching from bow to stern with purple and green lettering. The legend was at that time too indented on the public consciousness for it even to be necessary to read it. 'The ubiquitous suffragette,' Mr Balestier murmured with a slight air of disgust.

'What can be the point of their coming to Henley?' Mrs Hibbert observed. '*Boats* for Women?'

'My aunt, that's a thunderingly pretty girl!' The interruption came from Jack Cartwright, who had parted the overhanging willow boughs to get a clear view of the suffrage skiff. 'Shouldn't mind being the bobby who runs her in!'

'Oh, those Pankhurst people are quite clever enough to pick out a good-looking girl to send here.' Mrs Hibbert's tone was a shade acid. She put up her lorgnettes, but as the canoe was on the inner side of the double sculler, her vision was rather blocked. 'Well, I can't see your siren very well, but she doesn't strike me as so wonderful.'

'Yes, Mother, she really is. She is extraordinarily pretty – look, that one in the bows.' Ursula, too, had been peering out between the branches. Her praise, though decided, was surprised. This, as far as she knew, was her first introduction to the redoubtable 'militants'. She was not quite sure what she had expected them to look like, but certainly not like this! The 'siren' might be an exception, indeed, such beauty could not fail to be, but the four other occupants of the suffrage boat all looked refined and ladylike; indeed, they were quite indistinguishable from other girls in other boats. Was it possible that these were the raging viragos of whom the papers were full? Besides, the 'siren' was not only lovely; she impressed Ursula as being the most ethereal-looking creature she had ever seen. Yes, there was something flower-like about the slight figure, the pure, pale face with its tranquil expression – or was saint-like the truer description? A little smile was on the girl's lips as she sat trailing one white hand in the cool, green water. She was evidently quite unconscious of the scrutiny to which she was being subjected.

Ursula Winfield sat back with a jerk. The suffrage boat was moving away and she felt suddenly that she had been rude; she ought not to have stared. Still, when people came to Henley in a craft plastered all over with huge notices presumably they expected starers. She realised with surprise that Captain Talbot was enunciating quite a long sentence: 'Biggest crowd I ever was in, by Jove! Even if they'd only come for a rag, they had come, what? Men shovin' and singin' all round the Pankhurst girl's stand. Thought the whole caboodle would be over, but she never turned a hair. Some nerve, what?'

'The whole business is detestable – it degrades women.' Mr Balestier was speaking. Perhaps he thought that such seriousness verged on bad form, or perhaps he was merely bored with the subject, for he abruptly changed the conversation.

The afternoon passed very much as the morning had done. Ursula began to get rather tired of it all. A Henley day was so excessively long, and doing nothing so extremely exhausting. She would not have felt nearly as tired had she been working in her laboratory for the same length of time. They had arranged to leave by a seven o'clock train, but Ursula was not at all sure whether her mother intended to catch it. Mrs Hibbert had perfected the plausible missing of trains into a fine art, although nothing annoyed her more than other people's inopportune unpunctuality. Mr Balestier had now taken Captain Talbot's place in the canoe, and Ursula's heart sank as she saw that her mother was evidently appreciating his conversation after her previous escort's heavy, if admiring, silences. The girl found, however, an unexpected ally in Mr Smee, who was also anxious to get home in good time, and even inquired about the possibility of catching an earlier train. Between them they managed to hustle Mrs Hibbert on to the platform just as the guard was preparing to blow his whistle.

Ursula sank into her seat rather breathless. It was a good thing that Professor Smee had hurried on ahead and found places. As it was, he had only been able to secure three, each in a different compartment, but she supposed that the other men of the party had managed to crowd in somewhere. How hot it was in this packed carriage! Apparently her neighbour also felt it so, for she half rose to take off her cloak. Ursula glanced round carelessly. A tricolour suffragette scarf flared on her vision. Yes, and there was the 'siren' sitting beyond in the corner. What an odd coincidence!

As the journey went on, Ursula could not help overhearing a good deal of the suffragettes' conversation. It was amusing to get a view of Henley from this totally different angle. The races seemed to play an even less important part in their thoughts than in her own – indeed, she began to wonder if they knew that there had been races! They were talking about the owner of one of the houseboats they had boarded. 'She really seemed impressed,' the girl next to Ursula declared triumphantly. 'If only she keeps her promise and comes to Queen's Hall on Monday! She's quite important, you know, and very rich.'

The 'siren' gave a tired sigh – her real name was Mary Blake, Ursula had discovered. 'One is glad to do it, of course, but Henley is horrible. All those staring men!'

'That is because you are so pretty.' The friend's tone was calmly impersonal. 'But it's awfully useful really.' Whether she was referring to Miss Blake's appearance or to the visit to Henley, Ursula could not determine. 'Anyway, it was pleasanter than a raid!'

'I don't know.' Ursula looked up involuntarily at Miss Blake's words. 'At a raid one can just think of the Cause and forget oneself.'

'Well, I can't!' The other suffragette laughed. 'Not when a mounted policeman's horse is prancing on my toe. Why, aren't you black and blue all over after a raid?'

'Oh yes, of course, but I meant – ' Miss Blake's voice trailed away. She seemed too tired to explain, too tired to speak at all.

She began languidly drawing out her hatpins, and took off her hat, revealing masses of pale golden hair coiled round her head. Presently, as she leant back in her corner, her white eyelids began to droop.

Ursula felt interested; she was also puzzled. So these suffragettes really did not enjoy the publicity they courted; they seemed positively to dislike it. And how unpleasant it must be to find oneself 'black and blue all over'! They genuinely were doing these outrageous things for the sake of 'the Cause', as they called it. How could anyone feel that a vote was worth it? If it had been a question of sacrificing themselves for some scientific work, for the furtherance of a discovery, then she could have understood it. But if these girls were nice, as they seemed, it made it all the more tragic that they should be thus mistakenly lowering themselves, lowering the whole of womanhood by their antics. Involuntarily Ursula's gaze wandered back to Mary Blake. She appeared to be asleep, and she looked even lovelier than before. The peaceful purity of her clear-cut pale face, the curve of her lips, the long dark lashes curling on her cheek, quite took Ursula's breath away. Once more she sat staring at this girl.

Suddenly Mary Blake's eyes opened. She did not seem to resent the stranger's gaze, perhaps because she was still hardly awake. Her hand wandered to a large, limp, whitish canvas bag that lay on her lap. 'Have you seen our last number?' she said, pulling out a copy of the well-known suffrage organ. 'It is the only one I have left.'

Ursula took it reluctantly. She could hardly refuse, but she disliked being associated with the movement even to this extent. 'I never see your paper; I am not a sympathiser,' she said curtly.

Mary Blake smiled. 'Perhaps if you did see it, you would be,' she suggested gently.

'I hardly think so.' Ursula felt irritated by the girl's calm assurance. Perhaps something of the age-long antagonism between science and religion, between fact and faith, was rising in her. 'Still, I will try,' she added with an effort at fairness. The little paper was, perhaps, better written than she had expected, but it did not impress her much. Its arrogant tone of confidence was simply exasperating. And the way in which it acclaimed the suffragettes in gaol as heroines and martyrs. It was too ridiculous! Why, these women had only to promise to behave themselves for twelve months and they could all walk out. As soon as she decently could, Ursula folded the paper and handed it back with a cold, 'Many thanks.'

'One day' – there was a curious light in Mary Blake's eyes, a rapt note in her voice – 'one day you will come to us.'

CHAPTER FOUR

Charlotte Smee was sitting in the dining room of her little house in Clarendon Road – dubiously Notting Hill Gate. She had *The Daily Telegraph* in her hand, but she was not reading it. She read little at any time, and now she was too vexed to make the necessary effort. Her plump face was even redder than usual and her indefinite eyes looked moist. The ugly black marble clock on the mantelpiece struck; it was half-past eight. 'It's disgraceful of him,' she muttered angrily.

The Henley expedition had annoyed her from the first, although she had tried not to show it. Certainly, she detested boating and was very unlikely to have accepted. Still, Vernon's grand friends might have had the common politeness to ask her. Pride had kept her silent when her husband had told her of the invitation with a careless, 'they didn't mention you, and, of course, I knew regattas weren't in your line.' He had never noticed the hurt look on her face, nor had he realised since that her extreme irritability was due to a rankling sense of humiliation. No, he only wished, with an aggrieved discomfort, that Charlotte would stop bringing up every possible, petty grievance and nagging over it continuously.

Of course this was not the first time during the Smees' twenty-one years of married life that the Professor had struck up a friendship of this sort. There had been several other smart ladies at various times at whose houses he had been intimate, but who had shown no desire to extend the acquaintance to his wife. Repetition of the experience had not, however, accustomed Charlotte to it; rather a consciousness of increasing years and decreasing looks made it each time more painful. She was a little older than her husband, although the fact had passed unnoticed when he, as a precocious, impecunious lad of twenty-one had married her, a girl of twenty-five of tolerable appearance and good expectations. Her father, a prosperous Balham grocer, had been regarded as a 'warm man', and everyone, including Vernon himself, had considered the bridegroom to be the lucky one in making so good a match. But since then, not only had there been a strange reversal in their comparative social status, but the difference between their ages had unaccountably increased. On the last occasion that the Smees had gone to a scientific soirée, poor Charlotte had been asked after her 'distinguished son'. The tears still welled into her eyes at the mortifying recollection.

It was perhaps not surprising under these circumstances that Charlotte Smee was apt to resent her husband's woman friends. This time there was certainly some cause for resentment, although she did not know it; indeed, she misread, almost comically, the whole situation. For it was Mrs Hibbert whom she regarded as the attraction; the scientific daughter she believed to be a mere schoolgirl. When Vernon had told her of the Lowndes Square household, it was of the mother he had spoken, her gorgeous dress, her amazing youthfulness. In reply to Charlotte's query as to whether Miss Winfield were pretty, her husband had answered 'Not exactly', and the subject was dropped. Vernon had always been rather bored by young girls, his wife had thought guilelessly.

Even with regard to Mrs Hibbert, Charlotte Smee's objection was, so far, more to the type than to the individual. Mrs Hibbert was one of the grand ladies who had made Vernon so critical and discontented. In the old days when they lived at Leeds on the small income of a university demonstrator, Vernon had been fond of his home and proud of it. He used to admire her domestic management and tell her that he got better food in his own house than anywhere else. Quite frequently at that time he would bring back one of his friends to supper. They used to have such pleasant evenings, and Charlotte would sing. But since they had come to town about eleven years ago, Vernon had been so discouraging about her music that she had quite dropped it. He said, too, that entertaining in London was beyond their means, so no one was invited to Clarendon Road. Occasionally, indeed, he gave a men's dinner party at the Savoy – it was necessary for his position, he told her. As though she could not have done double the entertaining at home for half the cost, Charlotte felt resentfully. But, of course, she knew that expense was not the real reason why Vernon did not ask people to the house. He was ashamed of it; yes, he was ashamed of his home; he was ashamed of his wife! A tear rolled down Mrs Smee's fat cheek and plopped on the tight, sham-lace yoke of her silk bodice.

The clock struck three-quarters. General woes were swallowed up in the particular one – dinner would be ruined! Vernon's not returning became a greater crime than his having gone. Certainly he had said as he started that he might be a little late; that was why she had ordered dinner for half-past seven instead of seven as usual. But here it was getting on for nine! Nothing would be fit to eat and Cook would be furious. Very likely she would give notice and, except for her temper, she was such a treasure. A despairing memory came to Mrs Smee of a long series of incompetent domestics. How annoyed Vernon had been when the last cook had sent up whitebait boiled! And the other one who had put the asparagus through the sieve! Yes, most girls needed watching over hand and foot. Indeed, more than once during a servantless interval, Mrs Smee had been obliged to do all the work herself, helped by an accommodating 'char'. Not that she had minded it. Her cooking was excellent, and she took quite an artist's pleasure in it. Nor did she dislike the housework – the brasses and the silver never shone with so high a polish as during these domestic interregna. But her satisfaction was spoilt by the terror of being 'found out'. All the time she felt like a culprit. Vernon's friends would indeed despise her, she told herself, if they knew she ever acted in a menial capacity.

And if Cook left, no doubt Carter would leave too – so Mrs Smee's thoughts now ran on gloomily. Servants never could stand a change. Besides, Carter had only just come. She was not yet rooted. Mrs Smee was still dreading to hear 'I wish to leave at the end of my month, M'm,' every time the girl came into the room. And the expense was so enormous of changing servants nowadays. Procuring Carter had cost her over a pound – three and sixpence on a totally fruitless advertisement in the *Morning Post* and four registry office fees. Oh, those miserable registry offices with their crowd of anxious mistresses waiting vainly for servants who never came! It was all very well for people who could afford to give exorbitant wages or who kept a large staff; they, no doubt, could get servants easily enough. But when it came to cook-generals and house-parlourmaids with wages from twenty-two to twenty-six pounds a year, well, they absolutely didn't exist.

A taxi slowed up at the door. The fare got out. Charlotte recognised her husband's step. The driver's unusually polite, 'Thank you, sir,' caused her irritation to increase. Vernon always overpaid everyone so ridiculously. And then he considered himself economical! Mrs Smee's grievance was not without grounds, for her husband did get through a good deal of money. The Professor did not drink champagne, as he often mentioned, but he liked his claret good. He was not a great smoker, but his cigars cost ninety-four shillings a hundred. He did not have many new suits, but his tailor lived in Albemarle Street. The flannels he was wearing had cost just twice as much as his wife's 'Paris Model' gown.

Meanwhile, the taxi had palpitated off. Smee, having let himself in, was making a hasty toilette. He now opened the dining room door. 'Oh, there you are,' he called out gaily. 'Of course, you didn't wait.'

'Of course I did.' Charlotte's voice was sullen. 'Do you think I could ask Carter to bring up the whole dinner twice?

Well, as you *have* come home, you had better ring and let them know.'

'Carter saw me in the hall.' The brightness had faded from Vernon's face. This was all the reward he got for trying to be home early. Why, he had made a perfect nuisance of himself hurrying everybody to the station. And he hadn't had such a particularly pleasant day either. Charlotte needn't be in such a temper. He glanced at the clock. By Jove, five to nine! It was later than he had thought. Then he remembered his wife's irritating habit of keeping the clock a quarter of an hour fast. He pulled out his watch and compared it. 'That's all wrong,' he said aloud. 'It's not much after half-past eight.' The fifteen minutes gained gave him a feeling of virtuous punctuality.

'Even so, it does not make you in time for seven o'clock dinner.'

From being apologetic, the Professor grew injured. 'Well, I told you I should be late,' he grumbled. 'It's a nice thing that a man can't go to Henley without being abused like a pickpocket. It's seldom enough that I get a day's holiday.'

However, the meal was a pleasant surprise. Professor Smee ate with appetite. 'It is much better than what we had for lunch,' he observed.

A slight smile came over Charlotte's blotched face. When the dessert had been put on the table and Carter finally left the room, her mistress felt free to abandon her fictitious and garrulous gaiety. Perhaps the abrupt silence brought to Vernon a consciousness of his remissness, for he now looked up. 'I forgot to say that I am the bearer of all sorts of apologies for your not having been asked today. I explained that you didn't care for boating, but Miss Winfield was afraid you might have thought them rude. She told me to tell you that it was my fault for not having mentioned I was married.'

The look of relief that had crossed Charlotte's face at his first words, vanished as he went on. 'Miss Winfield? Didn't the apologies come from Mrs Hibbert?' she asked suspiciously.

'It was Miss Winfield to whom I was talking.' Professor Smee's conscience was so entirely at rest with regard to Miss Winfield's mother, with whom, indeed, he had hardly spoken, that he had no suspicion of his wife's interpretation. 'I didn't mention you to Mrs Hibbert,' he said carelessly.

'No, I suppose not. No doubt you had plenty of other more agreeable things to talk about!' Poor Charlotte rushed chokingly from the room.

Her one idea was to take refuge somewhere before bursting into a storm of tears. Her bedroom – no, Carter might be there turning down the bed. The drawing room would certainly be empty. She opened the door. There, sitting by the window, dimly visible in the dusk, was a substantial figure, motionless save for hands busily knitting. 'Susie!' she exclaimed, surprise routing her lachrymose intentions.

The sisters embraced with affectionate fervour. 'I didn't scare you, did I, Lottie?' Mrs Todd inquired. 'Not that I'd be likely to be mistook for a ghost!' Her whole fifteen stone of good nature wobbled with laughter.

'You dear old Susie.' Charlotte squeezed her sister's hand. 'Let's sit down and be cosy.' It would add to the cosiness not to have the lamp, she went on, her real reason being a desire to conceal her tear-stained face. She inquired solicitously how long her sister had been waiting and why she had not been told.

Mrs Todd was reassuring. She had not been there above ''alf a nour', as she put it. 'Don't you fret yourself, my dear, I 'ad my knitting'; she soothed Charlotte's apologies. 'At 'ome now I might 'ave grudged the time, for a biz is worse than a baby in the work it gives you. But on an 'oliday what does it matter? And it wasn't your gell's fault; she wanted to tell. But I said don't disturb 'em. A man likes to set quiet over 'is vittles.'

'But you *should* have let Carter tell me,' Charlotte urged reproachfully. Susie was so seldom in London, she said, that she must see a lot of her – 'no one can't 'elp doing that' – Mrs Todd interpolated with her fat chuckle. After that the sisters' talk then turned on family matters, Charlotte inquiring eagerly after the four young Todds. The eldest was in the paternal business – Todd *père* was a ship chandler at Southampton – 'an' the way the boy's took to it is something wunnerful. 'E's got a rare 'eadpiece, Frank 'as,' his mother observed proudly. The next sister, Florence, a teacher, was also doing remarkably well. The list of subjects in which she had recently passed examinations seemed to exhaust human knowledge. 'Not that I altogether 'olds with the edication nowadays,' Mrs Todd commented, 'it's too much smatterings with that there French, an' natural science, an' two M's an' three D's an' 'eaven knows what all! Simple an' thorough is my motter. It's just the same as with vittles, which everyone knows as meat an' puddin' an' come again is a deal 'ealthier fer the stomick than your grand dinners with dozens o' courses, an' 'ardly a mouthful to any one of 'em.'

Charlotte was here suddenly stung with a sense of hospitable guilt. 'Oh, but that reminds me, have *you* had your dinner, Susie?'

'Dinner? At nine o'clock at night. It does sound funny.' Mrs Todd laughed again. 'Twelve-thirty is *my* dinner hour, my dear, an' allus 'as been. Why, I 'ad dinner afore I left Southampton an' I've 'ad supper too at the hotel. An' now I expects I'll be thinkin' of 'aving bed.'

'Oh, no, no, you mustn't go yet.' Charlotte's vehemence was quite sincere. For the first time for days she was feeling almost happy. Besides being really very fond of her sister, she experienced in Susie's company an unwonted and refreshing sense of brilliancy and elegance. Her sister's naive admiration came as balm to her slighted soul. As Mrs Todd herself always humbly put it, she had not received Charlotte's advantages. There was a difference of fourteen years between the sisters, and their father, the grocer, had during the interval developed from a white-aproned assistant serving behind a counter into a black-coated manager already dreaming of the day when he would walk proudly around his own emporium. The transformation had been reflected in the education of the two daughters, for Susie, in her youth, had attended a board school, although the fact was afterwards suppressed, while Charlotte went to a young ladies' seminary of the most genteel description with lessons in dancing and the pianoforte a guinea extra. Nor had Susie been able later to supplement her scanty book learning. The care of a delicate mother and many short-lived little brothers and sisters had overfilled her girlhood. Then, when with Charlotte's growing-up she might have attained more leisure, she had chosen to marry Samuel Todd. Since that time her four successful children and the growing 'biz' had completely absorbed her.

As they sat there, the elder sister passed in review Lottie's married life. Of the first half, the Leeds period, she knew but little; the sisters had never once met during those eleven years. They had both been very tied; nor, in either household, had money been sufficiently plentiful to admit of long railway journeys. Even letters had been infrequent between them, for Charlotte was strangely dumb on paper, while the actual calligraphy was always an effort to Mrs Todd. Of course, the sisters had communicated to each other the central facts of their existence. Susan had known, for instance, of the five brief and tiny lives that had come to Charlotte during this time – lives so brief and so tiny that they could hardly be said to have existed. But she knew nothing more. When they had last met, as Charlotte did not refer to the subject, Susan Todd had been shy of doing so. Now the silence of years was broken. 'What a pity,' she murmured, 'that none of your little 'uns didn't live.'

The result of her words was unexpected. Charlotte broke into a perfect passion of weeping, utterly overshadowing her former grief. Her sister was absolutely alarmed. 'Poor dear, poor dear,' she murmured in remorseful surprise. 'I didn't know you still felt so about it. I didn't ought to have spoke of them.'

'Speaking of them doesn't matter when the thought is with me always.' The face that Charlotte raised, though blotched and distorted, had a certain dignity of woe. Her tragic intensity even brought a tinge of poetry to her commonplace speech. 'All these years I've been longing for them, aching for them. I dream of them at night – but then the empty morning comes. If they'd have lived, Vernon might have gone on caring, though I shouldn't have needed it so much. It isn't fair, oh, it isn't fair! I paid the price. I had the suffering. To give me five and to take them all. It isn't fair when I want them so.'

CHAPTER FIVE

On the following Sunday, Professor Smee went to call at Lowndes Square, 'a duty call' he phrased it to himself, demanded by Mrs Hibbert's recent hospitality. Unfortunately, as after Henley, he returned home hopelessly late for the evening meal, and this time found that his wife's annoyance had been acute enough to carry her off to her own room. Such exaggerated resentment only repeated its former effect of changing the Professor's sense of guilt into one of grievance. It was ridiculous of Charlotte, he felt angrily. As though it could matter his being unpunctual on a Sunday when they always had cold supper! Besides, it had not been his fault. When he had arrived at Lowndes Square, Mrs Hibbert and Miss Winfield had been on the point of starting for a motor run with the inevitable Captain Talbot to drive them. Mrs Hibbert had already established herself on the front seat, and when Professor Smee appeared, she pressed him to come too, offering with vicarious kindness a spare motor coat and cap of the Colonel's. It was a tempting day, and Vernon Smee would probably have accepted the invitation even had the vacant fourth place not happened to be next to Miss Winfield.

The Professor's opportunities of meeting Ursula had not been limited to this chance 'joy ride'. For she was still working at his College all day and every day. But although he constantly saw her there, he did little more than see her. The girl's absorption in her experiments was so profound that Vernon Smee often wondered whether she realised his presence at all, and as for the two youths he had assigned to her, he was certain that she regarded them as a mere part of her apparatus. Of course, when he addressed a remark to Miss Winfield on the subject of her work, she responded readily and even gratefully. These discussions between them invariably left each with a heightened opinion of the other. For Ursula was profoundly impressed by the Professor's experimental skill, and still more by his rapid grasp of a subject upon which he had previously worked so little. The fact that she herself was 'slow in the uptake' made this barrister-like quality of mind seem to her the more wonderful. And Vernon Smee for his part became increasingly convinced that Miss Winfield had the touch of genius with which, indeed, he had always credited her.

Consequently, genuine scientific interest, as well as a growing personal feeling for his new 'special student', caused the Professor to spend a great deal of his time in the small research laboratory. He would have been there even more, now that the vacation had set him comparatively free, but for a chance remark he had overheard. 'The Prof seems considerably attached to our group!' the younger of the two men who were working with her had said to the other. Vernon Smee realised with a shock that he must be more discreet. The next few days were spent in the correction of examination papers and the 'Prof' was hardly seen by Miss Winfield's 'group'.

But this separation during working hours made it still more annoying that he could never have a word with Miss Winfield at lunch time. For the proximity of the College to Lowndes Square, instead of proving an attraction, as he had urged, was certainly for him the reverse. It enabled Miss Winfield to go home in the middle of the day – at a very variable hour indeed – but still for lunch. 'Mother always has it put for me in the library,' she told him with an unusual burst of expansiveness. 'It is so deliciously quiet and nearly as quick as going to a restaurant. Of course I wouldn't do it if I had to go into the dining room. There are nearly always visitors, and I shouldn't be properly dressed.'

Professor Smee could not be surprised at her decision. Still, if her home had been more distant, she would have had to fall back on a restaurant. In this case she would have presumably have patronised the Museum, where he went himself; it was certainly the best place in the neighbourhood, and it had the further advantage of being barred by its prices to ribald young students. Indeed, Vernon Smee's habitual lunch room was fast becoming deserted, for most of the usual throng of professors had already left for their holidays. And his own lingering had nothing to do with Miss Winfield, he reassured himself. Did he ever start his annual Swiss climbing expedition until August? For one thing, his exchequer wouldn't run to more than three or four weeks of it. It was a nuisance that guides and everything made climbing so expensive, when it was really such a laudably simple recreation.

The next evening he was just walking along the corridor, when a strange lady suddenly bore down upon him. He recognised the type almost with a groan – the mother of a prospective student. Well, it was too late to beat a retreat now; he must ask her into his private room, though he knew she would talk and talk and talk. She did! Of course her young hopeful was a genius; of course he had evinced an extraordinary scientific talent at a marvellously early age. Mothers should be exterminated, the Professor thought wrathfully, as he listened to an outpouring of doting *infantilia*. Finally, as a climax, the boy's photograph was produced! However, soon after that he did manage to get rid of the woman. But Miss Winfield would certainly have left. Why, it was past seven. She never stayed until this hour. However, he would just go upstairs to make absolutely certain.

He opened the door. His heart gave a sudden thump. There she was. Her back was turned to him; she had not heard him come in. How beautiful her hair was – that great coiled knot and the little curling tendrils. It gave a man an insane desire to touch it, to –

Perhaps Ursula felt the slight current of air from the open door, for now she turned. There was a dazed look on her face. 'Oh, is it you?' she said almost as though she did not recognise him. 'My tests have come out so beautifully today. They are just what I wanted.'

Her oblivious impersonality had the effect of bringing Vernon Smee back to common sense. 'I am so glad,' he said, more or less in his ordinary voice. He noticed that Ursula's face, although happy, was very white. 'But you are looking rather used up. Why not come and have some tea in my room?' It was a sudden inspiration. 'I am sure the porter's wife would get it for me.'

Rather to his surprise, Ursula consented; he always called her Ursula now in his thoughts, the name suited her so well, he thought. She had already begun putting away and arranging her apparatus for the night. 'I *am* rather used up,' she said. Indeed, as she walked along the corridor beside him, he thought once that she swayed. As soon as she got to his room, she sank down into his big chair and shut her eyes. 'It makes me feel rather giddy when I have been working very hard for a long time,' she explained.

'You shouldn't work so hard, nor for such a long time.' Vernon Smee's tone was severely anxious. 'Is there anything I can do – or get for you?' This unexpected weakness affected him strangely. He had felt that Ursula was almost inhumanly above all ills. However, as she drank her tea she revived; the colour came back to her cheeks. She began to talk, but to his disappointment it was still about her work. She seemed too saturated with it for any other thought. But Smee said boldly that he would not allow any more shop tonight. She would be turning giddy again. He began to talk about Switzerland. 'I go there every year to do a little climbing.'

Ursula looked interested. 'I have always thought I should like climbing, although I have never done any. I have never even been to Switzerland. My stepfather bars any place without shooting, though I tell him he could stalk chamois in the Alps. Climbing must be a little like swimming, and I love that. Yes, I wish I were going to Switzerland.'

For the second time that evening Vernon Smee felt his heart beating. Perhaps this unusual intimacy in the deserted College predisposed him to romance. His solitary annual month in Switzerland was already the happiest part of the year. Now the thought came to him suddenly of what it would be if Ursula were there to share it. His face flushed slightly. But this would not do, he told himself. With an effort he dismissed the delectable vision. Charlotte was his wife. 'By the way, Mrs Smee is hoping to see you before very long,' he lied, not unpardonably.

A slight shade crossed Ursula's face. What a bore it was about the woman. However, of course, she must be civil. 'I hope you have explained to Mrs Smee how dreadfully busy I am just now,' she said aloud. 'Please don't let her think I am rude. I do mean to call on her directly after the holidays. Has she an at home day?'

It was the first and last Wednesday, Ursula heard. But the Professor did not drop the subject as she had hoped. He suggested, although dubiously, the possibility of her calling before the holidays. 'Mrs Smee is not leaving town for some little time,' he said. 'But I suppose you are too rushed?'

'I am rather.' Ursula hesitated. Professor Smee evidently wanted her to call. But she really did not see how she could manage it. 'You see, I must get my experiments here finished by the end of the month,' she explained. 'Mr Flecker and Mr Smith are going away then for their holidays' – these were the two students who were working with her. 'And after that I have got a lot of work to do at home before I can even start on my miserable paper. Yes, I find I shall have to write it all over again.' Her tone was despairing. 'Oh, I wish I had never thought of the BA. This being tied to a definite date is a perfect nightmare!'

'But surely the writing of a paper isn't so terrible when you have thought it all out,' Professor Smee suggested with his attractive smile. 'Why, I haven't begun yet to think of my show for the British Association.' He was giving one of the two big popular evening lectures this year. 'I expect I shall write most of it in the train coming home from Switzerland.'

But he did not want to go to Switzerland, he realised suddenly. He wanted to stay with Ursula. She had said that she was going to be in town all through August. Why couldn't he stop and help her with that paper? Then he would see her every day! Returning sanity told him that this was impossible. He had been afraid of whispering his secret in his sleep. Why, if he were to give up his trip abroad and devote August to Miss Winfield, it would be shouting it from the housetops. No, if only for the sake of appearances, he must have his month's climbing. But perhaps this year he wouldn't take it in Switzerland. He would be thinking of Ursula all the time. If he went somewhere that was quite new to him, it would take his mind off her. The Caucasus? That was too far and too expensive. Perhaps he would try the Black Forest. Of course there would be no real climbing, but he had always rather wanted to see it. Besides, it was near Switzerland. If he didn't like it, he could push on.

He was out of the Park now and walking along Notting Hill Gate. The flower-woman near the tube station was packing up her basket for the night. 'The larst bunch left, me dear,' she observed to nobody in particular, and held out about a dozen or more dark red roses. 'Reg'lar beauties, too.'

Flowers were a thing that Professor Smee never had occasion to buy. But it struck him suddenly that this dark red colour would suit Ursula. He would like to see her holding the bunch, or perhaps wearing some of them. If only he might have bought them for her. But, of course, he must not. 'Only a shilling and dirt cheap,' the woman urged persuasively, noticing his unaccustomed pause.

Well, why shouldn't he buy them, even if he could not give them to Ursula? They certainly were beautiful; he needed more beauty in his life. He would take them home and give them to Charlotte. He put the shilling in the woman's hand.

His wife was in the drawing room. Vernon went straight in and displayed the bunch. 'I've brought you some flowers, old lady,' he told her.

There was no reply; nor did Charlotte make any attempt to take them. It was rather disconcerting. 'Don't you like them? I thought they were rather fine ones,' he went on with determined good temper.

'Yes, they are.' Charlotte made a visible effort to pull herself together. 'Thank you very much. I will put them in water.' She took down two ugly vases from the mantelpiece, and, with her back turned towards him, began arranging the flowers.

Vernon Smee watched her idly. He saw that in some mysterious way the roses under this treatment seemed to be losing their beauty. But he did not see that the hands that held them were trembling, nor that on his wife's fat face there was an expression almost of fear.

CHAPTER SIX

It was a few evenings later that Professor Smee announced to his wife his intention of not going to Switzerland this year.
'Not going to Switzerland!' Charlotte echoed in amazement. 'Where are you going, then?'
'To the Black Forest. South Germany, you know.'
'Are there mountains in the Black Forest?' The question was not unnatural.
'No, not mountains.' Vernon suddenly remembered the ostensible reason why his wife did not accompany him on his yearly holiday. It was supposed to be too dull for her, as he was out all day climbing. But if she thought he was not going to climb, perhaps she would suggest coming. 'Of course there *are* mountains,' he contradicted himself hastily. 'I only meant there's nothing above the snow line.'
'I understand.' Charlotte really did understand. She had guessed exactly what had been passing in her husband's mind. The only point she did not quite grasp was why he was giving up his beloved Switzerland. However, that was a detail. At least he had made it sufficiently clear that wherever he went he did not want her society. One of her waves of

unreasoning anger swept over her. 'It is a great pity you ever married me,' she cried. 'Then you would not have been bothered with me either in the holidays or in the term time.'

Vernon Smee flushed with anger. He did not speak, but took up a book, feeling that this was the best reply to his wife's unbalanced outburst.

Mrs Smee meanwhile fidgeted angrily. Her husband's silence was more infuriating than any speech could have been. 'Have you nothing to say?' she burst out at last.

'No, you have expressed your opinion of me, and I suppose you must keep it,' Vernon replied coldly, and left the room.

The next day the quarrel had blown over, not so much because the Professor was forgiving as because he was indifferent. After the first irritation, Vernon discovered that he cared very little what Charlotte thought of him. For at this time every feeling and sentiment seemed to be merged into one – a craving to be with Ursula. As long as the girl was at College where he could feel her near, where he could sometimes see her, life was bearable. But what would he do after she had left? And that would be soon, he knew, for her experiments were almost finished. However, there was one gleam of light in the gloom that lay before him, namely the Laurent lecture at the Chemical Society. Ursula was going to be there – had he not already supplied her with the necessary introduction? Surely she would let him walk home with her afterwards. It was only this prospect that enabled him to keep calm when one day he went into the laboratory and found her packing up her apparatus. 'If you ever want to work at College again, remember this laboratory is always at your disposal,' he told her with what she felt to be an amusingly unnecessary earnestness.

After that, four blank days passed which he survived with what patience he could. Then the longed-for evening came. Really, it was ridiculous, Smee upbraided himself as he walked along Piccadilly, for a man of his age to be feeling like a boy going to a dance. He resolutely put Ursula out of his thoughts, and then, perhaps as a reward of virtue, he caught sight of her a little way in front of him. A few hurried steps brought him up to her. 'How is the work going now that you are back in your own laboratory, Miss Winfield?' was his first discreet, although rather breathless, remark.

'Oh, not very well.' Ursula's tone was doleful. 'There is something I can't quite make out. And that BA paper is coming nearer and nearer. Ugh! I can almost feel its dreadful claws! But I won't begin to tell you about my woes now; there isn't time. Aren't your friends on the warpath tonight?' she branched off suddenly as they turned in under the archway.

'My friends?' Vernon was uncomprehending.

'The suffragettes. I thought a deputation was going to the House to interview the Prime Minister in spite of his refusal? Why, there is a poster. Look, "Desperate Women Suffragists. Threat to Storm the Commons this Evening." I wonder you are not with them!'

'I thought I could hardly expect my students to attend lectures at Wormwood Scrubs – or wherever the dungeon might be in which I should find myself immured,' he laughed.

'I meant weren't you going as a spectator, not as a raider! I suppose one really ought to see one of these raids before condemning them so absolutely,' Ursula went on to suggest with unexpected liberality as they made their way upstairs.

In the meeting room they were, naturally, separated. What a ridiculous fetish it was, this seating of the past presidents on a particular bench as though they were a set of demigods. Strangely enough the point had never struck Professor Smee before; indeed, he had rather liked the custom. Soon the lecture itself began and took up his attention. He glanced at Ursula once or twice during its progress, but he did not like to stare across too obviously. She seemed deeply interested; at the end he saw her clapping enthusiastically. The speech that followed was dull, and he could not refrain from again looking in Ursula's direction. He did not see her! There was a male figure in her place. Hardly believing his eyes, he scanned the bench carefully. No, she was not there. But this was absurd, he told himself; she always stayed until the end of the meeting. Probably she had moved into a better seat. He gazed round the whole room, unmindful of appearance. There were only two or three ladies present, so the search was brief. Yes, Ursula had gone. Perhaps she had felt giddy again, he told himself with a sudden panic. A wild desire seized him to rush after her, to take a taxi to Lowndes Square. But what right had he to inquire about her movements? And, after all, it would be ridiculous to make a fuss. She had merely left at the end of the lecture without waiting for the discussion, a course that was always pursued by many of the audience. He remembered now that she had chosen a seat by the door. It must have been design and not accident. How absolutely damnable – not of her, of course; he broke off his thought almost shocked – but of fate.

Meanwhile, Ursula, quite unconscious of the storm of emotion she had roused in Professor Smee's breast, was walking briskly down to Parliament Square. Monsieur Laurent's lecture had been over earlier than she had expected, and had confirmed her half-formed intention of seeing for herself one of these much-discussed raids. Indeed, ever since she had travelled from Henley with the suffragettes, the idea had been in her mind. She must find out why these girls demeaned themselves by doing these horrible things. Naturally she had not communicated her purpose at home. Her stepfather and mother already found her mode of life sufficiently disconcerting. Poor little Mammykin would expire on the spot, Ursula told herself, if she knew that her daughter proposed even looking on at a suffrage scrimmage.

The crowd in the square as she turned in by Westminster Bridge was larger than she had expected. From her place on the outskirts, she could see nothing but a sea of heads ending in a line of mounted police. The latter were ranged along in front of the railings to guard the precincts of the sacred House. Everyone seemed quite good-tempered and considerably amused. There was a good deal of horseplay, but nothing more; occasionally Ursula heard a burst of cheering, but did not know its cause. This was no use, she felt impatiently. She must get into the centre of things, where she could see the suffragettes. Otherwise she might as well have stayed at the Chemical Society.

Insinuating herself forward was less difficult than she had anticipated. The crowd was not so dense as it had looked to her unaccustomed eyes. Also, people made way for her in a surprising manner. She heard, "Ere's another of 'em,' several times, but failed to apply the remark to herself. Presently she found herself right at the front. She now saw that there was a continuous double row of ordinary policemen as well as the men on horseback. She felt with surprise that the MPs must indeed be very alarmed by the suffragettes to be thus triple guarded.

As she stood there, a little middle-aged, quietly-dressed lady suddenly detached herself from the crowd and flung herself against the wall of police. Ursula's mind realised that this was a suffragette, but every instinct proclaimed the lady as a lunatic. It seemed such inconceivable behaviour. The constable had meanwhile tossed the little figure back. She again rushed forward. This proceeding was repeated four or five times, the policeman's rebuff, not unnaturally, growing rougher on each occasion, and the suffragette more frenzied in her efforts to break between them. Finally, one of the men caught hold of the lady's arm and said something, Ursula could not hear what. The futile struggle was immediately abandoned. 'She's arrested,' someone in the crowd exclaimed. Apparently none of the men could be spared to take away the prisoner, so she stood there waiting patiently beside the police and trying with hands that visibly trembled to repair her disarray. The appearance that the suffragette now presented was indeed what troubled Ursula the most. In her struggle her dress had been torn and her hat battered down over one eye, while her greying hair was straggling down her back in an undignified tail. From a lady she had changed suddenly into a street slattern. But for her composed stand no one would have believed she wasn't drunk. Ursula's indignation at militant tactics increased.

A stir now took place in the lines of the police. A man, evidently in authority, was riding down behind the lines and giving some order. The rows of constables parted in several places to let through some of the men on horseback. These turned their horses and began backing them with a curious sidelong gait into the crowd. At the same time the line of ordinary constables pressed slowly forward, calling out: 'Pass along please,' or 'Further back there, further back.' As far as she herself was concerned, Ursula felt unaffected. She was standing quietly on the pavement, the proper place for a pedestrian. It was the roadway that the police were trying to clear, or so she imagined. As she saw the horses backing into the people, she felt seriously, although impersonally, alarmed. However, the animals were extraordinarily well trained; despite a few frightened screams there really seemed to be no danger. Indeed it was pretty to see how carefully the beautiful beasts were stepping, how gently they moved. They were so dignified, so quiet amid that surging mass of small, shrill humanity that Ursula could not but think with some shame of Gulliver's Houyhnhnms.

Suddenly, to the girl's amazement she saw one of the mounted police on the pavement right in front of her. The horse was sidling down with its hindquarters almost against the railings. So they wanted to clear the pavement too. But how could she get further back, however much they wanted it? The crowd on the pavement behind her, reinforced by many stragglers from the roadway, was absolutely solid.

In another moment something satin-like brushed her cheek – it was the horse's neck. She was clutching a strange leg and stirrup leather for support. 'Get further back there,' an unmounted policeman shouted in her ear.

The tone roused Ursula's indignation. She had never been commanded before. 'It is you who are pushing. Get further back yourself,' she retorted. Her own words surprised her; she did not even know that she was speaking.

There was a laugh from the people round. 'Now then, none of yer lip,' the policeman growled, and roughly caught hold of her shoulders. Ursula felt herself spun round and rushed violently into the crowd.

She was trembling with anger as she came to an unsteady halt. She had only one desire, to turn and struggle with the policeman, but she found herself pinned in by the crowd, which had opened for her enforced passage. The moment's pause made her realise the idiocy of resistance; besides, after all, the man was only acting under orders. 'Them p'lice do chuck yer abawt something crool!' a young woman beside her observed sympathetically.

Ursula stared. She had a life habit of admiration for our celebrated Metropolitan Constabulary Force, although her chief personal acquaintance with it had been from her mother's carriage, an upraised blue-coated arm often facilitating the exit from the Park. This was a new view. But, certainly, she had just been 'chucked about', as her companion put it. 'That man's behaviour was disgraceful,' she agreed.

'Well, I don't know as 'ow you can altogether blame 'em tonight,' her new acquaintance went on cheerfully. ''Uman men won't stand there like punchballs an' not git a bit rattled. Though we all admires the pluck o' you suffragettes, miss, all the same.'

'But I am not a suffragette,' Ursula disclaimed hastily. 'I hope I didn't hurt you just now,' she added, remembering suddenly that 'action and reaction are equal and opposite.'

'Not a bit. But it's my new blouse I'm worryin' abawt. This is it, 'ere in this pawrcel.' The girl showed a brown paper package, partly hidden by her mackintosh, which she was obviously trying to shield from the pressure of the crowd. 'Like a silly I bought it on my way down, for I don't often 'ave the chawnce o' gitting to the West End. Three an' eleven three it was, an' a bargain. It's of pink silk with them new glass buttings what's all the mud' – it was some time before the explanation of these peculiar buttons dawned on Ursula – 'an' reel laice, too – why, the laice alone's worf the money, the young laidy said. No, I wouldn't 'ave it crushed up afore Benk 'Oliday for somethink, I can tell yer!'

All this time the line of policemen had been slowly pressing the crowd back foot by foot, and Ursula and her new friend could hardly have separated had they wished to do so. Ursula noticed that the constable who had handled her so roughly was still quite close; he evidently had his suspicions of her. Suddenly she saw the man's eyes rest on the half-concealed bundle in her neighbour's arms, and a quick, concerned expression crossed his red face. 'Now then, careful 'ere,' he shouted, and put out a shielding arm. As he touched the brown paper parcel, his face broadened into a harassed grin. 'Thought it was a baby you'd got there,' he explained good-temperedly.

The little scene mollified Ursula towards him. Indeed, soon after, the constable seemed to come to the conclusion that the supposed suffragette, despite her 'lip', was a less dangerous character than he had imagined, for he moved from Ursula's neighbourhood. At this point she also got parted from her new friend with the pseudo baby. This did not mean, however, that the crush had lessened; on the contrary it was momentarily growing more intense. Some dozen young men, probably students, had formed themselves one behind the other into a sort of battering ram. Each clasped the waist of the man in front, and with shouts of laughter and the singing of popular songs they charged aimlessly about in the crowd. These forced rushes naturally increased the congestion around, and, in addition, two convergent streams of people who were being pressed back now met at the corner by the hospital with a curious suffocating swirl. For the first time Ursula grew alarmed. She had been a fool to come! She would never get out unhurt. The enormous power of this congested mass of humanity was terrifying. She felt herself such a small, futile atom in the midst of it. And yet at the same time there was a certain contradictory exhilaration at being part of this immense force. She struggled on patiently, with the one idea of keeping her feet on solid earth; fortunately she was fairly heavy. In a little while the pressure began to diminish and she was again moving. A few minutes more found her at the edge of the crowd, where mankind was again separated into individuals.

There she stood motionless. She needed time to recover herself, her own ego. Suddenly for the second time that evening she heard her name from behind in Professor Smee's voice. She looked round in amused surprise. 'So you have come down to see the raid after all,' she said with rather a breathless carelessness.

'Thank God I have found you. Thank God.'

The amazement on Ursula's face stopped him short. He realised that he had betrayed himself. But Smee's lovesick imagination had been picturing such horrors, ever since, towards the end of the meeting, it had suddenly dawned on him where Ursula must have gone, that he had lost all self-control. 'I thought I should have to bail you out, you see,' he amended with a passably natural laugh.

A dubious look was replacing Ursula's blank bewilderment. She had been so taken aback by Professor Smee's first remark, and still more by its tone, that she had been absolutely bereft of speech. But now it occurred to her that the Professor, too, must have got into a nasty place in the crowd, and it had made him hysterical. That would account for his extraordinary greeting. 'Why should you have to bail me out, when you know I am not a suffragette?' she said, with perceptible coldness.

'You might have got carried away in the general excitement. But I ought to have known better,' he apologised, as Ursula looked scornful. The girl had genuinely forgotten how nearly she had got 'carried away.' Indeed, as it was, she had only just escaped arrest. 'Well, what is your impression of a raid?' Vernon Smee went on in his most ordinary tone.

Ursula was reassured. She must have made a mistake, exaggerated the oddness of his greeting. She hardly had an impression, she told him in reply to his query, or rather she had so many. It was all muddled, never-ending, unsatisfactory – 'just like a bad dream.' 'What can they imagine is the use of it all?' she went on musingly, 'those poor little individual women throwing themselves against a solid, stolid rampart of policemen. And they do come out of it so badly. The police seem almost unruffled, while the one woman whom I saw arrested looked absolutely deplorable. Still, she was not vulgar,' Ursula added. 'No, I was wrong about that.'

'Are people ever vulgar when they are in earnest?' Professor Smee suggested.

'Perhaps not. All the same I *cannot* understand why they should do it. Oh, look, here is another.'

A girl was coming towards them guarded by two policemen, each man firmly holding one of her arms. In spite of it, this suffragette did not look 'deplorable', perhaps because she had had the wisdom to don a little knitted cap and a long, close-fitting golf-coat. As the girl came nearer, Ursula saw that it was Mary Blake. Even after the rough and tumble of a raid her beauty was triumphant. The same little smile was on her delicately curved lips; her eyes held a strange happiness as they gazed at something very far away.

Ursula felt a sudden illumination. 'It may be a minor martyrdom, but it is not a mock one,' she announced. 'Being beautiful is an accident, but somehow that girl makes me understand.'

CHAPTER SEVEN

The last Wednesday in July saw Mrs Hibbert emerge from her bedroom at about four o'clock, patently on 'the warpath' as the Colonel styled it. Her ninon gown ranked as an art product; this and the marvellous confection that crowned her fair hair alike proclaimed her bound for some function of unusual importance. As she began to go down the stairs, she heard steps behind her, and looking round she saw her daughter. Ursula also was in outdoor dress, and her clothes, although not as perfect as Mrs Hibbert's, yet betokened unusual care. 'My dear child!' her mother exclaimed in evident surprise. 'Imagine seeing you at large and in Christian attire at this time of day! Wonders will never cease! Does this mean that you propose accompanying me to the Holland House garden party?'

'Oh, no, Mummy darling. I may be swell, but I'm not swell enough for that. But what a vision you are. "My word, Albert Eddard, ain't we a bloomin' torf terday!"' Ursula was quoting the latest *on dit* of the Court circle, a remark addressed to the King by a Piccadilly flower seller as he drove to a recent city banquet. 'Isn't that yet another new frock, and at the deathbed of the season? What does the Colonel say about it, you shamelessly extravagant woman?' She shook a warning forefinger at her parent with her usual admiring amusement.

Mrs Hibbert laughed – by no means displeased. 'But you haven't told me what *your* toilette signifies?' she persisted, as she put her hand through her daughter's arm and sauntered downstairs by her side. 'It must be something very extraordinary to drag you from your horrid experiments. Is the British Association paper done?'

'Hardly begun. But I am going – don't faint, Mother – I am going to pay a call! Yes, a regular, orthodox, twenty minutes five o'clocker with card case and parasol. I shall drink tepid tea and eat crumbly cakes and pursue all the other wild excitements inherent to the occasion!'

'My dear Ursula!' Mrs Hibbert laughed again. 'But on whom are you calling? Where?'

'Notting Hill Gate and Mrs Smee. This is her "day" – so behold me hastening to Clarendon Road, a pattern of meticulous propriety.'

'Mrs Smee? Is your Smee man married?' Mrs Hibbert was carelessly surprised. She and Ursula had now reached the hall, but although the footman opened the door, through some mistake the electric brougham was not there. 'Tiresome!' The mistress of the house tapped impatiently with her foot. Then she turned again to her daughter. 'Well, all I can say is Mrs Smee must be a regular charmer to tempt you from your lair!'

'She isn't. I believe she is appalling – the sort of woman who can only talk domesticity, the iniquities of the maids and what she pays for her meat per pound! What does one pay, Mummy? Have you any idea?'

Mrs Hibbert was quite vague. The butcher's book last month had been fifteen pounds eighteen, or was it eighteen pounds fifteen? Perhaps Alphonse could give the desired information, although figures were not the poor dear man's forte. Or if Ursula had up the book, could she work out the prices herself with her mathematics?

'It doesn't matter,' Ursula laughed. 'I can bear to live on in my ignorance.' The car at last made itself heard. 'Aren't you very early, Mum? I thought the Colonel was to meet you at Holland House at five.' A sudden idea suggested itself. 'Look here, Mammykin, why can't you come with me to Mrs Smee's on your way? Notting Hill Gate isn't as far as it sounds. And you are always able to talk to people so beautifully. Now do be an angel, and come!'

Mrs Hibbert hesitated. She had meant to call on Lady Tremoine, she said. Still, she did not get many chances of enjoying her daughter's society, and she really did enjoy it. And the Smee woman, as she termed her, rather excited her curiosity. 'Come along then, my dear,' she said gaily; 'we'll go and talk about New Zealand lamb. That's what people of that sort always eat, I've heard. *Revenons à nos moutons* – Clarendon Road, James; it's somewhere in Notting Hill Gate.' She tripped into the brougham, followed by Ursula.

Mrs Smee's house did not seem as near as Ursula had promised, but this was due to the ten minutes perambulation of the adjacent streets before they happened upon Clarendon Road. The Hibbert chauffeur had the usual insuperable objection of his kind to asking the way, and it was strengthened today by the feeling that it was already a sufficient degradation to be brought to these unfashionable wilds. The scorn both of himself and of 'James' for the neighbourhood was increased by the hopelessly bourgeois appearance of the house before which they stopped. 'Some of Urs'la's rum friends,' the footman murmured, secure of inaudibility with a closed brougham behind. Jumping down, he rang the bell, and then stood holding open the carriage door with the blank and rigid respect of the perfect automaton.

Charlotte Smee was sitting in her ugly drawing room embroidering a cushion cover. She much preferred plain needlework, but this she felt unladylike; indeed, she had many qualms as to the gentility of any employment in the afternoon. As the bell rang, a flutter of pleased excitement agitated her. On her last at home day there had not been a single caller. Half apologetically, she had explained to Carter that her acquaintances must have thought the day too threatening. The girl had received the words with a contemptuous sniff; indeed, a few drops of rain on a June afternoon did not seem an adequate deterrent. And this morning, when she had said that the silver tea-service must have an extra rub up, Carter had been quite insolent, muttering sulkily something about waste of time. As for the other preparations, the mistress of the house had wavered uneasily between her fear of asking Carter to do them and her fear of sinking in Carter's estimation by doing them herself. The flowers – that did not matter, many ladies did their own flowers – but poor Charlotte twice took off and replaced the drawing room loose covers before she decided that Carter's contempt would be preferable to her blank refusal. But now, as Mrs Smee heard the front door open, she felt joyfully that she would be reinstated in her servant's respect. Probably it was Mrs Lawson, the vicar's wife, who had for some time owed her a call. And the Lawsons were not just ordinary clergy people; they had considerable private means. Why, the son was at Harrow.

If it were Mrs Lawson or not, there was no doubt about Carter being impressed. As the girl opened the drawing room door there was quite an awed look on her usually arrogant face. Indeed she seemed so overpowered as to be almost deprived of speech, for her murmur of announcement was totally inaudible. Then, in an aura of chiffon scarves, delicate perfume, and soft silken rustle, Mrs Hibbert floated in.

Charlotte Smee guessed at once who it was. The hot colour flamed into her cheeks. Her forebodings had been bad enough, but the reality was worse – younger, lovelier, more alluring. A woman of this kind would never have come to see her spontaneously. Vernon must have asked her to call. Yes, they felt the dowdy wife had to be placated! The idea was unbearably humiliating. In her bewildered anger, Charlotte Smee was hardly aware that she had made no movement to shake hands with her guests. She replied with a sullen 'How d'you do' to Mrs Hibbert's airy, opening civilities and Ursula's bow.

Mrs Hibbert's eyebrows, delicately pencilled both by nature and art, raised themselves imperceptibly. The hostess was even more 'impossible' than she had imagined. And what an absolutely hideous room! 'May I sit here?' she asked lightly, moving towards one of the hard tapestry and plush armchairs. 'Or is it your own especial seat? My daughter says that I have a talent for picking out the most comfortable chair in the room – like a cat!' Her sweet, but rather artificial laugh rippled out.

'So I should think.' Charlotte had a sense of having said something pointed, almost clever. The unusual feeling rather cooled her anger. 'Yes, please sit down,' she went on stiffly, but more civilly. 'And you too,' she added, turning to Ursula, of whose entrance in her mother's wake she now became fully conscious. She still did not realise that the girl was Miss Winfield; her wooden mind, having once conceived Ursula as a very juvenile and rather unattractive science student, refused to associate her with this handsome and dignified figure. No, this was some friend of Mrs Hibbert's.

Although that little lady had been rather taken aback by the peculiar manners apparently prevalent in Notting Hill Gate, she now, with determined amiability, resumed her effort to make conversation. 'How nice and fresh the air is here! It really is a great advantage to live a little way out of town.'

It was evidently the wrong remark. The hostess bridled. 'I never heard Notting Hill Gate called "out of town" before. Why, by the tube, I get to Oxford Circus in twelve minutes and it only takes the Professor – ' Charlotte broke off suddenly. She had not meant to speak of her husband. Almost involuntarily her eyes sought Mrs Hibbert's face, but her visitor appeared quite unconcerned. What duplicity, Charlotte told herself. As she stared she became conscious of the exquisite perfection of the guest's toilette. It only increased her indignation.

Such a gown was quite in excess of a mere afternoon call. Mrs Hibbert must have worn it with the express purpose of humiliating her.

Carter now appeared with the tea, a welcome diversion. Mrs Smee always made it herself, so a silver caddy was added to the paraphernalia on the tray. Tea-making was a thing on which she rightly prided herself, but today combined nervousness and irritation caused her to chink the cups clumsily and to flood the tray with water. She had an uneasy feeling that making tea in the drawing room was perhaps plebeian, little knowing that for once she had stumbled into the extreme of fashion. 'How delicious this tea is,' Mrs Hibbert commented.

'Yes, isn't it?' Ursula, who had also been rather startled by the greeting accorded them, now thought it was time to launch a remark. 'It's ever so much better than what we have at home, Mother.'

Mrs Smee looked up, surprise for the moment overcoming her other feelings. 'You are Miss Winfield?' she exclaimed. Then, as her mind readjusted itself to the position, she decided, like most people, that the relationship must be a step one. Well, that made things even worse. This woman was not even weighted by a daughter of her own. However, the compliments about the tea were undeniably mollifying.

Unfortunately Mrs Hibbert's next remark undid all the advantages gained. 'I expect the secret of the tea lies in the making,' she observed smilingly, with the full intention of being ingratiating. 'I wish you could show my people how you do it, Mrs Smee.'

'Thank you, I have something better to do!' Poor Charlotte's voice trembled with rage. 'Putting me on a level with her cook,' she felt furiously.

Ursula made a movement as if to rise and then thought better of it, while a genuine colour reinforced the dash of rouge on Mrs Hibbert's cheeks. The hostess's remark had been so astoundingly, so gratuitously rude. Perhaps Mrs Smee had some misgiving about it herself. She made an obvious effort to regain her composure. 'Won't you have another cup, as you like it?' she said in an altered and more pleasant tone.

Mrs Hibbert declined, but politely. She had to go on somewhere, she explained. Life was such a rush, one had no time for anything. The season seemed to go on later every year; didn't Mrs Smee think so? However, in a few days she meant to run away whatever happened, although she couldn't prevail on her naughty girl to accompany her. But she was feeling quite done up, she must have her month at Homburg. An extraordinary sound from the hostess – something between a snort and a gasp – brought the voluble little lady to a sudden stop. Could the Smee woman be ill? She looked very odd. 'Is anything the matter?' Mrs Hibbert said aloud.

'Oh, nothing, nothing! Only Homburg happens to be in South Germany, does it not?' Charlotte tried to give a withering laugh, but only succeeded in producing rather a hysterical shriek. So this explained Vernon's change of plans, his sudden decision to abandon Switzerland! Though she really thought her husband had arranged to meet Mrs Hibbert on his holiday, she did not, consciously at least, put the worst interpretation on it. 'What a curious coincidence!' The attempt at a coldly satiric note again did not quite come off; it merely sounded silly.

The mother and daughter exchanged glances. The same thought had occurred to both of them. Mrs Smee was not quite responsible, not quite like other people. Mrs Hibbert rose in some trepidation. 'Well, goodbye, dear Mrs Smee,' she babbled in rather incoherent farewell. 'We really must be going. So nice to make your acquaintance. So sorry not to have seen Professor Smee – please tell him.'

It was the last straw. The empty civility seemed to poor Charlotte's jaundiced mind a deliberate insult. 'How unfortunate you did not come later, then you could have seen him,' she cried, trembling visibly. 'I wouldn't have interrupted your teet-a-teet.'

'No, no, of course not. Goodbye.' Mrs Hibbert fairly ran from the room, leaving her retreat to be covered by the more composed Ursula.

In the brougham it was her daughter, however, who appeared the more upset. 'Mother, how perfectly awful,' Ursula exclaimed as they drove away. 'Mrs Smee is as mad as a hatter! I'm frightfully sorry to have let you in for such a scene.'

'No, no, it's all right.' To Ursula's surprise her mother began to laugh, although a trifle tremulously. 'I thought she was mad, too, but a light is just beginning to break on me. My dear, I believe Mrs Smee does me the honour to be jealous, yes, tearingly, ragingly jealous! And of me!' Mrs Hibbert laughed again. 'Why, you know, Ursula, that I have not exchanged half a dozen sentences with her precious husband. He is your friend, not mine. Isn't it too delicious! I believe she thinks I am planning to elope to Homburg with him! Professor Smee of all men!' Mrs Hibbert fairly swayed with merriment. 'I declare the ridiculous woman tempts me to give her something of which to be jealous.'

'No, it would be disgraceful –' Ursula began hotly. Far from joining in her mother's laughter, she had looked shocked, even disgusted. But she checked herself. Long experience had taught her that indignant ethics were not the means by which her mother could be managed. 'I won't allow it, Mammykin,' she went on in her usual bantering tone. 'You must content yourself with your little soldier boys and leave my Professor alone. It is bad enough for the poor man to be afflicted with a wife like that, without being made to realise the entrancing possibilities he has missed.'

Mrs Hibbert dimpled. 'Now that was rather charmingly put, my dear. But isn't it you, in this case, who have verged on the "entrancing"?'

'Mother, you know I am not attractive to men, not in that way – thank goodness!' Ursula had flushed violently. 'But you are only trying to get a rise out of me,' she went on with forced calm. 'No, you must promise me not to be fascinating.'

'P'ease, I will be dood.' Her mother folded her hands in mock-childish penitence. 'When your professor comes I'll stand like Saint Sebastian on his column – no, Sebastian was the poor pincushion man – anyway, I'll stand with my hair un-Marcelled and my face unpowdered, a model of plain, middle-aged discretion.' The car, which had been moving slowly in the line of carriages, now definitely stopped and Mrs Hibbert jumped out. '*Au revoir*, my dear,' she cried, blowing a kiss to her daughter and looking very much the reverse of plain or middle-aged or, above all, discreet.

It must have been some tricksy fate that caused Vernon Smee to forget to tell his wife of a dinner engagement he had for that day – a staid male affair in honour of Monsieur Laurent's last evening. Indeed he had forgotten it himself; he was busy revising the lists of students' examination marks, when, with a shock of recollection, this dinner came to his mind. He had been feeling irritable already, for the new assistant, who had had the drawing up of these lists, had been disgracefully careless. It meant going through every figure again himself, and he was working against time to get the lists off to the printers by the country post. And this plaguey dinner was at some extraordinarily early hour, he remembered, for the guest of honour was catching the night boat. Where was the card? Oh, here it was – 6.15 – confound it. He'd never have time to get home and dress after polishing off the lists; and they must go this afternoon, they were late already. Why, he could telephone up and have his dress clothes sent to him. Of course that was the thing to do. What a convenience it was having been put on the 'phone, though Charlotte had been so set against it. He rang up Clarendon Road.

Rather to his relief, Carter, and not his wife, answered. It would save explanations when he was so pressed. 'Tell Mrs Smee I shall be out to dinner,' he called peremptorily. 'And please ask her to send someone down to College at once with my dress clothes – an express boy will do – at once, you understand.'

The dinner, beginning in such good time, was over correspondingly early. It was barely ten when Vernon Smee reached Clarendon Road. His earlier annoyance had passed; indeed, he was feeling particularly amiable as he let himself in. The dinner had been good, and the company most interesting. Rather to his surprise he had been asked to propose Monsieur Laurent's health, and he knew that his speech had been one of his best. The distinguished guest had been quite moved and had complimented him upon his 'so charming eloquence.' 'Well, old lady,' he exclaimed genially as he sauntered into the drawing room. 'You got my message all right?'

'Obviously, as you are wearing your suit.'

Her voice was so aggressive that Smee almost started. Could she have discovered how he felt about Ursula? His abiding terror, that he had spoken of the girl in his sleep, returned to him. But no, Charlotte had been all right at breakfast time. Apart from this, she could not have discovered anything, for there was nothing to discover. Oh, of course, it was because he had not come home to dinner that she was in such a fury. Charlotte never could bear the least change in her plans. 'I'm awfully sorry I had to bother you,' he observed apologetically. 'I forgot all about the dinner until the last minute.'

'You need not take the trouble to pretend that it was an old engagement.' His wife laughed unpleasantly.

His obvious astonishment gave Charlotte pause. But during these five hours of solitary brooding she had pictured so continuously what was happening – Mrs Hibbert 'phoning to Vernon, or perhaps calling on him at College; the invitation to dinner; the dinner itself, gay with lights and champagne and laughter – and she, Vernon's lawful wife, sat neglected, in the dark – Mrs Hibbert and Vernon alone together in some dim corner, a conservatory perhaps. It had all become more bitterly real than reality. 'I know you have been dining with Mrs Hibbert,' she burst out. 'So it is no good trying to hide it.'

'But I have *not* been dining with Mrs Hibbert!' Professor Smee smiled in the superior way that his wife always found maddening. 'It was the dinner for old Laurent tonight. Whatever made you think I was at Lowndes Square? Did Mrs Hibbert 'phone?' His wife was curiously silent. 'Surely she didn't call here, did she?'

'You know she did,' Charlotte snapped.

Yes, Charlotte really was jealous of Ursula's mother! The Professor smiled again. But what could have made Mrs Hibbert call? She certainly was not the sort of person to trouble herself about a humble professor's wife. A possible explanation suggested itself. Perhaps Mrs Hibbert had been giving a dinner party that evening and one of her men had failed her. She might have come round at the last moment to ask him to fill the place. This would explain Charlotte's anger. 'Did Mrs Hibbert want me to dine there?'

The words re-kindled all Charlotte's suspicion. So even if Vernon had not been dining with Mrs Hibbert this evening, he evidently was in the habit of doing so. There was an unconscious touch of eagerness, of regret in his voice that had not been lost upon her. 'No, Mrs Hibbert did not ask you to dinner tonight, but no doubt she will give you other opportunities.' Anger scattered poor Charlotte's small remaining prudence. 'I told her she should have called later in order to see you!'

'But did she want to see me?' Vernon felt mingled surprise and uneasiness. His guilty conscience now suggested that it was Mrs Hibbert who had guessed the nature of his feelings towards Ursula – but no, he had been too careful not to betray himself. 'What does Mrs Hibbert want to see me about?' he asked aloud.

Charlotte started to her feet, quivering with rage. 'Oh, I'm sick of your pretence. As if I didn't know why you are going to Germany!'

'Germany?' Smee began to get alarmed. His wife was behaving so very oddly this evening. He had heard that women at about her age sometimes grew peculiar. Had this happened to Charlotte? 'Look here, my dear,' he went on kindly. 'You can't be well. Hadn't you better see a doctor tomorrow?'

'I am well enough.' She was still shaking with emotion. 'It's no good trying to put me off like that! You have fooled me till now, but you are not going to fool me any more. I knew directly she said Homburg!'

'Knew what? Who said Homburg?' Certainly either Charlotte was losing her reason or he was.

His blank bewilderment penetrated even the angry woman's obsession. Was it possible that she could have made another mistake? 'Aren't you going to Homburg?' she faltered.

'Homburg? Why on earth should I be going to Homburg? There's nothing there to climb!' A sudden illumination came to him. 'Is Mrs Hibbert going to Homburg?'

At his wife's sullen acquiescence he broke into a shout of laughter. His amusement was not unmixed with relief. So Charlotte absolutely imagined him to be wildly in love with Mrs Hibbert. Well, all the better; she would be less likely to guess the true state of affairs. Besides, in some indefinable way his wife's misplaced jealousy seemed to excuse his erring affections; it justified him in his own conscience. Not that he needed justification, he again mentally assured himself. They weren't living in a French novel. Sometimes he wished they had been. But then it would not have been Ursula. Why, if Ursula were to guess his feelings, she would be even more outraged than Charlotte. She had come near to guessing them on the night of the raid, and it had changed her at once. She was so pure, so wonderful. As Smee's thoughts dwelt on the girl, on her young, straight beauty, her quiet strength, a look came into his eyes which it was fortunate his wife did not see. More to break the silence – that for him was growing too full – he asked Charlotte carelessly what she had meant about having told Mrs Hibbert to call later.

His wife's colour deepened unbecomingly. 'I thought Mrs Hibbert only wanted to see you,' she muttered. Vernon's laughter had, for the time, at least, shaken her suspicions; she began to wish that she had behaved differently. 'I didn't mean that I wanted them to go.'

'Them?' Smee steadied himself. He had been amused, if annoyed, at the interview that he had pictured to himself as having taken place between his wife and Mrs Hibbert; the latter lady's bewilderment at her hostess's incomprehensible remarks. But apparently Charlotte had been something more than incomprehensible. And 'them'? 'Was Miss Winfield with her mother?' he asked with ominous calm.

A few more questions, a few more reluctant answers dragged from poor Charlotte, and he realised it all. Mrs Hibbert had not dropped in to make up her dinner table number. It had been a regular call. It had been Ursula's call. Mrs Hibbert had come because her daughter had brought her. And Ursula – his pulses began to beat faster. Ursula, who was so busy, Ursula who hated calling. Ursula had come because he had asked her to come. She had been thinking of him. She had done it to please him. Darling – his thoughts were rapturously indiscreet. And in return she had been subjected to this welcome! She had been insulted, practically shown the door – his door. His wife's earlier rage suddenly transferred itself to him. He turned upon her savagely. 'You fool! You insufferable fool!'

'You have no right to speak to me like that. You ought to apologise.' Charlotte burst into a paroxysm of weeping and rushed from the room.

Vernon did not attempt to follow her. He had never spoken to his wife in such a way before, but then, he had never been so angry with her before. Far from wanting to apologise to Charlotte, the only desire he felt was to apologise to Ursula. He must go to Lowndes Square at once. But no – he pulled out his watch – a quarter past ten, it was impossibly late. Suddenly he remembered it was Wednesday, the evening on which Mrs Hibbert was always 'at home'. Of course Ursula would probably not be visible – still it might be one of her exceptions. In any case he would see Mrs Hibbert. What luck that he was already in evening dress! Without giving himself time for further thought, he caught up his hat and overcoat and rushed out to hail a taxi.

As Professor Smee was announced, Mrs Hibbert's delicate eyebrows raised themselves for the second time that day. '*Le mari qui vient faire ses excuses,*' she murmured to herself. The young man to whom she had been talking drew back as the new guest approached. 'I don't know what I can say, Mrs Hibbert – ' Smee began.

'Then why say it?' Mrs Hibbert gave her airy laugh. 'We are just starting bridge. I suppose you play? Or are you, like my daughter, too clever for such frivolities?'

'It may be cleverness on Miss Winfield's part, but *my* not playing bridge merely denotes, as Dr Johnson said, "Ignorance, Madam, sheer ignorance!"' Vernon's eyes had been roving furtively about the room; now he suddenly caught a glimpse of the familiar, erect, young figure. Ursula's back was turned to him, and she was half-hidden by other guests, but he would have known anywhere the set of the head on the full white neck, the great knot of curling brown hair. 'I fear my play would drive my partner to drink or suicide,' he babbled on to his hostess, not without intention. 'The only rule I know is always to trump your partner's best card.'

'In that case perhaps I had better leave you and my daughter to entertain each other as spectators.' Mrs Hibbert gave another shallow laugh as she flitted off.

Vernon Smee did not go up to the girl at once, although he moved his position to have her in full view. Ursula was, apparently, in violent disagreement with the man to whom she was talking; her cheeks were flushed with the heat of the argument. It may have been her unwonted colour, or the low-cut wine-coloured velvet gown, or the necklace of rough turquoise emphasising the deep blue of her eyes, but she looked absolutely beautiful. Vernon was startled, dumbfounded! It was the first time he had seen her in evening dress, he realised with quickening breath, except that time at the Royal Society soirée when he had been fool enough hardly to notice her. But it was incredible that she could have looked like this!

After a minute or two Ursula caught sight of him. Her face lit up, and she rather unceremoniously dismissed her companion. 'Oh, Professor Smee, how refreshing!' She came forward to shake hands. Then lowering her voice she nodded in the direction of the departing male form. 'That idiot has been talking in such an absolutely imbecile way about science; he treats it with a sort of condescending contempt. I wanted to brain him – but that would be impossible!' she added with a laugh. 'Anyway, to see you there seemed like water in a thirsty land.'

Vernon felt his self-control going. Despite his forty-three years he was still emotionally very young. He had come expecting to be received with cold displeasure – and she greeted him like this. He lowered his eyes, absolutely afraid of what might be read in them. 'I came because I felt I must tell you how sorry I was that you had been exposed to such – such unpleasantness this afternoon,' he said, plunging at once into his apology. 'My wife hadn't quite understood; she is sometimes a little – little difficult; perhaps she wasn't feeling well. Can you forgive her – us?' he stammered.

'There is nothing to forgive. I was only sorry.' There was a new gentleness in Ursula's expression. 'You don't play bridge? Let us sit down then and talk.' She led the way to a little recess at the end of the room. 'It is cooler here.'

The conversation that followed was more personal than any they had had before; the afternoon's incident seemed to have made a new link between them. And although no word was spoken to which a wife, even a jealous wife, could have objected, Smee's thoughts rioted wildly. Once or twice, despite all his care, they manifested themselves in a look or intonation that made Ursula a little self-conscious. It was not that she disliked this new intimacy, perhaps she rather liked it, but it did inject a sudden misgiving that she might be 'verging on the entrancing'. But, of course, that was absurd, she assured herself. It was only Mother who was like that. So she failed to apply to herself the wise counsel that she had given her volatile parent, as to not allowing Professor Smee opportunities for comparison. This man was her friend; that was her only thought. The fact of his being married to such an appalling person made him all the more in need of her friendship. Indeed, the girl felt sorrier for him than she had ever done for anyone in her life before. It had never occurred to her that the 'appalling person' might also need pity.

It was only a few minutes after midnight when Vernon again got home. His early return was not sheer virtue, for

Ursula had told him that when the clock struck twelve, she, like Cinderella, would disappear. He tiptoed up to his dressing room and moved about there with unusual care. Was Charlotte asleep? he wondered uneasily. If she were, he did not want to disturb her; still less did he want to disturb her if she were awake. The thought of another scene gave him a positive feeling of nausea. He was tired out with the long day's work and his many varied emotions. If only Charlotte had not resented his suggestion of a camp bedstead in his dressing room that he could use when he felt restless or was kept up late. The fact was – he realised it suddenly – he did not want to see his wife tonight. On the white pillow her fat red face half ringed with the tight little greyish knots of curling-pinned hair – it repelled him. He wanted to be alone; alone with his beautiful, impossible dreams. He was already in his pyjamas moodily staring at the closed, connecting door, so a decision of some sort was inevitable. Suddenly he took a pocket-book out of a coat, and tearing out a page, began to scribble something rapidly. There, it was done. If Charlotte did wake up and miss him, this would keep her from being alarmed.

Had Smee gone into his wife's room, he might have found the sight less unpleasant than he expected. Charlotte was sitting up in bed, and her face, though fat and red, was irradiated by a look that almost gave it beauty. After her hysterical rush upstairs, she had sat down for some time in angry sobbing. Then, as she grew calmer, and better able to review the conversation that had taken place, a growing certainty of her mistake came over her. Vernon really did not care for Mrs

Hibbert; his tone, even more than his actual words, had proved it. What then was she crying about? Why, all her fears and jealousies of the past few weeks were groundless. The relief was so great that at first she could hardly realise it. It was like the heavenly, blank, uncertain feeling that accompanies the cessation of acute physical pain.

Of course, Vernon ought not to have spoken to her in the way he had done. 'An insufferable fool', her eyes again filled with tears. But he had been irritated. When he came up, he, too, would be calmer. His departing slam of the front door had meant nothing to her, for her husband often went for a walk late at night in an effort to capture elusive sleep. No, for the first time for weeks Charlotte felt at peace – even happy. How lonely and miserable she had been! Somehow, except for Vernon, she seemed to be lonelier than other women. Her thoughts went back to those tiny, short-lived beings for whom she had suffered so much and so unavailingly. The first ten years of married life had been spent at Leeds, but one little baby, the last, had been born here in this very room. He had lived longer than any of the others; for three whole weeks she had lain with him in the cradle beside her, her body battered, but her soul steeped in an ecstasy of motherhood. And then – but she would not think of that tonight. She meant to be happy tonight. When Vernon came up she would tell him that she had forgiven him for his unkind words, and surely, in return, he would forgive her for her silly mistake. He would then understand that she had only minded because she cared so much. A tremulous smile came to her lips as she heard a faint, a very faint sound at the connecting door.

It did not open. What could Vernon be doing? How quietly he must have come up that she had not heard him before. Probably he had thought she was asleep; it was good of him to have tried not to disturb her. But now her aroused ear certainly caught his footsteps. He seemed to be going out of his dressing room, away along the passage. Perhaps he had forgotten something, and was going downstairs to fetch it. A minute passed – two – five. Still there was no sound. She switched on the light.

A little sheet of paper lay just inside the door, conspicuous on the dark carpet. It had evidently been pushed under the door, through the crack. Puzzled, Charlotte got out of bed and picked it up. 'Intend sleeping in spare room,' she read in her husband's handwriting.

CHAPTER EIGHT

Two women could hardly have pursued more different modes of life than Ursula Winfield and Charlotte Smee, yet they shared one peculiarity – both made a practice of spending August in town. In 1909 the 'close time' for the metropolis was still unrelaxed, and Mayfair and Notting Hill alike proclaimed at this season a genteel desertion, with their miles of shuttered windows, to which careful housewives added a further screen of newspaper. It is true that 'down Porterbeller,' or a little farther west in the Potteries, these conditions were changed. Here, far from the streets being deserted, the flood of child life, released from barrack-like schools, surged more densely than in any other month of the year. The teeming pavements were criss-crossed with chalked hopscotch lines, and primitive skipping ropes twirled gaily from area railing. Indeed, in these quarters, the whole roadway seemed to have become one great nursery, in which the youthful population, growing perceptibly more rude and ragged, if more rosy, as the holidays went by, disported itself all day and late into the evening with its games and shrill outcry.

But from such districts, Ursula and Mrs Smee were alike far removed, if not in distance, at least in social attitude, and so the presence of the two ladies in London during the 'close time' could only be put down to a common eccentricity. One difference there was between them; Ursula openly proclaimed her unconventionality, while Mrs Smee sedulously tried to conceal it. Indeed, poor Charlotte took such pains in hushing up her scandalous secret, she put herself to such an extreme of discomfort over it, that it was hard to see why she persevered in the practice, instead of yielding like other people to the decree of fashion. Her husband used to tell her that she stayed in town merely to acquire another grievance, and there may have been a certain truth in the rather brutal statement. The reason that Mrs Smee herself put forward, namely want of money, was clearly inadequate. For, although it was true that Vernon's Swiss visit was very expensive – it invariably cost at least twice as much as he had expected – still he would hardly have indulged in it had his salary not permitted of his wife's having a holiday too, if of a more modest nature.

Probably the true explanation of Charlotte Smee's remaining in town was that although she did not like it, she liked the prospect of going away even less. For where was she to go? Reasons connected with the 'biz' kept the Todds from having her in August, although later in the season she always spent a fortnight with them – the happiest fortnight of her year. To establish herself in a strange hotel or boarding house seemed to her alarming, for poor Charlotte, despite her homely middle-aged appearance, had unsuspectedly preserved the shyness of a girl. Besides, people would be sure to ask her about her husband – Vernon Smee's name was sufficiently well-known to make it inevitable – and then she would have to acknowledge that he spent his holiday in Switzerland while she stayed in England. She could just imagine the galling comment, the still more galling silence. At the mere idea her painful pride was up in arms. No, it might be dull to picnic in the back rooms in Clarendon Road – for the front of the house was shuttered like its neighbours, while the maids were sent off on a month's holiday – but, at least, here no one knew of her humiliation.

Although Ursula Winfield had no desire for concealment, she, too, during August, largely picnicked in back rooms. But then she so rarely used any rooms save her laboratory, her bedroom and sometimes the library, that the rest of the house being shut up made little difference, while the absence of the major part of the staff came as a positive relief. For although the great Alphonse duly departed on the first of August for his annual month at Dieppe, the kitchen-maid's cooking amply satisfied Ursula's simple palate. And with regard to the other servants, she much preferred the cheerful ministrations of the rustic little third housemaid to the haughty if more experienced attendance of the first and second, while the butler and footmen had always struck her as discomforting luxuries.

But chiefly, of course, what appealed to Ursula about August in town was the opportunity it afforded for uninterrupted work. Every year she indulged in a regular scientific orgy, her appetite whetted by the period of abstinence that lay ahead. For, on Mrs Hibbert's return from Homburg, she expected her daughter to accompany her to Dumdrochie, the Colonel's place in Ayrshire, and to stay at least four weeks. It was a good-sized estate, but the house itself was too small to allow of much entertaining, and Mrs Hibbert used to moan that without Ursula it was absolutely appalling; the stupid men were out all day shooting, and she had not a soul to talk to! The little lady was, indeed, always planning the addition of a large new wing to enable her to give regular house-parties, but the plan had never materialised, for the Colonel was unprecedentedly obstinate. The house had been good enough for his father, he said, and it was good enough for him. There was room to put up four guns; he didn't care for shoots being messed up with a lot of petticoats! So Mrs Hibbert had acquiesced, possibly because she did not really object to a spell of enforced quiet. 'This place may drive me to suicide,' she confided to her daughter, 'but it gives my complexion a new lease of life.'

This year, however, Ursula found her scientific debauch less satisfying than usual. As she had complained to Professor Smee, her experiments were behaving in a most unaccountable way. Every now and then the atmospheric nitrogen seemed to be liberated with a far greater readiness than at other times, and yet, as far as she could see, the conditions were the same. Until she could find some explanation of this peculiarity, she could not get on with her BA paper. It hung over her like a nightmare, quite spoiling her happiness in the experimental work. She used to dream at night that she was standing in a hall before a mass of people with absolutely nothing prepared. 'Ladies and gentlemen,' she would begin, and then hear herself talking the most arrant rubbish, until with a start she would wake, bathed in perspiration. Finally, however, the experiments grew so absorbing that the thought of the paper receded. Suppose it were not done, it would not matter so terribly. She could postpone it until the next year. After deciding this, she felt happier, although she was still sleeping as badly as ever. All night in her dreams she was pursuing the explanation of the puzzle.

And then one day it came. Ursula had been working very hard all the morning, hardly pausing for lunch. By about three o'clock the laboratory grew so hot and she was so tired that she resolved to stop. She switched off the current and, going into her bedroom, flung herself on the bed. She supposed that she dozed, but of this she was not certain. All she knew was that suddenly she found herself awake with the answer to the riddle crystal clear in her mind. She rushed back into the laboratory and began again to experiment in order to test the new idea. She was shaking all over with excitement, although she was quite unconscious of it, until she saw the carbon that she picked up oscillating in her hand. Well, it was impossible to work like that. She sat down and sipped some water with a resolute determination to be calm.

Presently the trembling ceased and Ursula began again. Now she was working quietly, almost mechanically. One after another, with deft familiarity, she carried out a series of experiments; they all explained, or rather were explained, by the new hypothesis; the previous vagaries fell into their place as normalities. It was beginning to get dusk when she heard a reproachful voice beside her, 'Your dinner has been waiting downstairs a long time, miss. Oh, miss, and you haven't touched your tea!' Ursula stared, first at the maid and then at the tea tray, with dazed incomprehension. How had it got there; she had never heard anyone come in. However, she now washed her hands and went down to dinner. The meal was eaten in a dream. Then she returned to the laboratory.

She worked on steadily as before. Yes, every result went to prove the theory – her theory. In her own mind she had felt secure from the very first moment; still this confirmation thrilled her with rapture. Time passed, but she went on unheeding. Just about midnight, as she was finishing a certain experiment, a wave of giddiness swept down over her. It receded, but left her with a dazed feeling of immense fatigue. She could hardly drag herself into the next room and to bed.

She fell asleep almost at once, but she did not sleep long. As she opened her eyes, the summer dawn was already clarifying the objects in the room. At first she lay in a state of drowsy semi-consciousness. Suddenly, with a rush of excitement, yesterday's supreme happening came back to her. A wild desire seized her to dash into the laboratory, to shout, to sing. She restrained herself. Why, it was only half past four; it was absurd to think of getting up. She reminded herself that working before breakfast always made her fit for nothing for the rest of the day, and today she meant to do so much. No, of course, she must go to sleep again. She turned over and shut her eyes, making a resolute but quite unavailing effort. She felt too light, too immaterial for sleep; it would hardly have surprised her had her body floated into the laboratory of its own accord. Certainly, her brain was there, carrying out fresh experiments, despite all her efforts to tether it. The hours sped by at a marvellous rate; in some curious way, she seemed outside time as well as outside space. It soon was seven o'clock, her usual summer hour for rising. She had made a habit of a walk before breakfast, and she saw no reason for breaking it today. Half an hour later she was closing the front door behind her.

The park was lovely. A shower in the night had freshened the air and the rather weary August greenery. Ursula wandered along beside the Serpentine. She had the whole place to herself. The matutinal riders, who, in the season, cantered along the Row at this hour, were all far away, and it was still too early for the crowds of country excursionists and London slum children, who, later in the day, respectively swarmed on the steps of the Albert Memorial or dotted the sward with little family groups. Although Ursula felt buoyant mentally, her legs seemed curiously heavy and tired. She was soon glad to sink down on to a seat. A little paper bag was in her hand that she had taken almost automatically off the hall table as she left home. Now she opened it and began feeding the ducks. The poor things were evidently ravenous; a large drake waddled up almost to her feet, quacking vociferously. The girl became conscious of a male figure passing, but she did not trouble to look up. 'Miss Winfield!' she heard suddenly, in an astounded tone.

Mr Balestier was standing in front of her. He was wearing grey flannels and a straw hat – evidently he considered London in August could be put on a country footing – and he looked very cool and big and altogether pleasant to the eye. And Ursula did feel pleased, although she was rather surprised at herself for doing so. Perhaps, as she had not had anyone to speak to for a fortnight, even her unsociability was sated. 'How astonishing!' she exclaimed gaily as they shook hands. 'I thought I was alone in London!'

'And I had a sort of Robinson Crusoe feeling too. How jolly to meet another castaway – at least, I feel it so.' This early and improbable meeting did seem to the young man to have a spice of adventure; an attractive, odd sort of intimacy. 'I suppose I mustn't ask to share your last crust,' he suggested with a twinkle, 'but I'd love to feed ducks too.'

'I will even give you the whole of it.' Ursula put the depleted paper bag in his hands. 'I don't feed the ducks for pleasure, horrid, greedy things, but I think they are badly treated. All the rest of the year they are so stuffed that they consider it a positive condescension to eat at all. And then in August the manna suddenly dries up. Imagine how disconcerting!'

Tony Balestier had seated himself beside her. He was throwing the bread in all sorts of unexpected directions in order to see the ducks clumsily race for it. 'I suppose the kiddies who feed them are away?'

'Yes, all the fat, frilly, rosy babies in immaculate prams have gone. Of course there are crowds of poor children; I see them if I come for a stroll in the afternoon. They have very good times too, better than the rich children, I think. It must be much pleasanter having a small, big sister for a minder than one of those cross, grey-uniformed nurses. The little slummers sometimes bring bits for the ducks, but generally they look as though they hardly had enough for themselves, poor mites.'

Ursula's companion glanced at her with interest. How mistaken he had been about Miss Winfield! He had thought her too coldly clever for any human weakness, and here he found her feeding ducks and sympathising with ragamuffins. Indeed, now that he really looked at her, he saw that that striking face of hers was not cold at all. Indeed, she had an expression of almost tremulous softness; surely it had not been there when he had seen her before. But how frightfully white she looked! 'And what are you doing in town at this time of year, Miss Winfield?' he asked. 'You don't look as though it quite agreed with you!'

'Oh, yes it does.' The unexpected personal note brought the colour flaming into Ursula's cheeks. It changed her more than ever. Balestier could hardly take his eyes off her. 'I am very well indeed,' she went on, 'and very – oh, most ridiculously happy. I think I shall have to tell you about it.'

So that was it. Balestier smiled. He was only twenty-four, but still he had enough experience to know what it meant when a girl talked like that. Who was the man, he wondered. Perhaps it was the X-ray professor chap who had been at Henley; she had seemed very chummy with him. If it were that fellow, he didn't think much of Miss Winfield's choice, but then girls were always getting engaged to the most unlikely sort of men. Somehow he wished that Miss Winfield were not engaged, especially if it were to Professor Smee – yes, Smee, of course, Vernon Smee, that was his name. 'I think I can guess your news, Miss Winfield,' he said aloud.

'I am quite sure you can't.' Ursula gave an unsteady laugh. 'I did not guess it myself until yesterday. But I expect you have guessed the sort of thing. You know I do chemistry?'

'Chemistry?' The young man stared. But then Smee was a chemist. Doubtless she was going to say that this had been the first link.

'I have been working over a year on the extraction of atmospheric nitrogen, and then yesterday, suddenly – ' Ursula broke off; her voice was trembling.

Well, of all the extraordinary ways of announcing an engagement! 'I suppose you have been working at it together?' Balestier suggested, as she was still silent.

'Together?' Ursula found her voice suddenly; her tone was surprised, indeed indignant. 'What do you mean, Mr Balestier? I have not been working with anyone. It is an independent piece of research.'

What a bit of luck that he had not said more! Could he be on the wrong tack altogether, the young fellow wondered. He stammered out an apology.

Ursula accepted it graciously. 'I only minded because women are never credited with being able to do anything new alone, and my discovery will be absolutely new. You see when the nitrogen – but do you know anything about chemistry?'

Balestier had to plead ignorance. His companion, however, was too brimming over with her new theory to be discouraged. Perhaps, indeed, she found it easier to confide in an outsider. 'You won't mention it to anyone,' she began, and then embarked on a long technical description. Fortunately, she had the gift of lucid explanation and Balestier was, after all, not a Balliol scholar for nothing. 'But I could show you so much better with my apparatus,' she said at last regretfully.

'Take me to your laboratory. I'd like to see the thing immensely.' The young fellow had become quite interested. 'Lowndes Square can only be a few minutes' walk from here, isn't it?'

Ursula jumped up – and then hesitated. It was not from any thought of outraged propriety; such an idea never even crossed her mind. Had not scientific acquaintances more than once visited her laboratory? No, it was only that she suddenly felt so frightfully hungry. She could not do her experiments until she had had some food; would there be enough at home to ask this young man to share it? 'I want my breakfast,' she murmured childishly.

'So do I. Let's get some.' Tony Balestier laughed. Then he noticed that the colour had again ebbed from Miss Winfield's face. She grew so white that he was rather alarmed. 'Look, there's the Kiosk,' he said more pressingly. 'I suppose one can still get breakfast there.'

They walked across the grass together. Yes, they could have breakfast, they were told. Ursula was immensely relieved. She felt so queer that she did not know how she could have got home. She wondered if she was going to turn giddy again, but when the coffee and toast came, she found she was only hungry. 'Have you really never done any chemistry, Mr Balestier?' she asked presently in a musing tone. 'You must be amazingly clever.'

It was Balestier's turn to get red, although Ursula's remark had been too detached to be really embarrassing. She seemed to be considering his mental capacity from quite an impersonal standpoint. Now it occurred to her that, although her presence in town at this unfashionable season had been explained, his had not. 'I have been talking about myself all the time,' she told him. 'What is keeping *you* in London in August?'

Apparently, in his own phrase, Balestier had had 'a bit of luck' too. As Miss Winfield probably knew, an important Government Commission was going out to India next month, and Stanley, Sir Philip Stanley, was taking him out as his secretary. Meanwhile he was getting up a lot of data for the Chief at the British Museum. And, of course, there was his kit to see about.

Ursula was interested. Mr Balestier must look rather out of keeping, she felt, among the queer denizens of the Museum Reading Room. It flashed across her mind that the hall of Greek statuary would be a more appropriate place. But how odd that any friend of her mother's should be reading at the British Museum. She was sure that none of the others had even crossed the threshold.

As soon as they had finished breakfast, they returned to Lowndes Square. It was still quite early, and the kitchen-maid, who was cleaning the steps, drew aside to let them pass with an astonished stare. Miss Winfield always shut herself up from all the gentlemen who came to see 'the Missus', and here she was bringing one of them home and taking him upstairs before ten in the morning. But although she was astonished, any idea of impropriety was as far from the kitchen-maid's mind as from Ursula's own. In the servants' hall Miss Winfield was always said to be a bit cracked. This, no doubt, was a form that her crackiness took.

Indeed, Tony Balestier, the originator of the visit, was the only one to whom it brought any misgiving. When he found himself being taken up to the top of an evidently deserted house, he realised for the first time that Miss Winfield was alone at home. However, he really was immensely interested in what she had been telling him and keen to see her experiments. Besides, he could, in any case, only stay a very short time. Short though it was, he found he outstayed his welcome. In a few minutes Miss Winfield was so absorbed in her work that she became clearly oblivious of his presence. It was a new, and perhaps salutary experience for the young man. For Balestier, although a younger son, had sufficiently good prospects to make him eligible in the eyes of matchmaking mammas, and their efforts had, at least, not been discouraged by the daughters. After all, it is difficult for a man to have the appearance of a Greek god and not know it. Thus the young fellow was both piqued and amused when he found that his murmured adieus received no reply. As he made his way downstairs, he wondered whether, later in the day, Miss Winfield would remember that she had left a man somewhere about in her laboratory and speculate where it had been mislaid.

CHAPTER NINE

Although Ursula was too busy all day, and too tired when she went off early to bed, to meditate upon her new friend, he was her first thought the next morning when she woke up out of a long, dreamless night's sleep. Would Mr Balestier be in the Park again, and would she see him? She would like to tell him about yesterday's successful experiments. But what was the weather like? She jumped up and pulled the spring cord of the blind. Reassuring sunshine flooded the room. Well, that was all right. She would get up at once.

As she dressed she was assailed by a horrible doubt. Would it look as though she were laying herself out to meet Mr Balestier? But, after all, she went to the Park every morning. Why should she be driven out of her normal habits by any young man, even if he were six foot two and an Adonis? Besides, why should she not lay herself out to meet him? He was very intelligent, and she liked him. In any case, he probably would not be there. There was no reason why an early morning walk should also be his practice. After making it perfectly clear to herself that she would not see him, she made straight for yesterday's bench. Yes, he was already sitting on it.

Her work was going splendidly, she told him, in reply to his eager inquiries. And her theory, if it were correct – and it must be correct – was not a mere theory; it would be of great practical importance. For instance, it pointed to the possibility of a new process, a chemical one, for the liberation of the atmospheric nitrogen – a process that might be used to extinguish fires – prairie fires. She pulled herself up; why was she talking in this indiscreet way? 'This is just a wild idea of mine. You won't ever speak of it.' She turned to the duck-feeding for which another providential bag of crusts had been supplied.

Mr Balestier must have guessed that she regretted having said so much. 'I don't know enough chemistry to give you away even if I wanted to,' he laughed, and again possessed himself of the bread bag. 'Why haven't I always fed ducks before breakfast instead of riding in the Row?' he continued meditatively.

'Or why aren't you riding in the Row now instead of feeding ducks?' was Ursula's suggestion.

But the answer was easy. Even if Mr Balestier had wanted to ride, he couldn't. The horses belonged to his brother, and were now naturally in the country. A mere impecunious younger son could not afford such luxuries. 'But I wonder that I never saw you,' he went on. 'I used to ride past here nearly every morning in the season.'

'I don't come here in the season; I go the other way and walk along the Embankment. My place isn't among the society butterflies!'

'That's one for me!' Balestier laughed boyishly.

'Reading at the British Museum sounds more like a bookworm than a butterfly. But I shall qualify as one if I stop here idling any longer.' She was deaf to all suggestion of again breakfasting in the Kiosk, and would not even let him see her home further than the park gates.

After that they met every morning, and the intimacy that developed was a new experience for both of them. Until now Tony Balestier had held himself more or less aloof from girls, perhaps because the wiles of the matchmaking mammas had been too obvious. He had no wish, indeed he had a very strong disinclination, to be captured. And, as for girls not of his own class, the shop assistants at Oxford, or the musical comedy stars whom most of his friends found so alluring, he was too fastidious to be much attracted by them. So his feminine friendships had been chiefly limited to young, or quasi-young, married women of the type of Mrs Hibbert, but of a brainlessness that was less affected than hers. For on one point Mr Balestier insisted with youthful dogmatism: intellect in a woman was a mistake. And now, behold, he found all his theories upset. For here was a girl of his own class into whose scheme of life the idea of matrimony obviously did not enter; here was a woman of intellect who, far from boring him, interested him profoundly. The fact that Ursula was not only a brilliant chemist, but also a beautiful girl may have played its part in the interest. For, although Tony Balestier chose to consider himself as a blasé man of the world and indifferent to feminine charm, yet at twenty-four the blood is apt to run hot. The very fact that Ursula ignored the sex factor in life may, by causing him to neglect his defences, have hastened his subjugation. At the end of ten days he found himself, for the first time in his life, deeply and unreservedly in love. Now that he had come across a girl who did not want to get married, marriage, from an irksome tie, shone before him as the greatest happiness in life.

And Ursula? Ursula was also experiencing a similar revolution, although she was more unconscious of it than Tony Balestier. Naturally, she could not fail to realise that the sight of the tall figure coming towards her across the grass each morning gave her keen pleasure. But why should she be so pleased, she sometimes asked herself in puzzled surprise. Of course, Mr Balestier was clever, and although unlike most of her mother's friends, yet he belonged to the same social set. His upbringing had been identical; he was equally conventional, equally smart, qualities she had always detested. She felt sure that his opinions on the subject of women and many other matters were as retrograde as Colonel Hibbert's own, although Mr Balestier had the sense not to parade them in her stepfather's fashion. But in any case her gods could not be Mr Balestier's gods, for he knew nothing of science. That she should be influenced by her new friend's appearance simply did not occur to her. Had she not often declaimed at the absurd way in which men were swayed by feminine beauty? The mere suggestion that she could be similarly swayed by a man's looks would have seemed to her an insult. So she continued to speculate unavailingly as to what could be the link between them.

But although Ursula knew that she enjoyed these early morning meetings, she was genuinely unaware of how much she enjoyed them, until the day that Mr Balestier failed to appear. As she sat on the familiar bench alone, a feeling of blankness crept over her that filled her with an angry dismay. After all, what did it matter if this stranger came or not. Why, in another fortnight he would be gone altogether. Far from finding the idea soothing, her depression unaccountably increased. Several times she tried to turn her thoughts off on to her experiments, but these no longer seemed so entirely important and engrossing. The feeding of the ducks took longer that day; it was considerably after her usual breakfast-time when she looked at her watch. 'Hanging about for him like a nursemaid!' She got up with an angry jerk and strode homeward at a terrific pace.

On the breakfast table lay two envelopes. One had a German stamp and was addressed in her mother's sprawling calligraphy. The writing on the other she had never seen before; yet she felt that she had always known it. Her heart began to thump in a most ridiculous fashion. The note was short and friendly. Mr Balestier wrote that his Chief had wired for him, but he expected to be back in town by Friday at the latest. He hoped that the experiments were going well; she must not take advantage of his absence to overwork. He would be feeding the ducks each morning in the spirit, although not in the flesh. He didn't know whether he or the ducks would find it the more unsatisfactory.

It seemed 'unsatisfactory' to Ursula also, although the letter itself was eminently the reverse. Somehow, she felt as unaccountably light-hearted as before she had been depressed. And what a lovely day it was! She had not noticed it before; the sun must have come out. She read her mother's letter – many pages of extremely small gossip in an extremely large hand – and then she again took up Mr Balestier's. Suddenly she felt an extraordinary desire to press it to her cheeks, her lips. She must be going out of her mind, she told herself, and firmly thrust it into her pocket. Her face was still crimsoned as, singing softly, she went upstairs to work.

On Saturday morning, as she expected, she saw him. But instead of being at their usual meeting place, Mr Balestier was waiting at the corner of Lowndes Square. 'Were you afraid I would forget the bread for the ducks?' she laughed, with some embarrassment. Indeed, they were both rather constrained. The three days' separation seemed to have made a curious difference.

'I thought if I met you here, you could leave a message about breakfast.' Ursula had several times refused his invitation to this meal on the ground that it would be waiting for her at home. 'You will come to the Kiosk today? Please!'

As they were sitting opposite each other at one of the little alfresco tables fringing the Kiosk, he told her he had been afraid she would have gone out of town. 'I suppose you *are* weekending somewhere?' he asked.

'No, I never do. It interferes too much with my work. Besides, I don't know many people.'

Her companion suggested, a little absently, that the Wednesday evenings at Lowndes Square hardly bore out the last statement. Mentally he was considering whether he should be ill or detained by work in his telegram to his weekend hostess.

'Oh, those are Mother's friends on the Wednesday evenings,' Ursula explained. 'Of course she knows crowds of people. Weeding her address book is her one agricultural pursuit.'

Balestier smiled. 'But what are you doing this weekend if you are not going away?' he persisted.

Working, she told him; just the same as in the 'week-middle'.

'How immoral! But you can't work on a Saturday afternoon in weather like this. It isn't 'feasonable' – that's what an old gardener of ours used to say. Come with me on the river.'

Ursula visibly hesitated. The river sounded very attractive. For the last three weeks she had been working tremendously hard. And now her experiments were practically finished; her theory proved. There only remained the actual writing of the paper – and, oh! how she hated it. She really did deserve a little holiday first.

But suppose they should run across any of her mother's friends up the river. It was permissible to have a house there even in August. And people were such idiots! If she and Mr Balestier were seen alone together, it might give rise to some ridiculous gossip. No, she was only safe within the four mile radius. Aloud she said that the river was too far. She blushed as she spoke.

Tony Balestier, who was watching her, felt a sudden thrill. He shrewdly guessed what was passing through her mind. The thought of their being thus coupled, and still more, the thought that she had thought of it, stirred him curiously. For it denoted a change in her; indeed, he had felt it from the first moment of their meeting this morning. She was less scientific, more human, more personal. He had thought he cared for her as much as was humanly possible before; now he found he cared a great deal more. And it began to seem not so utterly impossible that she should some day care for him. 'If it can't be the river, why not the Serpentine?' he suggested.

'You can't be serious!' It seemed impossible to imagine a young man of the Hibbert set boating in Hyde Park. Ursula laughed at the thought.

Tony Balestier was not quite sure whether he had been serious or not. Bucketing about on the Serpentine did seem rather an extraordinary proceeding. Still, he, too, felt the security of August. And in order to be with Ursula he would brave much. 'I'd like it awfully, if only you don't mind,' he said. He went off to reserve a boat.

As they expected, they were safe from recognition that afternoon, although this was far from meaning that they found solitude. Still, the Serpentine was less crowded than Henley, as Ursula observed; indeed, she boldly declared that she liked it better; it was more 'real'. Certainly as evening came they saw a sight more striking than any the more fashionable river has to show. At one point on the bank Ursula noticed a crowd of urchins assembling. They made an ugly dull blot on the landscape; it was a pity the London poor were so unpicturesque, she thought. Mr Balestier began to scull away rather precipitately, and so she had her back turned towards the shore. Presently a whistle made her look round. Over the green sward, with its background of dark shrubs and trees, streamed a flush of wonderful, gleaming humanity, which broke up at the water's edge into detached, slim, glancing bodies. 'How beautiful,' Ursula murmured, almost awed.

The Saturday afternoon on the Serpentine was followed the next day by another cockney expedition – to Hampstead Heath. But how could they get there? Ursula had demurred, for both the cars had already gone up North. Mr Balestier's proposal of hiring a motor or taxi for the day she absolutely refused. She did not know much about prices, but she was sure that such a proceeding was not for an impecunious younger son. No, she would only go if they 'bussed' it. So Sunday morning saw them waiting at St Mary Abbots for the blue omnibus and, when it came, waiting still longer for the procrastinating third horse to drag them up the Church Street hill. Indeed, the whole journey took hours; and yet they neither of them felt it too long.

It was the first time that Ursula had visited London's playground. 'Why, it is lovely,' she exclaimed in surprise, having expected a medley of trippers, donkeys and round-abouts. They wandered around until they reached a brack-ened dell, faintly sooty but otherwise sylvan. Here Ursula sat upon a fallen tree trunk, while her companion lazily lounged nearby. It seemed an ideal place for lovemaking, and yet he did not make love. Frankly, he was afraid. It was true that he was more hopeful today than ever before, but suppose he were mistaken. If she refused him – well, he simply could not face it, he felt boyishly. Anyway, they had another week before he sailed, and she had promised to come to Hampstead again with him the next Sunday.

Had Ursula given him the least encouragement, probably his resolution of silence would have broken down. But she, too, felt afraid, afraid of this strange, new thing that had come into her life. She had always been so independent, so emotionally self-sufficient. Besides, the present was very agreeable. Several times her eyes rested on her companion approvingly, as he half lay on the grass beside her. How big he looked, stretched out like that! He had taken off his straw hat, and although his fair hair had the regulation almost convict crop, a little curl struggled irresistibly. All the same, whenever the conversation even verged on the sentimental, the girl quickly turned it. It was very easy to talk to Mr Balestier, as she had long since discovered, perhaps because he was so surprisingly interested in all she said. She even told him today about her own life; and, unlike most women, Ursula usually felt this to be an almost impossible topic. Why was it she knew so few people, he asked her, referring to what she had said the day before; had she never made friends at school? So she explained that she had not been to school. As a child she had travelled a good deal and there had been a governess. When she was twelve her mother had married Colonel Hibbert and then, indeed, she did go to school, but only for a term. 'They called it a finishing school, and it nearly finished me,' she observed with a smile. 'I told Mother that unless she took me away, I should commit suicide.'

'What!' Tony Balestier looked startled, indeed shocked. 'Did they treat you so badly?'

'No, they bored me so badly.' It really had been rather an appalling place, Ursula went on. The girls had nothing whatever to think about except the boys at a college opposite. After she had left, there had been some scandal which made her mother glad she had taken her away.

And after that? Oh, after that, governesses again, and then Bedford College. That was where she had first discovered science. 'It was a revelation.' Of course, at College she had got to know other girls, but when she had asked them home her mother pronounced them 'impossible'. 'They weren't "impossible", they were very nice girls,' Ursula explained, 'but I could see that they did not fit in very well at Lowndes Square, and so we never became intimate. But, of course, I did not mean that I have no friends; there is Professor Smee.'

It was the first time she had mentioned him; nor had the man crossed Balestier's mind since the initial meeting. Now he felt a sudden, horrible dismay. Suppose, after all, there were something between this fellow and Miss Winfield. His thoughts went back anxiously to the day at Henley. 'Do you see much of Professor Smee?' He hoped his voice sounded as careless as he tried to make it.

'Yes, I have been seeing quite a good deal of him this summer, because I was working for some weeks at his College. And one day I went to call on Mrs Smee.'

'Mrs Smee?'

'His wife – now she really is "impossible". But Balestier was so overpowered by gratitude for the existence of a Mrs Smee of any description that he hardly heard her remark; indeed, he was conceiving poor Charlotte as an angel, however disguised.

They returned by the same lumbering and idyllic route, and with one of the unreal coincidences of life, at Kilburn Mrs Smee boarded their bus. Charlotte always found such a proceeding rather an acrobatic feat, but as she did not like walking, it was her only method of getting fresh air. Just as she was unsteadily progressing along the top of the omnibus towards an empty front seat, the horses started, and almost precipitated her on to Mr Balestier. Ursula, who was sitting on the farther side of him, naturally looked up, and her eyes and Charlotte's met. For the first moment the girl really did not recognise the Professor's wife. Then as the hot, angry-looking woman continued her lurching passage without any sign, she thought thankfully that Mrs Smee had not recognised her. Certainly it had been for the older woman to bow first. Perhaps the ordeal was still in store, but, for the moment, the good lady presented only an unbowable, and also an extremely unprepossessing, back. At Notting Hill Gate, Mrs Smee got off, but she was staring fixedly in front of her as she again passed Ursula. 'Isn't it odd? That was Professor Smee's wife, whom I was telling you about,' Ursula whispered to her companion. She fervently echoed his 'poor chap' with reference to the Professor.

On Wednesday Mr Balestier had again to go down to see his Chief. He returned on Friday as before, but this time he did not wait until the following morning. Mr Balestier had called, and might he come up to see Miss Winfield's experiments? This was the message brought to the laboratory during the afternoon by the maid.

Ursula told the girl to show the gentleman up. A rush of such happiness flooded over her that she felt quite weak. It was too absurd, she scolded herself. Of course she was only pleased because she was writing the paper, and that was work which she had always hated. Had she been doing experiments she would have resented his interruption. She had jumped up from her stool and was now looking at the fume cupboard, the glass of which, at a certain angle, gave a reflection. Yes, her hair seemed all right; it really was a comfort having curly hair, which did not look straggly even when it was untidy. She was wearing her long blue overall. Should she take it off? She undid the top button, and then did it up again. No, it would be silly! The proper costume in a laboratory was an overall. If Mr Balestier thought it hideous, well he would just have to think so.

The young man did not give the impression of disapproval as his glance rested on her. Indeed, the long lines of the overall admirably suited the girl's upright young figure, while its blue was of the colour which became her best. She did not look at him as they shook hands. 'You want me to show you that last experiment, the one with the high frequency?' she said in an offhand way, and then began clamping a carbon in one of the holders.

Tony Balestier was rather pale. 'Well, I really came to tell you that my Chief has suddenly decided on our going by sea all the way – the old fool!'

Ursula looked surprised; she had not grasped the full significance of the change of route. 'But why do you mind so much? I thought you liked the sea,' she suggested.

'I do – but it means starting a week earlier. I am to go down to Southampton today. We sail tomorrow.'

The carbon Ursula was clamping snapped. She got another from its wooden box. So this was their last meeting. He would not be in the park tomorrow morning – or any morning. There would not be another Sunday together. A sense of desolation bore down upon her. 'I suppose then you have not got time to see my experiment?' It was the only thing she could think of to say.

The young fellow got paler than ever. Miss Winfield's way of receiving his news was desperately discouraging. He had meant to propose, but was it of any use? However, the experiment would, at least postpone the moment of leaving her. 'Yes, I have got time. I'd like to see it,' he told her.

Well, she must get the apparatus ready then. She began to connect up an accumulator with unusual clumsiness. Her growing depression seemed to clog her movements. All at once she inadvertently touched one of the poles. The unexpectedness of the sharp shock made her cry out. She snatched away her hand.

'What is it?' Tony Balestier had caught hold of her hand, and was looking at it anxiously. 'What is it?' he repeated.

'Nothing. I forgot the current was on. It's only just pins and needles. It has nearly gone.' At least here was an excuse for stopping. 'I am afraid you will have to wait to see this experiment until you come back from India.'

Balestier was still holding her hand. 'It is not all I shall be waiting for,' he began with a sudden audacity. Ursula looked up. Perhaps he read in her face what she had tried so hard to conceal. Perhaps it was just that they were both young and standing hand in hand. Certainly further explanations seemed unnecessary.

* * *

'We are both of us black as sweeps. I believe you have been sitting on one of the carbons,' Ursula observed a little later, with a tremulous laugh, as they slipped down again to earth from their perch on the high laboratory bench.

CHAPTER TEN

The great drawback to the British Association, in Ursula's eyes, was the necessity it involved of planting herself upon strangers. Had she been a free agent, she would have stayed at a hotel or even have taken lodgings, but this was not permitted. Once, she had made the suggestion. It had reduced her mother to tears and Colonel Hibbert to an explosion of wrathful blasphemy. 'A young girl like you knocking around alone at an inn! Outrageous, by George! Never heard of such a thing in my life! Damn it all, it ain't respectable!' Her mother had been driven to proffer a weeping offer of accompaniment. After all, Mrs Hibbert reflected, if Ursula were an ordinary girl she would require chaperoning to Commem, or May Week; thus to be escorted instead to queer scientific gatherings was to some extent her due.

Mrs Hibbert's proposal had been accepted, indeed, accepted with pleasure. Ursula's affection for her volatile parent made her enjoy the prospect, although she felt that 'chaperoning Mother' – for so the daughter viewed it – might prove rather distracting. For the girl was sure that the Lowndes Square martial escort would speedily be replaced by a scientific train, while her mother in ravishing toilettes flitted busily from Section to Section. However, the plan came to nothing, owing to her stepfather's discontent. The Colonel did not like the prospect of being parted from his wife even for a week, nor did he appreciate the alternative of 'kicking up his heels at a confounded scientific pow-wow'. To end a difficult position, Ursula had put down her name on the list of those desiring 'hospitality' and an invitation had been promptly forthcoming. This readiness on the part of provincial hostesses to welcome a strange and unattached girl probably pointed to some knowledge on their part of Miss Winfield's social position.

This year the British Association was to be held at Plymouth, and her hosts were a certain Mr Thompson and his daughter. Ursula had not expected to see her parents until she joined them at Dumdrochie after the meeting. A telegram, however, arrived the day before she left town announcing that Colonel and Mrs Hibbert would break the journey at Lowndes Square. Ursula was genuinely delighted both to see her mother and, to a lesser degree, her stepfather, but her delight did not lead her to impart to either the two great events that had befallen her during their month of absence. With regard to the scientific discovery, her silence was chiefly due to a desire to surprise her mother. Her paper would surely make a sensation at the BA, and she would then send the newspaper accounts. Her mother would be much more impressed by these than by anything she could now tell her. And with regard to the other discovery, she and Tony had decided in that brief, rapturous, miserable hour of parting that everything should be an absolute secret until his return – or rather she had decided it and Tony had acquiesced. For to Ursula this new experience seemed too beautiful, too unreal for speech. Probably she would not have included her mother under the ban of silence, had she not had previous experience of the leaky nature of maternal secrecy. Indeed, she reminded herself, Mother would probably refuse even to try and keep such news a secret from the Colonel. And the mere thought of her stepfather's jocosity and banter – for this he considered the appropriate setting for any affair of this kind – made Ursula writhe. She would not have the mystery of her love cheapened and desecrated. That he would approve of the engagement would only increase his pleasantries; and, at the same time, the consciousness of approval seemed to justify the concealment. When Tony came home it would be time enough to tell people of the engagement – though for her part she wished that no one need ever be told. For Ursula hated in anticipation all the fuss that in the Hibbert circle was the necessary precursor of matrimony; the banal paragraph in the *Morning Post*, 'a marriage has been arranged' – 'arranged', what a hateful word! The portraits in *The Queen*; the clothes; and yet more clothes; the presents; the letters. When her lover came back to her, her wonderful lover, could not he and she together slip into their dream-world, unseen, unknown?

It was not surprising that emotions so different from any that Ursula had previously experienced should leave some outward mark. Mrs Hibbert, at least, was conscious of the difference, for that little lady, with all her follies, was no fool, and she loved her only child. There was a new softness, a sort of indescribable, suppressed radiance about her daughter, which she could not understand. In any other girl she would unhesitatingly have put it down to love, but Ursula was not like other girls. Besides, who could have been in London in August for Ursula to fall in love with? It did, indeed, occur to her that Professor Smee might have given up the trip to Germany – her lips twitched at the recollection of Mrs Smee's absurd, jealous imaginings – and perhaps he and Ursula had again been working at his College together. She had often thought the man was attracted by Ursula, and who could be surprised at it, with such an outrageous wife? But it would be too appalling were Ursula attracted by him. A chance remark of her daughter's, in the course of conversation, set her mind at ease. Ursula had not seen Professor Smee since that last Wednesday 'at home' and was obviously quite unconcerned about him. Then who or what could it be? The little lady studied her daughter's face with puzzled interest.

Whatever might be the cause of the change, the result was unmistakable – an immense improvement. The great fault in Ursula's face had been a certain heaviness; this had now gone. Indeed, all her features seemed more delicate, more spiritual, probably because she had grown slightly thinner. 'I never saw you look so pretty, my dear,' her mother now observed with disconcerting suddenness. 'August in London seems to suit you. I do wish you weren't going to a desert like Dumdrochie for your holiday, where there isn't a soul to see you.'

Ursula had blushed violently at her mother's unexpected encomium, thus adding to its truth. 'Never mind, Mammykin,' she laughed. 'There will be crowds of people at the British Association to be prostrated by my dazzling beauty!'

'Oh, stuffy scientists. I don't count them!' Mrs Hibbert gently waved into oblivion the whole British Association, unmindful of Ursula's protest. This was less vigorous than usual; perhaps the girl was beginning to regard her mother's attitude as hopeless. 'We ought to be able to have nice house-parties at Dumdrochie,' the little lady rippled on. 'George, dear' – she turned to her husband – 'we really must have that new wing another year.'

Ursula here broke in with an emphatic assertion that if there were a house party at Dumdrochie she would not go, thus earning a grateful growl from her stepfather. Indeed, their common antipathy to the threatened wing was the greatest link between them. 'Ursula don't want a lot o' people – likes trampin' around the moors – same as me,' the Colonel throatily ejaculated as he puffed at his cigar. 'Can't think why you don't try your hand at a bit o' shootin', Ursula, what? Knock over a bunny or two, or a bird when it rises. Seems silly not to, what?'

He did not seem to expect an answer, and Ursula made none. The moors! Yes, she did 'like trampin' around' them, as the Colonel said, although without his concomitant of slaughter. Indeed, 'like' was a poor word to express her feeling. She fairly revelled in the solitude, the expanse, the great silence with its continuous undercurrent of tiny noises. The mere word brought back the smell of the sun-warmed thyme; the feel of the cool, brown loch into which she plunged; the cry of the peewits circling overhead. And this year the moors would mean more to her than ever before. For only on the moors, she felt, was there space enough and time enough to hold her love.

But before Dumdrochie came Plymouth and the British Association. Very soon, Ursula found herself caught up in the familiar atmosphere of scientific papers, varied with the usual Association festivities. She found, with mingled feelings, that her paper had not been allotted a place until the last day; it gave more time for preparation, but it kept the nightmare hanging over her. Added to this was the suspense of waiting to hear from Tony. He had sent a wire from Southampton before he sailed, and in *The Times* she had seen of the boat's safe arrival at Brindisi, a day or two earlier than had been expected. Of course, she would get a letter from Brindisi; it would come direct, for Tony had noted her Plymouth address. The officials at the chief post office in Plymouth were rigorously examined on the subject of the Italian mail.

This double strain of expectation would have been almost unbearable but for the ideal hosts with which fortune had provided her. Mr Thompson was a rich businessman, extraordinarily active for his seventy years, and a singular contrast to his invalid, middle-aged daughter. His excess of activity, and Miss Thompson's lack of it, almost removed them from their young guest's cognisance. The final perfection of their hospitality, Ursula felt, was their having limited it to herself, doubtless on account of the hostess's ill-health.

In particular, Ursula was appreciative of her solitary breakfast, for Mr Thompson rose at an impossibly early hour and Miss Thompson at an impossibly late one. Thus the morning mail could be scanned unobserved, and an Italian letter, Ursula had learned, would come either by the first post or the last. But, apart from this consideration, she was thankful for a quiet opening to the day. Such acquaintances as she possessed were chiefly of the scientific world, and so the Association week was one of constant meeting and greeting. Her quiet life fitted her ill for a corporate existence. Conversation worried her; even with scientists she could not plunge straight away into technical discussions, and she could never think of other things to talk about. Of course Professor Smee was different; he was a friend, but she had hardly seen him. One day they happened to meet, and he told her that he was having no end of trouble over the installation for his Monday evening lecture. He simply could not get down to Section B. Some of his vacuum tubes were 'very pretty'; he wanted her to see them.

The Professor's avoidance of the Chemistry Section and, incidentally, of Ursula, was not entirely due to his lecture preparation, as he said. During his holiday, Vernon Smee had been taking stock of the emotional position in which he found himself. Away from the irritant of his wife's presence, and the attraction of Ursula's, he was able to consider the question more fairly. No, he had no business to be in love with Miss Winfield; moreover, nothing but unhappiness could come of it. The only thing to do was to try and get over his unlucky passion. By filling the days of his German trip with strenuous physical exercise and by keeping a firm hold on his night thoughts, he managed to achieve a comparative success. Ursula's image in his mind became much less insistent.

Paradoxically enough, he had been helped in this by a letter he had received from her. It was a mere cold request for the address of his student, Flecker. She wanted the young fellow to act as her assistant at the BA. Really, Miss Winfield seemed unable to give a thought to anything outside her work, he had felt irritably.

On his return to England, Professor Smee spent a few days at home prior to the British Association, and there his convalescence suffered a severe relapse; indeed the fresh attack of lovesickness had all the initial virulence. For this setback his wife was responsible. Poor Charlotte had, at last, realised the true objective for her jealousy. That Sunday evening, when she had seen Ursula on the omnibus, she had been struck by her beauty, emphasised as it was by the patent admiration of the man beside her. The realisation penetrated and increased Charlotte's humiliated fury at the supposed 'cut'. Suddenly it flashed through her mind that Miss Winfield must be the attraction at Lowndes Square. No wonder Vernon had seemed indifferent to the mother! And not only had he seen the girl in her home, he had had her working for weeks in his laboratory. What a fool they must have thought her! How they must have laughed! The sense of having been thus tricked made the new jealousy even more insupportable than the old.

Perhaps the fire of Charlotte's indignation might have died down had not Professor Smee, on the very evening of his return, unwittingly poured oil on the troubled flames. He was chatting to his wife about his forthcoming lecture and the Association generally. As Charlotte glanced at some of the printed notices he showed her, Miss Winfield's name caught her eye. Vernon had not told her that he arranged for his lady friends to be at the Association, she broke out angrily. Of course now she understood why he had never suggested his wife coming to any of the meetings.

'Miss Winfield's presence has nothing to do with me. As you see for yourself, she's down to read a paper.' Vernon Smee checked his anger. 'The BA is not in your line, old lady, that's why I've never suggested your coming. Miss Winfield is a scientist; her mother won't be there.' Not knowing that the *venue* of his wife's jealousy had changed, he imagined this information would be soothing.

'No doubt then Miss Winfield will enjoy herself all the more! Oh, you needn't stare. I know what your fine young lady is like! Didn't I see her with my own eyes carrying on with that young man on the top of the bus?'

Vernon's surprise had made him 'stare'. Now he laughed. The idea of Ursula 'carrying on' with a young man on the top of a bus or anywhere else struck him as simply ludicrous. 'If you saw Miss Winfield recently with a young man, it was probably Flecker, my student, who is working for her,' he said curtly.

But the mischief was done. Vernon Smee's thoughts had again been turned to Ursula, and he had, moreover, been forced into an attitude of championship. Besides, although he disbelieved the possibility of Ursula's 'carrying on', he felt that there might be something to justify his wife's statement. Charlotte was not deliberately untruthful even in her rages. Probably Flecker – if it were Flecker – had fallen in love with

Ursula. How dared he – the cub! Not that Flecker would have the ghost of a chance. No, if he himself found Ursula cold – and that letter he had got in the Black Forest had been confoundedly cold – he knew, at least, that he was more to her than a dozen Fleckers. If he had been free, why, then he felt almost sure – But he was not free. For the future their friendship was going to be a model of frigidity.

When the evening came of Professor Smee's lecture, he found himself repaid for his work. It was a brilliant success; everyone told him so, some even proclaiming it the finest lecture they had ever heard. Amid the congratulatory throng, Ursula took shape. 'You were wonderful!' she smiled at him. The evening's triumph had already excited Vernon emotionally. Ursula excited him still more. Other people, pressing forward to shake hands, separated them. When, a moment later, he looked round for her, she had disappeared.

Although Vernon Smee little guessed it, Ursula was as agitated as he. She had expected her letter from Tony three days ago; it had not yet come. Which had been the worst, the blank mornings, with the feeling of an endless, dreary day to be lived through before the chance of happiness came again, or the empty, shattering evenings? On Sunday, when the single post failed her, she had had to face both – a miserable twenty-four hour eternity of hope deferred. This morning she had felt quite certain – and once more nothing! But tonight it must come, her letter, her precious letter! Why, at the post office they had told her that it could hardly be delayed any longer. Yes, she would find it when she got home. Her heart was singing as she sat, outwardly calm, listening to the lecture.

It had needed a struggle to stop and speak to Professor Smee. Tonight! Tonight!

She could hardly sit still in the cab. Why didn't the man go faster? She wanted to call out to him, but checked herself. At least, she would have his fare all ready. There was no waiting on the doorstep, for the ideal hosts had provided a latchkey. Now! The hall table stretched blankly. But, of course, when she was late, her letters were put in her bedroom. She was starting upstairs when Mr Thompson appeared – his one failure in tact. He began to ask about the lecture. 'Supper is waiting for you in the dining room,' he suggested pleasantly.

Ursula shook her head. She felt that food would choke her. There was only one thing she wanted, to get upstairs to her letter. On the plea of fatigue, she escaped. The first flight was sedately mounted, then came a rush. She was breathing fast as she opened her door and switched on the light. The letter was not on the little writing table. It was not on the dressing table, it was not anywhere. It had not come. And she had made so sure of it. She sank down on a chair, sick with misery.

After a time, she began to pull herself together. Letters, especially foreign letters, were often delayed for days. If only this had not been Tony's first letter. For underneath her distress was a deeper distress. Suppose she had not got the letter because there was no letter? Suppose Tony had not troubled to write from Brindisi? Oh no, it could not be that – and yet – after all, what a little time it was that she had known him. Suppose on the ship – so many girls were prettier and more attractive than she was. No, no, it could not be that. She could not bear it! It would mean that Tony was changeable –

untrustworthy. If Tony were not what she thought him, that would be the worst of all. It would be worse than his dying – her heart seemed to stop. Was that why he had not written? How absurd, she scolded herself. He was young and strong; it was most unlikely that he should even be ill. Oh, why was she not with him? This separation was horrible!

The next morning she would not let herself hurry. There would be no letter, she kept repeating with a sort of dull despair. She was right. After breakfast she wearily journeyed down to Section B. An unused room had been assigned to her, and here she had installed her elaborate apparatus. She wanted to go through her experiments once more before her paper the next morning. 'Aren't you well, Miss Winfield?' Mr Flecker asked, amazed at her listlessness.

That evening the big Association soirée was being given in the Guildhall. Ursula wished that she had not arranged to go, but she could not alter it now. Her old Bedford College professor, Dr Tremlett, and his wife, had arranged to chaperone her. She had even got a new gown for the occasion. When she had finished dressing, she regarded herself critically in the glass. Yes, it was rather nice! But what was the use of looking nice? Why wasn't Tony there to see her? Why, oh why didn't he write?

Dinner, in Miss Thompson's company, seemed to drag interminably. After all, she was glad that she was going to the soirée. It would have been appalling to sit and listen to Miss Thompson's chit-chat all the evening as the clock crawled on towards the postman's knock. Although the meal had seemed so long, it was only eight o'clock as they left the dining room.

On the hall table lay a letter. Was it – could it be? Yes even at that distance she could see the writing – or did she feel it without seeing it? 'A letter for you,' the hostess said indifferently. She spoke as though it were just an ordinary letter.

Ursula picked it up. She hoped her hostess did not see that she was trembling. She hoped that her voice did not sound too changed. 'I must go and get ready. My friends will be coming.' She fled upstairs.

A maid was in her room turning down the bed. How maddening! The girl mercifully withdrew. As the door closed behind her, Ursula locked it. At last! At last!

The envelope was covered with re-directions. Oh, Tony had posted it to Lowndes Square. No doubt, as he had reached Brindisi early, he had thought that the letter would catch her before she left home. And the idiots at Lowndes Square had forwarded it to Dumdrochie. That explained it. The letter had taken two days to get up to Dumdrochie and two more days to get back to her here. It was not Tony's fault. Well, she had got it. At last!

She was almost afraid to open it; afraid to start reading it. Suppose it began coldly, disappointingly. She must be disappointed, she told herself; she was expecting too much. She read the first words. Apparently she was not disappointed. The colour flooded her face; she was kissing the page rapturously. After all, it was her first love letter.

But now she would read it straight through. She would sit down comfortably in the easy chair and savour it to the utmost. How beautifully long it seemed! She glanced through the pages. Why, it was a journal letter! Tony had written every day, several times a day. He had been thinking of her, thinking of her often. And what was this? A smaller, separate sheet had fluttered out. Poetry? 'To Ursula.' She flushed again. Never in all her life had anyone written her poetry. There was a knock at the door. 'Mrs Tremlett is waiting for you in the carriage, Miss.'

Well – But Ursula's sense of humour came to her aid. It really was rather funny, after waiting for her letter all these days not to be allowed to read it. She thrust it into safety and caught up her cloak. When she came home, there would be no one to disturb her. Then she could read it, read it again and again, her wonderful letter. Meanwhile, she did not mind so very much. For with every breath she drew, she could feel it lying over her heart.

It was a transfigured Ursula who made her appearance at the soirée in the wake of kindly, commonplace Mrs Tremlett. Vernon Smee was standing in the first room near the entrance. He was waiting for Ursula, although he would not admit it. Great heavens, how lovely she looked! He went up to her with a curious expression on his face, a sort of deepened quiet. But instead of talking to Ursula, he found himself entangled in conversation with Mrs Tremlett. That lady was renowned for a never-ending flow of triviality. Would he have to stand listening to this drivel the whole evening, the poor Professor wondered despairingly. Perhaps Ursula guessed his predicament, for she smiled as their gaze chanced to meet. It made her look even more dangerously adorable. The next time that Vernon ventured to let his eyes stray, he saw that the smile had gone, or rather it had become diffused into a strange, soft radiance out of keeping with the Tremlett monologue.

What was she thinking about? Smee wondered. But of course he knew. That afternoon he had been down to his neglected Section and had penetrated into Ursula's room. Perhaps he could be of use to her in her preparations for the next day. But he had only found Mr Flecker, who told him that Miss Winfield was tired and had just gone home. The young fellow had then gone on to speak of the new theory, evidently imagining that the Professor knew all about it. It was not easy to follow the excited explanation, nor had Professor Smee liked to question too closely. But as far as he could make out Ursula had hit on rather a remarkable idea: if she could really substantiate it, the discovery might be of immense importance. No wonder she was looking so happy. All the same, he resented this unvarying absorption in work. Would she never care instead for people – for a person?

Dr Tremlett now came up and, breaking in upon his spouse's eloquence, timorously suggested a move towards the music. Smee warmly seconded the proposition, only to find to his horror that he was paired off with Mrs Tremlett, while the Doctor escorted his old pupil. Smee did not know to which part of the arrangement he objected the more. Of course he could not seriously feel jealous of such a white mouse of a man as old Tremlett – he ignored the fact that he had not the slightest right to feel jealous of any man – and he recalled with some satisfaction the flippant Bedford College anecdote that Ursula had told him. The poor old doctor had once absent-mindedly opened the skylight instead of the door for the exit of his class. 'He thought we were angels already,' Ursula had laughed.

Even after the Tremletts were finally dispossessed, Vernon still found himself cut off from Ursula. For scientists are not a race apart, and the girl's beauty this evening kept a small, black-coated group constantly around her. Ursula herself was surprised at the attention she was receiving, and still more at the way in which she was receiving it. For she found herself talking quite easily and brightly, more in her mother's style than her own. She seemed so brimming over with happiness that it unconsciously flooded into speech. Was she being very silly, she wondered once or twice, as her little court laughed delightedly at her sallies. But she did not care! What did it matter? Nothing mattered but Tony's letter.

Probably this state of affairs would have continued all the evening, had not Vernon Smee, fired still further by the admiration Ursula was exciting, at last forced an opportunity. 'Let me take you to have some supper, Miss Winfield,' he said, masterfully offering his arm.

'Now you mention it, I am absolutely starving!' Ursula smiled at him gratefully. Her docility extended to eating the supper in a retired ante-room, where Professor Smee had already located two seats. 'I want to hear all about the Black Forest,' she observed.

They began chatting gaily, but Ursula soon became conscious of a certain discomfort. Professor Smee was staring at her in such a curious way. Of course there could not be anything really to mind. He was such an old friend. Besides, he was married. But she did wish he would not do it. She had lowered her eyes, but now she looked up to see if he were still looking. He was. Her cheeks grew hot. Besides its being uncomfortable, she felt as though in some inexplicable way she were not behaving well to Tony. She began to wish that Professor Smee knew about Tony. Should she tell him? If she did not mention the name, her secret would still be safe. But how was she to begin? It seemed impossibly difficult.

Her companion's very next sentence gave her the opening. 'You are looking so well tonight,' he murmured. The words were prosaic enough, but his tone made them almost a caress. 'So well and so – ' He hesitated.

'I look well because I am so very happy.' Ursula's head was turned away, and her voice a little indistinct. 'I want to tell you about it.'

'I think I can guess.' Vernon smiled. Now for the new theory. Still, Ursula was so lovely tonight, that as long as she would talk to him, he could bear the talk to be about her work. 'I must congratulate you.'

'How did you know?' The face Ursula turned on him was radiant, so radiant, indeed, that Vernon's breath came quickly, although he still did not question the cause of the radiance. By a curious parallelism of fate, he was as certain that she was telling him of her discovery when she was telling him of her engagement, as Tony Balestier had been that she was telling him of her engagement when she was telling him of her discovery. 'How could you have known?' Ursula repeated, as he did not answer.

'Flecker told me. Was he indiscreet?'

'Mr Flecker! Mr Flecker told you! But he couldn't; he doesn't know.'

Her bewilderment was obvious. Vernon Smee's face changed. For if Flecker could not have imparted the news, then it could not concern her discovery. What was it? 'We are talking at cross purposes,' he said quickly, trying to dispel a horrid apprehension. 'I thought you were speaking of your work.'

'My work? Oh no, it isn't my work.' There was a note of laughter in her voice, and of something besides laughter, that turned Vernon suddenly cold. But what right had he to mind? he asked himself miserably. What had he to offer her, he, a married man? But she was speaking to him. 'I have found out that there is something besides work' – her voice was strangely soft. 'Something even more wonderful. Now I expect you really can guess. Only I have not told anyone – I – he – ' She broke off in happy confusion.

'Yes, now I can guess. Well, I must still more congratulate you.' Vernon Smee was white, but Ursula did not notice it. 'I am glad that you have found this happiness. That you should be happy is my deepest desire.' It was the hardest speech that he had ever made, and, at the moment at least, it was true.

CHAPTER ELEVEN

Although Vernon Smee would have preferred not to see Ursula again until he had had time to accommodate himself to her shattering revelation, he felt that it would be too marked to absent himself from her paper the next morning. He had quite decided, however, not to take part in the afternoon's excursion to Dartmoor. His determination was only increased by the fact that he had been looking forward to it all the week, or rather to the opportunity it would afford for seeing Ursula. Instead, he would leave for town by an early afternoon train. And he would be alone at home, thank heaven! Charlotte had still another week to stay with the Todds at Southampton.

The room devoted to Section B held about a hundred and fifty people; it was rather more than half full the next morning for Ursula's paper. In this there was no ground for complaint; some of the best papers had been less well attended. Indeed, in scientific phraseology, the size of the BA audience tends to vary inversely with the depth of the discourse. For the large element, chiefly feminine, that finds in the British Association a week of pleasuring disguised as education naturally prefers the more popular papers.

A few of these camp followers of science were to be seen among Ursula's audience, attracted probably by a report of her youth and beauty or possibly by her social position. The bulk of those present were, however, genuine chemists, and among them the girl was gratified to see three or four of distinction. Of course Professor Lyall Fleming, as this year's president of the Section, was almost bound to be there. How he must hate it, with his anti-feminist views! No wonder he looked severe as he sat there, large and impressive.

The occasion naturally did not call for oratory, but Ursula's reading was good and clear. She had an excellent voice for public speaking, Vernon Smee decided, as he struggled to give a dispassionate, scientific attention. He wondered once or twice whether any man had ever been subjected to such an ordeal as his before. Indeed he was almost glad when a vein of disparaging criticism began to thread itself among his admiration. No, the paper was not well written – it was getting more and more laboured – all tangled up – perhaps owing to the lecturer's over-effort to make herself clear. Smee was surprised; that impromptu speech of hers at the Chemical Society had been perfectly lucid. He remembered what she had told him about nibbling up her pens in the anguish of literary composition. The thought brought a rush of tenderness. Confound it, this would not do. He must keep his mind on her work.

The first part of the paper was taken up with a description of the experiments and the baffling error that had kept appearing despite all precautions. Suddenly, after she had been speaking a considerable time, there came a startling suggestion. The error was not an error. It was an essential factor. Ursula gave her explanation, her new theory. There was a stir of interest. The three or four distinguished chemists were whispering to each other. Some of the younger men began to clap, and the camp followers, although too ignorant to understand the new theory, or even to recognise it as such, joined in the acclamation. Ursula went on to detail her proof. Perhaps she went on too long. The applause when she finally sat down was rather unexpectedly scanty.

Professor Lyall Fleming, as chairman, briefly opened the discussion. They had listened with the deepest interest, he said, to Miss Winfield's able paper. Her suggestion was extremely ingenious although he was afraid he could hardly consider it as proven. He would, however, reserve his remarks until later.

Three or four speeches followed. Not only were they all sceptical, but there was a distinct undercurrent of hostility. These male chemists may have unconsciously resented a woman's claim to discovery. Vernon Smee sat silent, torn by the most opposing emotions. He did not believe in Ursula's theory, and yet he longed to champion her. He felt the criticism she was receiving was unfair, and yet he too was conscious of a certain jealousy, a certain irritation. Her paper had been so cocksure, poor darling. When would clever women learn a little tact? Perhaps their attitude was caused by their forming intellectually the *nouveaux riches*.

At last Professor Fleming rose again and majestically reviewed the new theory. His judgment, based on the ground of pure mathematics, was more shattering than any that had preceded it. Not only was it adverse, in substance, but the tone of its delivery was of unmistakable, if courteous, contempt. He concluded with a suave reference to 'the well-known and not unpleasing habit of youth, and, if he might venture to say so, more especially of charming, feminine youth, to build its conclusions on insufficient foundations.'

Vernon Smee was on his feet. The sudden colour on Ursula's cheek brought him there. With his barrister-like aptitude he took up her arguments and immensely improved them. But with all his ability he failed to convince. How could he convince of a scientific theory in which he himself disbelieved? Still, Ursula had looked across at him gratefully. Perhaps it was as well for his own safety that in order to catch the afternoon express he had to leave the meeting before its close.

The chief reason for Ursula's gratitude had been that Professor Smee's speech gave her time to get her feelings into manageable order. She was bitterly disappointed; but she was more astonished than disappointed, and more angry than either. It was against herself that her anger was chiefly directed. Her belief in her theory remained absolutely unshaken, but she realised that her experiments were not, as she had imagined, conclusive. Well, she ought to have made them so. She ought to have worked up the mathematical side and have been able to refute Professor Fleming on his own ground. She had been horribly slack, she reproached herself unjustly. Her theory ought not to have been presented until it was impregnable.

Anger may have stimulated her, for the short closing speech was as well delivered as the paper had been badly delivered. She did not attempt to answer her critics, beyond making clear one or two points that had been obviously misunderstood. 'With regard to Professor Fleming's concluding remark,' she said with a smile, 'he must remember that reprehensible youth has, at least, time in which to strengthen unsatisfactory foundations. I trust by the next meeting of the Association, mine will be found able to sustain even Professor Lyall Fleming's weighty – ' there was a hardly perceptible pause, in which, however, a titter made itself heard and the Professor flushed as she added 'criticism.'

Ursula's sole desire, as she left the hall, was to return to London at once and start on her work of reconstruction. But this was impossible owing to her promise to join her mother. And when she reached Dumdrochie she found herself, after all, glad of the holiday. Simultaneous discoveries in love and in science had been more exhausting than she had realised. She needed this period of mental and emotional quiescence – a quiescence that was a good deal disturbed by Tony's weekly letter and would have been still more disturbed without it. However, by the end of a month the elasticity of youth had carried her over her fatigue, and she was panting to get back to her laboratory. Once there she threw herself upon the task, working, as she wrote to Tony, 'like ten thousand furies'.

During the winter Ursula had the Lowndes Square house almost as much to herself as in August. For her mother and stepfather stayed in the North until the snow put an end to the shooting, and then, after a few days at home, they started on a series of visits to friends capable of providing hunting. It is true that during their absence a chaperone was established for Ursula's benefit, but several previous winters of training had enabled the girl to reduce that mild functionary to a condition of negligibility.

Perhaps it was owing to being so much alone that Ursula fell into what her elders – had they known of it – would have considered most undesirable company. For her interest in the suffrage, or perhaps it should be said, in the suffragettes, began to revive. After the raid which she had witnessed, she had, for the next few weeks, been too much taken up with her own affairs to pay any attention to other people's. Moreover, during August, suffrage had been quiescent, at any rate as far as London was concerned. And Dumdrochie was too far away to catch anything but distant echoes of the movement, chiefly in the form of expletives from the Colonel as he read his belated *Times*. 'Scandalous, damn 'em, abs'lutely scandalous!' was his almost daily comment. 'Cabinet ministers not able to call their souls their own! Can't think what the women of England are coming to!'

'Perhaps they are coming to the Vote,' Ursula had once lightly suggested and then regretted the remark, for it had reduced the poor Colonel to the verge of apoplexy. Only her repeated assurance that she had not the faintest idea of herself joining the 'Shrieking Sisterhood' restored the domestic calm.

This assurance was easily given, for, far from wishing to become a suffragette, Ursula's dislike of the militant movement was almost as strong as her stepfather's; indeed, it was perhaps the only point, besides the detested new wing, on which they agreed. She, too, felt this persecution of Cabinet ministers to be disgraceful, and what possible advantage could the women hope to gain by it? Nevertheless, despite her disapproval, she could not help being amused at the idea of the Prime Minister scuttling to meetings through underground passages or along barricaded streets. His life seemed to be shadowed by plain clothes men; he played golf guarded by constables. Really, these suffragettes, in their passion for prison procedure, seemed to have converted the Prime Minister of England into something very like a ticket-of-leave man!

And then there was this new business of the hunger strike. It had been begun about the time of the last raid by a suffragette who was in prison for scribbling something about petitions on the wall of the 'House', so Ursula had read. How depressing that anyone could be so wrong-headed, so insane! Then twelve of the raid women, including Mary Blake, had followed the regrettable example. They had all been let out after a few days, to Ursula's profound relief. For although she disapproved of hunger striking, she could not go as far as her stepfather with his growl of: 'If they want to starve, let 'em starve, and thank God for the riddance!' Not that the Colonel was really more capable of such callousness than Ursula herself, for he was one of the kindest of men. It was this very fact that, when it came to the point, no one would allow a woman to starve, that made the suffragettes' behaviour so mean! They were taking advantage of people's good feeling. If they committed crimes, why could they not take their punishment for them like men?

At the end of September came the first report of forcible feeding. Ursula was distinctly shocked. But her stepfather was probably right; it was all a mere pretence, a way of enabling the suffragettes to break their hunger strike and, at the same time, retain their pride. Such behaviour made them seem meaner than ever.

Then, one day, when she was back again in town, she happened upon a picture-poster of forcible feeding. 'Torturing Women in Prison' it was called. Below you were urged to 'Vote Against the Government'. It was not a pleasant picture, nor did it seem a desirable method of evading imprisonment. Indeed, merely to look at it made Ursula feel rather sick. But, after all, she reminded herself, she had no proof that the process really was like that. The poster was issued by the suffragettes for propaganda purposes: their exaggeration was notorious. All the same, she felt uneasy. It was horrible to think of Mary Blake undergoing anything that even remotely approached that pictured scene. She must get assurance on the subject.

Every day newspapers appeared automatically on the library table at Lowndes Square. These Ursula now studied with a new interest. They contained no reference to forcible feeding; indeed, the more important among them hardly ever mentioned suffrage. What ostriches! Did they think that by ignoring the agitation they rendered it non-existent, Ursula wondered. She would be driven to reading the suffragettes' own publications. But how could one get hold of them? It was clearly impossible to give the order to the butler in the usual way. 'I want you to get me *Votes*, Jenkinson.' She could picture the man's stare of shocked incredulity! No wonder he would feel outraged when she herself did not like to face the suspicion of militancy by going into a stationer's shop and asking for it. But there was a WSPU seller, a little elderly lady, whom she had often seen outside High Street Kensington Station. To buy it casually of her in passing would be less embarrassing.

The Embankment had now been substituted for the park, with its oversweet tantalising memories, as the route for Ursula's daily walk. But the next day she turned in the old direction and finally reached Kensington High Street. The pavement was thronged with smartly dressed Christmas shoppers, but there in the gutter stood the little lady with her bag of papers. Feeling absurdly guilty and self-conscious, Ursula proffered a penny. The seller's face lit up. Perhaps business was slack, and even one customer an acquisition. 'It is a very good number; there is a wonderful article by Christabel,' she told Ursula with a friendly nod.

After that Ursula bought the paper regularly. Much of its contents still struck her as high-flown trash, but she also came across some arresting facts. The experiences of one woman in particular were profoundly impressive. For this lady belonged to a famous English family, a family which even Mrs Hibbert could not look down upon. Indeed, although the lady in question had been extremely gracious on the one occasion that Ursula had met her, the girl had a suspicion that such people looked down upon the Hibberts and all the rest of the former Marlborough House set. And now Ursula read, to her amazement, of this aristocratic, delicate-looking woman taking part in a suffragette row, being arrested, imprisoned, on hunger strike. After two days she was discharged without being forcibly fed. They could not do it, the prison doctors said; her heart was not sound. A cheap martyrdom, Ursula felt scornfully.

A few weeks later she came across more news. The same lady had again been arrested, but it had been in the guise of a working girl. None of the prison authorities had recognised her. She had again hunger struck. This time she had been forcibly fed. No one had troubled about her heart. The greatest roughness and indignity had been shown her. One day her real identity leaked out. The result was immediate discharge.

It was disconcerting. Clearly her stepfather was wrong. Forcible feeding was not employed to make things easier for the suffragettes. On the contrary, it seemed to be used to make things harder. And poverty increased your punishment. If this was the celebrated English justice, there might be some grounds for women wanting the vote!

Early in December a suffrage meeting was to be held at the Albert Hall. The huge notice outside had already caught Ursula's eye. Her new indignation decided her to attend. As instructed by her *Votes*, she wrote to headquarters for a ticket. She was a little surprised at being required to send half a crown, particularly as she had heard that there was to be a collection. Surely this was unusual at political meetings. These suffragettes must be very ardent to be willing to pay for the privilege of paying again.

The evening was fine – did not the militants boast that the weather was always on their side? – and Ursula was glad to walk the short distance to the meeting. But how ridiculous it was, she mused, for these WSPU people to have taken the largest hall in London. Probably it was done for effect; it was impossible that they could fill it. As she got nearer and found herself in a dense, hurrying throng, she wondered if the impossible might, after all, be possible. Her seat was reserved, and as it was still fairly early she halted on the main pavement in front of the hall to watch the incoming crowd. The motor 'buses were stopping just in front of her, each in turn discharging almost its entire freight; while nearby a continuous stream of private carriages, cabs, and taxis were turning up towards the main entrance. Ursula was rather surprised; she had not known that the Cause counted so many of the well-to-do class among its adherents.

More interesting than the vehicles were the actual people all around her. The great majority were naturally women – women of curiously diversified strata. There was a large element in so-called artistic attire, rather untidy, rather attractive – at least Ursula found them so, although she could not help remembering the well-known quip, 'O Liberty, what crimes are committed in thy name.' There was another numerous and distinct contingent, probably ladies from suburbia, the mammas stout and unintellectual looking, the daughters slight and equally unintellectual looking, but all alike wearing the then fashionable large hat and long coat, the latter usually of a deplorable cut. Under it, Ursula divined, a fussy white silk blouse, for on the rare occasions when Mrs Hibbert insisted or her daughter's presence at a theatre party, the girl, looking round at the pit and the upper circle, had seen them filled with women of this type, rows and rows of them. Another distinct class was present with which Ursula was less familiar, poorer women with sensible, worn faces and toil-coarsened hands. She guessed them rightly to be the wives of working men, probably mothers of large families. There was also a sprinkling of working girls, more noisy and even smarter than the young ladies from suburbia – perhaps hailing from East End factories. But in all these varying kinds of womanhood there was one similarity. As the girl stood there, she could not help noticing a certain enthusiasm, a certain uplift in all the faces around. There must be something in a cause that gave people that expression, she reflected.

Although men were in a minority, a few went by, and these Ursula studied with an even greater interest. For they were of a type quite strange to her: more unconventional in appearance than either her mother's friends or her own scientific acquaintances; more interesting – she could not but admit it. But how queer their loose tweed overcoats and soft felt hats looked in town! A small, middle-aged man, who now got out of a 'bus, was, however, irreproachably clad; indeed, Ursula would never have remarked him, with his spectacled, amiable face, but for several eager ladies who immediately rushed up to him. From their excited questioning he was evidently someone of importance in the suffrage world. 'Did he think the Government had really paid Mrs Pankhurst's fine?' 'What chance was there of turning Winston out?' Queries such as these reached Ursula's ears from the circling feminine throng. The driver of the halting 'bus was, like Ursula, watching the scene. 'Now then, Solomon, ain't you a-going it?' he suddenly shouted. There was a general laugh in which the victim joined.

Time was now getting on and Ursula thought she had better go in. At the main entrance the official, an elderly man in semi-evening dress, was opening and shutting the glass door, apparently in a state of frenzied indecision. As Ursula, with some difficulty, struggled up the crowded steps, he suddenly called out that everyone was to go round to the other entrance and firmly closed the door. There were protests, tickets were held up displaying a printed 'main entrance', but in vain. 'I thought the "General" was organising this meeting,' a surprised voice, near Ursula, observed. 'Oh, that idiot of a man goes with the hall,' another feminine voice replied. 'Yes, he has lost his head badly, poor dear. I must get a message round to the "General". At this moment a short, stoutish woman in the tricolour sash was seen through the glass talking to the agitated official. Apparently she soothed him, for the door was again opened.

It was the only hitch in the perfect organisation. Indeed, but for this, Ursula might not have realised that there was any organisation – everything ran with such automatic smoothness. Girlish stewards posted at frequent intervals piloted her through the confusing circles of the hall to her seat. Placed on it was a little donation card with a green pencil suggestively attached.

Ursula looked round curiously. There were more empty spaces than she had expected, for it had been announced that every seat was sold. A woman sitting next to her explained that the empty places belonged to lifeholders. At other political meetings these people were willing to give up their seats – 'but they won't let *us* have them – the brutes!' the woman exploded. However, despite these blanks, the great hall was a wonderful sight with its solid human floor ringed with rising circles of faces. Above were the tiers of bursting boxes and finally the unreal, doll-like band of figures in the top gallery. These had come, Ursula supposed, to see, for they could not possibly hear.

A tremendous roar of applause announced the arrival of the leaders, applause that burst out again and again during the speeches that followed. Frankly, Ursula thought it undeserved. The speeches were good, but not great as she had expected. Then she realised that the fact of being able to move ten thousand people to a frenzy of emotion without supreme oratory was in itself greatness.

But for one item in the programme Ursula could feel nothing but an amused scorn. The Leader – so the announcement ran – was to decorate each hunger striker with a medal 'For Valour'. The Leader herself in her speech had referred to the women in a way that the girl had felt pitifully theatrical. 'Oh, God of Battles, steel my soldiers' hearts,' she had cried amid a tumult of applause. Nevertheless, when the white-robed procession crossed the arena towards the platform, natural human curiosity impelled Ursula to look round. Suddenly she found herself staring, shocked, aghast. She wanted to cry out, and, at the same time, she could not cry out. For this was not theatrical. As at the raid she had come across something that was real, horribly real. It was not so much that the women looked ill – though they did look ill.

Ursula had seen illness before. No, these women with their straight, colourless faces, with their straight, angular figures looked – looked – she did not know how to express it. Then the word came to her, a word that she had always scoffed at the suffragettes for using. But it was the only word. These women looked tortured.

The strange row of white gowns and grey faces was meanwhile moving along towards the platform. As each woman received the trumpery decoration, the chairman announced her name. 'Mary Blake,' Ursula heard suddenly. She stared still harder. Where was Mary Blake? That could not be she, that girl who was getting a medal. Why she was not beautiful. She was almost ugly. Now she was moving away. The new Mary Blake had caught hold of the back of a chair; she was hardly able to walk.

'That's Miss Blake.' It was Ursula's neighbour who was speaking. 'She has been forcibly fed a hundred and forty-two times. Her release was really due last week, but they kept her until this Tuesday to pay her out for hunger striking. And they knew her mother was dangerously ill. Aren't they beasts?'

Ursula did not reply. She, too, was filled with a sort of rage, but not so much against Mary Blake's gaolers as against Mary Blake. How dared the girl thus have misused herself! How dared she have spoilt her wonderful beauty! It was wicked, criminal! And when her mother was dying – but perhaps she had not known about the mother. Of course, it was rather amazing that Mary Blake, that all these women, should be willing to go through such suffering. In a way it was fine, even although it was insane.

To Ursula the rest of the meeting seemed of small importance, but probably most of the audience found in the collection their central moment. Indeed, it could hardly be called a collection – there was no need to collect. Money flowed to the platform, the incoming cheques being thrown so rapidly into the large waste-paper basket that several fluttered to the ground. The amounts themselves were scored up by slipping cardboard figures into a huge frame, such as is seen on a football field; at the end it showed a two with three figures to follow. Ursula had not meant to contribute – she was not sure enough about her attitude – but she found herself scribbling a promise for ten pounds. How could she do less when that band of white-gowned, grey-faced women, who had already given so much, were now giving money as well?

And yet, when she got home, the girl regretted her gift. For although she might admire, she still did not approve. What need was there for these extreme measures, for all this noise and violence? Women's Suffrage would surely come with the gradual emancipation of women. Where was the hurry?

CHAPTER TWELVE

Christmas was not a festival that was regarded with favour at 57 Lowndes Square. Ursula condemned it as an interruption to her work, while Mrs Hibbert moaned over the expense and declared her intention of forming a Society for the Suppression of Santa Claus. Certainly the servants' Christmas presents ran away with a good many sovereigns and even one or two fivers, while an army of unsuspected tradespeople started up from their yearly oblivion to claim a remembrance in tips. To make matters worse, at this season the soaring tendency of the household books became even more pronounced, and this without affording anybody the slightest gratification. For the delights of the old-fashioned Christmas with its turkey, mince pies and plum pudding are necessarily reserved for the underfed. To those who have always more to eat than is good for them, Yuletide cheer merely brings an unpleasant sense of repletion.

The one redeeming feature of the depressing season, in the eyes of Ursula and her parents, was their mutual interchange of gifts. For the devoted Colonel always bought his wife some article of jewellery, and Mrs Hibbert shared the savage's passion for shining stones. She, on her side, yearly presented her spouse with a box of cigars, usually a questionable feminine gift, but in her case beyond criticism. The Colonel was indeed wont to maintain that he'd 'back Vi's choice in baccy against any man's, by George' – another testimony to the practical sense that lay behind little Mrs Hibbert's fluffy frivolity.

With regard to the presents that passed between mother and daughter, these for a good many years had given dubious pleasure. Each seemed unfailingly to hit upon something that the other did not want. At last, one Christmas, Ursula with a smile handed her mother a weighty package. When opened, it revealed the latest work in German on the transformation of nitrifying organisms. After a moment of stupefaction, Mrs Hibbert took the hint. She thanked her daughter effusively for the 'ducky' volume, but suggested leaving it in the laboratory. She herself had seen the sweetest thing in gold-chain purses, which she proposed buying for Ursula. But perhaps for safety it had better be kept in her own jewellery safe.

Immediately after Christmas the Hibberts were off again to fresh hunting fields and coverts new. But nature having so inconveniently claimed the spring for the replenishment of her stock of targets, a pause soon ensued in the Colonel's round of destructive activity. Mrs Hibbert utilised it each year to carry him off to the 'South of France', which, in defiance of geography, was in her circle synonymous with Monte Carlo. Thus her daughter was almost continuously alone – save for the subjugated chaperone – during half the year.

But this winter, for the first time, Ursula was not only alone; she was lonely. Part of her depression was due to her work. For Ursula had set herself to study her subject from the Lyall Fleming basis of pure mathematics, and she was discomfited at her own ignorance. She had specialised in chemistry too early, she now realised. She ought first to have taken her degree.

But chiefly, of course, Ursula's loneliness was due to her lover's absence. When Tony had left her, he had said that the Government Commission would be away six months. Almost his first letter had informed her that the time was prolonged to eight. One of the Commission – 'an old fool of a Parsee', as the indignant Tony had styled him – was of such high caste that he could not cross the sea. As the Report had to be a joint production, this meant the rest of the Commission, and the luckless Tony in its wake, staying in India to write it. With a feeling of almost sick disappointment, Ursula switched on her joyful hopes from March until May. Then one day, soon after her mother had gone abroad, a letter arrived in which Tony announced another change of plan. His Chief, Sir Philip Stanley, was not going straight home from India. He had arranged to visit British East Africa and the Cape to take up the vexed question of Indian Emigration. There was no chance of getting through with this before September. If Ursula wished it – so Tony wrote – he personally could leave Stanley once the Report was finished and come back to her in May as had been settled. Only he was not quite sure if it would be playing the game. Stanley might have difficulty in replacing him out there; the old boy obviously liked him and depended on him a good deal. Besides, the work would be tremendously interesting; it was also important with regard to his future.

At this point Ursula collapsed. Putting her head down on the laboratory bench, she sobbed as she had not done since her childhood. Tony must come home in May! She could not go on any longer without him. It was impossible. But it was still more impossible that Tony should come home in May. She did not in the least care about Sir Philip Stanley's convenience. But this was Tony's work. To give up such an opportunity might ruin his career. How dear it was of him even to have suggested it. That he had done so was her one comfort.

After that she was lonelier than ever. Probably her love for Balestier was developing her emotionally, for she began to realise for the first time how few friends she had. She had hardly seen anything even of Professor Smee this winter. He never stayed on now after the Chemical Society, so there had been no more walks home together. At first Ursula thought their not meeting was accidental; then she realised that the Professor must be purposely avoiding her. Probably he imagined she was too much taken up with her engagement to want his society. Well, it was very stupid of him. He might have guessed from her always being alone that Tony was out of England. As a matter of fact, her loneliness made her want to see the Professor more than she had ever done before. If she ever had an opportunity for a moment's private talk with him, she would tell him so.

Even the human interest afforded by the suffragettes seemed to have passed out of her life. In January there had been a general election, and the WSPU with its usual highflown verbiage had proclaimed 'a truce'. Ursula was amused, and, at the same time, profoundly thankful. The new light that had been thrown on hunger striking had caused her constant uneasiness. At the same time, her disapproval of this and of every form of militancy had, if anything, increased. Now she could happily dismiss the whole question from her mind.

So the weeks went on. March, that year, instead of marking the beginning of spring, brought back winter in all its severity. Ursula almost envied her mother, who wrote of basking in the Riviera sunshine. Her regular constitutional was nothing but a penance in these days. If it were like this tomorrow, she would stop at home she decided, as she tramped along the Embankment one raw, foggy afternoon. She noticed that one of the benches had an occupant, an elderly, respectable-looking woman in black. What an extraordinary proceeding to sit out of doors in such weather!

Ursula passed. But she had only gone a little way when she decided to turn. It was really too horrid out; besides, it looked as though it were going to snow. Was the old woman still sitting on the bench? It was too foggy to see. After a few yards, the seat with the erect little figure upon it again became visible. She must be an inverse salamander!

As though conscious of Ursula's criticism, the woman at this point got up. Had her speedy return disturbed the reverie, Ursula wondered? But no, the old lady had not looked in her direction, and her steps on the greasy pavement could not be audible so far. Was the queer old creature coming towards her or going away? She did neither. Instead she stepped briskly across to the parapet bordering the river. Then, to Ursula's utter amazement, she began to struggle up on to it. Did the old lady mean to continue her meditation sitting on the wall? Or perhaps it was a new suffragette tactic? Suddenly the little black figure vanished. She heard a splash!

Ursula had been standing still in her astonishment. Now she began to run. She had never run so fast before. As she ran she was automatically pulling open her long, fur coat. She flung it off as she reached the spot where the woman had disappeared, and, almost simultaneously, kicked off her shoes. What luck that they were shoes and not boots, flashed through her mind. She could see over the parapet. Yes, there below, something was bobbing in the water, a black bonnet. She, too, scrambled up. There was a second splash.

Ursula had often jumped into water from a height, and thus she was expert enough to keep herself from going down far. Even before she reached the surface again, she had caught hold of something – a gown. Mercifully the wearer was not struggling; probably she was unconscious. By turning the woman on to her back and holding her close underneath, Ursula managed to support her with one arm and strike out for the side. But how horribly, how frightfully cold! Indeed the cold had been so intense that, at the first plunge, it had hardly given her the sensation of cold; rather it had struck her head like a blow. The thickness of her clothing had, for the moment, kept the chill from her body. Now an icy grip fastened on her; her heart seemed to stop; she could hardly breathe. But the exertion of swimming helped her; her breath came back. Half a dozen strokes brought her to the wall. By pressing her hand against the roughened masonry Ursula found herself supported. But what was she to do next? The wall was impossible to climb. Even unimpeded she could not have done it. As far as she could see – which, indeed, was not far in the fog – it stretched on unbrokenly. She began to feel like a rat in a trap. She would not have minded so much had the water not been so fearfully cold. Already she was getting numbed; her burden might slip. To restore her circulation, she let go her hold and struck out desperately, keeping alongside the wall as she swam. A faint sound from above reached her. Why had it never occurred to her before to call for help? She tried to do so, but her teeth were chattering violently. Only a croak came.

"Ullo.' A small boy's head appeared over the parapet. 'You in the water?' he asked in a pleasant, conversational tone.

'Where are the nearest steps?' The words came in gasps.

'They ain't so fur; jist along a bit. Want to git out?' The head vanished like a jack-in-the-box.

The swimming had made Ursula warmer, except for the arm that grasped the old woman's inanimate form. She shifted the burden to the other and went on as before. Suddenly the little boy's head bobbed up again a dozen yards or so lower down. He was evidently too small to look over without raising himself.

'Shall I bring yer coat and shoes, Miss?' He disappeared again abruptly. Probably his foot had slipped.

'Bring help,' shouted Ursula. She was not sure whether the child had heard, but she had no breath to call again. The burden she supported was growing very heavy. The steps seemed a very long way. Suppose the little boy was fooling her. Suppose there were no steps. A shrill, two-fingered whistle came hopefully to her ears. The urchin was evidently trying to attract someone's attention. Then perhaps he had sense enough to be right about the steps. If only her skirt did not drag so round her legs. Could she unfasten it and let it slip off? By treading water this was managed. It was much easier now. She again changed the arm that supported the old woman and swam along with renewed energy. At last, in the gloom, she thought she saw a break in the interminable smooth wall. Yes, it was a break. There were the steps. A final spurt and she had reached them.

The little boy was already there at the top, jumping up and down with excitement, and much involved with the fur coat and shoes. One of the latter he now dropped; it bumped from step to step and splashed into the water. 'Kitch it, miss, kitch it quick,' he shrieked to Ursula, who was vainly trying to hoist her burden on to the slippery ironwork. To her relief a man now appeared. She had thought as she swam that she had heard answering shouts to the boy's catcalls. The man thumped down his bag of tools and clattered to the bottom of the steps; then catching hold of the motionless form in Ursula's arms, he managed to drag it up. Ursula, too, was able to scramble out, now that she was unweighted. She drippingly followed the man, a middle-aged artisan, as he carried up the old woman.

There was a convenient seat at the top, near one of the circular gas lamps, and on this they laid the unconscious figure. The little ragamuffin was still holding the fur coat, and Ursula put it on. She hated herself afterwards for having done so; of course, she ought to have wrapped it round the old woman. But the action was as instinctive and unconscious as taking it off had been. Indeed, her only thought was the good fortune in having something dry and warm that would also conceal her knickerbockered condition. Even the sight of the artisan divesting himself of the outer of his two shabby jackets and wrapping it round the poor old creature's legs brought to Ursula no suggestion. They both leant down to hear if the motionless figure were breathing; ought she to make an attempt at artificial respiration? But at this moment the wrinkled eyelids quivered; for a moment they were raised. 'You'll be all right now, missus,' the workman observed cheerily.

A policeman had meanwhile been approaching with an unhurried tramp, a notebook in hand, ready for all emergencies. 'What's this – a party in the river?' he began leisurely, moistening his pencil. 'Anyone here know her name and address? And yours, too, please, miss?'

'Idiot!' Ursula fairly stamped her one shod foot. 'Don't stand asking addresses. Get her to a hospital. She'll die of cold. Call a taxi.'

The small boy again saw his opportunity. 'I'll git one for yer, miss,' he piped, and scurried off. The workman also went in search, leaving Ursula face to face with the angry policeman. She tried to look dignified, although it was difficult with wet wisps of hair dangling round her face and a pool of water marking the spot where she stood. However, her handsome, dry fur coat had an impressive effect. Moreover, it gave Ursula herself a slight, but sustaining, sense of returning warmth. 'Have you any brandy?' she continued sharply.

'No, I 'aven't.' The policeman, although hidebound, was not as inhuman as Ursula imagined. He had been fumbling at the straps of his rolled mackintosh; now he spread it over the old woman, while Ursula chafed the icy hands with fingers that were scarcely warmer. She started at a sudden piercing note. It was the constable blowing his whistle, but whether it was to summon a taxi or merely another policeman she did not know. Between his blasts, he again demanded information. This time, as there seemed for the moment nothing further to be done, Ursula could not refuse to supply brief particulars. 'You'll be notified when your presence is required in court,' the policeman told her at the end.

'Court?' Ursula's bewildered brain could only picture some ceremonial reward for saving life. After all, her stepfather had received the DSO in the African Campaign for rescuing his Colonel. 'Do you mean at Buckingham Palace?'

'Buckingham Palace!' It was now the policeman who was bewildered. 'No, p'lice court, Bow Street, most like – when she's charged, you know.' He jerked his thumb at the prostrate figure. 'You'll be the chief witness.'

It was still more incomprehensible. 'But why should she be charged?' Ursula asked feebly.

'Attempted sooicide. It's a serious offence. I 'ave 'eard that it's a capital one by law, though, of course, they don't never enforce it.'

'They hang you for committing suicide!' Ursula suddenly wanted to laugh, despite the fact that she was shivering. It was all like a Gilbert and Sullivan opera. 'But how do you know this woman wanted to commit suicide?' she protested.

'It's likely she'd be setten' on that wall in this weather for pleasure!' The policeman grinned. 'Mostly though they does it lower down the river. Here's your cab now, miss.'

He seemed to take it for granted that Ursula would go off in the taxi alone to Lowndes Square. This she absolutely and angrily refused. They must drive the old woman first to St George's Hospital; then she herself would go on in the taxi. The driver was distinctly grumpy when he realised for what he was wanted. It would mess up his cab, he said. He wouldn't get another fare that day. Ursula's well-filled purse had been in her coat pocket. She put in her hand and found it still there. The driver was soothed into golden acquiescence and the honest small boy sent off beaming. Only the workman refused the silver she pressed upon him. 'Glad to do my bit, miss,' he said civilly.

As they lifted the little black figure from the bench, the eyes again opened. 'Where am I?' the old woman asked feebly. She repeated the question when she and Ursula and the policeman were in the taxi.

'Where are you? Where you was before you were, and a nice lot of trouble you've given us getting you there,' the constable scolded. 'It's this young lady you've got to thank for being 'ere at all.'

Suddenly the old creature began to cry. 'But I don't want to be 'ere. Oh, miss, you meant it kindly, but why couldn't you 'ave let me be? It would all 'ave been over by now.' Sobs choked her voice.

'There's gratitood!' The policeman's voice was disgusted. 'Don't notice 'er, miss.'

Ursula did not hear him. Despite her physical condition – and never in all her life had she been quite so cold and uncomfortable – she had been glowing with a sense of having done something rather fine, of having saved a fellow creature's life! And now the bubble was pricked. The fellow creature told her she would rather not have been saved. This old woman would rather have gone down into the icy, black unknown than go on living. It was incredible! For the world was such a delightful, interesting place; why should anyone want to die? There must be something very wrong somewhere, Ursula felt soberly.

CHAPTER THIRTEEN

When Ursula jumped into the river after the drowning woman, it was not with the smallest idea of acquiring credit for herself; but neither did she expect her action to be viewed with an almost universal condemnation. Apart from the poor old creature's own reproach and the constable's deterrent formality, it would be difficult to imagine anything more rebukingly horror-struck than Jenkinson's stare as he opened the front door with a gasp of 'Miss Winfield, miss!'

Ursula certainly did look a peculiar figure. She had no hat, and her damply dishevelled hair hung round her face, while the absence of one shoe gave a queer limp to her gait. 'I have just been pulling a woman out of the river, Jenkinson,' she observed airily.

'Yes, miss.' But the explanation seemed rather to increase than to diminish Jenkinson's disapproval. As he himself afterwards put it, in all his years of service he had never heard of no ladies swimming around in Chelsea. And as for pulling a person out, everyone knew that the class of them that fell in was not at all fitting for Miss Winfield to associate with. However, although the young lady had forgotten what was due to her position, Jenkinson knew the proper conduct in his. This precise experience might not previously have befallen him, but gentlemen, and ladies too, often came home soaked through after a wet day in the hunting field. So he now observed with deferential sympathy, 'You will wish me to inform Denyer, no doubt miss, that she is to prepare a hot bath immediate? And may I take the liberty of suggesting that a glass of brandy and hot water strong is what's considered the best after immersion?'

It was not only the domestics who considered that Ursula's conduct had exceeded the bounds of decorum. The meek chaperone was almost tearful in her agitation. Even Mrs Hibbert, when she heard of the incident, seemed dubious. 'Of course, it was perfectly splendid of you, darling,' she wrote, 'but wasn't it a weeny bit unnecessary? Surely the policeman or the boy or someone could have pulled out the poor old woman?' The idea of Bow Street completed the parental disapproval – how Ursula regretted having mentioned her comic Buckingham Palace mistake. The Colonel even suggested rushing home to England to chaperone his stepdaughter to such a dubious resort. In her violent objection to this proposal, Ursula rather ungratefully overlooked its kindness. But she felt that the ordeal before her was tiresome enough in itself if only on account of the waste of time, without being complicated by the Colonel's presence. After a rapid passage of letters, a compromise was reached. Ursula was to be accompanied to the police court by Mr Joliffe, the family solicitor, a portly, polite gentleman of later middle-age. Really, from the way everyone was behaving, Ursula told herself pettishly, she might be suspected of having pushed the old woman into the river instead of pulling her out. Would Tony, too, take the general view that the incident formed rather a discreditable chapter in her career? But it would be weeks before Tony got her letter telling him about it and months before she could receive his reply. How horrible it was his being so far!

Ursula's unusual irritability was largely due to a severe chill that had followed her 'immersion' despite Jenkinson's panacea. If the cold had made her ill, what must be the condition of Mrs Bennett? – this Ursula had learnt, was the old woman's name. A note of inquiry was sent to St. George's Hospital, but a reply came that the patient had already been transferred to Holloway Gaol. Ursula was amazed and indignant, although too unwell herself to deal with the matter. And almost the first day she was up again, a formal notice arrived, instructing her to attend at Bow Street the following Tuesday at Martha Bennett's trial.

As in duty bound, Ursula forwarded the communication to Mr Joliffe. He suggested calling at Lowndes Square on Tuesday to escort her. This proposal Ursula refused, saying that she would meet him at Bow Street instead. The plea was to save his time, but her real object was to get there before him in order to secure a private talk with Martha Bennett. The old woman's parting words still troubled her. Why should she have said that she did 'not want to be here'? What was the reason for the desire that it should 'all be over'?

The police court was a more dignified building than Ursula had expected. The stone facade, although dirty, looked solid and respectable compared with the ramshackle

Covent Garden precincts around. A little knot of people and two or three policemen were standing on the pavement outside, and the square entrance hall was crowded. Rather to Ursula's surprise, no one had questioned her admittance, and she now looked about her wonderingly. Two archways faced her, but the passage through to the stone staircase beyond was cut off by a railing, which also served to safeguard an incongruously domestic perambulator and a harmonium standing on the farther side. Another exit from the hall suggested itself in the wooden, box-like structure on Ursula's left. Making her way towards it, she found that the two sides were indeed swing doors, through one of which people were passing. A policeman stationed near surveyed the scene with a coldly superior air. 'Can I see a person called Martha Bennett? She came this morning from Holloway Prison.' Ursula asked.

The reply was curtly negative. 'You'll see her fast enough in the dock.' Another case had to come on first. 'Now then, no blocking up the gangway,' the constable admonished her rudely.

Two painted wooden seats were fixed along the opposite wall of the hall, one on each side of a radiator. That on the right was fairly full, but the other had for its sole occupant a slight young girl with a babyish face. As Ursula crossed to sit down, the girl quickly moved to make room for her; she moved so far that she was almost pressing against the pipes.

'I don't need the whole bench, thank you,' Ursula smiled. She was doubly grateful for this courtesy after the policeman's churlishness.

The girl stared as if in surprise. 'Ow, I'm all right,' she said and tittered. It seemed to be more with nervousness than with amusement. The poor little thing's eyes were swollen with crying, Ursula now noticed. This probably accounted for the embarrassment. 'Can I help you?' she asked, half-surprised by her own rush of protective pity. 'You look so young to be here alone.'

The girl again stared, but she did not seem displeased. 'You don't look so awfully old yerself,' she suggested.

The naive retort amused Ursula. 'I am twenty-three; that must be a good deal older than you! Besides, I have been about a lot alone.' Then she reminded herself that her companion, despite her infantile appearance, was doubtless earning her own living; she could not be quite so inexperienced as she looked. What was she? Not a servant; she had not the manner; nor did she suggest a factory girl. Perhaps she was in a shop. 'If I can do anything for you, do let me,' Ursula said aloud.

'Thank you, I'm sure.' The girl giggled again unnecessarily, but there was real gratitude in her tone. 'But I ain't here by meself. I'm with a lady friend of mine. She's just gone to ask about when the case I've got to do with comes on. There she is now, waitin' for me.' There was a moment's pause. 'Thank you ever so all the same.'

Before Ursula could say any more, her companion got up and strolled towards a rather bold-looking dark girl, who was standing at a little distance. An expression of surprise was also on this second girl's face, mingled with a certain obvious amusement. She evidently began to question her friend about the recent conversation and broke into rather a coarse laugh at her reply. Then they both sauntered across towards the entrance door – 'not for a good hour,' Ursula heard the 'lady friend' observe as they passed out.

At this moment Mr Joliffe appeared. He was evidently perturbed to find Ursula already there. 'You must have arrived very much in advance of the appointed time, Miss Winfield,' he told her reproachfully. 'I do not know what Colonel Hibbert would say.' He beckoned to a constable, who unlocked a door and then ushered them into an empty waiting room. It was the same man, Ursula noticed, who had previously rebuffed her; now he was polite to the verge of subservience. Recognition was mutual. 'Wasn't it you, miss, who wanted to speak with one of the prisoners? It's against the rules, you see.' He turned to Mr Joliffe apologetically. 'You'll tell the young lady as I couldn't 'elp it, sir?'

'No, no, of course not – your request was quite irregular, Miss Winfield,' Mr Joliffe went on with a certain severity, when the policeman had withdrawn. 'The constable could not arrange such an interview on his own responsibility.'

'But he need not have been so rude about it,' Ursula commented. 'He is quite different now.'

The lawyer was all apology. Doubtless the policeman had mistaken her for a suffragette. These terrible women were bringing the whole sex into disrepute. A message that the Bennett case was coming on closed the anti-suffrage tirade.

Ursula found herself sitting in a sort of pew at the side of a large room. The walls were high, painted grey above and oak-panelled below; a big domed skylight formed the greater part of the roof. In front of her to the right was the magistrate's seat, showing an attempt at state and dignity, which its good-looking, white-haired occupant successfully maintained. In front of her to the left, and thus facing the magistrate, was what she recognised with a thrill must be the prisoner's dock with its suggestive iron bar. Almost at once, Martha Bennett was conducted into it and the bar replaced.

The poor old creature looked very ill – this was Ursula's first thought. Indeed, she hardly seemed able to stand. It was shameful to have dragged her here in this condition! Otherwise the little figure looked as neat and respectable as it had done that afternoon sitting on the Embankment, and this despite the fact that the rusty black cape and gown had in the interval served as a bathing costume and almost as a shroud. Her voice, as she now answered the magistrate's questions, matched her attire; it, too, was worn and decorous.

There was a queer little stand with a flat, wooden canopy directly opposite Ursula on the other side of the court. This she was now asked to occupy. When she reached it, a book was produced, and a man began to gabble something which she did not catch. Just as he had finished, she realised that the book was a Bible and that she was being sworn. Had she any desire to depart from the truth, such a perfunctory ceremony would hardly awe her into keeping it, she felt.

'On the fifth of March, you saw the prisoner loitering upon the Embankment?' the magistrate began interrogatively. As the simplest way of answering his questions, Ursula started upon a terse account of the afternoon's procedure. The magistrate was listening with obvious interest. The whole court was listening. Purposely Ursula laid as little stress as possible on her own performance, but naturally it could not be eliminated. Her simple, 'so then, of course, I jumped in,' evoked an admiring murmur. As she told of – at last – reaching the steps, there was a distinct breath of relief. 'Thank you for your extremely lucid description, Miss Winfield,' the magistrate observed at the end, with a slight, courteous inclination in her direction. 'Undoubtedly you may feel that, under Providence, this unfortunate creature owes her life to your courage and presence of mind.'

It was not unnatural that Ursula was conscious of a certain elation as she went back to her seat. A glance at the dock dispelled it. She knew, if the magistrate did not, at what value the 'unfortunate creature' held her life. Besides, she ought to have said more in Mrs Bennett's defence, Ursula reproached herself. She might have pointed out that there was no absolute proof of attempted suicide. Perhaps they would send the poor old woman back to prison. Yes, she had bungled her evidence!

There was no means of rectifying the omission. Another witness was in the box, an elderly man with a kindly, breezy manner. This was Thompson, a police-missionary, Mr Joliffe whisperingly informed her. Mr Thompson was stating in jerky, illiterate phrases that he had known the prisoner for a number of years. He had always considered her a most respectable person. Her husband had died eighteen months ago. Since then the prisoner had done government work – territorial and police uniforms and such like. At this point the witness consulted a little notebook in his hand. The rate of pay the prisoner had received was threepence three-farthings for finishing trousers, a matter of four hours' work. A farthing a pair for footstraps to cavalry overalls; these took her half an hour. Riding breeches eightpence a pair – six or eight hours –'

'It is scandalous!' Ursula was on her feet despite Mr Joliffe's agonised 'Miss Winfield!' and his monitory hand on her arm. 'I did not know anyone could be paid so little! No wonder she wanted to end it. It is the people who give such prices who ought to be sent to prison!' The outburst had apparently electrified the court into impotence, but now an usher decisively drew near. 'I will be responsible for finding Mrs Bennett properly paid work in the future,' Ursula finished quickly, and sat down.

The magistrate was concealing a smile under pretext of stroking his chin. It was all highly irregular, but how handsome the girl had looked as she stood there with her flaming cheeks! Like most old gentlemen on the bench or off it, the magistrate was not impervious to feminine appearance. Besides, he was acquainted with Colonel and Mrs Hibbert, a fact of which Ursula was unaware, and the reports he had heard of the beautiful daughter who lived immured in an attic had made him interested to meet her in the flesh. But he had not expected such an outburst. Not that it had made any difference. After Thompson's report he would, in any case, have discharged the old woman! 'Very well, Miss Winfield, I understand that you will take charge of the prisoner's future. The next case.'

Acting on Mr Joliffe's advice, an interview with the police-missionary followed. Mr Thompson advised that, for the present, the old woman should go to a convalescent home. He could arrange it all if Miss Winfield would pay. 'Thank the young lady,' he told Mrs Bennett, who, with a white, dazed face, was standing silently by.

She dropped a half-curtsey. 'Thank you kindly miss, thank you, sir.' Suddenly she began to cry. 'But I'd sooner go 'ome.'

There were difficulties, it appeared. An enigmatical conversation followed. It ended in Mrs Bennett producing a shabby purse stuffed with a quantity of small cardboard squares. The police-missionary began sorting them. 'Five bob, two and six, eight,' he murmured. 'Four pounds would pretty near cover the lot. That chair's run out.' He lowered his voice. 'I suppose you don't care to run to it, miss?'

A vista of ambulatory furniture with herself in pursuit passed before Ursula's eyes. Further explanation revealed that Mr Thompson merely wanted four pounds. This would procure Mrs Bennett her home. It seemed extraordinarily cheap. And what a relief to be able to do something she wanted for the old woman at last.

Mr Joliffe, conscious of an imminent appointment had been fidgeting impatiently. He did not feel his duty to Colonel Hibbert complete until Miss Winfield was safely escorted from the police court precincts. Now he could disengage her. A taxi was passing outside. As Ursula declined it, he deprecatingly went off in it himself.

When she parted from the worthy solicitor, Ursula had every intention of going straight back to Lowndes Square. But a few yards down Bow Street, she almost ran into her little acquaintance of earlier in the morning. The girl, together with the 'lady friend', was evidently returning to the police court. Quite a lot of people were going in. The next case must be of interest, Ursula supposed. Why should she not wait and hear it herself, suggested itself suddenly. She probably would never be in Bow Street again. Her day's work had been spoilt already.

The inner doors were opening and shutting rapidly. Ursula passed in with the stream, chiefly made up of young men, and found herself standing at the back of the court. Here, in the crowd, she was pleasantly inconspicuous. The dock, which stood in the line between her and the bench, screened her still further. The prisoner, of whom she had a back view, was a rough-looking man with a torn coat. The case was just ending. 'Twelve months' hard labour', the magistrate pronounced.

The man in the dock gave a clumsy bow. 'Thank you, yer Worship.' His tone was cheerful and husky. 'Much obliged. This ain't our fust meeting, and it in't likely to be our last.'

'A case of many happy returns of the day'; the magistrate's cultured voice came in contrasting response. There was a roar of laughter. How would the court express its appreciation if a magistrate made a good joke, Ursula scornfully speculated. A decent, elderly man was standing beside her. Of him she inquired particulars. What had the prisoner done?

'Stole a pair o' boots.'

'Stolen a pair of boots!' Ursula was amazed. The offence seemed so ridiculously inadequate to such a sentence. 'Well, I shouldn't give twelve months hard labour for that; I should give the boots.'

'That 'ud 'ardly do, miss.' Her informant laughed indulgently. 'Why, this was 'is twenty-third conviction. But it wouldn't 'ave been so 'eavy, if it 'adn't been for 'is assaulting the copper.' A surge in the crowd stopped the conversation.

A fresh inrush of people through the swing doors was marking the close of the case. Ursula began to feel not so much comfortably obscured as unpleasantly crushed, when she noticed a little space at the end of one of the two long benches that stretched across the court in front of her. By the time she had squeezed into the seat, the new case was in full swing. From where she now sat, she could see the prisoner in profile. He was comparatively well-dressed – perhaps a city clerk – and might be considered good-looking. Personally Ursula was intensely repelled by him. She preferred the former rude occupant of the dock.

The first witness was called – 'Lily Smith'. Ursula saw her little acquaintance crossing the court. The gabbled formula of the swearing in again afflicted her ears, but Lily Smith's kissing of the Book was reverent. Indeed, the poor girl was visibly trembling. 'What is your occupation?' the magistrate asked.

'A prostitute.'

It was perhaps the most amazing moment of Ursula's life. Naturally she was not entirely unaware that prostitutes existed, but she had never consciously thought about them. They seemed as remote from life as the two-headed monstrosities or limbless infants whose birth she had occasionally seen recorded in scientific journals. But this girl was just like other girls, indeed she looked nicer than many.

It was impossible, Ursula told herself. She had made a mistake.

Perhaps the magistrate also was surprised, or he may merely not have caught the low-toned reply. 'What's that – your occupation?'

'I am a prostitute.'

This time there was no possibility of mistake. Even more astounding than the girl's statement was the calm way in which the magistrate accepted it.

'Oh yes, a prostitute,' he acquiesced, as though it were a perfectly ordinary calling. 'And how long have you known the prisoner? Two years?'

Ursula's face was white. It grew whiter as the case went on. She sat there frozen and sick with horror. She had known that prostitutes existed. But she had not known that men could live with prostitutes and upon their shameful earnings. The prisoner was such a man. Lily Smith herself had denounced him. 'You had had a quarrel, I suppose?' the magistrate suggested carelessly.

A clerk sitting at the table just below the bench here rose and said in a low tone that the quarrel was connected with the second charge. The magistrate, putting on his pince-nez, turned to his notes. 'Er, yes, I see – criminal assault. Yes. That will do' – this was to Lily Smith – 'I will now take the child's evidence. I suppose she is in Court?'

A little girl of nine or ten was sitting on the front bench not far from Ursula. An usher now approached her and said something that Ursula did not catch. The child burst into tears and clung to the woman beside her. 'Mother, don't let him take me! I don't want to tell them.' The magistrate was again conferring with the clerk. 'All women to leave the Court,' came the peremptory order.

There were two ladies sitting near whose suffrage badges had already attracted Ursula's attention. At this decree they grew excited. 'Monstrous!' one of them shouted. 'It's the men who ought to be turned out, not women!'

The magistrate looked annoyed. 'Silence in the Court,' he said severely.

A burly policeman appeared magically beside each suffragette, and shepherded each one, still shrilly objecting, out through the swing doors. Ursula followed them. All feeling had been lost in a state of dazed incomprehension. Why was the little girl crying? What could she have to do with it?

In the outer hall the two indignant ladies were standing, still talking violently. Some remarks reached Ursula as she passed – 'having to give her evidence alone before all those men, poor little thing. It's time we did have the vote!'

Ursula's one idea had been to get out, out into the fresh air, away from all this filth. Probably only a sense of physical numbness had kept her in her seat so long. But now she hesitated. A scientific training is not conducive to leaving problems half-solved. 'Excuse me.' She went up to the irate ladies. 'I do not understand. What is the matter with the little girl?'

The required explanation was given, indeed, given with alacrity. The suffragettes were too accustomed to speaking on these subjects to realise the feelings of the girl who had questioned them. Details were elaborated; one of the ladies knew the child's mother – 'such a nice woman, absolutely heartbroken.'

No, no, it was impossible! Although Ursula stood there silent and motionless, her whole being was crying out in revolt. This was a nightmare, not reality. Such things did not happen, not today, in England. They belonged to savage countries, to history books. 'But you cannot be certain; children romance,' she stammered at last, white now to the lips.

'Physical facts do not romance.' The suffragette gave a semi-hysterical laugh. 'There is a house near here – ' further searing revelations followed – '"fallen children" they call them,' she concluded bitterly. 'And then they wonder that we are militants!'

Ursula turned away blindly. She must sit down; she was trembling all over. Why, this was the same bench on which she had sat earlier this morning. Was it only this morning? Then the world had been a clean and pleasant place of healthy men and women. Now it had become rotten, crawling with obscene abomination. These suffragettes talked of the vote – as though the vote could help! If people were so vile and bestial, nothing could help, nothing! It was all horrible. She did not want to live. Science was dead, futile. Everything was tainted – even Tony.

After a while she grew more rational. After all, whatever the suffragette ladies might say, it was not certain that the man was guilty – at least, not of that ultimate horror. The case was still *sub judice*. She would wait and hear the verdict. Until then she could keep the last hope.

Presently, as she sat there, she became conscious of a sound which up till then she had been too overwrought to notice. Someone, not far off, was weeping. Leaning forward, she saw Lily Smith sitting on the other bench, her face buried in a handkerchief, her body shaken with sobs. Her friend, the bold-looking girl, was patting her shoulder in a not untender attempt to comfort her.

Ursula stared for a moment and then sank back into her corner. Her emotions seemed exhausted. She could only feel numbly that life was beyond her. She recalled the particulars that she had heard in Court. Lily Smith herself had denounced the prisoner. The quarrel had been in connection with the second charge. It flashed through Ursula's mind that a prostitute must then also have a moral code. Lily Smith apparently drew the line at assaulting little girls. But why, if she denounced the man, should she now be crying heart-brokenly? Was it conceivable that she could care for him, for that vile brute who had lived upon her shame? If she did care for him, then was not that just a little redeeming? And he, to have made her care, must surely have some spark that was not utterly evil. Indeed, was 'evil' the right word at all? Ursula wondered suddenly. Such a man seemed too incredibly wicked to be wicked. The thought brought comfort. He was insane.

There was a sudden emergence through the swing doors. The case was over, and the men, who in virtue of their robuster sex had been allowed to stop and listen, came pouring out. They were laughing and talking over the spicy details they had heard. At another time Ursula would have been revolted by their attitude, but now her only thought was of the verdict She got up and went forward. 'Is he guilty?'

The youth whom she had accosted leered unpleasantly. He probably was going to say something familiar, or even indecent. But Ursula's aspect, her set, grey face, seemed to check him. Instead he answered, civilly enough, that the prisoner had been found guilty on both counts – 'three months for each to run consecutive.' Jerking his bowler awkwardly, he passed on.

Ursula remained staring. Even horror was lost in amazement. This man who assaulted little girls, who lived on a prostitute's earnings, had got three months imprisonment – not even years – months! After three months he would again be at large. Why, it was not safe when the man was insane! And if he were not insane, then it was still less safe. Did they think that three months' imprisonment would terrify or reform him into morality? Twenty-three imprisonments had not reformed that other man even of stealing boots. And the other man had been given twelve months! The magistrate must be insane too! They were all mad together!

The two suffrage ladies, who were still lingering in the lobby, now learnt the verdict. 'Three months – that's all they think a little girl is worth. I'd like to kill the brute,' one loudly exclaimed. 'We'll expose it in *Votes*. Let us go round to Clement's Inn at once,' the more composed friend suggested.

How absurd they were! Still, Ursula felt it must be a comfort to take any active step. If only she could do something. It seemed impossible to go back and work in her laboratory in this new world of enlarged maniacs and crazy magistrates. But, after all, was it the magistrate's fault? He only administered the law. Probably the punishment for such an offence was specified. Certainly it had not been the magistrate, but the law, that had dragged poor old Mrs Bennett to prison. Then it was the law that was insane, or rather the lawmakers. Yes, and Mrs Bennett's starvation wages had been paid for government work. The suffragettes were right. There was some connection between such things and the Vote.

The policeman in the Strand gave a weary smile at Ursula's inquiry for Clement's Inn. She was too intent to notice it, too intent to be surprised at the size of the suffragette headquarters. It was uncertain whether the Leader could be seen. Would she wait in there? A door was opened for her.

The room was large, with a window at the far end. The sunshine, streaming through it, fell upon a girl in blue, who knelt, surrounded and half-hidden by a surging mass of open, white umbrellas. The unexpected sight surprised Ursula into attention. What could she be doing? The girl now rose. It was Mary Blake, but the hunger-look had been wiped away; she stood there serenely beautiful. Her hands were filled with short, bright-coloured strips; doubtless to keep them from falling, she had clasped them to her breast; the white cloud-shaped umbrellas seemed to billow at her feet. There was a moment of silence. Then came Mary's gentle voice. 'Do I know you?' she asked.

Ursula pulled herself together. 'Yes, that time in the train. You lent me *Votes*. You told me that one day I – '

A sudden transfiguring radiance shone in Mary's face. She held out her white hands, showering to the ground their gay, trivial contents. 'And you have come,' she said.

CHAPTER FOURTEEN

Ursula's having penetrated into the suffragette headquarters did not mean that she had changed her views as to militant tactics. Indeed, had not the 'truce' been in force, it is unlikely that she would ever have taken such an incriminating step. She expressed herself boldly on the subject in an interview she had with the Leader a couple of days later – the great little lady had been found to be out on her first visit. 'I cannot see that violence is any argument, and I hate it,' Ursula protested.

'You cannot hate it more than I do, Miss Winfield.' The Leader smiled. Her delicate, worn face and her slight figure in its well-fitting gown gave emphasis to her words; it seemed impossible to connect her with violence in any form. 'Moreover,' she went on, 'all the violence in connection with this Union is done against us, not by us. Is it violent to walk peaceably down Parliament Street, or to ask a perfectly legitimate question at a public meeting? Yet for doing this, our women are set upon, knocked down, kicked. My own girl was made ill for weeks by the treatment she received. Is it violent to refuse food in prison? No, the violence lies in the forcible feeding – an abominable and outrageous form of violence! Have you ever seen our hunger strikers when they come out?'

'Yes.' Ursula stopped. The recollection of those gaunt women at the Albert Hall came over her. Also, although she did not like being declaimed at, there was something curiously moving in the suffragette leader's voice; the fact that it was hoarse and strained with excessive speaking only enhanced the effect. An understanding came to Ursula of the attitude almost of idolatry that existed in the Union. Yet, curiously enough, the very fact that she was touched alienated the girl. Emotion was not reason, she told herself angrily. She felt that she was being jockeyed into an unreal sympathy. 'Surely breaking the law, as the suffragettes do, is a form of violence,' she suggested.

To her amazement the charge of lawbreaking was denied. According to the Leader, all the illegality also was on the other side. Statutes of Edward III, of Charles I, of Victoria, rattled in Ursula's ears. The effect was only to make her grow colder. This defence was a quibble. When people committed actions with the declared object of getting arrested, how could they pretend that they did not break the law?

Perhaps the Leader had felt the lack of sympathy, for a note of irritation came into her voice. She paused, and suddenly changed her standpoint. 'We are not lawbreakers, but we are quite prepared to become so,' she announced suddenly. 'Why should women respect laws which they have had no share in making? I would break every law in the land – with this reservation. No damage must be done to any living creature. So long as I have any voice in this Union, we shall stop short at that. Women know too well what life costs to wish to destroy it. They have had to pay the price. Why, it is this feeling that lies at the back of our whole movement. We want the Vote so that we may lessen the suffering, the abuse of life, that we see all around us. That is why I am asking you – I am asking every woman – to help us.'

The phrases had no doubt been used at public meetings without number, but, even while guessing this, Ursula was stirred by them. She had come too recently into contact with the 'abuse of life' not to feel the force of the argument. Still, she was not absolutely convinced. 'If I felt that every legitimate way had been tried – ' she began dubiously.

'But we are trying every legitimate way all the time,' the Leader broke in. 'Nine-tenths, ninety-nine hundredths, of our work is absolutely constitutional. All that our members are pledged to is not to support the candidate of any political party in parliamentary elections until women have obtained the vote. Surely you can come with us so far, Miss Winfield?' she smiled.

As Ursula had never in her life had the faintest desire to support any political candidate, the stipulation did not seem hard. Soon, although still a trifle dubious, the girl found herself signing the small perforated card enrolling her as a member of the National WSPU. The Leader looked pleased. She had had judicious inquiries made, and knew that a girl of Miss Winfield's wealth and social position, not to mention her scientific attainments, would be an asset to the Cause. But apart from this, the Leader's insight developed further possibilities. Miss Winfield had a good presence, a good voice, a clear head. Here were the makings of a first-rate speaker. When Ursula left, she found herself booked for a meeting a few days later. 'They will only just want a few words. Miss Blake is the speaker of the evening,' the Leader had explained. In addition, Ursula had consented to sit on a newly-formed local committee, and to write to a dozen leading scientists, including Professor Smee, inviting their signatures to a suffrage manifesto. 'How could I have been such a fool?' the girl groaned as she thought of her interrupted science.

Her sentiment was repeated with still greater emphasis by Colonel Hibbert at 'Monte' when his wife, almost in tears, showed him the letter containing Ursula's confession. Indeed, his vocabulary grew so sultry as to be unrecordable. 'But, George dear,' Mrs Hibbert babbled, trying to subdue the explosion, 'it is quite true what Ursula says, the suffragettes haven't been so outrageous lately; not that I don't regret it all as much as you do; I think they are the most dreadful creatures! Still, dear Ursula does say that whatever the others do, she will keep entirely to constitutional methods, as she calls them. And, after all, you know, George, quite good people are going in for that sort of thing nowadays, look at Lady Florence Howard.'

'Pack o' tomfoolery. What do women want with politics? Let 'em mind their own business. I won't have Ursula mixed up with those yelling idiots – that's flat. I shall write and tell her so.'

It was perhaps fortunate that Colonel Hibbert was not a ready letter-writer, for a communication thus worded would have been likely to provoke in his stepdaughter a rage at least equal to his own. But before he had braced himself to the necessary effort, the world, and more especially the social world of the Hibberts, was shaken by an event which caused Ursula's delinquencies to be almost forgotten. The unexpected news of King Edward's death found the Hibberts just arrived at Paris, for Mrs Hibbert was breaking the homeward journey in order to purchase her new gowns for the season. 'The dear, dear Prince,' she exclaimed, wiping away real tears with her lace pocket handkerchief. 'It seems too dreadful. Always so kind, so tactful. Please 'phone at once to Maison Fouquet cancelling all my frocks. To think that one day more and it would have been too late.'

'I suppose, then, we can get off home tomorrow?' the Colonel suggested, as he returned from the errand. Even the *ville lumière* possessed little attraction for his insular mind, now that he had reached the decorum of happily-married middle life. 'No point in hanging round here all the week, what?'

'Why, of course, there is all the more point.' Mrs Hibbert's tone was plaintively surprised. 'You know, George dear, I haven't a single rag of black, and so I must get everything new. Our happening to be in Paris seems almost providential. Haven't I always said that English people have not an idea of what can be done with mourning? Even Bird's things are unutterably dowdy and hideous and almost as expensive as Fouquet.' Speculation followed as to the probable date of the royal funeral. Naturally they must be at home for that.

The royal demise did not awaken in Ursula the same emotion as in her mother. Indeed, as the girl turned disgustedly from the daily outpouring of journalistic lamentation and adulation, she began to reproach herself with an unnaturally stony heart. For, after all, she, unlike most people, had had a personal acquaintance with the departed sovereign. It was true that, since his accession, the King had only twice honoured Lowndes Square with his presence, and then Ursula had been in abeyance, but in her childhood a stout, smiling gentleman had often patted her on the head, while she was bidden to make a hated curtsey to 'the Prince'. Probably the exalted personage had been no more interested in the sulky little girl than she in him, for Ursula still remembered how quickly he had always resumed his interrupted conversation with her mother. Well, it had been rather nice of him to appreciate her little Mammykin, Ursula now reflected. Still, that did not make him the newspaper combination of hero, saint, and genius, and she could not pretend to lament.

Indeed, far from lamenting the King's death, from the suffrage point of view Ursula unfeignedly rejoiced. For the political hush that followed facilitated the formation of the 'Conciliation Committee' to draft and introduce a new Women's Suffrage Bill. That this Bill would speedily become law, few were doubtful, for, like Ursula, suffragists felt that the anachronism of tax-paying but voteless women could not survive into a new reign. Even the militant organ came out with a number headed 'Peace?' Yes, these horrible raids and hunger strikes were finally done with, the girl told herself jubilantly.

It was this feeling of the whole agitation being transient, that caused Ursula to yield herself so completely to the moral press-gang of the WSPU. Otherwise she would probably have told herself that scientific work was as useful to the world as suffrage activity and, to her, of far greater interest. But for a few months, until the Bill became law, she would devote herself to pushing it. For it was not as though her own work had been going well of late, she reminded herself. On the contrary, it had been going abominably. Somehow she seemed to have lost her old power of concentration. Instead of working out mathematical formulae, she found herself working out the number of days until September! With suffrage work it was easier. While she was speaking at meetings, sitting on committees, chalking pavements, or even, like Mary Blake, pasting inscriptions on procession umbrellas, her thoughts could not veer away to Tony. So the paper for the British Association was definitely put aside. She would give it the following year instead. For on one point she was determined. She would not again bring forward her theory until the proof was absolutely irrefutable.

Had Ursula not found herself adapted to her new activities, she might, after all, have returned to science. But the Leader had been right in her surmise; the new recruit quickly developed into a speaker. To that first suffrage meeting Ursula had gone feeling sick with fright. She had meant to write out a couple of carefully considered pages, but had put off the hated task and then, at the last moment, something had prevented her. Now she would have to speak impromptu. She couldn't do it. Her teeth were chattering with fright during Miss Blake's rambling but movingly sincere discourse.

The first stereotyped sentence was known by heart. Then came a moment of anguish. The whole world seemed blank. Suddenly Ursula found herself speaking easily. The audience was interested. Although the girl did not know it, the mere fact of her newness to the Cause was an asset. Her speech was free from the usual suffrage clichés. 'Splendid,' Miss Blake whispered at the end. Several people came up and complimented her.

Ursula was pleased and surprised; at the same time she was far from satisfied. She could do better than that. The thoroughness shown in her previous scientific work was now transferred to suffrage. The next speech was not only written out beforehand, but committed, word for word, to memory. It was a dead failure. And it deserved to be! She would not attempt to write a speech again, Ursula decided, although the framework should be prepared. Impromptu speakers never stopped. But first she must get up her subject. Soon she could rival the Leader in her crushing flow of statistics and statutes. Lessons in voice production followed. Then came a by-election, a frenzied week of 'chairing' on rickety platforms in the pouring rain. It gave her confidence. Presently she found herself the chief speaker at various small meetings in inaccessible suburbs. Once she occupied a pulpit. It avenged her for hours of childish boredom during the reign of a pious governess.

At one meeting there was a surprise. Ursula had been asked, at the last moment, to replace a speaker and on arrival found that Professor Smee was in the chair. The surprise was mutual, and perhaps also the pleasure, but Ursula's was more frankly outspoken. Afterwards they met at several suffrage functions. It was curious that the new work, like the old, brought them together. Once, as they were returning late from a meeting at Croydon, Ursula again spoke of Tony. Vernon Smee listened with profound interest. 'I suppose your fiancé is a suffragist?' he asked a little curiously.

'Oh, of course. At least, I know he will be.' Ursula did not explain her rather contradictory reply. The fact was that the question had never been brought up between them that glamorous August fortnight, incredible as the omission now seemed. It had not even figured in her letters until she attended the Albert Hall meeting. Then, in the same words that Professor Smee now used, she had 'supposed' that Tony was a suffragist. Of course, she knew he disapproved of militancy.

Her lover's reply naturally had not reached her for two months. It might have worried her more, if she had not, by then, largely forgotten the wording of her own letter. For Tony had not assented to her supposition. Might it not be a mistake, he had suggested with guarded vagueness, for women merely to follow in the footsteps of men? It seemed to him that no work could be greater than that to which women were already called. 'But it is too big a subject to write about, darling,' he had broken off tenderly. 'We must talk it all over when I come home. Of one thing you may be certain – my sympathy in any movement that will really benefit your sex.'

Ursula had been satisfied, and the subject again dropped. Indeed, as Tony said, it was impossible to carry on a discussion with eight weeks interval between the sentences. At the end of March had come the trial and the impetuous joining of the WSPU. Of course she had written to Tony about this, and at enormous length, but although she heard from him by every mail it had not yet been in reply.

However uncertain Ursula might be as to Tony's attitude, she had been left in no doubt as to that of her stepfather. When the Colonel and Mrs Hibbert had returned from Paris, there had been a tremendous storm. 'If you ever take part in one of those d – d raids, you needn't trouble to come back here,' the Colonel had exploded. However, as weeks passed and the militants continued to 'behave themselves', as he put it, he grew less violent. As for her mother, she had from the first been more tolerant than Ursula had dared to hope. This was in part due to a lack of realisation, for Ursula was discreet in her disclosures, and poor Mrs Hibbert never pictured her daughter promenading Whitechapel with a lighted lantern at the end of a long stick, or chalking West End pavements with notices of meetings in the small hours.

But one night when Ursula came home, she found her mother sitting alone in her boudoir with an obvious air of distressed reproach. It could have no connection with this evening's meeting, for it had been a decorous debate between the Leader and the chief of the Antis, a lady of almost monumental respectability. She began to chat about its humours to her mother, but evoked no response. 'Well, Mum, what is it?' she asked at last. 'Wherefore this sombre mien?'

'I am getting old.' Mrs Hibbert's face was turned away.

'You old!' Ursula laughed at the unexpected reply. It seemed merely absurd in connection with her exquisite little parent. 'What has put that idea into your head?'

'The King's death.' Mrs Hibbert's shoulders quivered. Ursula expected some jest. Suddenly she realised to her amazement that her mother was crying.

How could anyone as remote as the King touch Mother in this personal fashion, Ursula speculated in bewilderment. But, of course, she was thinking of the old days, when he was the Prince. Perhaps his death seemed like the turning over of a page, the end of the chapter of youth. Yes, that must be the explanation. Now she came to think of it, Mum had been different ever since she came home from Paris – less talkative, graver. And although, of course, little Mummy would never be old, she certainly did not seem quite as extraordinarily young as she used. Surely those lines around her eyes had not been there before. 'Poor Mammykin!' Ursula went over, and, perching on the arm of her mother's chair, began to coax her back into cheerfulness. 'Shall I buy you a shawl for your poor old shoulders and a pair of spectacles for your poor old eyes? Wouldn't the Colonel have a shock? Where is he tonight?'

'Where he always is. At his Club! I don't see how you can expect me to be very cheerful,' Mrs Hibbert broke out pettishly, 'when I am left alone evening after evening. You know I never did like living in barrels like that Demosthenes man. Of course, one can't entertain this year, but if you were like any other daughter, I should have your society at least. It was bad enough when you were cooped up in the laboratory all the time, but then you did occasionally emerge for a meal. Now you might be at the South Pole for all I see of you!'

'What nonsense, Mum!' Ursula laughed again. 'Haven't you got my society now?'

'It isn't nonsense.' Mrs Hibbert started off afresh. 'I never have the least idea where you are or what you are doing. I know absolutely nothing about you.'

'Why, I am just "suffragetting", you know that. I don't talk much about it because I think it will bore you – or shock you! Though I really don't make a practice of bowling over bobbies.'

Despite her careless words, Ursula's conscience had given her a sharp stab. For what her mother had said was true. Mum did know nothing about her. The suffrage reservations were unimportant, but what about Tony? Somehow, as she had not spoken at first, it had seemed increasingly difficult to do so. It was not as though she and Tony were seeing each other, she had told herself. Her letters were no one's concern but her own. She felt suddenly that she had been wrong. Her mother ought to have known. Besides, a little excitement might cheer Mum up, help her to shake off this queer mood of depression. But it was awfully difficult to begin. Involuntarily she got out of her chair, and moving to the mantelpiece began to examine the Dresden china figures with fictitious interest. If only her heart wouldn't thump so; it made her feel almost choked. 'There *is* one thing that you don't know about me, Mum darling. I am engaged to be married.'

Mrs Hibbert sat up straight. 'What? Who? Break it to me quickly. I am prepared for the worst. A dishevelled male suffragette? Or a dowdy little chemist?'

'Neither.' Ursula coloured furiously. 'Mr Balestier.'

'Mr Balestier? Not *my* Mr Balestier? Tony Balestier?' Mrs Hibbert's voice rose in an amazed crescendo. It was probably the greatest surprise of her life. 'Why, he is quite nice.'

'That's what I think.' Ursula gurgled with amusement.

Her mother took no notice of the reply. 'But Tony Balestier is a good match,' she went on incredulously. 'Though he has nothing much now, some day he'll come in for – But where on earth, Ursula, did you run across him? I thought he was in India.'

The girl related the story with stiff brevity. She was hurt by her mother's mercenary tone, while Mrs Hibbert was hurt by her daughter's long reticence. When the account was finished, the elder woman gave a short laugh. 'Well, you are a funny girl, my dear. Talk of hiding talents in table napkins! I suppose if you had picked up some perfectly impossible person, you would have rushed to proclaim your engagement from the housetops.'

'But as, according to you, I have "picked up" a prospective gold mine, it isn't surprising that I kept it quiet.'

The bitterness in her daughter's tone did not escape Mrs Hibbert. 'You wouldn't despise money if you had none,' she observed sagely. 'However, I never said that Balestier's only eligibility was financial. Why, I consider him a perfect model of virtue – he has never even made love to me! And then, of course, he is frightfully handsome, besides having brains. Good, clever, beautiful, going-to-be-rich – what an impossible perfection it sounds – quite fatiguing. Really, Ursula, although you are my daughter and a genius, I consider you are rather a lucky girl.'

'Yes, I am – the luckiest girl in the world.' Ursula's voice broke. 'If only it weren't so long until September.'

Mrs Hibbert's expression was of amused surprise. Now she

got up, and gave her daughter a kiss, not devoid of tenderness. 'You always did take things badly, my dear! Measles – you nearly died of it. And then there was mumps!'

If Mrs Hibbert had been pleased about her daughter's engagement, Colonel Hibbert was even more so. 'Balestier!' he almost shouted when his wife told him the news. 'Why, he's as good a fellow as they make 'em, and quite a decent shot. Besides, he's a gentleman, thank God, which is more than can be said for most of Ursula's crowd. By George, I never thought the girl had so much sense!'

The Colonel's gratification was even sufficient to make him follow his wife's advice and refrain from speaking of the engagement in public or joking upon it in private. 'Ursula is in one of her intense states.' Mrs Hibbert warned him. 'She already has misgivings because Balestier isn't a pauper. She'll find some high, romantic ground for breaking it off if we aren't careful!'

'I'll be precious glad when she's married, seeing it'll be to a decent chap like Balestier,' growled the harassed Colonel. 'Not that I want to get rid of old Ursula,' he hastened to add. 'She and I have always been good pals, what? But the fact is, Vi, we've given the girl her head too much. Do her good to run in double harness.'

Double harness for Ursula will be tandem with herself in front. But Mrs Hibbert did not express this prophecy in words. It was part of her policy to let men imagine themselves lords of creation. She would complain with a smile of her husband's domestic tyranny, while the Colonel's fondest boast was of being master in his own house. Yet, during their thirteen years of married life, the one invariable conclusion whenever their desires had conflicted had hardly supported these utterances. 'Building on to my little place at Dumdrochie,' the Colonel was now telling his cronies. 'Only had room to put up four guns – not enough to keep down the birds, what?'

Not only did Ursula find her stepfather unexpectedly tactful on the subject of her engagement, but he seemed to have become quite rational with regard to her suffrage work. Certainly he chaffed her a good deal, presenting her with a fresh variety of voice lozenge almost daily, but there was no trace of his previous heat. Had she guessed the reason for his acquiescence, she would hardly have been so undisturbed. 'Ursula will chuck the whole bally business fast enough when her young man comes home,' Colonel Hibbert confided to his wife. 'Balestier can't stand this suffrage tomfoolery no more than me. Heard him say so myself.'

Mrs Hibbert looked surprised. 'Perhaps Ursula will refuse to "chuck it"' she suggested airily.

'Not she.' The Colonel laughed. 'There's one thing that's certain, Ursula's head over heels in love with Balestier, though she'd bite off my nose if she heard me. We're hardly worthy to mention his name. Thinks him God Almighty! I'd never have thought it of old Ursula, what? Fact is, women are pretty much the same, science or no science. Not that I've ever met one that's in the running with you, my dear!'

All this time Ursula had not heard Tony's opinion of her suffragette development. She began to think that the long letter in which she had told him of joining the WSPU must have got lost, perhaps, indeed, others also, for he was complaining that he had not had a line from her since he landed in East Africa. 'I know it is the fault of the post, and that you have written, darling,' he assured her. 'Only it makes me determine what I had already determined. I will never go abroad again until I can take – my wife.'

Naturally it was not only in these initial letters that Ursula had spoken of her new activity. Every time she wrote she was increasingly full of it. For the Union was now her world. Her scientific work had been entirely put aside. Sometimes a wave of homesickness for her laboratory came over her, an intense yearning for her own work, but it would be impossible and tantalising, she felt, to combine the two lives. Nor did she really want to do so. For her police court experience, and the facts she had since learnt, had fired the girl to a white heat of revolt. The contagious enthusiasm of fellowship, the excitement of battle, added their stimulus. Until the Vote was won, Ursula felt she neither could, nor would, turn to anything else. But it would not be for long, she again thankfully reassured herself. Their Bill would be through this session. Then she would be free; free to give science her working day – and Tony the rest.

On 18th June there was to be a great procession. It must surpass anything they had ever done before, the Leader said. Thus, by showing the strength of the women's demand, they would make the Bill safe. The co-operation of other suffrage societies only increased their work. Clement's Inn seethed with activity. Ursula almost forgot what an armchair was like.

It had been after one of the very hardest days that, coming home late, Ursula found a letter awaiting her in the beloved handwriting. How divinely restful and comforting! She took it into the library to read over her solitary supper. The envelope felt thinner than usual – but quantity was nothing to quality! Joyfully, she tore it open.

She stared, almost too taken aback to read further. 'Dear Ursula' – Tony never began 'Dear Ursula'! – 'I gather from the letter, which I have just received, that you have joined the Women's Social and Political Union. I can only say that I am utterly amazed. How could you possibly have taken such a step without in any way considering or consulting me? I cannot think that it augurs very well for our future happiness together. Perhaps this is what you wish me to understand.'

Ursula's hand dropped with the letter in it. She felt cold and rather breathless. How could Tony? How could he? Why, it had been impossible to consult him. It had never even occurred to her to do so. Tony himself had said that you could not discuss such subjects by correspondence. It would take too long. She had been doing suffrage work for three months, and she had only just got this letter. If she had waited to consult him, these three months' work would have remained undone. It was absurd. She would not read his letter. But how could she not read it? She again raised the sheet, but found her eyes were too dim to see. Impatiently she brushed her hand across them.

'I realise,' Tony went on, 'that one or more of your letters have not reached me. They might possibly have put your action in a different light, although they could not have altered the central fact. You may not have realised how little sympathy I have with Women's Suffrage. Out of consideration for you, I have been trying to keep an open mind on the subject, so as to discuss it with you when I get back. But, at least, you knew that I absolutely detested the so-called militancy, and I thought you did too. Yet you have deliberately joined a militant society. I notice you say that the work of the WSPU is now non-militant, but how can you ensure its remaining so? Possibly you have stipulated that you will leave the Society if militancy recommences. I sincerely hope that this is the case? But, darling, don't you understand what a risk you run in mixing yourself up with these people at all? Don't be too much hurt by this letter. Sweetheart, if I could only hold you for a minute in my arms, I am sure you would see it all as I do.'

Ursula was crying now, but this time with sheer relief. So Tony did love her still; she almost felt as if nothing else mattered. If only they could be together, as he said, why then she would be able to make him understand. Tony was a reasonable being. He had been just vexed at hearing of her action so suddenly. Perhaps he was right, and she ought to have consulted him – how blissful it was to be able to blame herself. After all, he had consulted her before deciding to go to East Africa. But then he had had more time. Only she might have cabled. Yes, of course, that is what she ought to have done, although it seemed impossible to see how she could have explained the position in a cable! At any rate she would cable now – tomorrow. She would tell him she was sorry – not, of course, for having joined the WSPU, she was glad of that – but sorry for having hurt him. Then she would say 'much love' and tell him that the Conciliation Bill was sure to pass and her connection with the WSPU would then be over. The Conciliation Bill – the name took on a further meaning! It would be a very long cable, she realised, and frightfully expensive, still that could not be helped. Perhaps Mrs Hibbert was justified in thinking that her daughter only despised money because she had it.

The cable was sent, and the one that came in reply made Ursula happy again. Still, the strain of the abortive quarrel, coupled with the rush of her work, left its mark. Colonel Hibbert was rather horrified at his stepdaughter's appearance when he met her in the hall one evening, his return home having happened to coincide with her own. 'You look about used up. Ursula, what? Have a whisky and soda?'

Ursula was tired enough to accept the offer, stipulating for a very little whisky to a great deal of soda. As she subsided into an armchair, the Colonel continued to stare at her uneasily. 'You're getting thin,' he told her. 'Go on like this and there won't be anything left of you when your young man comes home. I don't know that I've ever congratulated you and all that,' he branched off. 'But Balestier's all right, one of the best. When d'you reckon to fix it up – the Matrimonial Stakes, what?'

'One of us might get "scratched".' Ursula laughed with a sudden flushing of her cheeks. 'But if we are both "running", I suppose the event will come off this winter. Patience does not seem to be one of Tony's strong points!'

'Quite right too, what? There's a lot said against marriage nowadays' – the Colonel seemed to be in an unusually discursive mood – 'but there's a lot to be said for it too.' He helped himself to a second whisky and soda, mixed in inverse proportions to his stepdaughter's blend. 'Of course, marrying ain't all beer and skittles, but then neither's not marrying. Get hold of the right person and you won't regret it. Look at your mother and me, though there was once all that scandal – '

'All what scandal?' Ursula interrupted in astonishment.

The Colonel pulled himself up. Although not in any way intoxicated, he had had enough to over-loosen his tongue. 'That don't matter,' he told her hurriedly, 'I always knew it was all right. I'm saying that here's your mother and me been married thirteen years, and I've never regretted it for an instant, bless her! And I don't believe she has either.'

'I am sure she hasn't,' Ursula agreed heartily. The Colonel's devotion to her mother had always touched her. The 'good night' that followed was quite affectionate.

Perhaps it was the mollifying effect of this interview that made Colonel Hibbert take up his stand at the Club window the next day when the Suffrage Procession came in sight, instead of seeking refuge in the most distant part of the building as had been his previous practice on such occasions. A good many other elderly gentlemen were also grouped around, and much raillery of a rather ponderous and not too delicate character was passing between them. The 'Prisoners' Pageant', headed by Mary Blake, formed the first contingent, and although the six hundred white-robed figures with silver wands might be theatrical, they were effective. The chaff died down. 'Damn it all, they look like those classical thingummies – Temple fire business,' one man suggested. 'Vestal Virgins', another amended, who had retained a trifle more of classical lore. But that was only the beginning. Detachments followed from the different societies, from different countries, from different professions. As the nurses in their uniforms passed, the Colonel found himself taking off his hat – an army man with the Crimea tradition could hardly do less. But still the women came, rank upon rank, four abreast, rank upon rank, rank upon rank. 'By God, there's more of them than I thought,' the Colonel exclaimed, startled.

One of the other men was looking at his watch. 'They've been passing for an hour and three-quarters, and I can't see the end of them yet. Not a hitch either. They can organise, confound 'em!'

'We shan't get home for dinner tonight,' a third man grumbled.

The Colonel was silent. A sudden idea had struck his not very active brain. Suppose he had had to do this organising! An uneasy recollection of various manoeuvres came to him at which his men had only been saved from hopeless confusion by the smartness of the sergeants. But could any man have run this procession better? And if women could run a procession, why not – of course, it was absurd. The Colonel did not know how nearly his mental attitude resembled that of the two road-sweepers who were a this moment watching the women graduates pass, the MA's, MD's, DSc's, all in their distinctive gowns. 'Well, Bill,' one was saying to the other: 'I don't see why they shouldn't have brains just the same as we.'

Despite his attention, the Colonel had not distinguished his stepdaughter amid the passing host, but perhaps Mrs Hibbert's maternal eye was quicker. On the pretext of a drive in the park, she, too, viewed the whole procession and could almost have touched Ursula as she passed by. The girl, all in white, was carrying a banner; and she looked rather fine, Mrs Hibbert thought with a throb of pride. Nor did Ursula seem tired, although it must have been a long tramp to Knightsbridge right from Northumberland Avenue. Rather, something seemed to be uplifting her, some inward dream that was shining in her eyes. What Ursula had felt when she saw Mary Blake at the raid, Mrs Hibbert now felt when she saw Ursula.

It was considerably later when the girl got home, for an Albert Hall meeting had followed the procession, but she found her mother awaiting her. 'Oh, Mum, I'm glad that's over,' she cried, weary at last, and sank into a chair. 'But we raised five thousand pounds! Think of it! Five thousand! I suppose you didn't deign to see anything of the procession?'

'Yes, I did.' Mrs Hibbert pulled the pins out of her daughter's big hat and took it off, that the girl might lean back more restfully. 'Oh, yes, I saw you marching along with your head in the stars, although you didn't see me!' She laughed with a shade of malice. 'What were you thinking of – the Vote or your Tony?'

'I suppose it was both.' Ursula's voice was grave. 'I suppose it is because of Tony that I feel I must try and make the world a little better for other women – for the women who have no Tony!'

CHAPTER FIFTEEN

August this year was spent by Ursula under very different, although hardly more conventional circumstances than the previous August. For it found her in poky Margate lodgings, together with Mary Blake and a certain Sarah Burnley, a factory lass from the North. The Conciliation Bill, the peg of suffrage hopes, had passed its second reading the month before, and with a majority beyond their fondest expectations. Only the Chancellor of the Exchequer failed them; as a democrat he voted against the Bill on the ground of its enfranchising too few women. The Prime Minister, on the contrary, as an Anti-Suffragist, objected to the Bill on the ground of its enfranchising too many women, and refused to give facilities for its passage into law.

More processioning and a great Hyde Parl Demonstration were alike unavailing. There was fury at Clement's Inn, the behaviour of the supposed friend being even more resented than that of the avowed opponent. A return to militancy was vehemently demanded. Nothing else would stop this political quibbling. Moreover, the war-chest needed filling. For, as Ursula now learnt to her surprise, the supposedly unpopular raids were the one thing than brought contributions pouring in. But the decree was firm. No militancy until the Bill was irrevocably lost. *Votes* contented itself with a mild cartoon of 'Whatever I do and whatever I say, Aunt Tabitha tells me that isn't the way.' The Leader flashed through the Highlands, speaking an incredible number of times a day. Members were to spend their summer holidays 'keeping the flag flying' in every town and village of the kingdom.

It was not only Ursula's first experience of a holiday campaign, but her first experience of a holiday resort. Her initial introduction to the sands struck her motionless with astonishment; there were no sands! The sea was fringed by a dense mass of men, women, children, bathing machines, donkeys, minstrels, coconut shies, sweet-sellers, lemonade vendors, photographers, ice-cream stands – 'a gradely place for us,' Miss Burnley observed with satisfaction, and, by instinct, picked out the best site for their stand.

This was easily set up. The paraphernalia was carried by the girls themselves – a couple of wooden folding chairs, a folding table, a white tent-umbrella, sandwich boards, and a mass of suffrage literature. Miss Burnley and Mary Blake now donned the sandwich boards, on which the meeting was announced, leaving Ursula to plant the umbrella and set out the papers.

A crowd quickly gathered. The minstrels had finished and this new diversion was welcomed. 'I don't like the look of them. I hope they won't be rough,' Mary Blake whispered. She took the chair by the simple process of standing on it.

There was an immediate uproar. The audience was out for

a holiday and meant to have it. Catcalls, mouth organs, popular songs entirely drowned the chairman's gentle voice. 'Call on me,' Ursula advised in an undertone. 'I can shout them down.'

She failed; indeed, the disturbance increased. A missile flew through the air; it plopped harmlessly on to the umbrella. The next was better aimed, coming full at Ursula's face. By some lucky chance she caught it – a large, unripe plum. The feat had produced a momentary lull. She took advantage of it. 'Thank you,' she called out gaily, 'a few more of the same sort will bring down my housekeeping bill! And that's what giving women the Vote will do, bring down the nation's housekeeping bill.'

There was a laugh – with her, not at her – and the first step was won. Thenceforward the disturbance from being continuous became intermittent. There were encouraging admonitions of 'Quiet there; let's 'ear the young lady.' But Ursula felt it unwise to tempt providence too far. After a few minutes she brought the meeting to a close with 'Tomorrow at the same time and plenty of plums.'

After that each day brought an improvement, the audience growing continuously larger and more attentive. By the end of a fortnight the huge crowd practically kept itself in order. Occasionally there came a relapse. One windy day, when it was already difficult to make oneself heard, an uncouth-looking man made it still more difficult by constant interruption. 'Look here, sir, we can't both speak at once,' Ursula called out good-temperedly, secure in the sympathy of the meeting. 'I'll have my say, then you shall get up and have yours.'

The man agreed, although sulkily. 'Now it is your turn – but only five minutes,' Ursula told him presently, and vacated the chair on which she stood. It was a wobbly platform, especially in a wind, but practice had given Ursula security. She was as astonished as the man himself when his jump up was immediately followed by a jump down again! Rather red and disconcerted, he tried once more, this time grasping the pole of the umbrella to steady himself. 'Ladies and gentlemen – the speech we've heard, although doubtless well meant, can only be described by one word, drivel, absolute driv – '

A roar of laughter drowned the speaker's words. His hand, which clutched the umbrella pole, was indiscreetly pressing the spring. The umbrella was slowly closing. For a moment an angry, incomprehending face was visible; then he was literally shut up.

Ursula, too, could not help laughing as she helped to disengage her luckless opponent. He proved himself a man of determination, and returned to the attack. This time, by keeping his body absolutely rigid, he managed to preserve a precarious foothold without the aid of the pole. Presently, carried away by his theme, his caution relaxed. 'Women can't vote because they haven't the physical force to uphold their decisions,' he shouted, sawing the air with his arm. The gesture was fatal. Only a clutch at Ursula's shoulder saved a fall.

There was another delighted roar. 'Anyway she's upholding you all right,' came a voice. Ursula had meanwhile disengaged her shoulder. She grasped the back of the chair and put one foot on the rung. 'That's steady. But you've only two more minutes,' she murmured.

The man started afresh, or rather he reiterated what he had already said. 'Time's up,' Ursula presently told him. He took no notice. 'Time's up,' she repeated, louder. He, too, went on louder and still more volubly. She wondered how she would enforce her ruling. Unconsciously, she let go of the chair. The speaker lay sprawling at her feet!

The crowd yelled; it almost sobbed with delight. Such a gale of merriment was too much even for the orator's assurance. He got up and slunk away. Ursula was again standing on the chair. 'As the gentleman's arguments have fallen to the ground, I need not waste your time by answering them,' she observed gaily amid sympathetic laughter. 'It only remains for me to pass a vote of thanks to the chair.' The few who saw her meaning laughed again.

It was not only from her work that Ursula derived satisfaction; the new comradeship was delightful. As she had once told Tony, she had never had a girl friend; now she found one in Mary Blake. Miss Burnley, too, whom she had at first felt to be rather an unwelcome third, soon won her admiration. For the humble textile worker was endowed with a sense for advertisement that bordered on genius. It was to this, as Ursula realised, that their huge daily crowds were due, far more than to any power of oratory she herself possessed, or to Mary's loveliness and touching sincerity. And Miss Burnley was so amusing! Her racy talk opened up a whole new world, a world in which little bread-winning girls of eleven pattered down to 'th' mill' in headshawl and clogs at an hour when the Hibbert household might just be going to bed. But, for that matter, Mary Blake's life as the daughter of a poor dissenting minister was, to Ursula, almost equally unfamiliar. And yet they all three got on so well together. How little difference class really made!

But Ursula's greatest happiness during this Margate month came from something different, a sheet of thin yellowish paper, the cable to tell her that Tony had sailed. Now every hour, every minute, every second, was bringing him nearer; the thought made her want to dance for joy! Perhaps she would have done so, had not every available surface in the tiny sitting-room been covered with precarious ornaments. Thirty-nine on the mantelpiece alone – she had counted them one day with an amused air. 'But what's amiss wi' 'em?' Sarah Burnley had asked, puzzled.

September 3rd was the date that Tony had given for his arrival. To be on the safe side, Ursula had arranged to go up to town on the First. An afternoon drawing room meeting at the house of an important local lady, whom they had succeeded in converting, was to form a triumphant close to the campaign. But to Ursula's dismay the lady stipulated September 2nd. The Union Castle Line was consulted by wire. No, there was little chance of the boat arriving before the expected date. That settled it. Invitations for the meeting with Miss Winfield as the speaker were sent to a number of the leading residents.

The Second of September came. Ursula was combining a hasty lunch with a final glance at her notes when the landlady brought in a telegram. It was from Tony. He would arrive at St Pancras that afternoon at six.

Ursula had jumped up; she was looking at her watch. She

knew that there was a train leaving Margate at about two o'clock. Could she catch it? Yes, there was ample time. That was all right.

For the moment she had forgotten the meeting. But, of course, she couldn't go, she now reminded herself. She had to speak. She would not be able to get to town until the evening. Tony would come and not find her. How absolutely damnable!

The meeting was a success; that was some comfort. Still more was the fact of catching the earlier of the two possible trains to town. It was barely half past eight when she reached Victoria. She had an absurd hope that Tony might be on the platform, although, as he knew nothing of her movements, it seemed hardly probable. But the platform, although crowded, was blank. He would be at Lowndes Square. She frantically hailed a taxi. Yes, Mr Balestier had called, the maid said who opened the door. He came about half an hour ago. No, he had not waited; there was a note.

'Give it to me.' Ursula tore it open. Tony was disappointed, but not reproachful. He supposed that his telegram had been delayed. 'Your maid says you are at Margate – why Margate of all places on earth? – but that you are expected home tonight.' He would be round early in the morning, he went on. They would breakfast together at the old Kiosk.

Well, that would be lovely, but she could not wait until the morning. It was still quite early, not yet nine o'cock. But where was he? In one of his letters he had said something about going back to his old chambers at the Temple. 'Don't pay the taxi, I am going on,' she told the astonished maid.

The Temple was quickly reached, although Tony's address took some time to locate. It would have been reassuring had she been able to read the board of names at the entrance, but for this it was too dark. However, she started hopefully up the many flights. On each successive landing she found the oaken doors all shut. They were more inhospitable-looking than any doors she had ever seen, with their absence of bells and knockers. How did one make the people hear? she speculated. Well, she would make Tony hear if she had to yell through his keyhole!

This desperate expedient was unnecessary. On the top landing 'Mr A Balestier' in painted black letters was plainly visible. The oaken door stood wide open, revealing a much less impenetrable inner door with a customary knocker. This Ursula wielded rather tremulously.

The door opened at once. There stood Tony himself, Tony very big and clean and good to look upon. It was more than she had dared to hope. 'Tony, Tony.' 'Ursula!' For the moment all else was forgotten. They were twelve months in arrears.

It was Tony who first found coherent speech. 'Someone is with you, downstairs?' he suggested. 'Your mother?'

'Oh, no, mother is at Dumdrochie. No one is with me. Are you pining for further society?'

He did not take up the jest. Indeed, he looked singularly grave. 'But, dearest, you can't be here alone like this.'

'I am not alone,' she laughed. 'I am with you! And why don't you ask me in?' They were still standing in the little hallway. As he made no movement, she laughed again. 'Tony, you surely aren't worrying about Mrs Grundy? She's quite extinct – anyway among suffragettes!'

'I will walk home with you.' There was an uncomfortable decision in Tony's voice. He took his hat off the rack. Then as he turned again to open the front door, he caught sight of Ursula's hurt, astonished face. The straw hat went down recklessly. 'Darling, you can't think that I don't want to keep you.' The tone of his voice, and still more his kiss, did make the idea seem improbable!

Ursula emerged flushed but comforted. 'Well, I certainly think you are very ridiculous! And if I weren't so outrageously happy, I should be exceedingly cross!'

The next day made partial amends with its Kiosk breakfast, although they were both too busy to spend much time together. The following morning found them travelling to Dumdrochie, secure of nine, blissful, united hours. By dint of bribery and corruption a compartment was secured for the greater part of the way, a difficult feat in a corridor train. 'What fool invented them?' Tony muttered when, at last, intruders appeared.

Then came a fortnight that was the happiest Ursula had ever known. Her first joy was Tony's announcement that he had not brought his gun and did not mean to shoot. This decision he adhered to despite his host's shocked protests. A love that went to such lengths seemed to the Colonel hardly proper. He and the two cronies who completed the party, for the new wing was still unfinished, shook their heads sadly over the decadence of modern youth.

If Ursula had loved the moors before, what did she feel

now, as she rambled over them with Tony, showing him her best-beloved haunts, her most wonderful views? Sometimes they followed along the wooded bank of a rushing, dashing burn, a perfection of forest glade and rugged rock in miniature. More often they would climb the fells, solitary save for the hundreds of black-faced, browsing sheep that had formed the tracks which their steps trod. At the top they would sit, breathing the air that was in itself a joy, gazing sometimes at a singing circle of great hills, sometimes at a wide distance, moor and scanty field and woodland, with here and there a gleaming scrap of water, and very far away the shining glamour of the sea. Then they would tramp down again, very damp from squelching through the numberless tiny brooks, very dusty from clambering over the many loose stone walls, but supremely happy with the world and with each other.

Yet it was in connection with one of these stone walls that they had their nearest approach to a quarrel, as well as their only adventure. Ursula was a little ahead when they came to it; she scrambled up unconcernedly, for this wall, like the rest, had convenient footholds formed by the larger projecting stones. At the top, however, she hesitated, surprised. On the further side it was much higher, and hung over disconcertingly. 'It's a regular precipice, Tony!' she cried.

'Wait for me.' Balestier's tone was peremptory – too peremptory, for Ursula immediately jumped. Her skirt caught on one of the loose upper stones. There was an immense continuing crash. Ursula and a large part of the wall disappeared together.

In an incredibly few seconds Tony was standing beside her. 'Are you hurt?' He was breathless.

'No, I don't think I am hurt.' Ursula was already staggering to her feet. She was slightly astonished at being alive; it had seemed as though the whole hillside were coming down on top of her. 'No, I am not hurt,' she repeated more definitely, 'but I will sit down for a bit.'

They sat in silence. Although Ursula was not hurt, she felt exceedingly shaken and also rather a fool. Perhaps had she not been so taken up with her own sensations, she would have paid more attention to her companion. For Tony was so white that it might have been he who had had the fall. 'It was all the fault of my horrid skirt,' Ursula presently observed. 'Skirts are a frightful handicap. If either sex wear them it ought to be the men, as they are stronger.'

'Your skirt would not have caught if you had waited for me.'

'Tony!' Ursula was amazed, angry, not so much at the words as at the tone. She had never heard him speak in such a way before. 'Your being there would not have kept my skirt from catching! All that would have happened would be stones falling on you.' A sudden realisation came to her of what she would have felt had the stones fallen on Tony – a sickening vision of his lying there stretched upon the grass, unconscious, his face cut, crushed. But perhaps this was what Tony had felt about her. Besides, the accident had really been due to her carelessness; her skirt would not have caught had she been in less of a hurry. 'I am sorry, Tony,' she said childishly, and slipped her hand into his.

He was not implacable. 'And another time you will wait for me, darling?' he urged.

'If ten mad bulls are charging, I will stand and scream helplessly, like a perfect lady,' she assured him.

It had only been by a display of great moral firmness that Ursula had secured a holiday disentangled from suffrage. But, indeed, apart from all question of Tony, she had felt that it was necessary. Five months of incessant work had brought her near the end of her physical resources. But after arranging for an absence of at least three weeks, it was disappointing to find that Tony could only spare ten days. The report on Indian Immigration must be got out as soon as possible, he said. He would be down at the Stanleys' country place slaving at it most of the autumn. He went on to tell Ursula that Sir Philip wanted him permanently as his private secretary. Probably he would take the job until he went into Parliament.

'Are you going into Parliament?' Ursula interrupted in surprise.

Apparently it had been settled long ago. He would stand for Rivenden, the family place. His brother wished it and would make it financially possible. Yes, Claude was his half-brother really, there was nearly twenty years difference in age between them. Claude said he was to go in at the next election.

'But suppose the electors don't say you are to go in,' Ursula suggested.

Tony scouted the idea. The seat would probably not even be contested. No one stood much chance against a Balestier. Nearly all the voters were tenants.

'How immoral!' A hot discussion followed. No, it was not a case of illegitimate influence, Tony insisted. Their people felt that a Balestier could represent them better than a stranger. Why, his family had been there for five hundred years. Besides, Ursula was looking at it in a wrong light. Being an MP wasn't a personal advantage; that was why he loathed this idea of the payment of members. A fellow went into Parliament – Tony grew rather red and embarrassed – well, because he owed a service to the country.

'I understand.' Ursula did understand. She had the same feeling about suffrage, although in her case the service was not to her country but to her sex. She did not make the analogy aloud. The great subject was to be banished during the holiday, she had decided. Her jaded mind needed a rest; if she once began to talk of it, she would talk of nothing else.

Thus suffrage remained practically untouched between them, to Tony's intense relief. It was not until the last day that Ursula brought it up, and then it was only in connection with her own plans. 'Directly the Conciliation Bill is through, I shall feel free to go back to science. You can't think how I sometimes ache for it.'

'You feel certain that the Conciliation Bill is going through?' Tony was picnicking with her in a sort of grass lane formed by two of the high, treacherous walls running parallel along the bare hillside.

'There can't be any doubt about it. The second reading was passed by a majority of a hundred and ten.'

Tony was silent, but unconvinced. Colonel Hibbert had observed one day – fortunately not in his stepdaughter's hearing – that the Government might be fools, but they weren't such d – d fools as to give women votes. This remark, in Tony's opinion, represented pretty accurately the feeling of the great majority of his countrymen. Had he never met Ursula, it would probably have represented his own. Even now, although he had made the greatest effort to be sympathetic, he could only feel that Women's Suffrage was an experiment, and a very doubtful one. However, this Conciliation Bill, according to Ursula, would only enfranchise a million women. If the matter stopped at that, it could not do much harm. And, of course, as far as his own personal feelings went, the sooner the Bill passed the better. Had not Ursula just said that she would then give up political work and return to science? At the bottom of his heart, Tony felt that he would much prefer her not to do either; his ideal had always been his dead mother, a gracious, gentle, home-keeping lady. But he realised that a woman of exceptional talent like Ursula must pursue her vocation – although it had been no part of his original scheme of life to marry the exceptional woman. However, as he was certainly going to marry Ursula, he would have to resign himself to her working. Only it would be far pleasanter if the work left her quietly in a laboratory at home, instead of taking her about the country making speeches at political meetings.

'Yes, the Conciliation Bill is certain to be through by Christmas,' Ursula began again, abruptly breaking in upon his thoughts.

'And my Report will be through by Christmas,' Tony laughed. 'There will be nothing left to fill up the time, except to get married!' He moved even nearer to Ursula, while a black-faced sheep that was cropping hard by, with an elderly lamb in tow, broke away with a sudden scurry, evidently considering that this was no place for the young. 'You will marry me at Christmas?'

Ursula had been depressed all day with a consciousness of the diminishing hours of Tony's stay. 'Yes, but will it ever be Christmas?' she said lugubriously.

CHAPTER SIXTEEN

As Tony Balestier had anticipated, he had little leisure in the time that followed for seeing Ursula. The Stanleys' place in Shropshire was too remote to permit of flying visits to town; moreover, Sir Philip was, in Tony's words, a 'godless, fourth-commandment-breaking sinner,' who worked seven days a week and expected his miserable secretary to do the same. At last there came a happy Saturday, early in November, when the taskmaster was summoned away, and Tony found himself with thirty-six hours of freedom. By an exhausting series of changes, he caught the late express from Birmingham and reached London at midnight. He had already wired to Ursula that he would be with her on Sunday morning to spend the day together.

That Ursula, on her side, might not be free to do so, had never occurred to him. More than once in her letters she had mentioned that she was refusing all engagements except suffrage ones, and these he did not imagine invaded the Sabbath. As a matter of fact, when the telegram came, Ursula's joy was largely mixed with dismay. She was definitely engaged for two open-air meetings the next day. By means of spending her dinner hour in frantic telephoning, she procured a substitute chairman for the afternoon meeting on Wimbledon Common. But the morning meeting at Jack Straw's Castle was unalterable; there she was the chief speaker. Perhaps Tony would arrive in time to accompany her. Did she or did she not wish him to, she speculated. On the one hand it was hateful to think of missing any of their precious hours together. But then to have Tony in her audience – the idea overwhelmed her with nervousness. Apart from the ordeal of holding forth in her lover's presence, there was the fear of the crowd being hostile. Alone, she felt equal to coping with any number of hooligans; but suppose Tony tried to protect her! He might lose his temper; that, she knew from experience, was fatal. A horrid vision came to her of her lover struggling in a mob of roughs. However superior he might be to them in strength and in science, he was only one man; what could one man do against fifty? It was even said that the stronger a man, the more danger he ran of getting hurt. Had not a certain Mr Hawkins, a member of the Man's Union, had his leg broken quite recently when the stewards flung him out of a Cabinet Minister's meeting? And even if Tony received no serious injury, Sir Philip Stanley would be annoyed at a secretary with a black eye! Indeed, Ursula felt, with a smile, that she would not like it herself. Her Tony was too beautiful!

The risk was avoided, for Balestier had not appeared when the time came for Ursula to start. She did not get home again until nearly two – never had there been so many tiresome people wanting to ask questions. Then she found him. 'Oh,

Tony, I am so sorry! They told you about my hateful meeting? Have you been waiting long?'

'About three hours!' Tony gave a rueful smile. 'I didn't know that there was any place open for a meeting on Sunday morning.'

'It certainly was open – Hampstead Heath! We have had meetings there every Sunday, and get enormous crowds.' She stopped as she caught sight of her lover's face. 'What is the matter?'

'I had not pictured you as a stump orator.' The tone was cold.

Ursula did not notice it. She was too surprised by his ignorance. 'Why, I speak much more out of doors than indoors!' she told him. 'At Margate we were always on the sands. Didn't I ever mention it? I suppose I took it for granted that you knew. You see, my voice is very strong, so it is better to leave the indoor speaking to people who haven't such good lungs.' Her companion was still pointedly silent. 'Tony, what is it? Do you dislike open air speaking? Surely you can't be shocked!'

'Yes, I am. I suppose it is old-fashioned, but I simply hate to think of you standing there to be stared at by every passing Tom, Dick and Harry!'

'But, Tony – ' Ursula wanted to laugh, but she refrained. Nor would it do to express a wish that the rudeness of every passing Tom, Dick and Harry was limited merely to staring. Instead she substituted lightly that no one *passed* while she was speaking, and that even in a hall she would still be visible. Her lover continued to pace the room in evident agitation. 'But anyway, Tony, it won't be necessary for me to speak in public at all once the Bill is through,' she comforted him. 'And I am sure I shall only be too glad to get back to my peaceful Tom-Dick-and-Harry-less lab. Did I tell you about our Albert Hall meeting next Thursday week? It is going to be an enormous success; practically every ticket is sold. When the public reads about it, they will at last realise the strength behind our demand. Once they do that, the Government will be forced to give up their endless evasion and shilly-shallying.' The luncheon bell cut short her tirade.

Very soon after lunch Tony pulled out his watch. Apparently the Sunday journey back to Shropshire would be even more lengthy than the journey up. 'You can't go yet, I have hardly seen you,' Ursula protested, regretting more than ever the wasted morning. 'Anyway, promise me that you will come again soon. Only it would be no use before November 10th – that is the Albert Hall meeting. Till then I shall be so frightfully rushed.'

In no case could he get away before that date. Tony assured her. Then he hesitated. Before leaving he had meant to ask her not to speak again out of doors. He did not imagine that Ursula would refuse such a simple request, an entirely natural request as it seemed to him, but still she might wish to discuss the matter, and he had very few minutes left. 'I don't want you to go,' Ursula murmured suddenly, and clung to him, half laughing at her own childishness. Looking down, her lover saw tears in her eyes. By the time he had kissed them away, even the catching of his train was in jeopardy.

As Ursula had foreseen, the days preceding the Albert Hall meeting were filled with work to overflowing. On the evening itself, as head platform steward, she had to be at her post before six o'clock, and a couple of strenuous hours followed before the meeting began. She had no time to attend to the earlier speeches – latecomers had to be found places, an almost impossible task. But by the time the collection was called for, she felt herself comparatively free. As usual the money came rushing in almost faster than the figures could be changed on the great scoring board. But this time the collection would be larger than ever before. Why, it had started with an anonymous gift of five thousand amid an excitement that was almost painful. Six thousand – how splendid it would look in the papers. Seven thousand – that would influence public opinion. Eight thousand – perhaps even the Government would come to its senses. Nearly nine thousand – at last the limit had been reached.

The most important speeches were to follow. With her usual wisdom the treasurer had placed them after, and not before, the collection. Ursula listened with growing enthusiasm, with growing wonder. These speeches were finer than any she had heard. 'Suffrage militancy is not the militancy of murder which Christ condemned, but the militancy of suffering which Christ recommended.' Yes, that was the difference, Ursula told herself. Why had she never thought of it? Once, she remembered, the Leader had called upon the God of Battles. But it was not the God of Battles whom they served; it was the God of Calvary.

The exaltation in which Ursula went to bed was still with

her the next morning. She was down even earlier than usual in her anxiety to see the papers. Even if the reporters failed to convey the extraordinary spiritual uplift of the evening, the speeches themselves would be there for people to read – and the amount of the collection! At last the public would understand. And Tony too; she would send him all the fullest accounts.

Strangely enough, in her own daily paper the report was not as apparent as might have been expected; she had thought that it would nearly fill a page. She began to scrutinise more closely, first each sheet, then each column, then each paragraph. She turned to the list of contents. It was incredible, but there did not seem to be a single word about it! Perhaps the reporter had been ill or forgetful. How angry the editor must be!

The meek chaperone was not yet down, but the illustrated daily that she patronised lay beside her place. Ursula commandeered it. The search in this took less time. It yielded the same result – an absolute blank.

But this was too absurd! In the servants' hall, as Ursula happened to know, they patronised a well-known – a too well-known – halfpenny publication. She now rang and asked for its loan. Again the same incredible silence! Had the meeting ever taken place? Or had she dreamed it? But she certainly was not brilliant enough to dream those speeches! She rushed upstairs and put on her hat.

The newspaper shop at the corner was assailed with a breathless demand for all the morning papers. At last, in an obscure corner of one of the lesser dailies, Ursula found a brief report. *The Times* also contained a few lines of small print with an expurgated list of the speakers. It had, however, found space for an enormously long quotation from the *Anti-Suffrage Review* and several letters. Yes, and when the Antis had had a comparatively small meeting a few weeks ago, Ursula reminded herself, all the papers had had columns about it. How monstrously unfair! What was the use of constitutional work if no one were allowed to hear of it? Such treatment was enough to drive one to militancy; there, at least, the boycott was raised.

It was about a week later that Ursula was told one morning that the Leader wished to see her – not at Clement's Inn, but at home after office hours were over. The Leader's home at this time was a small flat lent to her by a supporter, for the modest salary that she allocated to herself from the Union funds hardly admitted of paying rent. Ursula found the little lady sitting with her usual trim erectness in a wasted armchair. 'I have been hearing great accounts of your speaking of late, Miss Winfield.' She greeted Ursula with a charming smile. 'And do you still disapprove of militancy?'

'I am not sure,' Ursula laughed. 'The way the press treated the Albert Hall meeting hardly encourages a constitutional frame of mind.'

'No, indeed!' There was a pause. 'Of course, you know, Miss Winfield, of Sir Edward Grey's reply to the Berwick-on-Tweed delegates – that it is impossible for the Government to give facilities for our Bill this year?' Ursula nodded. 'And that in consequence I am leading a deputation to the House of Commons? Will you come?'

'Oh, I don't think I can.' Ursula was conscious of the feebleness of her answer. But although she had half-suspected the object of the interview, she had not been prepared for such a direct attack. 'I really don't think I can,' she repeated.

'I know that I am not asking an easy thing of you.' The Leader's instinct had told her the right way in which to approach this possible recruit. 'To serve on this deputation will probably mean arrest and imprisonment. It will certainly mean rough handling, physical humiliation. I do not want anyone to volunteer in ignorance.'

'I know. It is not that, but I do not think that I ought to serve.' Ursula grew clearer. 'There are my people.' Though she had said 'people' she was thinking of Tony. 'They would disapprove frightfully. After all, one owes them some consideration.'

'Unless it clashes with a higher consideration.' The Leader was horribly ready. 'Others in the deputation, Miss Winfield, also have "people" to whom their action will give pain, from whom it will bring estrangement. It is part of the sacrifice. Do you remember what Garibaldi said? "Come with me. I offer neither pay, nor quarters, nor provisions; I offer hunger, thirst, forced marches, battles, and death. Let him who loves his country in his heart, and not with his lips only, follow me."'

'The deputation is next Tuesday?' The question did not mean that Ursula had agreed, but that she wanted to gain time. The quotation had moved her horribly.

'It was to have been next Tuesday, but my daughter thinks that the House may have ceased sitting by then. We are going tomorrow.'

'Then I can't go.' Ursula's tone was triumphant; she felt immeasurably relieved. 'I should not have time to let – anyone know. My people are all away. It would not be fair on them.' Yes, if ever she were going to take such a step, she was telling herself, Tony had, at least, the right to know of it beforehand. 'And in any case I do not feel absolutely certain about the deputation – I mean, as to whether it is wise.'

The Leader recognised the note of finality. She was acutely disappointed; she had quite thought the girl was on the point of yielding. Also, being unused to contradiction, she was annoyed. 'Then it is useless to discuss the matter further,' she said coldly. 'Only you have not forgotten, Miss Winfield, that one sometimes deludes oneself – quite genuinely – into thinking an unpleasant task is unwise.'

Ursula flushed. 'But also the fact of its being unpleasant does not necessarily make it wise,' she retorted.

'No. I only wanted to put you on your guard. I know you could not bear to be, in any way, sheltering behind other women, women who *are* paying the price.'

Ursula's flush grew deeper. 'I shall not do that.' At the moment she felt as though she hated the Leader.

Although she had refused to go on the deputation, Ursula naturally attended the Conference the next day at Caxton Hall. It met at noon, simultaneously with the re-assembling of Parliament. Presently a woman hurried into the hall and up on to the platform. She began speaking to the Leader in a low voice. This was the messenger bringing the report of the Prime Minister's speech. The Leader rose. 'As we expected,' she said, 'the Prime Minister has omitted all reference to

Women's Suffrage. Further, he has announced the dissolution for next Monday.' There was an outburst of hisses and groans. The Leader raised her hand. 'The motto of this Union is "deeds not words". The deputation will start at once.'

The total number of volunteers for the deputation was over three hundred. It had, however, been arranged that it should be divided up into detachments of not more than a dozen, starting at a few minutes' intervals, so as to keep within the legal number. Thus the hall only emptied itself slowly. Ursula sat on for an hour, and then, getting tired of waiting, went off to see what was happening. The crowd, as she went down Victoria Street, was noticeably less dense than at the previous raid, probably because this one had been less advertised. Parliament Square itself had been cleared by the police. Presently, looking across the green, she saw a little group of women standing straight in front of St Stephen's entrance. She recognised the Leader and most of the first detachment, all women of a certain age and celebrity. So they had not been admitted. It was extraordinarily stupid, if nothing else, of the Prime Minister, she reflected.

By this time she had worked her way sufficiently near the front of the crowd to see clearly what was going on. Policemen at intervals were keeping back the people; then came a clear space, and then a continuous line of stalwart, dark figures. As on the previous occasion, a woman here and there was trying to press her way through the cordon of police. There was one doing it just in front of her. But it was different from the last time – Ursula felt it instinctively. She saw the policeman raise his fist. The woman thudded on to the ground. He had deliberately knocked her down!

Ursula's heart seemed to stop beating. Even through her recent experiences she had never before seen a woman struck. And this woman had grey hair. For one moment a lamentable heap lay in the road and then she was up, and again rushing forward. This time Ursula could not quite see what the policeman did to her; the result, however, was the same. Again the woman was lying in the road. But now she did not move; she was evidently hurt, perhaps stunned. Ursula vainly tried to press through to her assistance. Then she saw a gentleman, who was standing in the front row, step forward. That was all right, Ursula felt with relief; he looked strong; he would be able to help the woman better than she could herself. The gentleman approached the prostrate figure. He lifted his foot. There was time for a flash of puzzled speculation to dart through Ursula's brain and the boot swung heavily into the woman's back.

'You brute! You brute!' Ursula's exclamation was hardly audible; she was half sobbing. 'Let the woman alone,' a working man shouted more effectually. 'The perlice can do their own dirty work.' 'Garn – serves 'er right!' This was from yet another source and was followed by some outrageously foul remarks. Meanwhile, the kicker had retired back into the crowd, satisfied apparently with his achievement.

All this time the woman on the ground had lain silent and motionless. Now she suddenly sat up. Blood was running from a cut in her forehead; probably in falling she had struck against the kerb. She got to her feet and stood swaying, her hand pressed to her head. Then she staggered – forward.

There was a cheer. The woman's courage had impressed the crowd. 'Let her through.' 'Why can't you arrest her?' came in angry shouts. 'They've had orders not to arrest,' someone near Ursula volunteered. 'That's why they're knocking them about.' 'They'll kill her then before they've done with her!'

The police, too, may have feared this result; the streaming blood probably impressed them. There was a hurried consultation between two constables as the woman weakly pressed up against them. Then followed a merciful arrest.

The scene that Ursula had just witnessed had certainly no bearing on the primal question of Women's Suffrage, nor even on the secondary issue of the desirability of militant tactics. At the most it only showed what one woman was prepared to suffer in order to gain the Vote, and how, under present conditions, she might be treated. And yet, illogically enough, nothing before had ever fired Ursula with such an irresistible passion for Women's Suffrage, with such a burning faith in the value of militancy. The Cause, from being an intellectual desirability, suddenly became a religion. Militancy was no longer tactics; it was martyrdom.

The rest was simple. When the thing was viewed in this new light, how could she remain out of it? Yes, she had been sheltering behind the other women, as the Leader had said, sheltering behind this grey-haired woman whom she had seen lying there kicked and bleeding. She wanted to rush to Caxton Hall – to volunteer on the spot – the last detachment could hardly yet have left. But the thought of Tony came, and even at this moment withheld her. She owed it to Tony to write to him first. After all, it was not as if this was her last chance.

She had already heard it announced that if Parliament dissolved next week without considering their Bill there would be another deputation. She would go on that deputation, but now she would go home.

Ursula went to bed very late that night, but before she went she had decided. The fateful letter to Tony was written. There it lay, stuck up and stamped, all ready to be posted in the morning. The letter to the Leader would go the next day, or even on Sunday, it would reach her at the office equally soon. And to her mother! Poor little Mammykin, all unconscious up there at Dumdrochie. On second thoughts Ursula decided not to write to her mother until the deed was done. Of course, if Mother had been alone in the world it would have been different. Then she would have felt about her as she did about Tony – that it was only fair to let her know. Besides, in such a case, Mother might have been cajoled into acquiescence, or, at least, into resignation. But the Colonel made the idea hopeless. It was impossible to argue with him. Indeed, he never did argue, he only exploded. And, after all, although she was fond of him, he was not her own father. No, she would not tell them anything beforehand. Her stepfather had laid down his terms – that if she took part in a raid she was never to return to Lowndes Square. By that, of course, she would abide. It would not really be such a deprivation. She only lived at home to be with her mother, and her mother was almost always away! There was her laboratory, she remembered regretfully, but she had been in it so little of late that it no longer seemed very important. As for the servants and all the luxuries with which she was surrounded, she would be only too glad to have done with them. But what a comfort it was that she had four hundred a year of her own. The real sacrifice must be for women with no money.

Certainly there was a sacrifice for her too, a very great sacrifice, that of distressing Tony. But she had written to him so carefully; when he read her letter he would surely sympathise. And even if he failed to do so, even if he were hurt, angry, he still would understand. He would realise that, feeling as she did, she could not act differently. And, after all, it would make no practical difference. She had already decided that they could not be married until the Vote was won. For this reason she had never allowed him publicly to announce the engagement. When that happy day of Women's Suffrage came, she could stop all the things of which he disapproved. Until then their love must make the bridge between them.

The next day was one long rush. Ursula had hardly time to live, far less to think. She was so tired that she slept all night and late into Sunday morning. A speech had then to be thought out for an afternoon meeting in Battersea Park. Sunday evening found her for the first time with leisure to write her letter to the Leader. 'I offer myself for the next deputation. I feel after all that you were right.'

She put the envelope on the hall table and settled herself by the fire with a sensation of profound relief. So that was settled. Tony must have got her letter that morning. The Leader would hear the first thing tomorrow. There was a sudden ring at the bell.

Who could it be? So few people came to the house when her mother was away. The meek chaperone was at evening service and would not be back for another hour. The front door was opened. She heard a familiar voice, a familiar step. 'Mr Balestier,' the footman announced and withdrew.

'Tony!' Ursula was trembling. She did not know until she saw him how afraid she had been lest he should be angry. But instead he had come to her. 'Oh Tony.' She almost flung herself into his arms.

'Darling.' He kissed her. 'But you have frightened me horribly with your letter. Of course, the idea is absurd.'

Ursula drew back dumbfounded, dismayed. Tony had not taken her letter seriously. At least, he must have taken it seriously or he would not have come rushing up to London, but he did not accept her decision. He thought he could persuade her to give it up, even persuade her easily. 'Tony, I told you in my letter – it is all settled,' she stammered.

'It is *not* settled.' He controlled himself. 'You said in your letter that you had not yet given in your name for the deputation. Have you done so since?'

'Yes.' Then Ursula remembered that her letter was still waiting to be posted. 'At least they have not got it yet, but I have written.'

Tony hurried into the hall. Doubtless he had seen the letter lying on the slab as he came through. He reappeared smiling. 'So there is no difficulty at all,' he said gaily, and put the envelope into Ursula's hand. 'Darling, you will tear this up and make me happy again, won't you? It really would be frightfully foolish. I can assure you that these raids are doing your Cause irreparable harm.'

The argument was still going on an hour later when the

timid chaperone appeared. She knew, of course, that the young people were engaged, and finding them both hot and indignant she fled with an even greater promptness than she would otherwise have shown. Her brief entrance, however, had had the effect of putting a brake on the discussion. 'Tony, it is no good.' Ursula's voice was pitiful. 'You don't think that Woman's Suffrage is very important, and I think it is the most important thing on earth. You think militancy does harm, and I have come to think that it is the only way to success. What is the use of our arguing any more? We shan't change each other.'

'No, and we won't argue any more.' Tony came closer. 'Keep your opinion, dearest. I only want you not to take part personally in the militancy. There is all the other work that you have been doing.'

'But, Tony, listen.' Ursula remembered that he did not know of the incident on Friday, the incident that had changed her whole point of view. She had felt that she could not write to him about it; perhaps she ought to have done so. Well, she would tell him now. . . . 'and as the woman lay there, a man – he looked like a gentleman – went up and kicked her.'

'Don't. You make me feel sick.' Tony had indeed got paler. Then he gave a short laugh. 'And you think that after hearing this, I could let you expose yourself to similar treatment?'

'You won't understand! Tony, can't you see that I feel it a question of honour? I could not love you, dear, so much – ' she stopped chokingly.

'Please don't drag in that hackneyed quotation! I certainly cannot see much honour in rolling in the gutter!' Tony checked himself. Ursula had covered her face with her hands, and, despite his anger, he felt brutal. Crossing over, he sat on the arm of her chair. 'Forgive me, dearest.' He gently possessed himself of one of her hands and began kissing it. 'I know that your motives are fine. But you would not have helped that poor woman by putting yourself in the same position. And that is all I am asking you, darling, not to let yourself get knocked about. Surely it is not very much to give up for my sake?' It seemed so little, indeed, that he smiled.

But Ursula had risen. 'I can't, I can't. I must go.' Her voice was strangled.

This time Tony did not control his anger. 'You only care for your blind self-will,' he exclaimed hotly. 'My wishes are nothing to you. Marriage under such circumstances would be absolute folly.' The door shut behind him.

CHAPTER SEVENTEEN

Tuesday morning found Ursula again at Caxton Hall. She had not been acutely unhappy after Tony had left her, for her mind had simply refused to entertain the idea that everything could be at an end between them. It was impossible, she told herself. She and Tony were too closely linked. She could not live without him. She had written to him again, almost directly after he had gone, reiterating her love and re-explaining her suffrage position. When he got this letter, he *must* understand. It had occurred to her that perhaps she was wanting in proper pride to be writing to him at all after what he had said, but pride seemed so meaningless and insignificant in connection with herself and Tony. She had hoped the night before to get a telegram in reply; as it had not come, she guessed that the primitive postal arrangements in the Shropshire village had delayed it. But soon after breakfast this morning, the footman had come in with a silver salver bearing the expected reddish envelope. She waited until the man had left the room; even then she could hardly bring herself to open it. A feeling of breathlessness had come over her, almost as though she had been running. She was telling herself that perhaps in another moment she would be happy. Perhaps she would read, 'Darling, I understand' or would Tony think 'darling' too compromising for a telegram? It was difficult to tear the envelope, her hands were shaking so. How badly it was written. The words grew clearer. 'I feel position arising from course you propose would be impossible. You must choose between the two alternatives.'

But that left no alternative. The possibility of withdrawing from the deputation did not even occur to her. Why, in an hour she would be starting! Tony had simply cut her off. She could not write to him again. She could not see him. She could not *ever* see him. Mechanically she journeyed down to Caxton Hall and took her place in one of the special rows reserved for the deputation. There she now sat, numb and dazed with misery.

She was so miserable that the speeches hardly penetrated to her understanding. Her stony face must have betrayed her, for presently Mary Blake came up and squeezed her hand. 'It will be all over in a few hours, dear,' Mary whispered. 'That's what I always tell myself. It makes it not so bad.'

Ursula looked up uncomprehendingly. 'What will be over?' she asked. Then she remembered, 'Oh, the raid; yes, I had forgotten the raid.' She almost laughed. She had forgotten the thing that was the whole cause of her despair. 'I don't think I shall mind the raid very much.' Indeed at that moment the idea of physical pain came as a positive relief.

It was soon after this that a messenger came in and handed a white envelope up to the platform. It contained the expected suffrage statement that the Prime Minister had just made in the House. The Committee withdrew to consider it. It was half an hour before they came back; they had been securing further details. The Leader's first announcement was that the House of Commons had risen. There was a shout of 'Cowards!' and a good deal of laughter. Then the Leader read the statement. The Prime Minister promised facilities for the Bill – not for this session – not for next session – but for the next Parliament! 'It is an absurd mockery, an insult to common sense,' came from the Leader's daughter. 'We hurl it back to them. We declare war from this moment.'

Even Ursula had by now lost her apathy. As she joined in the great burst of cheering Tony was, for the moment, forgotten. The deputation would go to Downing Street, the Leader announced, since the House was empty. Ursula took her place in one of the 'fours' that were forming outside. In an incredibly short time they were marching up Tothill Street. No one stopped them or particularly interfered. The police, doubtless, were expecting another raid on Parliament; this new procedure had taken them by surprise. As the procession approached Downing Street, policemen had barely time to make a single line across the entrance. The Leader pressed forward resolutely, unseeingly, with the weight of her three hundred behind. The police cordon wavered. It broke, and the women rushed through.

It was then that the struggle began. Reinforcements of constables came up at the double. The fact that their line had been broken made the policemen's difficult task still more difficult and, moreover, it had, as a start, irritated many of them into a frenzy. By a lucky chance, before Ursula was stopped, she had got to Number 10. She grasped the railings while three large policemen dragged at her from the back.

Naturally, she was quickly detached. She fell upon the pavement. Then she was up, and again trying to catch hold of the railings. This time one of the policemen gripped her by the throat. He shook her until she was dizzy and gasping.

When the mist cleared, she found that she was out in the road in the midst of a band of young men. She had imagined that she would not mind the raid; she had not been prepared for this. The indecency of their buffeting made it the most horrible experience of her life. Afterwards she found that most of the other women wore a protective cardboard armour under their clothes. Suddenly another suffragette, with a very white face, was standing at her side and pressing something hard into her hand. 'Break a window,' this woman whispered, 'then they'll be forced to arrest.' Ursula stared, only half understanding. 'A bit nearer,' her companion went on. 'Make sure there's no one inside to be hurt.'

Together they forced their way a few paces on through the horrible, lewd crowd. A ground-floor room in front of them was clearly empty. 'Now,' the other suffragette announced. Despite the authoritative manner, she was clearly unused to throwing, for her missile fell harmlessly into the area. A crash marked the passage of Ursula's stone through the selected window.

As the suffragette had foretold, almost at once they felt heavy hands upon their shoulders. 'Come along quiet now, or it will be the worse for you,' an angry voice growled. Considering how hard they had tried to get arrested, the remark seemed to Ursula superfluous. They were hustled along a few back streets and presently found themselves entering a police station. It seemed like entering heaven.

A few of the other women were already there, and a number more were brought in during the next hour. One or two fainted on arriving; they all were more or less damaged. There was no grumbling, however, only sympathy and a hubbub of excited talk. Ursula, at first, took part in it. Then suddenly the thought of Tony came back to her like a weight falling upon her soul. She became conscious, too, that physically she was bruised and aching from head to foot.

She sat there on the floor – the room was too crowded for most of them to find seats – her dejection steadily increasing, and, with it, a yearning to be alone. This keeping up of appearances, this never-ending chatter, was more than she could bear! Every now and then a policeman looked in. Ursula seriously considered asking one of them to show her to her cell. But she supposed it would not do. Besides, she had heard that later in the evening they were all to be bailed out. Would that time never come? The day's proceedings, as they passed through her mind, began to get dulled with a sense of horrible futility, probably the result of fatigue. Was it possible, after all, that Tony might be right, and militancy a mistake? Did Women's Suffrage matter so frightfully? At that moment she felt that she would have sacrificed every cause on earth to see Tony come in at the door.

Eventually the bailing out took place. A male supporter arranged it, a gentleman of some standing. As he appeared, he was assailed with questions by the assembled ladies. There had been about a hundred and fifty arrests, he told them. Yes, the Leader had been arrested, and three men. It was all over now. Ursula did not wait to hear more. Her only idea was to reach the little hotel off the Strand, where she had engaged a room for the night. She was so utterly miserable. But she was also utterly exhausted. She had hardly got into bed when her misery faded into sleep.

Eight months before Ursula had thought it an adventure to be at Bow Street as a witness. Now she found herself there as a prisoner. On the first day she never got as far as the court; the long hours dragged themselves through in the waiting room. This was a spacious apartment, very different from the little room at the police station. Indeed, save for there being wooden forms instead of chairs, it might have been a ladies' club, with its gentle occupants reading the papers, writing letters, or conversing in cultured tones. The congestion with which the day started, rapidly thinned, for every few minutes women were summoned away, usually singly; but sometimes in groups. A few came back, the cases of wilful damage or assault, which were being held over until the next day. All the rest, the great majority, who were charged merely with obstruction or resisting the police, were discharged. This so-called leniency on the part of the Home Secretary filled the suffragettes with fury. First, instead of being arrested they were knocked about; then their cases were withdrawn in order to conceal from the public the brutality with which they had been treated – this was how they viewed it. Ursula felt too dulled to share the indignation around her. 'You'll get your chance. As you broke a window, they'll have to hear your case,' Mary Blake said to her enviously.

The next morning, as Miss Blake had foretold, Ursula was standing in the coveted dock. She still felt in a dream. There was only one real thing in life – that Tony had cut her off. She heard herself charged with breaking a window to the value of five shillings – the unconscious feminine instinct for economy had caused her to pick out a small pane. Naturally she pleaded guilty. The magistrate was about to pronounce the sentence, when Ursula remembered that this was her 'chance'. With an effort she pulled herself together. 'Will you allow me to explain that I am not in the habit of breaking people's windows,' she began with a disarming smile. 'On Tuesday afternoon I was taking part in a peaceful deputation. If the deputation was in order, we ought to have been received. If it was not in order we ought to have been arrested. Instead of which the police assaulted us. I broke this window in order to be arrested. Moreover, I felt that it is more justifiable to break a pane of glass than for the Prime Minister to break a promise.'

'We have nothing to do with politics here,' the magistrate interrupted. 'We have to administer the law.'

'It was to enforce the administration of the law that I broke the window,' Ursula retorted. 'The behaviour of the police was illegal.'

There was laughter, for many of those present were members of the WSPU. 'Silence.' The magistrate was clearly angry. 'If there is any more of this unseemly noise the court will be cleared. A fine of five pounds or one month's imprisonment.'

For Ursula, as for any other suffragette, this meant imprisonment. It was curious that again, so soon, she was being offered an impossible alternative. But, indeed, she almost thought that she preferred prison. At least there she would be alone; she would be at liberty to be miserable. No doubt the physical discomfort would be great, but what did physical discomfort signify?

When, after more dreary hours of delay, and a long, jolting drive in a Black Maria, she at last reached Holloway, she found the discomforts less than she had imagined. The imprisonment during the last four years of articulate women, some of whom were even of good social position, had produced many reforms. Moreover, at this time special privileges were being accorded to suffragettes, among them that of clean bedding. It is true that Ursula's bed, although new and clean, was the hardest she had ever slept in, and her cell was both cold and stuffy, but her healthy young body adapted itself with surprising rapidity. No, to her surprise she found that it was the thing for which she had yearned, the enforced solitude, that proved in practice the most unbearable. Other suffragettes had spoken of this terror of prison life, but Ursula had thought herself superior to it. 'I should like to have so much time to think,' she had said. Now it was from her own thoughts that she wanted to escape. For in those interminable, solitary hours, her misery grew and grew. And the cell was so small, so unexpanding. Sometimes she felt that if she could not get out, out into the fresh air, out among other living, human beings, she would go mad. One evening, lying awake, she grew so desperate that she began to beat her head against the stone wall. 'I am too unhappy; I can't bear it,' she was sobbing wildly. Suddenly the sound of the 'Marseillaise' reached her. Some of the suffragettes were singing in the street outside to cheer the prisoners. Never had the gay, dauntless air been more needed. Ursula heard muffled, answering voices echoing from the cells around, and she, too, with quivering lips, took up the refrain. As she sang, she grew ashamed of her recent feeble frenzy. After all, her own happiness or unhappiness was but a little thing, a pinprick in the infinite. It was the Cause that mattered, the Cause that was to make all women happier.

After this, the girl did not again let her self-control slip, but it was some words spoken by the wardress that finally aroused her to face life. She had been sitting dully in her cell, brooding over the blankness of existence, when the woman happened to unlock the door and look in. 'You don't seem as 'appy as most suffragettes 'ere,' was her unexpected remark.

'Are most suffragettes happy here?' Ursula felt a stab of conscience. Had she been showing the white feather, letting down the Cause in this woman's eyes?

'Oh, yes. When I sees an 'appy faice among the prisoners I knows it's one of you ladies. Not that I 'olds with your doings,' the wardress went on severely. 'You don't seem to 'ave no consideration about what it means for us. Not that we'd object to two or three at a time like, spread out over the year, but these big crushes makes the work for us something cruel.'

'I am sorry.' Ursula was looking interested at this new point of view. 'It does seem too bad. They ought to give you extra help after a raid. That is one of the things that we shall improve when we get the Vote,' she branched off. 'Women will be able to insist on decent hours and decent pay.' The suffrage discussion that followed was only cut short by the wardress declaring that if she was caught there chattering to a prisoner she'd get into 'horful trouble'.

Even a Holloway month must come to an end. One morning, after hours of the aimless waiting which seemed an inseparable part of prison procedure, Ursula found the great gates opening to let her out together with some twenty-five of her comrades. Despite the long delay, it was still only eight in the morning, so the girl quite expected to walk into a street, empty save for step-cleaning maids and brisk, rat-tatting postmen. Great was her surprise when she saw the thick crowd, while a sudden burst of cheering startled her unaccustomed ears. What could it be? Was some royalty passing? Then she realised that these were friends, members of the WSPU, who, despite the early hour, had journeyed up to greet the outcoming prisoners. How good of them, she felt gratefully. Another moment and she was driving off in a beflagged carriage amid fresh cheers. They were going to the Criterion, she was told, for the 'Welcome Breakfast'. It certainly would be welcome after Holloway fare and the early start, Ursula laughingly retorted. Naturally the dense throng at the prison gates did not extend far, but the route was thinly fringed nearly all the way. For the most part the onlookers were silent, though here and there a boo made itself heard, or the shrill salutation of a partisan.

As Ursula had stepped into the carriage, a bundle of letters had been pushed into her hand; they had come for her to the office. She now glanced at them, but without any great curiosity, rather, indeed, with a sort of resentment. What did letters mean to her now? Tony – with a violent effort she switched off her thoughts. Her mother and her stepfather? She had not heard a word from them all the time she had been in prison, and so had made up her mind that they, too, had cast her off. These letters would only be requests to speak, or congratulations from other suffragettes, or abuse from strangers – yes, there were sure to be some anonymous, indecent postcards. Suddenly she caught sight of her mother's large, ornamental handwriting. But it might be only a formal disownment, she reminded herself, trying to check her rising hopes.

No, little Mum was staunch! A glow of happiness warmed Ursula's aching heart. Although her love for her mother was hardly of a filial character, it was both real and deep. Even as a baby, she had gazed with solemn eyes of wondering admiration at the exquisite little figure that flitted at rare intervals into her nursery. As she grew older, the wonder changed into amusement, but the admiration remained. No one appreciated little Mrs Hibbert's beauty more than her daughter, while Ursula, unlike most people, recognised that her mother combined sound commonsense and even brains with her taste for folly and flirtation.

But how characteristic this letter was; an involuntary smile came to Ursula's lips. 'I did not write to you before,' her mother said, 'because I was so fearfully rushed getting off from Dumdrochie: Jenkinson becomes more asinine every year, and I didn't suppose they would let you have letters in that horrible place. Your stepfather was furious, of course; indeed, he still is. He wanted me to have nothing more to do with you, but I told him that was absurd. I disapprove of prison as much as he does, but it doesn't make you stop being my child. I don't suppose you can return to Lowndes Square, but I shall come and see you directly we get home. We are staying with the Mountcalm Lees until the 23rd. I told your stepfather that if he made a fuss about it, I should have to break a window too, and then I should be sure to meet you. I am dreadfully worried about your hands. Did you remember to take your manicure set to prison? You have such nice nails: it would break my heart if you spoilt them picking oakum. By the way what is oakum? Can you eat it when it's picked? Ever your loving Mother.'

Another pleasant surprise awaited Ursula that morning. When they reached the restaurant, she heard, rather sinkingly, that breakfast would not be for another half hour. The guests, some two or three hundred in number, were assembling in an adjacent room. She shook hands with several enthusiastic sympathisers, and then, too tired for more compliments, retreated to a retired corner. Suddenly Vernon Smee stood before her. 'You?' she exclaimed delightedly, then she half-wondered at her own delight. But a well-known face seemed such a relief among all these recent acquaintances. Mingled with the pleasure was surprise. Although the Professor had now spoken several times from WSPU platforms, Ursula had thought that he would have disapproved of the renewal of militancy, and had certainly never dreamed of his attending this official welcome.

Vernon, meanwhile, had been contemplating her with some concern. 'You are tired,' he said. 'Do sit down again.' He fetched another chair for himself and put it near to hers. 'I hope you haven't been hunger striking?'

He was obviously relieved at her denial, but still seemed worried. But although he thought that Ursula was looking ill, there was no doubt that she was also looking very handsome. His misgivings about coming to this breakfast faded. For, as Ursula had guessed, he had had misgivings. It was not so much that he disapproved of the raid, but he felt, with justice, that it did him professional harm to be mixed up with such doings. He had yielded to the Leader's pressing invitation partly out of interest in the Cause, a little, perhaps, to annoy his wife, but chiefly on Ursula's account. For although he had got over his old passion, or thought he had, he still felt about Ursula as he did about no other woman. Someone had told him that Miss Winfield's action had led to a quarrel with her people. Did 'her people' include her fiancé. He must find this out. Now that he saw her, he rather thought that it had. There was a hint of tragedy in her face that was new. 'I never expected to see you at a gathering of gaol-birds,' Ursula remarked with an effort at jocularity.

'I never expected it myself. But then I never expected that you were going to develop into that *rara avis*. Of course, on such an occasion I felt that as an old friend I must come and greet you.'

Ursula's eyes suddenly filled. Prison is demoralising; also she was very hungry. 'You are really a friend,' she said unsteadily.

Nothing more passed between them of a personal nature; nor was it necessary. Vernon had found out what he wanted to know. Ursula's engagement was at an end. While he was profoundly sorry for her, he could not help a certain faint feeling of excitement, even of pleasure. Of course, Ursula being free did not make any real difference. He was still tied. Besides, he felt vaguely, that although Ursula might have broken off her engagement, she was not the sort of woman to care again. He remembered her face at the BA soirée when she had told him of her engagement. But now he and she could be friends in a way which a fiancé or a husband would have made impossible. Yes, they would be 'really' friends, as she had called it.

CHAPTER EIGHTEEN

It seemed ironical that after Ursula had sacrificed so much in order to become a militant, the year that followed her November raid was again one of 'truce'. In the spring a new Conciliation Bill of an even more conciliatory character was introduced, and it passed its second reading by a still greater majority. But this did not complete the similarity. The triumphant Bill was once more absolutely ignored. The WSPU grew restive. Worried statesmen then began to reflect that a suffragette outbreak would harmonise badly with the Coronation festivities. So a compromise was reached. A promise was given of a week's facilities for the consideration of the Bill in the following year.

Although there were no raids, there was an immense amount of hard work. In April had come the Census Protest. If women were not intelligent enough to vote, they were not intelligent enough to fill up a Census Statement, the suffragettes declared. Women householders returned blank forms. Those who were not householders passed the night away from home. Ursula's scientific sense was exercised by this new form of protest, yet she joined in it. At half past two in the morning she found herself making a speech to a packed, enthusiastic audience at the Aldwych skating rink. An hour or two later she was eating stewed apricots in Drury Lane. What strange happenings suffrage entailed! Then she made her way home – for some time now she had shared the flat of a suffragette friend in Adelphi Terrace. As she opened the front door, she saw the hall carpeted with slumbering forms outlined under rugs and cloaks. It was quite difficult to pick her way among them. The rooms seemed equally congested, perhaps more so, for the dining table afforded the possibility of a double layer. There really did not seem to be space for a single other sleeper. She had better return to the Aldwych rink, especially as skating was one of her few accomplishments. The dim dawn revealed her busily cutting backward eights with a sense of light unreality among a circle of intimate strangers.

June, the month of the Coronation, witnessed the greatest procession suffrage had held; the greatest procession ever held some enthusiasts declared. All the societies combined, and forty thousand women assembled to march for the Bill. Ursula herself was a Section Marshal and so, to her disgust, could not take her honourable place among the seven hundred prisoners. However, her mother would be relieved, she consoled herself.

For, as Mrs Hibbert had informed her husband, she had entirely refused to be cut off from her only daughter. Ursula did not go to Lowndes Square, but Mrs Hibbert frequently made dazzling, if brief, appearances at the Adelphi Terrace flat. 'I must say you've made yourself very comfortable here,' the little lady used to exclaim, almost enviously. The flat was, indeed, charming, for Ursula's friend was a woman of artistic taste and sufficient means. 'Why can't I live like this?' Mrs Hibbert would sometimes plaintively add. 'No worry of entertaining or looking after a houseful of lazy servants!'

'Celestine would never allow it,' her daughter laughingly reminded her.

'No, I don't suppose she would. That woman is a perfect tyrant.' The possibility of dispensing with the French maid did not present itself.

But Mrs Hibbert was not the only visitor from the girl's previous life, nor, indeed, the most frequent. As Professor Smee had foreseen, he and Ursula had become real friends. He had formed a habit of coming on to see her after the council meetings at the Chemical Society, alleging brazenly that Adelphi Terrace was only 'round the corner'. They naturally also met when Ursula herself went to the Chemical Society, but her attendance at the Thursday evening meetings was now of rare occurrence. There was often some suffrage engagement that stood in the way, but apart from this, it was doubtful if she wanted to go. These brief returns to the scientific world depressed her. It was not only that they brought a longing to return to her own work, but she was seized with a horrid doubt as to whether she could do her own work even if she did return to it. She certainly found it almost impossible to follow these papers on the work of others. In vain she told herself that her present scientific dullness was due to preoccupation. How could her mind turn to chemistry when it was filled with the Cause? In suffrage she was doing good work. They were obviously pleased with her at Clement's Inn; at meetings she nearly always held her audiences. But while she thus reassured herself, she was conscious that some power in her, some gift of creative divination, had gone. She sometimes thought that sorrow had killed it.

Whatever might be her shrinking with regard to chemistry, it did not extend to chemists, for she welcomed Professor Smee. Apart from her increasing liking for him as an individual, it was a rest and a stimulus to meet anyone not of the regular suffrage world. The intimacy between them might in some circles have been questioned, but Mrs Grundy was not a suffragette. Moreover, Ursula had a chaperone, for the owner of the flat was a married lady with an adequate, if absent, husband in the Indian Civil Service. Certainly, convention might have cavilled at the chaperone's imperfect attendance, for the Cause also held Mrs Forsyth in thrall, and more often than not Vernon found Ursula alone. It must be a dull way for a distinguished man like Professor Smee to pass his time, she sometimes reflected, after an evening spent together in the pretty little sitting room. In the old days she could have told him about her work, but now what had she to say of interest? Once as he rose to go, she put her thought into words. 'Do you really like wasting so much time on me, Professor Smee?'

'Perhaps I do not consider it wasting time.' Vernon had flushed slightly, but Ursula did not notice it. Then he laughed. 'Do you know your calling me "Professor Smee" always makes me feel so immeasurably antique! Would "Vernon" be impossible?'

Ursula looked as surprised as she felt. Not that calling a man friend by his Christian name struck her as odd. Although she had never done it herself, it was a common practice both in the Hibbert set and in her present suffrage *milieu*. But Professor Smee! She was still young enough to feel his forty-five years as elderly, although he certainly did not look forty-five. Still, "Vernon" struck her as hardly suitable. She intimated this to him and was surprised that he seemed almost vexed. 'Of course I will say Vernon, if you like it better,' she hastened to assure him, 'but then you must call me Ursula. Otherwise I should really feel antique! You would be giving me the position of your maiden aunt.'

'And a very suitable position,' he bantered her. 'Still, I will comply. Good night – Ursula.' This time something in his voice, his look, penetrated even Ursula's incomprehension. Had her permission been indiscreet, she wondered.

There was one aspect of the friendship with Vernon which did not occur to Ursula – its effect on Vernon's wife. Or if she considered poor Charlotte, it was as an added reason for the friendship. Being tied to such a woman must be almost as miserable as being separated from Tony. She and Vernon must try and cheer each other in their common loneliness. Naturally she would not permit herself any vulgar criticism; the wife's name was never even mentioned between them. As for visiting at Clarendon Road, she was thankful that Mrs Smee's own outrageous rudeness had made that impossible.

Although Ursula saw a fair amount of Professor Smee when she was in town, there were also considerable periods when she did not see him at all. For weeks on end she would be away at by-elections or on suffrage speaking tours. It is doubtful, however, whether these intervals did not cause the friendship to ripen even more rapidly. For, to Smee's surprise, Ursula proved herself an excellent correspondent. And not only was he surprised at the length and frequency of her scribbled letters, written for the most part in the train; he was still more surprised by a certain intimacy that underlay them, an occasional, almost tender sentence that made his breath catch, and for which the stereotyped beginning and end of 'Dear Vernon' and 'yours sincerely' found him utterly unprepared. Professor Smee would have been less puzzled, and also less pleasantly excited, had he guessed the explanation – that Ursula was unconsciously using him as Balestier's understudy. For, during the absentee engagement, the girl's daily letter to her lover had become a part of her life. She had treated it as talking to Tony on paper – not as hated literary composition – and so to stop writing to him had hurt almost as much as to stop seeing him. Now she slid back into the old habit.

And there was so much to say! Her suffrage tours, although tiring, were full of interest. The constant succession of strange hosts in itself provided material for correspondence. Personally, Ursula would have preferred the more restful monotony of hotel life. It was not the expense that deterred her; she had discovered that her four hundred a year was comparative wealth in her present sphere. But the Leader urged her to accept local hospitality, no doubt feeling shrewdly that the ardour of supporters was increased by entertaining anyone of Miss Winfield's appearance and social status. Once or twice the girl again found herself staying with people of her mother's world; more often her hosts were well-to-do business folk, only differing from the rest of their class in a passion for 'causes'. For Ursula found, to her distress, that a whole series of what she termed silly fads – vegetarianism, anti-vivisection, anti-vaccination – almost invariably co-existed with a suffrage sympathy. Could people not see that whatever their views might be, they must concentrate on the one great issue, she felt indignantly.

All the same, she extracted a good deal of amusement out of these 'fads', Vernon received a comic description of a dinner at which the fare offered was a saucer of chopped apple and a Brazil nut. 'I had had nothing but a few sandwiches since breakfast,' Ursula wrote, 'and two hours of speechifying loomed ahead! Imagine how my heart sank – if heart be the right organ! I suppose my hostess noticed the stony look of despair settling on my countenance, for presently she murmured something about there being other food for the servants. At last a small boiled egg and a slice of bread and butter appeared. This I consumed under the reproachful gaze of seven infant nut-eaters, who evidently considered my orgy as a cross between sacrilege and cannibalism!'

Another experience was almost as painfully humorous. It was a cold, damp evening, and Ursula's meeting, held in a cold, damp hall, was but sparsely attended. The audience, such as it was, may also have been damp; it was certainly cold: only once could she arouse the faintest enthusiasm. Thoroughly chilled, she left the hall to find the rain coming down in sheets, and a long tram journey necessary to reach the suburb where dwelt her night's hosts. On arriving at the house – a place of some pretensions – she was cheered to be offered supper, but, as was not unnatural at such an hour, the meal was cold; also water was the only beverage. Afterwards she was conducted to her bedroom, a vast, freezing chamber with three great windows on which the rain beat furiously. The general icy feeling was deepened by the furniture, a monumental mahogany suite, and the two washstands, one with the usual china equipage, which included two jugs and two carafes of cold water, the other with fixed nickel taps, labelled hot and cold, but from both alike issued the same frigid flow. On the great round centre table stood a decanter of cold water ringed with glasses, while upon the little bed table a thoughtful hand had placed a tumbler already filled with water so cold that the glass was dimmed. Ursula was staring shiveringly at the immense glacial expanse of the bed, and summoning sufficient fortitude to undress, when there came a knock at the door. Hot milk? Hot soup? Ursula's thoughts soared hopefully. At least a hot water bottle? 'I thought you might like a glass of cold water, Miss Winfield,' came in her hostess's solicitous tone.

After seven months thus filled with varying experiences and continual strenuous work, it was not surprising that by August Ursula felt the need of a holiday. To go with her mother was out of the question. Indeed, Colonel and Mrs Hibbert were already at Homburg, the usual yearly purge being more than ever necessary after the Coronation celebrations. No doubt Ursula could have found some suffrage friend to go with her, although Mary Blake was booked, but it would be more change, she felt, to get away from all her everyday associates. Cornwall? The unknown 'duchy' had always attracted her. The chance hearing of good farmhouse lodgings in a picturesque fishing village decided her.

When Ursula had packed her trunk, she had really thought that she would enjoy a month of rest and solitude. Had she not always done so? Now she found that she was no longer happy enough to be alone. The old yearning for Tony resurged with its first intensity. Life was only bearable when she could imagine him there, sharing her rambles, her picnic meals, as he did last year at Dumdrochie. Sometimes in her thoughts they were staying there together in a yet more intimate relation. But such dreams were madness. They only left her more miserable. At the end of a week she fairly fled back again to town.

Here was work, at least, and in work, forgetfulness. The depleted office welcomed her with open arms. There was practically no one left to sell the paper, she was told. Ursula beat up and organised recruits. She herself took up a site. Indeed she took up several, moving steadily eastward. The West End might be empty, but the East still swarmed. To her surprise she found a readier sale in these poor neighbourhoods than she had ever done in Kensington, although each copy sold often meant the clubbing together of three or four customers. But although business was brisk, it was also fatiguing. This was the summer of un-English heat when the thermometer rose above all recorded heights. And Ursula spent it standing for hours beneath a brazen sky on a scorching crowded pavement bearing her heavy bag of *Votes*.

It was little wonder that when Vernon Smee came home from Switzerland he was concerned at her pallor. He himself had only taken three weeks abroad instead of his usual four – he had not been able to keep away from Ursula any longer. 'You ought to have stayed in Cornwall and have had a proper holiday,' he told her.

'It takes two to make a holiday.' Ursula flushed furiously. 'At least, what I mean is that it's awfully dull holiday-making alone. Another year I shall join a Cook's tour!' She laughed without mirth.

Vernon had got up and was looking out of the window. Had Ursula guessed the tumult that was going on in his mind, she would have been utterly amazed. Yes, it did take two to make a holiday. How he had felt it! Had Ursula meant that? Returning sanity told him no. She was fond of him, but only as a friend. Perhaps some day – but it would always be impossible. He was bound, chained for life. This was what he told himself. But he knew very well that if Ursula ever cared for him, he would not resign himself to the impossible.

'What are you looking at out of the window so intently?' Ursula's words broke in upon his thoughts.

'I was thinking what a depressing place London is compared with Switzerland. And I was also thinking of how we could get you away for a holiday without recourse to Mr Thomas Cook.' He had not been thinking of either of these things, but now he began to do so. A sudden inspiration combining the two flashed across him. It was staggering, dazzling! Had not Vincent, a scientific colleague, urged him for years to join the Swiss party that he and his sister got up every winter? And had not Miss Vincent once spoken to him of Ursula with admiration? 'Miss Winfield is such a wonderful speaker' she had said. He propounded his scheme; he and Ursula should both join the Vincent expedition in the Christmas holidays.

Ursula clearly found the idea attractive. As she had said once long ago, the unknown Switzerland appealed to her. Mountains, so big and cool and quiet! And winter sports! Without conceit, she knew herself to be a good skater. Yes, winter sports would be delicious – especially by contrast with this torrid August. Besides, it was quite true what Vernon was urging, that she had had no proper holiday this year. If she went on too long without one she would only break down. Still, she demurred. 'But I hardly know Miss Vincent or Professor Vincent either. How can I foist myself upon a lot of strangers?'

'I shall be there, and I am not a stranger!' Vernon was struggling to make his voice casual, to keep out of it the intensity of his desire. 'It will be a great "spree".' Ursula, do come.'

'It will be rather a "spree".' She smiled. For the first time for months there seemed to be a looking forward in life. Though but a second-best, friendship was yet a pleasant thing. She had been surprised this afternoon to find how glad she was to see Vernon again. Yes, she would enjoy a Swiss holiday in his society. She would go at Christmas if the Vincents asked her, she told him.

That autumn Ursula spoke more than ever. The local organisers in all the south coast towns clamoured for her presence, she did not know why. Personally, she disliked these southern audiences; they were both less intelligent and less well behaved than those in the north. No wonder up in Lancashire they talked of the 'Silly South', she reflected at a great Worthing meeting at which neither she nor any other speaker was able to make a single word carry. What a pandemonium – shouting, stamping, singing, dancing, music of every sort and description. Finally, Ursula's senses got so deadened that she almost ceased to notice it. The sound beat like the waves of the sea; it was no effort to sit there in smiling unconcern.

The next night she was in Southampton; this was to be a much smaller affair, with herself as the only speaker. In this town there was a large hostile element. But they did not expect any trouble tonight, a rather agitated organiser told her. The door was well policed. Entrance was by ticket only, and the audience would practically all be sympathisers.

If meetings were limited to sympathisers it was hardly worthwhile to hold them passed through Ursula's mind; but she did not increase the organiser's agitation by putting her thought into words. One cause of the poor girl's perturbation now transpired. The lady at whose house Ursula was to have stayed had suddenly been taken ill. 'Some people called Todd have asked to put you up,' the organiser went on. 'They are awfully kind – the Miss Todds are two of our best workers. But they are rather humble and live over their shop – ship chandlers. I do hope you won't mind.'

Ursula reassured her. Indeed she genuinely felt that to visit over a shop would be an interesting experience. And what would her mother have said? The idea added a touch of malicious glee to the prospect. She was almost sorry to hear that she was to dine at the organiser's own 'digs' and only go on to the Todds after the meeting. Whether this was to save her hosts trouble, or to limit her own stay over the incriminating shop to the smallest dimensions, she did not know.

When, later, they reached the meeting, they found a large band of noisy roughs already gathered outside, although at a respectful distance from the door at which stood several solid policemen. The organiser's precautions had been wise, Ursula felt, when she found that the hall was not on the ground floor and could only be reached by a long, curving flight of steep stone steps. Horseplay, such as had taken place the night before, would here be frightfully dangerous. 'It is the only hall that will let to suffragettes,' the organiser explained.

The place was already fairly full, even though, as the organiser proudly stated, there had been a sixpenny charge. Indeed, her theory was that you got a bigger audience in this way. 'If people have to pay to come, they think it must be worth coming to.'

'Even if it isn't!' Ursula interpolated laughingly.

The audience was not only sufficiently numerous, it was also more enthusiastic than Ursula had expected. She found herself speaking well, undisturbed by bursts of noise from outside; these, however, were largely muffled into insignificance by the distance from the ground and the closed windows. Her speech was long – over an hour. She was ending on the note of the prisoners – their sufferings. With a speaker's second consciousness, she knew that her audience was moved, indeed, the hall was dotted with white, mopping handkerchiefs. Suddenly, a crash – a sharp shivering of glass! A flaming body rushed through the air. Women screamed, started up – now literally moved! The fiery object had fortunately fallen in the empty space between the front row and the platform. It lay there fizzling ominously. There were shrieks, 'A bomb! A bomb!' and a stampede towards the door.

Ursula also had risen. She shouted: 'Keep your seats,' and sprang down from the low platform. There was but one thought in her mind – to get rid of this thing that was alarming the audience. Another second and she had reached the sinister black object. A leaflet happened to lie on the ground nearby. Automatically she snatched the 'bomb' up in it. Afterwards the thought of this intervening piece of paper amused her; what possible purpose could it have served? Running across the room, she threw the disconcerting visitant out of the window through the hole that its flaming entry had made. 'We won't deprive the donor of his kind gift,' she called out cheerfully.

The rush to the door had already stopped. Curiosity being almost as strong as fear, people had waited to see what Ursula meant to do. Now that the supposed bomb had been put outside, they probably felt that they would be safer inside. Certainly, the majority resumed their seats. The few who still made their way to the door did so quietly. The real danger, that of the steep, curving stairs, was over.

Ursula finished her speech, but her peroration was spoilt. So much the would-be wrecker had accomplished. But her action, illogically enough, did more for the Cause than any words. 'Weren't you frightened, Miss Winfield?' several ladies asked admiringly, and gave in their names as new members. Their enthusiasm was hardly diminished by the explanation that the supposed bomb was merely a large firework. As a matter of fact, Ursula herself had not realised it at the moment. She had simply had no time to be afraid.

There was a good deal of delay after the meeting; the organiser had to interview the police, soothe the hall proprietor, discuss the insurance of the window. Presently she was free; she grasped the speaker's suitcase, and prepared to escort her to her night's abode. Ursula protested, but feebly; she had found that organisers were distressed if she attempted to carry her own luggage, however much better fitted she might be for the task. Fortunately, the Todds' shop was not far.

Here the organiser made her farewell, leaving her seated at a bountiful supper dispensed by the two Misses Todd. They seemed nice girls, Ursula thought; although her mother would hardly have considered them even on the level of 'impossible'. They had been at the meeting and were clearly overpowered with admiration, either at their guest's exploit or at her speech. Formerly such an attitude had made Ursula shy, but now she was used to it. 'Ma and Pa hoped that you would excuse their not sitting up,' the younger Miss Todd suddenly apologised. 'This seems late to them.'

'It seems late to me,' Ursula smiled. It was, indeed, nearly eleven. A rise was made.

There seemed very little space in the bedroom to which Ursula was escorted, but she was too busy assuring the girls that there was nothing more she could possibly require quite to take in the situation. After they had left her she looked around curiously. It was not that the room was so extraordinarily small, but it was so extraordinarily full! Never in her life had she seen so many objects crowded into an equal space. Her astonished gaze travelled over three brocaded armchairs, blocking every inch of passageway, a bed with two satin eiderdowns, a chest of drawers and a mantelpiece chock-a-block with vases, clocks, ornaments of all kinds, and finally a dressing table groaning under silver-backed brushes, bottles, pincushions, trays, ring-stands – there were even two jewelled rings! A sudden explanation struck her. The whole house had been denuded of its most valued properties to adorn the chamber of the guest.

She slept soundly – after removing both satin eiderdowns – and it was broad daylight when she woke. Her watch showed her nine o'clock. How unpardonable! For the Todd girls had told her that they breakfasted at seven, although they had certainly added that Miss Winfield must not dream of getting up so early. A large can of hot water stood outside her door. She had been called then and had not heard. She was in a very apologetic frame of mind when she hurried down half an hour later.

A stout, capable-looking woman, presumably her hostess, came into the hall and greeted her with reassuring geniality. 'I'm that glad you've 'ad a nice long sleep, my dear, if I may call you so. You must 'a been fair wore out. But I must see to your breakfast; it won't be more nor a minute. Jest you set down inside there an' make yourself at 'ome.' She bustled off, and an appetizing frizzle soon made itself heard.

Ursula complied with Mrs Todd's instruction and took a seat in the stiff little dining room. The table with its clean cloth was only laid for one. But Ursula imagined the earlier breakfast cleared away; it did not cross her mind that the Todd family had had it in the kitchen. Nor did she realise that her own meal was being personally prepared by her hostess, until the good lady suddenly appeared with a large tray and a beaming smile. Ursula jumped up again, conscience-stricken. 'Oh, you should have let me help.'

'No, no, my dear, you set down.' Mrs Todd put the tray on the table and almost pressed Ursula back into a chair. The teapot and toast were deftly transferred. 'You do your work and I'll do mine' – a tempting plate of eggs and bacon revealed itself – 'then we'll both be easy like.'

Only after her guest's every want was satisfied would Mrs Todd consent to sit down. 'Mostly we do 'ave a gell,' she related cheerfully, if a trifle breathlessly; 'for the young ladies is set on it, though I tells 'em that for every 'ands turn o' work a gell does, I does two in gettin' 'er to do it. But the young ladies don't think it looks well for me to be going to the door. "People will look down on you, Ma," they sez. "If people looks down on me for opening my own 'ouse door to 'em, they can stop away," sez I. However, for the sake o' peace an' quiet, I gives in. And them gells mostly don't stop long – that's one mercy. In between times I can 'ave a bit o' comfort and my kitchen to myself.'

Ursula was smiling at the new aspect of the servant difficulty. She felt curiously attracted by this sensible old body. 'I have sometimes thought that I should like to do without servants too. Only not in town; everything gets so dirty.'

'Yes, other folk's smuts are a discouragement,' Mrs Todd assented. 'Some day I 'opes to live in the country, when we makes over the business to our boy Frank. A nice little cottage is what I've always wanted, and a garden with cabbages an' 'olly'ocks and a – But there, the young ladies don't like me to speak o' that,' Mrs Todd broke off mysteriously.

'Oh, do tell me.' Ursula really felt curious. There had been such a tender, wistful look in the old woman's eyes.

'Well, then it's a pig.' A note of defiance was in her voice. 'All my life I've 'ankered after a pig. Maybe it's because in the business I've 'ad such a deal to do with lard an' taller. A pig's such a comfortable creature, companionable when alive, an' every bit of him of use when dead. But the young ladies thinks pigs is vulgar.'

'My mother thought suffrage was vulgar, but she has got used to my working at it. I expect your daughters would get used to your pig.' Ursula laughed at this strange bond of union, and Mrs Todd, who evidently possessed a sense of humour, chimed in with a fat chuckle. 'But bacon, even from your own pig, could not be better than this!'

The hostess beamed. 'That's what Mr Todd sez, "Give me one o' mother's rashers an' I'll die 'appy". Certainly what we 'ad at that grand Lunnon hotel 'e took me to weren't fit to set before a dog and that's a fact. But you'll 'ave a mite more, won't you, my dear? You needs plenty o' vittles to keep up your strength with all this travelling round an' speechifying – more especial if you often 'ave sich goings on as last night. I 'eard all about it from the young ladies; they couldn't say too much about you. That's what I likes, a bit o' courage. I often thinks that courage should 'ead the commandments, for you can't keep none of 'em without it.' Mrs Todd bore away her guest's empty plate.

What a delightful old person. As Ursula sat awaiting the promised second helping, her eyes wandered idly round the room. A large framed photograph of a wedding group caught her attention. Wasn't it hideous? She supposed from the dresses that it must date from the eighties – probably it was the Todds themselves. Suddenly something about the bridegroom struck her as curiously familiar – the attitude – the set of the head. She jumped up to examine more closely.

How extraordinary! Of course the bridegroom could not be Vernon, but it was astonishingly like Vernon – at least, like what she imagined Vernon must have been. Indeed, you had only to add a few wrinkles to the face, to take away a few wrinkles from the dreadful suit, and there stood Vernon. The bride? Here Ursula was uncertain. The girl in the photo was slight and even pretty; her face wore an expression of beatific happiness – it did not tally with her recollection of Vernon's wife. But then she had only seen Mrs Smee twice, and both times in a rage. 'This photograph is so extraordinarily like a great friend of mine,' she said aloud, as her hostess returned.

'It's my sister, Mrs Smee, on 'er wedding day.'

'Then it is the same! How curious! And Mrs Smee is your sister?' The fact of the relationship was almost as surprising as the identity of the photograph. She had not pictured Vernon's wife coming from so humble a class. Besides, it was almost impossible to conceive nice, sensible Mrs Todd being so closely related to that virago.

Fortunately Mrs Todd misunderstood the surprise. 'Yes, you see I was the top of a long family, and Charlotte the tail, so there was a deal o' difference in our ages. You may say I've been more like 'er mother than 'er sister. And you're a great friend o' Charlotte's, are you, dear? Well, now, ain't that nice? I don't think she's 'appened to speak o' you.' Mrs Todd, although increasingly cordial, was clearly puzzled.

'Oh, no, I hardly know Mrs Smee. I have only seen her once or twice. It is Professor Smee who is my friend. We meet very often. I used to work in his laboratory.' Ursula was intentionally stressing her acquaintance with Vernon in order to lead the conversation away from his wife. It would be dreadful if dear Mrs Todd guessed her true feelings towards her sister.

'Yes, I know as 'ow 'ee 'as lady students.' There was no diminution in Mrs Todd's friendliness, but her words were a trifle absent; a keen observer might have noticed a slightly worried look on her kindly face. She settled herself in a chair, this time with a certain air of permanence, and, producing a large, half-finished grey sock, began to knit. 'I think I've 'eard of you then, my dear, though not by name. My sister was staying 'ere a week or two back. You're the young lady, ain't you, who is going on a sort of excursion party like with 'Im at Christmas?'

'Yes.' Ursula looked surprised at this knowledge of her plans. But, of course, it was natural that Vernon had told his wife of the arrangement, and she, no doubt, had mentioned it to her sister. As a matter of fact Vernon had not told his wife; Charlotte had discovered it by chance, and the resultant row had eclipsed all previous ones. 'Professor Smee and I have both been invited by some mutual friends to go with them to Switzerland for two or three weeks.'

'Yes, that was it.' Ursula's tone had been a little stiff, but Mrs Todd did not appear to have noticed it. She was still knitting placidly. 'I dessay you needs an 'oliday after all your 'ard work – and 'Im too, after 'is.'

'Yes, we do.' Ursula's face lit up as she spoke. She was really looking forward to this trip immensely. It would be such a relief to get away from the English atmosphere of work and mud into the bright Swiss sunshine. She was longing 'to try her foot at skiing,' as she had told Vernon. And the jolly talks they were going to have together! 'I think we shall enjoy it tremendously.'

'I'm glad o' that, my dear.' There was a pause. Then Mrs Todd's equable, cheerful voice went on. 'But don't it seem a pity rather to get your enjoyment by making anyone as un'appy as you're making Charlotte?'

'What do you mean?' Ursula flushed violently. She would have been furious with anyone else, but it was difficult to be furious with Mrs Todd. 'I am not doing anything to make your sister unhappy. Of what does she accuse me?'

'Oh, my dear, she don't accuse you of nothing.' Mrs Todd was still knitting imperturbably. 'She just sez 'er 'usband's in love with you.'

'How dare she!' Ursula choked.

'Well, ain't 'ee? It's nothing so surprising. You're very 'andsome, my dear. And I'm not saying you're in love with 'im; I can see pretty clear you ain't. If you was, it would seem more respectable to me.'

'I don't understand you.' Ursula stared, surprised out of her anger.

'It seems such a waste like to embitter an 'ome an' make Charlotte so un'appy jest to be friends with a man. Leastways that's 'ow I sees it.'

'But it is entirely your sister's fault for being so unhappy when there is nothing on earth to be unhappy about!' Ursula retorted indignantly. Why was she arguing with this old woman, the girl wondered; she ought simply to walk out of the room. But there seemed to be something constraining in Mrs Todd's genial passivity, in the regular click of her knitting needles. 'In any case,' she went on triumphantly, 'my friendship gives *Professor* Smee a great deal of happiness.'

'Does it now? Are you sure, dearie?' Mrs Todd was still entirely unprovocative and unprovoked. 'I ain't seen Charlotte's 'usband just lately, but when I did, 'ee didn't look to me so 'appy. I thought 'ee looked worried like an' a lot older. Seems to me there can't be much satisfaction for a man in being friends with the woman 'ee's in love with.'

Mrs Todd paused, presumably for a reply, but none came. A horrible conviction was forcing itself upon Ursula. Yes, Vernon had been looking worried and ill of late. He had admitted himself that he was sleeping abominably. Could their friendship be to blame? Suddenly Mrs Todd spoke again and in an altered tone; for the first time the imperturbability had gone; even the knitting stopped.

'But it ain't the friendship being bad for 'Im that I'm thinking about!' Her voice shook. 'It's my sister, my little Charlotte – for she'll allus be that to me. When she was 'ere she spent 'alf 'er time crying – crying becos o' you. You've taken away all the 'appiness of 'er life – an' that weren't over much.'

'And do you think my life has so much happiness?' Ursula's bitterness showed itself in her voice. This woman wanted her to give up her Swiss holiday, the one thing in the world to which she was looking forward. She wanted her to give up her friendship with Vernon – and now for the first time she realised what a solace, a pleasure, this friendship had been. She wouldn't do it; she couldn't. She had sacrificed too much already. 'Life isn't such a frightfully cheerful business for any of us, Mrs Todd.'

Mrs Todd was looking at her compassionately. 'Ain't it, dearie?' she said, and the inflection was tender. 'An' I was thinking of your life as brimming over with good things; it shows 'ow little any of us knows of the other. But leastways you 'aven't 'ad poor Charlotte's trouble – bearing five little 'uns to 'ave 'em all dead.'

'What?' Ursula gripped the table. The calm words were overwhelming, incredible. The possibility of the Smees having had children had never occurred to her. Childless marriages were so common in her mother's set. 'Did you say – did you mean – the Professor and Mrs Smee – ' She broke off, speechless.

Mrs Todd entered into details without exaggeration or emphasis. The babies had only lived a few hours or days. 'Charlotte weren't made right to bear 'em,' she explained simply. With each one the doctor had said that she might not live through another such experience. 'You've maybe noticed a little scar on my sister's lower lip,' Mrs Todd observed. 'That was where she bit it through the last time to keep 'erself from screaming.'

'But it is horrible! How could Professor Smee? How could he?' Ursula's voice was strangled.

'Well, my dear, I don't know. In my experience such things is mostly six o' one an' 'alf a dozen of the other. But maybe I oughtn't to be speaking to you like this,' she apologised, 'only in these days the gells seems to know more nor their mothers. And I just wanted to make you understand about poor Charlotte – how it's extry lonely like for 'er, if 'er man's took away.'

'But I haven't taken him away.' In spite of Ursula's new pity, she could not let this accusation pass; it was too monstrous. 'Why, I only see Professor Smee about once a week.'

'That's once too often. An' it ain't the amount you sees 'Im, my dear, that 'is wife minds, but 'is thinking of you all the time. I know what you are going to say, that you can't 'elp 'is thoughts; but you just take an old woman's advice and try. Out o' sight is a wunnerful long way towards out o' mind. Just put yourself in my poor sister's place, though for that matter it ain't your charity I'm asking of you, but simple justice, which is a lot the 'arder to give. For, a'ter all, you must remember 'ee's Charlotte's 'usband, dearie, not yours, an' the father o' Charlotte's children. Menfolk is born silly, but that's why we women 'as got to stand up for each other. Ain't that what suffrage mostly means?'

'Yes, that is what suffrage mostly means,' Ursula agreed slowly.

CHAPTER NINETEEN

Mrs Todd's dictum as to advice making folks do the opposite proved itself false for once. Ursula did give up her friendship with Vernon Smee, although it was feeling rather than reason that constrained her. Mrs Todd's arguments had left her unconvinced, but the account of the five dead babies, each the outcome of so much suffering, filled her with an immense pity for the mother, and an anger that was almost repulsion against the father. Mrs Todd in her mellowed wisdom might consider these useless births to have been due to 'six o' one an' half a dozen of the other,' but Ursula's youth and suffragette training unswervingly put all the blame for them upon the man. It was horrible of Vernon, she felt indignantly. Whatever his wife might now be like, the least he could do in reparation was to devote himself to her.

The break would have been more difficult, it might never even have been achieved, had not Ursula, on her return to Clement's Inn, been asked to join Mary Blake in 'taking charge of Wales'. This meant becoming a paid organiser, and Ursula was glad of it, for a regular post would give a greater definition to her life; while the salary, the idea of which troubled her at first, could, after all, be returned as a donation to the fund. Her headquarters would now be Cardiff, she was instructed, and she was to start on the new work at once. That evening, when Vernon Smee called at the flat, he found Ursula busily packing her few books and pictures. 'There will be a frightful lot to do down there,' she told him. 'I don't suppose I shall have a moment for writing letters.'

Vernon stared. He was already dismayed to find that Ursula was leaving London, but this suggestion of not hearing from her, after their almost daily correspondence, was incredible. Even at that moment Ursula's last letter was, as always, in his inner breast pocket. 'You are not implying that you won't have time to write to *me*!' he said with a laugh that was a trifle forced.

'Yes, that is what I do mean.' Ursula felt guilty, not at her decision, but at her excuse for it. It was not quite truthful. But how could she help it? One could not tell a man to his face that one thought him wrong to have had children. 'You see when I was a speaker, letter-writing was a change,' she went on hurriedly. 'It filled up the time on those interminable railway journeys. That is why you had such screeds inflicted on you! But now I shall be in an office writing letters all day long. I shall be sick to death of the mere sight of pens and paper!'

He disregarded the elaborate explanation. 'Ursula, what have I done? Why are you treating me like this?'

'I am not treating you like anything, but you don't want to treat me to writer's cramp!' She laughed nervously. Why wouldn't he let her pass it off as a jest? He was making it very difficult. Suddenly her native honesty asserted itself.

'No, there is another reason, but I can't tell it to you.' She blushed.

'Ursula!' His heart was beating. An idea had suggested itself, a rapturous idea. Had she found out that she cared for him? Was that the reason for her strange behaviour? 'Ursula,' he repeated passionately, and took her hand.

The idea was shortlived, for Ursula snatched away her hand. A sudden vision had flashed before her of the five little dead babies – that poor woman's babies and his. 'Don't. I don't like it. I – you are not to.' She blushed more deeply than before, but this time with anger.

A second illumination came to poor Vernon, even more erroneous than the first. Of course that was the explanation! She had made it up with Balestier. Doubtless she had promised her lover to abstain from militancy. Perhaps that was why she was going to Cardiff, to be out of the way of temptation. And now that she had Balestier, she did not want a mere friend! Well, she might have let him down more gently. To write to a man every day, and then – It was rather heartless. But she had always been rather heartless. He tried to laugh. 'It shall not happen again. I now understand the position. And I certainly don't want to give you writer's cramp. I shall not expect to hear from you. Good luck, then, and goodbye.'

'Goodbye.' Perhaps Ursula felt that she must seem a little heartless. She certainly felt that she was going to be very lonely. Had Vernon tried to take her hand again, she might not have pulled it away. But he was already opening the door. 'Goodbye,' she repeated. He did not hear the quiver in her voice.

Ursula had no sooner reached Cardiff than the suffrage world was struck by a bombshell, which dissipated not only her regret for the lost friendship, but every personal feeling whatsoever. This was the proposed Manhood Suffrage Bill, with its proposal to enfranchise millions more men who were not asking for the Vote, while passing over the women, who were sacrificing everything to win it. Such an idea not unnaturally aroused every suffragist in the kingdom to fury. It was no comfort to be told that a Women's Suffrage amendment could be added. What chance, the leaders pertinently asked, would a non-party amendment have when tacked on to a Government measure? No, Manhood Suffrage was an insult, a trick devised to wreck the Conciliation Bill. The Government itself had broken the truce.

A protest demonstration was called for November 21st, but, instead of being encouraged to volunteer, Ursula found she was now forbidden. An organiser could not be spared, the Leader wrote. After further correspondence, a reluctant and qualified consent was obtained. Either she or Miss Blake might volunteer, she was told, but in no case both of them. The one who took part in the demonstration must resign, at least temporarily, her post as paid organiser. 'Of course it would be idiotic for us both to leave the work here just as it is starting so well,' Ursula acquiesced as she discussed the matter with her friend. 'So I shall go.'

'No, I shall go.' Mary Blake, in her gentle way, was as determined as Ursula. 'You will be of much more use here, dear. Any fool can be in prison.'

Ursula could not deny her greater competence, but she

would not submit. Each was determined to take upon herself the greater sacrifice. 'I am stronger than you,' she urged, 'and better able to stand being knocked about. Besides, suppose they hunger strike. You have been through it once. Now it is my turn.'

Mary did not think that a hunger strike would be necessary. It had been used as a protest because suffragettes were not treated as political prisoners. Rule 243a had now improved matters. Though, of course, one could never be sure, she admitted. But the only effect of the possibility was to make her the more decided. At last the girls agreed to draw lots. Mary won – and sent in her name.

Fortunately Ursula's anxiety proved needless. The demonstration on this occasion took the form of organised window-breaking. In consequence the women were arrested and not manhandled. In prison, under the recent rule, they were accorded most of the rights to which they considered themselves entitled. But Mary never even got as far as prison. An unknown sympathiser in Court paid her fine. Two days later she was back at Cardiff, enraged and humiliated. 'The penalty of beauty,' Ursula laughed at her.

Ursula was naturally overjoyed at her friend's return, although she could sympathise with the discomfiture. Yes, it was very sweet to have Mary, Mary with her great beauty both of face and soul. And yet somehow Mary's presence did not keep Ursula from being horribly lonely. The ache for Tony was always there, dulled by time, but like an old wound ready to start into pain at any unlucky touch. And, in addition, she missed Vernon even more than she had expected; she missed the daily letters, the weekly talks. Dear Mary might have many virtues, but she had no conversation. Indeed, Mary's whole friendship seemed by comparison curiously insipid. No doubt this was due to Vernon being an unusually brilliant person. Ursula would not admit that the difference in sex could have been responsible for any of the previous piquancy.

But despite the shortcomings of Mary's society, Ursula found herself still more lonely without it. Early the following March another great demonstration was announced. Again an unwilling acquiescence for one volunteer was wrung from headquarters, and again the girls drew lots, for Ursula protested even more vehemently than before that it was now her turn, while Mary stubbornly urged her right to wipe out the former failure. Apparently chance favoured Mary, for once more she won. This time there was no question of the fine being paid, for no fine was allowed. In an access of thoroughness Mary had broken windows to the tune of a hundred and ninety-eight pounds. As she read the charge, Ursula was amazed. How could gentle Mary have managed it? Once she had found her friend almost in tears because there was a mosquito on the wall and she could not bring herself to flick it. A hundred and ninety-eight pounds of glass. What a crash!

In view of the damage, Mary's sentence of six months did not seem preposterous. But why, because the sentences were longer, should Mary and all the suffrage prisoners be deprived of the privileges accorded under Rule 243a? There was a deputation to the Home Secretary, petitions, remonstrances – in vain. The women waited a month. Then came what Ursula had dreaded. At first those outside did not know. Then, one by one, the women began to come out. They had gained their point – but at what a cost!

It was while Mary was in prison that Ursula was distractedly summoned to the Crewe by-election. It was difficult to leave her own work in Wales, but she felt that she ought to go. None of the chief figures in the WSPU could be present. One was in hiding; the others were all too ill after their hunger strike. Not that Ursula imagined she could replace them. It was impossible for anyone to do that!

But in the WSPU they had a trick of doing the impossible. For the Leader herself could not have done better than Ursula and the two other girls who were running the campaign. As a start they captured the best committee rooms in the town. They held meetings at every hour of the day and almost of the night. They paraded the streets, followed by crowds of adoring factory women and bands of singing children. The growing rage of the Liberal agent testified to their success.

On the evening before the poll, the three girls held an immense open-air meeting on Catholic Bank. A hostile Liberal element was undoubtedly present, but it soon became submerged in the sea of sympathisers. Before Ursula's turn came, the interruptions had become negligible; indeed, their only effect was to arouse her fighting spirit and make her speak the better. She opened on a defiant, half-humorous note. 'Prison was now the only place for any respectable woman!' Presently her tone changed; it became, for her, unusually emotional, rather a risky procedure with such an audience. But, as she stood there, the flood of encircling faces had suddenly faded. She saw only Mary, Mary in prison, Mary undergoing perhaps at that very moment her daily torture. 'I have never hunger struck myself,' she cried, and her voice thrilled her hearers. 'I have never been forcibly fed. I might not have the courage. For it seems to me wonderful that human beings are capable of such endurance, that they can make the soul conquer the flesh. It is a great, a supreme thing for any country to have this martyr spirit in its midst – and we can only find place for it in prison. For whether you think that militant tactics are wise or foolish, whether you think they are right or wrong, there can be no two opinions as to the spirit that lies behind the tactics, the spirit that is a sacrifice of self, a following of the ideal, a seeking of those things that make for the ultimate ennobling of – '

Ursula stopped dead. There had been no sound, no interruption, although there now came a burst of clapping. Tony stood there! He was quite distinct, although at a considerable distance, for his height made him top the crowd. Besides, a street lamp was shining full on his face; it lit up his fair skin, his clear-cut features. And he was looking straight at her; he was looking as though he cared. She forgot the crowd, she forgot everything. For an instant their eyes met. Then Tony turned, and hurriedly pushed away.

The audience was still clapping. Few of them had heard the final preposition; they thought the speaker had reached the end of her sentence. Ursula looked round dazed. Where was she? What had she been saying? She had not the least idea. Her mind refused to work. She sat down.

Meanwhile, Tony, as he retreated down the nearest side street, was upbraiding himself for his carelessness. He had thought himself invisible in the gathering twilight, and had been too absorbed to notice the lighting of the lamps. His presence, in the first instance, had been entirely accidental. Sir Philip Stanley's place was within a motor-ride of Crewe, and the Conservative candidate happened to be an old College chum. It was to attend his friend's meeting that Tony had come that evening, but afterwards, as his way lay past Catholic Bank, curiosity had taken him into the suffragettes' crowd. There had been much talk at dinner of the militants and their disgraceful proceedings. 'All the same, I'm precious grateful to them,' his host had said with a laugh. 'Whatever rampages they may have been up to, this lot are awfully nice-looking girls, and as clever as they make them! The way they are turning votes is something wonderful.'

But, although, in consequence, Tony had ventured into the suffragettes' circle, he had not expected to find Ursula there. Chance gossip had recently mentioned in his hearing that she lived at Cardiff. Why then should she be at Crewe? Or had there been a faint, unacknowledged hope that he might see her? In either case it was a strange coincidence that, as he turned the corner, it should be she who was speaking from the suffrage wagonette. She was all in white, save for her tricolour badge, and as she stood there, a straight young figure against the fading sunset sky, something about her, something virginal and at the same time gallant, brought a sudden rush of the old feeling, a sudden catch in his throat. And how well she spoke, although he was almost too far off to hear properly. He pushed cautiously nearer. Oh, she was on the hunger strike tack – well, he utterly disapproved of it! But what she was saying did put the matter in rather a different light. At any rate her unselfish admiration for her friends was fine. So she herself had not been in prison again – he was glad, at least, of that. And she doubted her own courage to hunger strike. She needn't. If he was certain of anything, he was certain that when she did get to prison she would go through with it, the whole horrible, revolting business.

Then suddenly, startlingly, there came the recognition – Ursula's utter breakdown. Tony was certainly remorseful, but he was also stirred; above all, he was astonished. For during all this time he had been reproaching Ursula with her hardness. He had thought that she had never really cared for him. Resentment had almost dominated his pain. And now he found that she had cared for him, that she still cared for him, that the mere sight of him was sufficient to blot out her world. He was moved almost past endurance.

And yet he went away that evening and made no further effort to see her. What would be the use? For although she loved him and he loved her, although he began dimly to perceive her standpoint, he still was opposed to it. And Ursula understood his keeping away; indeed she was almost grateful for it. To meet him could only have brought fresh pain. Even had he been a sympathiser, a member of the Men's League, it is doubtful whether she would now have become engaged to him. For she felt that the Cause demanded the whole of her. She was consecrated to its service. Yet, although the momentary meeting had led to nothing tangible, it brought to each a hope. Some day when the Vote was won – so Ursula told herself. Some day, when the miserable business was chucked – so Tony phrased it. But their thoughts united on the shadowy 'some day'.

It almost seemed as though the Fates, like other ladies, must have had a weakness for Tony in the efforts they made to keep Ursula out of prison. The result of poor Mary Blake's hunger striking experiences necessitated many subsequent months in a nursing home, and during this time Ursula had perforce to stick to her more or less constitutional work in Wales. Often she wondered whether she were right to do so. Was it really cowardice that was keeping her, and not obedience to the Leader? But every week she expected to hear of Mary being well enough to return and take over the campaign. Then, at last, she would be free!

At the end of the year Mary did return, having by this time been nursed back into something like normal health; complete recovery was impossible. But although Ursula now came to London, and had leisure for prison, the Fates did not cease their protection. For the girl found a new policy in force at headquarters; a policy of mischief instead of martyrdom; or rather the martyrdom now only commenced when prison was reached, and that was postponed as long as possible. Do as much damage as you can without getting caught, the Leader openly proclaimed, although life in every shape or form was still to be held inviolate.

These new tactics left Ursula rather dubious. She considered, in a very literal sense, that it was dangerous to play with fire. At any rate she would not take such a responsibility upon herself, even in its modified form of dropping phosphorus into pillar boxes. It is true that she visited a golf green at an unfashionable hour and left behind her indelible marks of her suffragette presence. But although there was no danger to anyone in this proceeding, she was not sufficiently convinced of its utility to repeat it. Interrupting cabinet ministers was a less debatable action; she did it on several occasions, to their mental, and her extreme physical, discomposure. And once, on some public occasion, she contrived to thrust a petition into the carriage of astonished royalty itself!

But for the most part Ursula confined herself to constitutional work at the new office in Kingsway. Thus she remained at liberty and felt ashamed of it. 'The only way is Hollo-way,' ran a line in one of the suffrage ditties, and Ursula believed it true. 'The blood of the martyrs is the seed of the Church.' Had it not been the sufferings of the women in prison that had first drawn her into the movement, and that still kept her at fever heat? Recently these sufferings had been immensely increased by the 'Cat and Mouse' Act. 'The Prisoners' Temporary Discharge for Ill-health Act' was the official but unused title. Prisoners who had forced their release through a hunger strike were now automatically re-arrested after a few days. It was impossible to allow the women either to terminate their own sentences or to kill themselves, the authorities explained. What fools, Ursula felt passionately. Did they imagine that any human body could stand an indefinite number of hunger strikes alternating with being nursed back to health? In the end, these imbeciles in authority would be faced by the same problem as at the beginning – they must let the women go or they must let them die.

Perhaps the Fates got tired of their solicitude on Ursula's behalf, for in June she at last achieved imprisonment. But this, oddly enough, was not as a result of any militant action, it seemed rather in recognition of her constitutional labours. One day the office was 'raided', and all the chief workers arrested, Ursula among them. On the advice of the Leader, they gave a temporary undertaking not to take part in any violence or incitement, and the promise was afterwards renewed at the police court. This enabled them to remain on bail until the 'conspiracy' trial itself, which took place at the Old Bailey six weeks later. It lasted several days, and most of the accused spoke in their own defence. The jury were obviously moved, and recommended them strongly to mercy. Ursula's sentence was nine months in the third division – a queer sort of mercy, she felt. It seemed familiar to find herself in the reception cell at Holloway; the medical examination, the giving up of property, the signing for it in a book – it was all as before. Then she was taken to her cell, and that, too, was identical with the previous one. Only now a difference would begin. For this time Ursula meant to hunger strike. She was going to try and keep all knowledge of the fact from the authorities. 'If you get ill enough before they find out, they aren't so likely to forcibly feed you,' so her friends had told her, and the prospect of forcible feeding was the one thing that filled her with terror. To her dismay the wardress, when she brought in her reception meal, seemed to guess her intention. 'Now do be sensible and eat this up,' the woman said, not unkindly, as she set down the tin pot. 'You makes it so unpleasant for everyone if you starves yourself.'

Ursula waited until the wardress had gone. Then, getting up on to the table, she pushed aside one of the tiny sliding panes of the window and threw out the contents of the pot. The waste worried her; she hoped some stray cat might profit. Otherwise the small slab of tinned meat and the larger slab of bread had not been very alluring. A bell soon rang and the wardress came back. 'That's eight o'clock. You must put down your bed and make it,' she said, indicating the plank bedstead upright against the wall. If she guessed what had happened to the food, she made no comment.

It was with the next morning's breakfast that the trial began, which was increased by the obviously superior quality of the fare over the ordinary prison diet. But the mug of tea was the real temptation. Although Ursula had slept well, she had a headache, and tea was just what she needed. After all, drinking was not eating; why should it matter? She had the mug in her hand when suddenly realisation came to her that if this tea passed her lips, it would be failure. She would have betrayed her Cause. She tipped it out of the window.

The wardress now came in, and Ursula heard, to her surprise, that she was to be sent by train elsewhere. Two other women, presumably wardresses, and a man accompanied her in the taxi to St Pancras. In the train a carriage was reserved. Ursula asked more than once what her destination was, but her companions refused to answer. It was a useless reticence, for when, after travelling several hours, they got out, she saw the name of the station. Another long drive ended in another prison.

This prison compared badly with Holloway; at least with Holloway as improved and enlarged for its suffragette clientèle. Here the reception cell was dirty; the matron, with her hard features and rough manner, positively repellent. This woman immediately asked Ursula whether she meant to hunger strike. Ursula was prepared to forgo food, but not truth, so she kept a compromising silence. She was then told that she would lose all her privileges and was curtly ordered to strip. After a moment's amazement, she as curtly refused. Two wardresses were summoned and instructed to 'remove Number 251's clothes'.

The resistance Ursula made was merely technical; indeed, the appearance of the prison garments was in itself sufficient to account for a certain reluctance. Each article was stamped with a date; one petticoat bore an unmistakable 1878. Were the fleas contemporary, poor Ursula wondered.

After these preliminaries, she was taken to her cell. The doctor came and saw her, but did not stop long. Presently a meal was brought. The normal porridge and bread looked so unpalatable that it repelled rather than tempted, but the added mug of Bovril was horribly appetising. She must open the window quickly and throw it out. In any case to open the window was the first step, for the cell was appallingly close. But how was she to reach it? The table here was a fixed board let into the opposite wall. Perhaps she could manage by standing on the little triangular shelf above the rolled-up bedding in the corner. She hastily removed from it the regulation objects; brush, comb, drinking pot, slate, Bible, Prayer Book and letter box, and scrambled up. Eureka! She could just touch the window. If only the wardress did not come in, or look through the hateful spyhole! She began to push at the minute panes. These were much thicker than at Holloway and of ribbed glass, so they let in but little light. Not one moved; probably they were stiff from want of use. Indeed, the cell felt as though it had not been aired for years. It was only after she had struggled with each of the fourteen panes in turn, that it dawned upon her they were fixtures!

But this was monstrous. They had not the right to asphyxiate prisoners! When she had heard of her friends breaking cell windows, she had imagined they did it as a protest, not that it was their only method of getting fresh air. Well, she had better break some of these panes. But, after all, would it be wise? As she was hunger striking it might be better to limit herself to that. Anything else would complicate the issue. Besides, if she had to starve, it was of no great importance also being suffocated. Not, of course, that she would literally be suffocated; there were two obvious ventilators. But it was certainly horribly stuffy.

The Bovril still mocked her; indeed, the exertion of her fruitless effort made her long for it more than ever. She must get rid of it, if possible in such a way that the wardress would think it drunk. An ingenious paper funnel was constructed, reminiscent of chemistry days, and by its help she manœuvred the liquid down the ventilator. And now for a long draught of water – but the water pot was empty.

She rang the bell. After a long pause, a wardress came. No, she could not bring water, the woman replied snappily in answer to Ursula's request. Nor could Ursula go outside and fill her pot from the tap in the passage. She was not to leave her cell at all, even at 'slopping time', to empty her washing bowl. Milk would be given her, or Bovril, as much as she liked. Ursula did not know that this decree was illegal. She contented herself with asking whether she was also expected to wash in milk or Bovril!

Up till then Ursula had been drinking water freely, for the thirst strike had not yet become a suffragette practice. Now she realised that a thirst strike was forced upon her. And already her mouth was uncomfortably dry. It was going to be a good deal harder to be thirsty than hungry. Still, she could bear it. She could bear anything but forcible feeding – and she might have to bear that.

That night she slept badly. It worried her to have been taken from Holloway. She felt as though she were cut off from all support. Chiefly, however, what kept her awake was actual physical craving. Whenever she fell asleep it was to dream of wonderful meals spread out before her, and, more especially, of brimming jugs and glasses; then when she stretched out her hand to grasp them she woke. But the thought of giving in, of grasping, when awake, the real food and drink so plentifully supplied, never even crossed Ursula's mind. The suffragette hunger strike was based on the ground that it embarrassed the government and aroused sympathy in the country, but Ursula had long since ceased to reason. She simply felt herself suffering for the Cause; the more she suffered, the deeper grew this conviction. In some illogical way, the future happiness of women seemed to rest on her present unhappiness. A sense of exaltation supported her. Only a coward, a traitor, would yield.

The following night, hunger ceased to worry her, but the thirst was horrible. Her lips were like wood, and her tongue seemed to have grown too large for her mouth. She had a backache, too, as well as the headache, which had got steadily worse. And she was so cold; most of the time she was shivering. When the doctor came in the morning, he looked at her sharply. 'I don't believe she is drinking that milk,' he told the wardress.

'I don't know what she's doing with it then, sir.' The wardress was clearly aggrieved. 'They're that artful,' she grumbled.

The doctor approached Ursula. She started back and held out her hands to ward him off. 'You're not to touch me! You're not to do it! You can't without my consent.' She was trembling violently and her heart beat like a hammer. She thought that this was the preliminary to forcible feeding.

The doctor contented himself with feeling her pulse. Then he humanely withdrew and there was another blessed period of solitude. Presently the wardress returned accompanied by two others. 'You're to go to see the Governor, Number 251,' she informed Ursula. 'Follow me, and none of your tricks.'

Ursula was conducted by the gallery which ran along the face of the block and into which all the cell doors opened. There were four of these galleries, one above the other. Across a narrow street-like space was another similar wall, also with rows of cell doors giving upon galleries. This space between the two prison buildings had a glass roof, turning it into a sort of hall. Halfway up, wire netting was stretched across. This, Ursula already knew, was to break the fall if a prisoner jumped. Down below a number of women in prison clothes sat sewing. Their unnatural silence was the most noticeable thing about them.

The little party went down the whole length of the gallery. At the end was a door with a less aggressive lock, and without the usual sliding shutter and spy hole. Here the wardress stopped and knocked. A portly gentleman in a black morning coat was sitting writing at a desk. Almost as soon as Ursula got inside, he began a tirade against suffragettes in general and 'number 251' in particular. He was talking utter nonsense, Ursula told herself, but her head was aching too much to try and argue with him. Indeed, she found great difficulty in standing there at all; everything was swaying about in the most unaccountable fashion. At last he began to read something. A few words reached her ears with a certain distinctness '... persist in your refusal to take nourishment ... punishment cell for three days on bread and water.'

She gave a sudden laugh. It really was too delicious. For refusing all food and drink, she was threatened with being limited to bread and water! Then the floor began to go up and down to such an extent that she was obliged to concentrate on it her whole attention.

Although the sound made by 'Number 251' had been rather croaking, its nature was clearly recognisable. The

Governor flushed with anger. 'Possibly you will not find it so amusing as you imagine,' he said severely. 'Remove the prisoner.'

This time, instead of going along the gallery, Ursula found herself being taken down several flights of open iron stairs. They led to the floor of the hall where the women were sewing. She looked around eagerly, trying to see a familiar suffragette face. But these women all seemed to be ordinary prisoners; one had such a round, babyish countenance that Ursula felt a stab of pity. 'Come on now, Number 251; no loitering.' The wardress hurried her along a passage and down more steps, this time of stone. A door was unlocked.

Ursula had thought her other cell dark and stuffy; this one was darker and stuffier; her first impression, indeed, was of a cellar. Certainly there was a window, but so little light penetrated that it must have looked out into some sort of area: like the other cell window, it did not obviously open. Save for one seat without a back, and a fixed table, the place was utterly and blankly bare. 'This is the punishment cell that you thinks so funny,' the wardress said, taking her tone from the Governor.

At any rate, she would have no temptation here to break her strike, Ursula reflected. That was something to be grateful for. But her gratitude was premature. The door was suddenly unlocked and a can of water and half a loaf thrust in – the punishment diet of which the Governor had spoken. Suddenly, Ursula realised that he had been right; it was no laughing matter, it was a punishment, a most horrible one. The bread, she didn't want it; but the water – she must have the water! And why shouldn't she? Why must she condemn herself to thirst as well as starve? But then she had already gone on so long. If she could only resist, it would mean that it would all be over the sooner. The chance of forcible feeding would be less. She gave a sudden push with her foot and overturned the pot. The water spread in a pool on the stone floor.

The next moment she was kneeling beside it. She felt mad, mad with thirst. She put down her head, ready to lap from the dirty stones like a dog. But the water had all run away under the door. The check brought back her senses. What was she doing? She was disgracing the Cause. She dragged herself on to the seat, first pushing it against the wall to have a support for her back. But it was still too uncomfortable; she felt too ill. Almost without knowing it, she found herself lying on the floor.

When at eight o'clock the bed was brought in, Ursula found it little softer than the floor. Her back ached agonisingly. This night she did not sleep at all. The next morning, when she tried to get up, she fell. The wardress, who was in the cell, looked frightened and called another wardress. Later on, she came in with the doctor. There was a good deal of low-toned conversation. During it, Ursula lay shaking with terror; she expected to hear every moment that she was to be forcibly fed. Where should she find the strength to resist or even endure? However, it ended in her only being taken to the hospital.

The bed here was far more comfortable. The ward, too, was light and airy; otherwise the situation remained unchanged.

For Ursula still refused all nourishment. Different delicacies, grapes, beef tea, were thrust upon her. At last, tired of waving them away, she hid her face in her pillow. She had even got past wanting them. Her hard, swollen throat now seemed normal. A chaplain came and talked to her for a long time, but, had she wished to, she could not have followed him. The doctor came; he came again. Finally, after he had given his solemn assurance that she should not be forcibly fed, she allowed herself to be examined without resistance.

The doctor disappeared. A blank seemed to intervene. She must have fainted, Ursula realised. Then she suddenly heard herself talking, talking in such a queer, thick voice that at first she did not know whose it was. This frightened her. A suffragette must keep control over herself. Otherwise they might trick her into taking food, they might certify her as insane. With a great effort she managed to get herself in hand, to stop the babbling. But surely she could not go on like this very long. Soon she would die. She would die that the Cause might live.

It was getting dark when she again heard male voices. She opened her eyes, and saw a face she knew. Yes, it was the Governor. He was reading some paper aloud. 'The terms of your licence – you are discharged,' came explanatorily in the doctor's voice. He was holding a glass to her lips. And then – painfully – she drank.

CHAPTER TWENTY

Naturally, Ursula's discharge had only been under the 'Cat and Mouse Act'. In less than three weeks she was back in Holloway with the whole business to go through again. This time her thirst strike was deliberate from the start. It was harder even than before, although she would have said that was impossible. Fortunately, it was also briefer. On the third day a prolonged fainting attack alarmed the authorities. Once more she found herself free.

This time Ursula was so ill that she went straight to a small nursing home kept by suffragette sympathisers at Golders Green. A lady doctor, also a suffragette, examined her, and enjoined absolute rest for several months. The patient's heart was affected. Ursula suggested that this might rather be a reason for returning to prison than for keeping out of it. The doctor, torn between professional and suffrage consideration, looked harassed. However, it ended in Ursula's acquiescence. She felt too ill to make the necessary effort to go to prison and die.

After Ursula had been in the nursing home about a week, her mother came to see her. The Hibberts had just returned from Carlsbad, having taken the cure earlier than usual this year owing to the Colonel's indulgence in an inopportune attack of gout. 'Think of it, being torn from London in June! I am sure it is a sufficient ground for divorce,' Mrs Hibbert had laughingly complained. The news of her daughter's two imprisonments had reached her, dimmed by distance; certainly she had never realised the form they had taken. Thus she was utterly unprepared to find Ursula in bed, hollow-cheeked and grey. 'My dear child, what have you done to yourself? You look twenty years older.' She burst into tears.

'Don't cry, Mummy. You are so blooming, you might be twenty years younger. The average is all right. Perhaps I'll attain my heart's desire and have you mistaken for my daughter.' Ursula smiled wanly, and felt for her mother's hand.

The rare affectionate gesture and little pleasantry only increased Mrs Hibbert's woe. 'You have lost all your looks,' she moaned.

'I will live on the credit of yours.' Ursula's fictitious gaiety faded. With a weary gesture she pushed back the hair from her forehead; with a hand that was painfully transparent.

'You must have been hunger striking. How could you be so wicked!' Suddenly Mrs Hibbert noticed her daughter's intensified pallor. She dabbed her eyes carefully with a lace handkerchief – even grief did not make her unmindful of art – and opened a small parcel. 'I have brought you some guava jelly. Isn't it like a Christmas supplement? Nonsense, the doctor won't mind, real guava jelly can't hurt anyone.' She proceeded to administer it.

The jelly seemed to justify the praise, for after a spoonful or two Ursula did look less ghastly. 'Now, my dear,' Mrs Hibbert began firmly, 'we must have this out. What possible connection is there between starving yourself and getting the Vote, except that the one makes people quite sure that you are too silly for the other?'

Ursula raised herself in bed. The occasions were so rare on which her mother discarded the ostentatious fluffiness and revealed a certain intellect, that it gave the argument interest. She told herself that 'Mum' had more brains in her little finger than the Colonel in his whole body – and *he* had a vote! She was trying to generalise her thought into less disrespectful language, when a wave of fatigue again swept over her. 'I am too tired to talk,' she said faintly. 'But starving oneself does show that one is in earnest; that is the connection. Why has anyone ever died for anything?'

The last words were too much. Even the complexion was forgotten as Mrs Hibbert sobbed out, 'Yes, and that is how it will end. You will kill yourself.'

'Poor little Mum.' Ursula again found her mother's hand and squeezed it. There was a silence, as she racked her brains for something comforting to say. 'Can't you think of me as – as a soldier?' she began at last hesitatingly. 'Suppose you had a son in the army and there were a war.'

'Don't be ridiculous.' The remark had certainly checked Mrs Hibbert's grief, although not quite in the way that Ursula had intended. 'A soldier has to fight, but no one wants you to. Besides, he fights in a proper way; he doesn't go about breaking people's windows! Now, my dear, do for my sake stop all this silly business and go right away. Oh, yes, I know you are under arrest, but they'd be glad enough to have you leave the country. I am certain there would be no trouble and we could all be happy again. Germany, now? You used to be always raving about the laboratories there.'

Had Ursula wanted to carry out her mother's plan, she was in no fit state at present. However, she unhesitatingly refused. But Mrs Hibbert's distress caused a compromise to be effected. Ursula would not run away, but neither would she provoke arrest, at any rate, until she had quite recovered. 'I'll just "lie low and keep on sayin' nuffin',"' she told her mother, and with this poor Mrs Hibbert had to be content.

The period of quiescence was much longer than Ursula had imagined when she made the compact. The whole autumn and winter passed, and still the doctor would not pronounce her cured. She stopped on at Golders Green, for she liked the women of the nursing home, and there was nowhere else in particular to go. Besides, these people had got used to having policemen with studied, ponderous unconcern hanging around the house; other hosts might be less accommodating. Save for these policemen and an obvious plain clothes detective who occasionally followed her on her short walks, Ursula was left unmolested. Spring came, and at last the troublesome heart mended. And now, Ursula told herself, she must again play a fighting part.

The weekly afternoon meeting at this time was held at the Knightsbridge Hall. One Monday Ursula suddenly appeared on the platform. There were cries of 'A Mouse! A Mouse! Miss Winfield!' and enthusiasm enormous for the size of the hall.

When it had subsided, Ursula made a speech. It could hardly be called inciting, yet nothing could have stirred her hearers more than this simple account of prison experience. 'Probably today I shall again be arrested,' she said at the end amid a deep hush. 'I do not know this time how it will end. But I do know that whatever happens to me, perhaps a little because of what happens to me, the Cause will go on. I do know that over our dead bodies, women will one day reach their goal.' She stepped off the platform. A male hand with a dark blue cuff grasped her shoulder.

Doubtless by now the harassed authorities were getting a little tired of their 'cat' rôle. They had found that it did not frighten the women from militancy as they had hoped, and it was distinctly unpopular in the country. Even anti-suffragists criticised the repeated hauling back of women to prison; it seemed unsportsmanlike, out of keeping with the British character. But if the women were not to be hauled back, then they must not be allowed to go. For it was impossible to have sentences of many months transformed into sentences of a few days. Forcible feeding must recommence.

Thus the fate that Ursula most dreaded overtook her. It equalled her anticipations. She never liked to speak of that time afterwards. It was best shrouded, so disgusting was it, so horrible. At first the process took place twice a day; after she had lost twenty-five pounds in weight, it was increased to three times. Still the loss in weight continued, although less rapidly. But getting so thin that her bones protruded was the least part. Was it conceivable that she could live through nine months of this, Ursula speculated tremblingly. She was terrified – not by death but by life.

If Ursula was suffering in prison, her mother was suffering, although perhaps hardly to a comparable extent, outside. At first Mrs Hibbert in her ignorance had been relieved at hearing of the forcible feeding. Now her silly girl would not be able to starve herself. Then one day in a railway carriage she saw a copy of *Votes* – it was extraordinary how the paper managed to penetrate – even into the first class. The picture on the cover attracted her horrified gaze. 'What's that filthy rag?' the Colonel thundered and threw it out of the window. Mrs Hibbert made no remark. She left her husband at the Club – and bought another copy.

That was the end of any peace of mind for poor little Mrs Hibbert. Had she been able to talk about Ursula, she might have found it easier. But the Colonel would not allow his stepdaughter's name to be mentioned. Doubtless he would equally have resented any variation from the usual social round of entertaining and being entertained, but indeed it never occurred to Mrs Hibbert to make it. Superficially, at least, it was with even more than her usual gaiety that Ursula's mother laughed and flirted through this London season.

It was at the last big dance of the season that the vivacious little lady ran across Tony Balestier. He was looking bigger than ever, she thought admiringly, and so sunburnt that a sharp hat-line marked his forehead. 'Where have you been hiding yourself?' she greeted him. 'I haven't seen you for centuries!'

'I only landed last night. My Chief has been globe-trotting again, West Indies this time, so, of course, I've had to globe-trot after him.' There was a barely perceptible pause as Balestier wondered whether he must ask for a dance. He would hear about Ursula, perhaps, but did he want to hear about Ursula? And Mrs Hibbert was so very much made up tonight, so very *décolletée*; he hadn't remembered her being so outrageous; it wasn't a style he appreciated. However, as he heard her saying to some man when he met her, that she hadn't the 'teeniest weeniest extra left', there wasn't much risk in being polite. 'I suppose I am too late for a dance?'

'You are, but I'll cut one for you.' She smiled at him.

The favour made him feel less anxious for it than ever. When the time came, she was flirting so obviously with her last partner that he had thoughts of tiptoeing away and leaving them undisturbed. However, she had seen him. 'Let's sit it out in the conservatory,' she said sweetly. 'We shall be alone there.'

So he was expected to go on in the same style. Well, he wouldn't, not, at any rate, with Ursula's mother. He sat stiffly in rather a disgusted silence.

'I am so miserable about her, Tony. There is no one else I can talk to. They are killing her.'

'What? Is she in prison now? Hunger striking?' The unexpectedness of the remark had taken him off his guard. His tone was of shocked horror. Even the absence of a name was revealing.

Mrs Hibbert told the story with tears. But she was not too overcome to glance at her companion curiously. She had confided in Ursula's former fiancé merely to relieve her own feelings. It was incredible that he, that any young man, should care for a girl to whom he was not even engaged after such a separation. Yet his voice had sounded very queer. Was it possible that Tony Balestier was that phenomenon she had hitherto considered confined to fiction – a constant lover?

'Can't you – can't anyone persuade her to eat?'

'Persuade her, when she thinks it's her duty to starve! You know what Ursula is.' Indeed he did, poor Tony felt ruefully. 'You might as well try and persuade the Albert Memorial!' An aggrieved consciousness of all that her daughter had thrown away came over Mrs Hibbert. 'Ursula is an idiot,' she said almost viciously. Suddenly her eyes again filled. 'But she is rather a splendid idiot!'

Meanwhile Ursula, in entire ignorance of this interview, was carrying on her life in Holloway. One day she told the doctor that the torments of the damned now possessed for her no terrors. He looked incredulously shocked, but the words were hardly an exaggeration. Apart from the actual period of feeding, she was continuously conscious of pain from head to foot. But it was the suffering of her comrades, and not her own, that formed the greatest trial. Three times a day she had to listen to the shrieks coming from the neighbouring cells. She would stuff her ears, roll her head in her gown; nothing would keep out the sound. Even before her own cell door opened, she would be white and trembling with helpless sympathy.

It might have been out of unsuspected pity; more probably it was to check communication between the suffragettes, that, in July, Ursula was moved to another cell. Here she heard nothing, saw nothing, except the two doctors and the wardresses. Although she dreaded the sight of these people more than she had ever dreaded anything in her life before, she bore them no personal grudge. Rather she pitied them for the hateful task they had to perform. No wonder they were surly with her, she told herself, with a rather unusual stretch of sympathy. At first they had also been very rough; now that one of her teeth had been broken, it was no longer so difficult for them to prise open her mouth. And she had grown so weak; she could make little more than a show of resistance. One of the doctors would still sometimes argue with her, trying to point out the folly of her ways. But, as Ursula had told her mother, she was too tired for argument, too tired for thought. She could only cling blindly to the example of the Leader. Hers was the stubborn faith of exhaustion and despair.

But a few days later, despite her condition, Ursula began to be conscious of some curious change in the prison atmosphere. The wardresses, and still more the doctors, seemed to be excited, preoccupied. One pleasant form their altered attitude assumed was a lessening of the immense amount of fluid they had hitherto insisted on administering. 'I can't spare the time,' one doctor said to the other. 'Next week I expect – ' the rest was inaudible. As a matter of fact, from the medical point of view the decrease was a benefit, for the lesser amount gave a better result. Ursula wondered if her friends could be right who had told her that overfeeding was used on the principle of the mediaeval torture.

It was the next day that Ursula heard some wardresses talking outside her cell in high, agitated tones. 'Troops' – 'declaration of war' – came distinctly to her ears. 'Is there actual fighting in Ireland?' she asked, as the women came in.

'Ireland? No, it's – ' the woman broke off tantalisingly. 'You don't deserve to hear nothing, giving us all this trouble, at such a time too,' she grumbled.

Well, whatever it was, it could not concern her much, Ursula felt. Probably there was more trouble in the Balkans. The wardresses were already preparing the horrible implements. She must nerve herself for the ordeal.

After it was over, and Ursula was, as usual, lying faint and exhausted, a distant sound of cheering reached her. She thought at first it was a delusion; in these days the borderline between the real world and the imaginary was very indistinct. Then it occurred to her that it might be suffragettes. She pulled herself together to listen. There was a band – people singing – what was it? Oh yes, that new music-hall tune; wasn't it called 'Tipperary' or some such name? Suffragettes wouldn't be singing that. It could not be anything of importance.

That evening the third feeding was omitted. As she was not prepared for her good fortune, this only meant an almost unbearable prolongation of the period of suspense. The next morning, instead of the usual group of doctors and wardresses with their dreaded paraphernalia, the Governor appeared. He read out her discharge. 'For how long?' Ursula asked wearily. She did not want to be discharged. Could they not kill her now and have done with it?

The Governor told her that it was a complete discharge. Ursula would have been amazed, but she was too weak even for amazement. The Governor went on pompously. 'Probably it is imagined that the gravity of the situation will induce some return of sanity, even among the members of your Union.'

His taunt went disregarded. 'The gravity of the situation?' Ursula repeated, puzzled.

'The situation due to the war.'

'What war?'

The Governor looked amused. The prisoner was, after all, an educated woman and living in London. It seemed so incredible that she should know nothing of the world-shaking events of the last few days. 'Are you not aware that we have declared war?'

'On whom? Russia?' Even Ursula's inertia of weakness was shaken.

'Russia! Of course not. She is our ally. On Germany.' Details followed. It would be the greatest war in history. The country was responding splendidly. There were long queues at the recruiting stations. The first contingent was believed to be already in France.

Ursula said something. The Governor was not quite sure if he had heard aright. Or was the prisoner wandering? He gave place to a doctor. The words had been, 'But won't they break windows?'

CHAPTER TWENTY-ONE

It was three months later. Ursula was lying on the sofa in her mother's boudoir, if, indeed, that formerly dainty apartment could now be dignified by such a name. In lieu of the Dresden china ornaments, the mantelpiece was piled with rolls of coarse khaki knitting, while male flannel undergarments in various stages of completion littered the tables and stood stacked in bundles against the walls. Here, every afternoon, fashionable ladies met and plied slow needles and quick tongues. The results had driven Mrs Hibbert to add the services of two professional needlewomen. 'Men may be willing to die for King and Country, but not in shirts doing up at the back with two left arms,' she had explained gaily.

These working parties by no means limited little Mrs Hibbert's war activity. When Ursula had arrived from the nursing home that morning, she was amazed to find that her mother was already out. 'Mrs Hibbert leaves the house at six o'clock a.m. for the canteen, miss,' Jenkinson had informed her. 'We all thinks it very good of her.' The war seemed to have shaken even his impeccable aloofness.

Ursula was still meditating on this first human remark that she had ever heard emanating from a butler, when a familiar rustle of silken skirts caught her ear. But whatever Mrs Hibbert's underwear might be, her visible costume was severely tailor-made and also fashionably unfashionable. 'Mammykin!' Ursula had jumped to her feet.

'Now, don't get up, darling.' Mrs Hibbert pressed her daughter back on the sofa. 'Oh, yes, I know that you are a Hercules, but you don't look it.' Indeed, Ursula's appearance was still fragile, although she was pronounced cured. 'I'll take this comfy chair beside you.' A pile of gaily-patterned hospital bags that the chair had been harbouring was unceremoniously tipped on to the floor. 'Now tell me things.'

'But I want to hear things. Jenkinson says that you go to a canteen every morning at break of day. What do you do there? Wash plates! Mummy! Aren't you absolutely worn out? You'll ruin your hands!'

Mrs Hibbert rippled with laughter. 'Isn't this a delicious reversal of our usual rôles? Now I shall start preaching to you about the sanctity of work with a big W. Why do I do it? My dear child, I must do my bit!' The little lady suddenly grew grave. 'There is nothing else left to do. All my beloved boys have been killed – all the nicest ones, anyway. I can't believe it. It seems so impossible. And there is your stepfather back in the army and moving heaven and earth to get sent out too. Not that he'd be the faintest use, but the War Office is such a fool, one can't count on its not sending him. Meanwhile London is a desert. No dinners, no dances, no evening frocks, no anything. Life has just crumpled up!'

'Poor Mum.' Although Ursula sympathised, she had been secretly amused at her mother's wifely candour. 'However, if the Colonel weren't so taken up about the war, he might not have relented towards me,' she suggested consolingly.

'Yes, that is my only comfort, all your horrid suffragette business coming to an end – no, we won't discuss it,' Mrs Hibbert broke off hurriedly, seeing argument in her daughter's face. 'It is no use.'

'No, it does not seem of much use.' Ursula lapsed into obedient silence. It was strange how the Cause, for which she had given up everything, had been swallowed up in this vast upheaval. The very fact of her presence here at Lowndes Square proved it. Not that the Colonel had exactly forgiven her – she could hardly have brought herself to accept forgiveness – he seemed rather to have entirely forgotten her crime. And his attitude was that of the country at large. The iniquity of the Hun had blotted out the iniquity of the suffragette. As far as Ursula was concerned, the war had only increased her sense of the importance of Women's Suffrage. To what chaos the world had been reduced by this government by men alone! If women did not do better, at least they could never do worse.

But despite this feeling, Ursula sincerely agreed with her mother that it was useless talking on the question. For the time being, suffrage had better be dropped. And, unlike most suffragettes, she found herself unable to transfer her activity to war work. Now that everyone approved of militancy, she found herself disapproving. Was she fated always to be in a minority? The fact that human beings were purposely mangling one another haunted her with a sick horror night and day. 'Thou shalt not kill' rang in her ears accusingly. Then came the report of Englishmen outnumbered one to eight, fighting as they gave ground, fighting mile after mile, fighting doggedly. And these were the gilded youths of her mother's whom she had always so despised – well, if they had not known how to live, at least they knew how to die. The German atrocities in Belgium began to leak through; they numbed her almost into acquiescence. The world had gone mad, she told herself despairingly. Then the letter came from Mrs Hibbert asking her to come home. Little Mum's wanting her seemed the one healthy reality in a phantasmagoria of horror.

Meanwhile, Mrs Hibbert, who was entirely ignorant of her daughter's attitude on the great subject, was chatting pleasantly. She was full of talk about the canteen. 'Mrs Smee –' she began. 'Did I tell you that Mrs Smee was running our canteen?'

'Not Professor Smee's wife?' Ursula was surprised into attention. 'Oh, Mum, how awful!'

'It isn't awful in the least.' Mrs Hibbert bristled. 'Of course Mrs Smee isn't exactly Vere de Vere – and I'm thankful for it! All the dear Tommies say that ours is the best canteen in London, and it is entirely due to Mrs Smee. She goes down to Billingsgate and those places and buys the food herself every morning. The woman is a genius, my dear.'

'A genius!' Ursula was almost speechless with amazement.

'Yes, but she is terribly severe. I come off pretty well, for she has found out that I am not such a fool as most of the others. She almost told me so.' Mrs Hibbert looked gratified.

Ursula gave a sudden laugh. It was a long time since she had laughed, but it was too comical for her mother to be pluming herself on Mrs Smee's approval. 'Mum, how funny!' she gurgled.

'Well, it is no laughing matter, darling. We all positively tremble before Mrs Smee! There was such a scene the day before yesterday. Lady Diana Findon – have you ever met the fair Diana? – a little idiot with overworked eyelashes and a lisp, but everyone kowtows to her on account of her father. Well, Lady Diana descended on the canteen and said she had come to help. She proclaimed herself a 'prothessed cook', so she was sent off to make rock cakes – all Tommies adore rock cakes. I don't know what she did to them, left out the baking powder probably, but she brought back a trayload of lumps of putty. Mrs Smee picked one up in an awful silence. Then she slowly tasted it. "While I am in charge of this canteen, the men are going to be given food fit for human beings," she said, and tipped the whole lot out of the window.'

'How drastic!' Ursula looked increasingly interested.

'"Drastic" – that was the very word Tony Balestier used when I told him about it.'

A slight rigidity came over Ursula, otherwise she made no sign. But if her mother had suddenly fired a pistol at her head, she could not have been more startled. She did not even know that Mum saw Tony – and then this casual and unexpected mention of him. 'I met the dear boy in Victoria Street yesterday,' Mrs Hibbert rattled on in an airy manner, although, had Ursula been less dumbfounded, she might have detected a touch of unusual nervousness. 'Mercifully, when I related the anecdote, I didn't mention Lady Diana by name. Just in time I remembered that she is Tony's aunt, at least his aunt by marriage. She was old General Findon's second wife, you know, and centuries younger. They had a frightfully smart wedding, oh, it must be three years ago, and he died a few months after – no wonder, poor man! But Tony is actually staying with his aunt now; he happened to mention it. He looked so handsome, the dear boy, in his khaki; I fell in love with him again on the spot. I suppose you saw that he has got his commission – so ridiculous his ever joining as a Tommy. He is on active service leave, he told me; going over at once. As this is his last day, I asked him to look in.'

'Mother!' Ursula leaped from her sofa. 'How could you?' Her voice was strangled.

'Oh well, *you* needn't see him. I don't profess to be superior to all human feeling, and I want to say goodbye. Do you know what life the insurance people are giving subalterns at the front – three weeks?' Mrs Hibbert dabbed her eyes. 'Tony isn't as stony-hearted as you are,' she announced quaveringly. 'When I told him in the summer that you were killing yourself with your ridiculous suffrage, he didn't stand staring like a sulky oyster. He was most sympathetic.'

'Mother, what – there is the front door bell now,' Ursula broke off with an accent of despair.

'Oh yes, that will be Tony. I said come early. Well, I must change – I couldn't bid anyone farewell in this hideous frock; it makes me look a hundred. Tell him I won't be a minute.' She flitted off.

'Mr Balestier.' The announcement came before Ursula had time to collect her dazed thoughts. It was the most impossible moment of her life. Yes, khaki did make him handsomer than ever; the thought flashed involuntarily through her mind. But the unaccustomed uniform, however becoming, estranged him. She felt him unknown. Was he the old Tony at all? As they shook hands, she realised that Tony was as taken aback as she had been. He was actually blushing. 'Mrs Hibbert said that you were still away,' he stammered.

His confusion put her at her ease. And if he had imagined her away, he would not think that she had been involved in the invitation. But did he mean he would not have come had he known she was there? The thought crushed her; she felt speechless with anguish. Her mother had said – well, Mother was wrong. If Tony had shown himself sympathetic when she was hunger striking, it had been merely with Mum's grief. He had not minded for himself. Indeed, why should he? Was it likely that he would still care? Probably, by now, he was engaged to some other girl. Oh, how could Mum have asked him? It was not fair to subject her to this. 'I only came home this morning.' She had managed to say it, and in a fairly normal tone; indeed, if anything, her voice had been unusually cold and indifferent.

'I see. I am afraid what I said sounded rather rude.' He laughed, although in an embarrassed fashion. The laugh was so familiar that Ursula suddenly felt as though her ears had been hungering for it. A flood of emotion swept over her; she did not know whether it were joy or pain. She glanced up again and their eyes met. The other girl to whom he might be engaged was forgotten. How well he was looking, how absurdly boyish! He was blushing more than ever. The little curl in his close-cropped hair was still irrepressible; it moved her in the old ridiculous fashion. Tony – the name was not uttered aloud, but her whole being was crying it!

'I meant that if I had known you were here, I wouldn't have butted in without your permission.'

'Yes; won't you sit down?' Of all the absolutely banal remarks! Ursula felt positively enraged. But what could she say? It was all too difficult.

They sat facing each other almost in silence. Although Ursula did not know it, Tony's mental attitude was extraordinarily similar to her own. He, too, had at first been conscious of estrangement. Then the old, inexplicable attraction began to be felt, an attraction only increased by the new delicacy which he saw in Ursula's face. But, no doubt, she had long since ceased to have any feeling about him; the coldness of her remarks convinced him of it. Well, it was better that it should be so. Tony, too, knew of the insurance agents' three weeks; war engagements in the face of such a fact disgusted him. If a fellow were engaged already, that was a different matter, but no man going on active service ought to ask a girl to marry him. Even if one came through, which was unlikely, one probably would be maimed, blinded perhaps. To think of tying Ursula to a helpless hulk!

'Mother said that you are expecting to go out to France almost at once?' Ursula observed, still with polite calm.

'The day after tomorrow.' Tony stared. However differently she might feel towards him, it seemed impossible that she should be talking to him like this. Her face was half-averted, so he could now glance at it with impunity. 'You are still looking ill.' The thought expressed itself involuntarily.

'I am quite well now, thank you.' Suddenly, Ursula, too, felt that to keep up this sort of conversation was impossible. Even if Tony no longer cared, she could not treat him like a casual afternoon caller. He was a friend, someone with whom she could talk, really talk, and how she wanted to talk! For months, it seemed to her, she had been bridling her tongue, bottling up her real feelings. No one understood, not even Mary Blake, nor the suffragette nurses at the home where she had been staying; indeed, they were all ultra-militarist.

'If I look ill, it is because I am so frightfully miserable about the war'; the words burst out. 'I know that other women have more cause to be miserable. They have sons out there, or husbands. But then they don't seem to feel that it is all wicked in itself, as I do. That is what makes it so dreadful. They think it is worth dying for. But I disapprove of war.'

'Good heavens, don't we all?' Tony was looking interested, touched, perhaps in the faintest degree, amused. He might also have been irritated, had he not been disarmed by Ursula's distress. Besides, anything was better than the former unreal talk. But how like her to take up this unexpected standpoint, especially to him, a soldier! 'Isn't it because we disapprove of war that we are fighting?' he suggested gently. 'If a burglar breaks into one's house, and still more into one's neighbour's house, one is bound to defend it.'

'I thought that you would feel about it like that.' Yes, Tony was taking it from the idealistic standpoint, she told herself gratefully. 'But a still deeper disapproval of war might keep us from fighting at all. Perhaps that would be the highest courage.'

'Do you stand outside recruiting stations giving white feathers to the men who *have* joined up?' Tony asked with a smile.

'No, I don't go as far as that.' Ursula also smiled. Then she grew grave. 'But is it ever right to hurt people, to kill them?' she broke out passionately. 'I suppose I feel about it as you did about suffrage militancy. The methods are too horrible for any end!'

Well, it was lucky that he did not approve of war engagements, Tony was reflecting rather bitterly. For even if Ursula had still cared, obviously she would not have had him. Of course, the simile to suffrage was absurd – but had she felt it like that? Had suffrage militancy to her seemed like enlisting to him, an elemental and incontrovertible duty? For the first time he fully realised her idealism, which, however much they differed, was yet so akin to his own.

'Don't think I don't understand – your enlisting, I mean.' Ursula's words cut through his thoughts, almost echoing them. 'Feeling as you did, you could not do anything else. It was your duty. I – I even admire it.' At that moment, indeed, she was admiring so much that mental detachment was difficult. 'Especially your enlisting as a private. But you have taken a commission now.' There was a note of regret in her voice.'

'Then you disapprove less of a private. Why?'

Ursula flushed. 'Oh, a private – you know,' she broke off

incoherently. 'Only I really don't understand why, if you meant to take a commission, you didn't do it at first. Mother spoke as though you had had the choice.'

He did not reply. In the strained silence there came back to Ursula's mind that other remark of her mother's, the three weeks of life that the insurance companies were giving to subalterns. But among privates surely the casualties were not so high. No, she remembered herself having noticed the disproportion in the lists. So that was why. Yes, that was Tony. 'You need not tell me,' she whispered. 'You took a commission because there is more risk.'

'Oh, I don't know. Officers just seemed to be needed.' Tony quickly began to talk of something else.

But Ursula did not hear him. More risk, she was repeating to herself; so much risk that it only gave three weeks. Three weeks – three weeks – three weeks – the words were hammering themselves in her brain. Tony was going the day after tomorrow – and then three weeks. He looked so strong, so splendid, so utterly removed from death – three weeks – three weeks.

Suddenly Balestier stood up. This silence of Ursula's was making the position unendurable. And she was looking so horribly white. Could it be possible that she did still care for him? 'I am afraid that I can't wait to see Mrs Hibbert. Please make my excuses.'

Ursula also had risen, almost mechanically. Her lips parted, but no sound came. As he saw her stricken face, Tony knew that his guess was right. Yes, she cared! He wanted to take her in his arms, to forget the past, the future. But his scruples re-asserted themselves. It wouldn't be playing the game. 'Goodbye,' he said gently.

Still Ursula did not speak. She could not. The old giddiness had suddenly come over her; it had never been as bad before. Everything was swaying; she could hardly stand. A half-amused thought shaped itself at this trick her ill-used body was playing her. Was she going to faint like a despised early-Victorian young lady? Then blackness closed upon her. 'Tony,' she gasped. He caught her as she fell.

She was never quite certain afterwards whether she was actually unconscious. In any case, it was but for a moment. She could not spare more time, she told Tony with a weak smile, as she lay on the sofa and he knelt beside her. Indeed, the half hour they had together was preposterously short, if immeasurably long. 'But we can write to each other now,' Ursula said, as the time for parting drew near. After the blank years such a prospect seemed almost rosy. She smiled at him again. 'I suppose we are engaged, Tony?'

'I ought not to have allowed it.' Tony almost groaned. 'Darling, I am engaged to you, of course, but you are not to be engaged to me. It isn't fair on you. I won't have you bound.'

But Ursula laughed. 'It is the only thing that is fair on me,' she said. 'It is the only thing that makes me able to bear it, the feeling that I am bound.'

CHAPTER TWENTY-TWO

Tony was one of the lucky ones. For the three weeks given by the insurance agents passed and passed again; they multiplied themselves into months, and yet he remained alive and unscathed. Not that the fact was surprising, for he had never reached the front. He had been posted instead to a battalion at a Base Camp 'somewhere in France' that was patently Boulogne. 'I suppose you will think it good news,' he had written to Ursula. 'That is my consolation, for personally I consider it rotten. We have nothing to do, and we spend all day doing it. It is simply a continuation of Minster and Epsom. I didn't join up to hang about French watering places.'

Yes, Ursula certainly did consider it good news, in spite of Tony's discontent. She felt, indeed, rather like a prisoner on the scaffold in face of a sudden reprieve. Of course she could understand her lover's feelings; her own suffragette experience came back to her. At the same time she felt that Tony was being absurd. As she truly wrote to him, an army has got to have a base, and someone must form it. 'Besides,' she added casuistically, 'if you want so much to be in the trenches, the greater sacrifice is keeping out of them.'

Tony smiled as he read the words. It was a sacrifice that a good many people seemed prepared to make. One reason for his discontent was the society in which he now found himself. The best men were all at the front. This crowd struck him, for the most part, as shirkers, who had 'wangled' themselves into a 'cushy' job. A set of young fools, and immoral fools to boot! The way they tore about the country with flamboyant women in government cars disgusted him. And although Tony did not tear about with women, and tried to do his work intelligently as far as was permitted, he could not feel himself much better. Nothing excused his being there in safety while other men were agonising.

Tony's self-condemnation was increased the next spring by hearing, in rapid succession, of the deaths of three of his friends. One of them, killed while leading a very gallant attack, was especially mourned. Indeed, poor Tony's depression overcast the joy of the first meeting when he came home on leave. 'I wish you had known Seaton, darling,' he said to Ursula. 'He was just the sort of man you would have liked – very able and an idealist. He, too, hated war, yet he enlisted in the first week.'

'Yes, I wish I had known him' Ursula's tone was gentle. 'Did you say he was married?'

'Married, with two kids and no private means. And they sent *him* to the trenches and keep *me*, with no responsibilities, wrapped up in cotton wool. Pretty idiotic!'

Ursula felt a tightening in her throat. The words had hurt her, but she would not show it. Tony was right to put duty first. Besides, their love was not a 'responsibility'. 'But, Tony,' she argued, after a pause, 'although it was idiotic sending poor Mr Seaton to the front, it really isn't idiotic not sending you. I don't think any of the cleverest men ought to be in the first line. The country cannot spare them. If I were Kitchener,' she went on with rather a forced gaiety, 'I would have an entrance exam for the trenches – only the failures admitted.'

'Well, one could always achieve failure,' Tony suggested with a smile.

The flaw in the argument was admitted. Raising the age limit was Ursula's next airy suggestion. 'Only men over seventy ought to be eligible for active service – the 1845 class. You see, they have had their lives already; it wouldn't matter so much their finding heroes' deaths. Besides, it would improve the nation's health, for all the men would have to be kept alive and fit up to three score years and ten.'

Tony laughed outright. 'It is to be hoped that the Boches would be obliging enough to follow your lead, or our veterans would have a thin time of it. Think of the poor old boys toddling into action with shawls and thermos flasks.'

That Ursula could speak jestingly about the war – although her words were not altogether a jest – showed a modification of her previous tragic attitude. But, indeed, had that first misery persisted, that ever-present consciousness of men being mangled to death, she would have gone mad. Like others, she had become hardened. Or was it that the thought of Tony, and still more Tony's actual presence, dimmed the world tragedy?

And Tony, too, although he had come home saddened, yet forthwith recovered. How could two lovers be unhappy when they were together in a world where summer sunshine was gilding the flowery hopefulness of May? The war and all the years of pain and separation that preceded it were blotted out. They were once more in the time when they had first found each other.

Consciously, as well as unconsciously, they turned back life's pages. Their old Kiosk was closed, either for lack of patrons or of provisions, but they boated as of old on the despised Serpentine. 'Only no one would think it extraordinary of us now,' Ursula mused. 'It is conventional to be unconventional. Besides, everything is allowed to a khaki hero!'

'Even to upsetting his lady passenger when she is impertinent!' Tony rocked the boat perilously. 'And he can then show his khaki heroism by rescuing her. But pulling people out of the water is your speciality, isn't it, darling – although you do land them in jail.'

Another day there was an encore outing to Hampstead Heath – the horse bus had now been replaced by a less dilatory motor. Despite the danger of repetition and a somewhat embarrassing pervasiveness of saluting soldiery, they enjoyed it even more than that long-ago day of the past. For their picnic tea they found a spot ringed with bushes and so secure against military invasion; there they afterwards dallied, Ursula making a pretence to read and Tony stretched on the ground at her feet. It struck her suddenly that he was even better-looking than he had been in the past; but perhaps she was biased, she told herself naively. How well khaki suited him. 'I don't think that I shall ever be able to bear seeing you again in ordinary clothes.'

'And you a pacifist. Shame! As we are on personalities, I may say that you look rather nice today.' The words were intentionally banal; the look accompanying them ardent. Presently Tony mentioned how long this expedition was overdue. Had Ursula forgotten that when they came before, they had meant to repeat the programme the following week, only he had been dragged off to India instead by his 'brutal Chief'. 'Yes, and I had arranged to propose to you that Sunday,' Tony related. 'I had composed a most beautiful proposal! But having to do it in a hurry, up in your laboratory, quite rattled me. That was why I could only kiss you – and subside on your carbons.'

'Weren't you in a mess?' Ursula smiled reminiscently. 'But I didn't know that I had been cheated out of a grand story-book proposal.'

'Would you like it now?' Tony spread his handkerchief on the grass and knelt on it with ridiculous care, murmuring that this time he should emerge from the ordeal unspotted. 'Miss Winfield, conscious as I am of my unworthiness, an ardent and ever-growing attachment emboldens me to request the honour of your hand in marriage at such a time as may witness the subsidence of the present lamentable European upheaval.'

'You know I'd marry you tomorrow, only you are such a ridiculous goose, you won't!' They both laughed at the unromantic reply, Ursula a little ruefully. It was quite true. Tony persisted in the opinion that marriage ought not to be undertaken by a man on active service. 'You would have had a much more decorous reply before,' Ursula went on lightly.

'"Oh, give me a little time, Mr Balestier, this is so sudden." But now it is you who express that sentiment!'

'Anyway, however an acceptance is worded, it is always supposed to have the same conclusion,' Tony suggested and came closer. He kissed her with a sudden intensity. Both felt too much for speech.

It was soon after Tony's leave was over, and he had gone back, that Mrs Hibbert first began to reproach her daughter with heartlessness. Ursula was surprised and a little contrite. 'I suppose we were rather childish and irresponsible,' she half apologised. 'I was so frightfully happy to have Tony that it made me forget.'

'You might know that I am not speaking of that.' Mrs Hibbert's voice was quite unusually snappish. 'Of course, when the dear boys come home it is one's duty, if one is engaged to them or not, to give them as nice a time as possible.' No, Ursula learnt it was her refusal to take part in Red Cross work that was the cause of her mother's displeasure. 'But, Mammykin, I should be no use at your working parties,' she protested. 'You know that I can't sew.'

'As if that mattered in the least. You would be showing a proper spirit,' was the vexed retort.

Finding that her mother was seriously upset, Ursula suggested, as a compromise, that she should pay for a needle-woman. Those early days of the war found the dressmakers idle and their assistants thankful for work. But her substitute was to make sandbags, the girl stipulated. For Ursula had heard on unquestionable authority that for lack of sandbags men were being killed. The idea began to haunt her. Of what use was her one little needlewoman? Ought she not herself, qualified by suffrage experience, to take in hand a sandbag campaign? Then to her relief she heard that the thing was being already done. Sandbags were soon pouring in; the flow had even to be checked. It seemed strange that two obscure maiden ladies living in a London suburb had been able to succeed where the War Office failed.

Although a sop had been thrown in the matter of the working parties, Ursula was still not left undisturbed. Indeed, little Mrs Hibbert was genuinely shocked by her daughter's apathy. 'I wouldn't say a word if you were doing anything for the country, anything at all,' she exclaimed, almost tearfully. 'I could quite understand your preferring to make munitions to socks. Oh, my dear, why don't you? Lady Lonsdale's daughter and lots of the nicest girls are working in factories now. That sort of thing would be just in your line.'

'Killing people is not in my line.' Ursula's tone was short. 'I should think socks preferable to munitions, but really Mother, I don't intend to make either.'

Mrs Hibbert was, not unnaturally, affronted. But, although she dropped the subject, it was only for the moment. That very afternoon the little lady began again in her most airy and unruffled tone. 'I have thought of something to which you can't possibly object, darling.'

'What is it, Mum?' Ursula hoped that she didn't sound as disagreeable as she felt.

'Why, I am sure you wouldn't mind being the chief programme seller at my Kingsway matinée for the Serbian Red Cross next week. Oh my dear, most of the girls are such fools; it would be such a comfort to me to feel there was someone sensible in charge. I shan't have a moment myself, for I have to be in attendance on the Princess, you see.'

Ursula hesitated. She might have capitulated, but for her mother's next remark, which showed indeed an unusual lack of tact, but Mrs Hibbert was carried away by her theme. 'And the programme sellers' costumes are absolutely dinky – I designed them myself from a book of Balkan travels – those white headdresses, you know, with gold ornaments – so becoming! You'll look perfectly fetching, my dear. No man will be able to resist you.'

'He won't have the chance.' A heated argument ensued. It was disgusting to dress up in order to wheedle money out of men, Ursula insisted. 'I'd as soon be a prostitute,' she burst out. Mrs Hibbert dissolved into tears.

'Oh Mum, I didn't mean it. I am sorry.' As soon as the exaggerated words had been uttered, Ursula had regretted them. The fact was that her temper had been frayed by Mrs Hibbert's patriotic persistence. 'I expect that my high moral motives are merely a delusion,' she exclaimed penitently. 'If I felt it in me to be a successful programme seller, I should probably jump at it. Only, you know, Mammykin, I never could say please. My forbidding aspect would cause a panic! They would think I wanted their money *and* their life.'

Mrs Hibbert was with difficulty assuaged. Indeed, it was several days before the easy intimacy between mother and daughter was re-established. But Ursula's outburst had one advantage, her mother made no further attempt to conscript her into war service. The only approach to it was when the poor lady had a party of Belgian peasants landed upon her at a moment's notice. 'My dear, whatever shall I do? There are seventeen of them!' she gasped, rustling into her daughter's laboratory. 'Of course I told Lady Ditchling that I would take in one family, and these say they are all one family and so can't possibly be parted! I have sent Jenkinson off to hire beds and 'phoned round to all the agencies for charwomen and people – a sort of SOS call, Send On Servants! But what I came in to say was that some of the Belgies must sleep in here.'

'In my lab? Oh, Mother!' Ursula looked round in dismay. She was not doing any scientific work herself – she hardly was strong enough yet to make the effort of starting after all these years of abstinence – still she did not like to feel that the possibility was to be taken from her. Only in face of her mother's dilemma, how could she be selfish enough to protest? Not that the Belgians would approve of sleeping in a laboratory, she reflected, any more than she approved of their doing so. Then a brilliant idea struck her. 'But Mammykin, you'll have to put me somewhere, unless I am to camp out amid Belgians. Why not give them *my* bedroom, it's nearly as big; and let *me* sleep in the lab?'

'Oh my dear, I couldn't allow you to make such a sacrifice.' To her amusement Ursula found that her interested suggestion had turned her almost into a heroine. 'How can you dress without a long glass?' her mother protested. The maids' faces were almost awed as they moved in her clothes. 'I do think it's right down good of her,' Ursula heard one of them observe to another.

For a week Lowndes Square seethed. A babble of strange talk could be heard all over the house. Strange smells of cooking – rather savoury for the most part – issued from every room. Strangely habited figures with babies and baskets bustled noisily up and down the front steps – the back ones were firmly ignored. 'Going out at all hours of the night,' the outraged household protested, regarding as nocturnal a day that started at five a.m. Ursula, secure in her fastness, felt the invasion less than the others. The laboratory, indeed, was the only room that the afflicted Belgians would consent to leave unvisited. They seemed to regard it with misgiving, possibly imagining that unholy rites were there practised by their heathen hosts.

On the eighth morning Mrs Hibbert was confronted by a solid phalanx of maids. Either they or the Belgians must go. It was an ultimatum, and the maids, as they doubtless knew, were secured by the present wartime domestic dearth. Even Jenkinson supported them, poor Jenkinson, the last of the male staff, whose one object was to avoid attracting attention, lest, on a wave of his mistress's vicarious patriotism, he should find himself carried into the army. But he now voiced firmly the intolerable position: 'Much I can stand, Madam, and I knows in these days it's our duty to stand. But I draws the line at saucepans on the drawing room mantelpiece or pigging it indiscriminate, male and female, in one room like the Garden of Eden.' His words caused the hasty dispatch back to headquarters of the ramifying Belgian family, there to be sorted and re-issued in smaller and less unconventional groups, preferably to households without marble mantelpieces.

A lull in Mrs Hibbert's philanthropic activity followed this disaster, or rather a return to her abandoned canteen. Once more eulogies flowed of Mrs Smee. 'She really is a most wonderful woman,' Ursula was told by her mother in a voice that was quite awed. 'Do you know, my dear, that she has never missed a single day at the canteen? *Le mari* appeared one afternoon, your pet Professor' – thus the little lady rattled on. 'I showed him round and told him something of what we think of Mrs Smee. Oh, I rubbed in his inferiority – I always did dislike that man! You should have seen his face when I asked him innocently whether he wasn't very proud of being Mrs Smee's husband. Though I believe he has been working hard too.' The admission was grudging. 'They say he is on a scientific committee, inventing poison gases and things for the War Office. By the way, he looks years older; his hair has gone almost grey.'

So Vernon, too, had got caught up in the war. The war – it seemed to Ursula a gigantic Moloch that was gradually engulfing every human being in the world. It absorbed their brains and energies even when it did not actually batten on their bodies. And all for what? What possible quarrel had the mass of English people with the mass of German people or the mass of Austrian people? Why, every nation said, and probably really believed, that it was fighting for the same thing. One day she read of a shipwrecked traveller who, after long wanderings, arrived at an inhabited Pacific island. 'Europe has gone mad,' they told him. 'All the people there are killing each other.'

Yes, that was it, Ursula felt, Europe had gone mad. The view seemed disloyal to Tony, but she could not help it. All these little shopmen, these humble labourers, these lowly artisans, who were tearing and torturing each other, were simply mad. Or if they were not mad themselves, they were hypnotised by mad rulers. Anyway, she was not going to take part in any orgy of insanity. And to produce these horrible gases in safety was, she felt, worse than being a soldier. How could Professor Smee justify himself?

Despite this self-sought seclusion, Ursula did not entirely lose sight of her old suffrage comrades. True, Moloch had gripped them nearly all into his service either at home or abroad. Or could they be considered in his service, she wondered, puzzled, these women who were carrying on a campaign of healing and succour? When she read of them in every war-zone, gallant and serene, braving hardship and danger, she felt a glow of pride. And not only were Englishwomen to be found with our armies; discouraged by the War Office, they worked for the Allies. Ursula smiled bitterly when she heard of two well-known women doctors of her acquaintance for whom no work in the British Army could be found. A year later, when they had been tested by the French and found to be not only innocuous but strikingly successful, the War Office repented. A great military hospital in London was put under their charge. It was run entirely by women, many of them ex-suffragettes. Mary Blake, who had long since finished her training and had been on a hospital ship at Gallipoli, was now established there as a nurse. It was primarily to see her friend again that Ursula visited the place.

She was appalled! It was her first experience of Moloch's handiwork on the large scale, and although she had known what it must be like, yet it found her unprepared. Mary, who looked more Madonna-like than ever in the nurse's blue dress, was overflowing with pride in 'our hospital', and so did not omit a single ward. What endless beds in these long, long double rows! It seemed to Ursula that there must be miles of beds. And to think that each one held a man who, a few days, or weeks ago, had been at the top-note of life, had been in the glory of youth and strength. Now he lay there, helpless, broken. And people had done this on purpose! They had done it in a world that already held pain and disease. That was what made it so incredible. 'Yes, we are mad,' Ursula murmured incoherently.

Mary stopped. They had just left a ward and were standing in the empty, white-boarded corridor. 'I had forgotten that it was new to you,' she said. 'Would you rather not see any more? I used to feel as you do, but one gets used to it. I hardly notice now if a man has one arm or two. It sounds heartless' – her tone was apologetic – 'but really it is better. One cannot be useful if one is minding too much.'

'Yes, I understand; it has become your work.' Ursula had regained her self-control. 'And I know how splendidly you are doing it.' The Commandant had told her of Mary Blake's excellence but, indeed, in going round the wards, it had been obvious. Again and again the white faces on the pillows had brightened as 'Nurse' drew near; there had been salutations of respectful flippancy to which Mary had given gentle, smiling replies. 'The men seem to love you.'

'*I* love them.' Mary's face shone. 'They are such boys, such babies. Sometimes, out there, when one of them was very bad, he would ask me to hold his hand. And he would cry as though he were a little, hurt child and I were his mother. One boy really thought I was his mother – he was delirious, of course. He kept calling, "Mum, Mum, I feel so rotten, Mum. Give me something to make me better."'

'How can you bear it?' Ursula's voice was strangled.

'I don't know. And the way they think of one – their unselfishness – it is wonderful. The other night there was a man in my ward – just an ordinary Tommy. I had been doing things for him for a good while and suddenly he said: 'Set down, Nurse, you must be getting tired.' Three hours later he died.'

'Don't. It makes it worse. It is too hateful.' Rage against Moloch shattered in Ursula every other emotion.

'How do you mean hateful?' Mary looked puzzled; with her Moloch was as much taken for granted as an earthquake would have been. 'You mustn't think that it is all sadness here,' she elaborated, conceiving that possible sympathy with a nurse's lot was making her friend so angry. 'Why, I often feel that the hospital is the most cheerful place in London – the only cheerful place in London! As soon as the patients get the least bit better, they are laughing and skylarking about like great schoolboys. They are quite happy then – unless they are getting so well that they think they will be sent back to the front. That is rather heartbreaking! But even then they don't say much. And you never hear a single bitter word from them against the detestable Boche.'

It was manifest before the tour of the hospital was over, that Mary herself could not claim this lack of bitterness which she praised. The girls had reached the last ward. This was her own, Mary explained. She was night nurse here, but she had only started this week; previously she had been attached to the operating theatre. Despite her recent advent, the friendly grins that greeted her were even broader than in the other wards, the salutations still more hearty. 'Hello, Nurse, what are you doing around at three o'clock of an afternoon?' called out a one-legged Canadian. 'It ain't proper for a young lady like you to be up at this time of day.' Embroidered table-centres of terrible hues, wallpaper beads, wool-work canvas belts and squares with regimental crests were held up for her to admire. A young fellow whom they called 'The Terror' was busy knitting a particularly innocent-looking, fluffy white scarf. 'Want to get it done tonight,' he observed to the rather laboured accompaniment of his clicking needles. 'And want to get married tomorrow so there'll be someone to wear it,' jeered his neighbour.

But at the last bed, the one in the corner, no fancy-work was displayed, nor did any greeting come from its occupant. As Ursula approached she saw the reason – she had hardly been able to credit her eyes before. The object lying here was a mere swathed block, a crude overturned image resembling futurist sculpture; nowhere was there visible the faintest trace of skin or eyes or hair. Was the thing human at all? passed through her mind. Compared with its white, shapeless inanimation a museum mummy would seem lifelike. Yes, it *was* human, for when Mary spoke there came a slight, a very slight movement in reply. 'Mary, what is the matter with him? He can't be bandaged like that all over?' she demanded of her friend when they stood once more outside.

'He is.' Mary's gentle face grew almost fierce. 'It's the new liquid fire that those fiends, those devils, are using! When he first came in, his skin was black – charred like burnt wood. The doctors think now that he will live. But his eyes – he doesn't know it, but he is blind.' Her voice shook.

It was curious that this time Ursula seemed the less moved of the two. Suddenly, for her, as well as for Mary, the horror had become 'work'. For her friend's words 'liquid fire' had suddenly rapt her out of the hospital into the serene realm of science. With a rush that old idea came back to her – the discovery of some process for the liberation of atmospheric nitrogen that could be used to extinguish fire. Only would she now be able to take up such work? she asked herself in anguish. Would she ever be able to do research again? Her scientific mind was so rusty, so clogged with disuse.

Those suffrage years had been unavoidable – she still clung to this – but why, oh why, had she not returned to scientific work directly the war came on, or, at least, directly she was strong enough? Idleness, she reproached herself. But it had not been idleness. Rather, she had been determined to do nothing in connection with the war, and, at the same time, had felt that nothing else was worth doing. Science? What was the use of science in such a mad world – indeed, science had only promoted this misery and slaughter. No, Tony was the only comfort, Tony still mercifully safe at the base. So she had snatched the happiness within her grasp and had numbly let all else slip.

But now had come this experience, this tragic, bandaged figure. To devise a means of checking such a crime would surely not be working for the war, but against it. Thus she had felt in connection with her nurse friends; she felt it now still more strongly about herself. And yet she was not certain. Perhaps those people, those Quakers for instance, who refused to take any part in war were really the more logical. However this might be, she felt that she could no longer stand aside. For this man in the hospital all help was now too late, but there were the others. Suppose other boys should be burnt, 'charred like wood,' blinded – and her work might have saved them!

She hurried home and locked herself in her laboratory.

CHAPTER TWENTY-THREE

No one had ever yet been able to reproach Ursula with lack of industry, once she was started on a piece of work, and this time proved no exception. Not that taking up scientific research again was easy. As she had foreseen, her mind was rusty; it refused to function. Although the apparatus was set up, she remained blankly void of ideas. Despair almost overcame her. Finally, with dogged determination, she dragged herself through several series of her old experiments. At last she began to be absorbed. Her brain seemed to shake off some hazy weight and to move as of old.

As far as outside conditions went, nothing could have been more ideal. Ursula had not told her mother on what she was working, fearing an indiscreet betrayal, but Mrs Hibbert guessed that her daughter's sudden industry was in some way connected with the universal cause. From that moment Ursula's peace was secured. Never had she been so free from pressgang efforts to hustle her into a service, formerly social, and, of late, charitable. Indeed, maternal solicitude guarded her laboratory almost as a shrine.

To Tony Balestier the girl had been more explicit, and

here again she had received exhilarating support. 'The news about your work gives me more pleasure than I can say, dearest,' he wrote in happy contrast to his former attitude towards her suffrage activity. He had felt so strongly, he said, that in this crisis everyone should be giving their time to the country. With her talent, he was sure that she would devise some means of protecting our men from 'that devilish Hun invention'.

Early in the New Year, Tony's leave again became due. One afternoon he arrived unexpectedly and made his way straight up to the laboratory. To say that Ursula was not enraptured would have been untrue. For as much as half a minute, as he held her in his arms, she forgot her work. Then, with an exclamation, almost of dismay, she turned back to her apparatus.

If Tony were surprised, he said nothing. Indeed, he himself was genuinely excited about the work and full of eager inquiries. No, she had reached no satisfactory solution as yet, Ursula told him presently when a pause came in the experiment, but she felt that she was on the track. She must just go on 'soaking' herself; then one day she would suddenly find all was clear. That was the way in which ideas always came to her. But it was really most curious; a stream of technical detail followed. But she would show him. She switched on the current. Then he would understand better what she meant.

Despite Tony's interest, he would have been hardly human if, towards the end of his brief leave, he had not begun to feel distinctly ill-used. One afternoon Ursula did consent to go out with him; but although her body walked by his side, her thoughts were obviously still in her laboratory. At last he asked a trifle bitterly if she was aware of his being there at all.

'Oh, Tony, do you think that I have been horrid to you?' Ursula suddenly became aware of what might be her lover's point of view. 'But it has been rather horrid for me, too, having to go on with my work instead of being able to enjoy you. You see, when I am doing a piece of research, the rest of life becomes rather like a dream. I can't help it, dearest. Besides, with this work, there is the feeling all the time of what is behind it – of the men who are being hurt. I never told you properly about the boy I saw at the hospital.' Although several months had passed since her experience, Ursula's voice shook as she spoke of it. 'Oh, Tony, I still see him,' she finished pitifully. 'I see hundreds and hundreds of him. It is only when I am at work that I can forget. And every minute that I stop I feel is making more of them – more of those spectres, blind and bandaged, charred logs of wood. Mother says I must be possessed to work so hard. Tony, I think I am.'

'Poor darling.' Under cover of her muff, Tony pressed her hand. 'Yes, I understand. You mustn't think of me at all. Let us go home now, dear, to the laboratory.'

Still, on the last evening of Tony's leave, Ursula did take a holiday. After all, she owed something to her lover; to herself. For although Tony ran little risk at Boulogne, at any time he might be sent off to the front without their seeing each other again before he went – or ever. During all his leave she had been conscious of this possibility, but had deliberately put it from her. It was too horrible, too unnerving; it would interfere with her work. Her work had to come first. She might not have felt justified even in giving up this last evening had she felt less tired. But she was dazed with fatigue after the double strain of these last few days, so dazed that her spectres and Tony's possible danger alike faded from her mind. How restful it was to sit in silence with Tony's arm around her, Tony who 'understood'. He was going tomorrow, but still Boulogne was near; he would soon be back; he would be safe.

Tony also was thinking of Boulogne, of its safety and its nearness, but for him the reflection was the reverse of soothing. What an extraordinary thing it was that he should still be there after urging again and again to be sent to the front. Yes, he was still there, skulking at the base, when every decent man he knew was in the trenches. 'It's a comfort that one of us will be of some use in the war,' he said aloud suddenly. 'I can't flatter myself that my services are making much difference to the country!'

The bitterness in his tone pricked through Ursula's exhaustion. She made an effort to rouse herself. 'What nonsense, dear,' she said lightly. 'It is because you are of so much use as a commissariat officer that they don't send you to the front. An army triumphs on its tummy.'

Tony smiled at the paraphrase, and there was another restful silence. He was unconvinced, but he and Ursula had argued the point so often, and he knew that she was tired. Presently he gave a short, half-reluctant laugh. 'Has it ever struck you as being rather comic, darling, that I, who rushed to enlist on the first day, sit around and do nothing at

Boulogne, while you, the pacifist, who disapprove of all things military, slave at war work for eighteen hours out of the twenty-four?'

'I don't!' Ursula sat up straight. Such a suggestion made her forget her fatigue. 'At least I do slave, but it isn't at war work. My work is humanitarian.'

'If you can bring off your idea, it will be war work right enough, and jolly important war work too. Of course, I know what you mean, darling,' he went on soothingly, seeing that Ursula looked seriously disturbed. 'Your work is defensive, not offensive, and I am awfully glad of it. Although I don't share your views about women making munitions – I think it is quite right of them – still I simply hate their doing it. And suppose you had been an arch-munitionist, inventing poison gases and that sort of thing – I don't know how I could have stood it!' He broke off and kissed her fingers. 'Of course, I know I am hopelessly illogical.'

'You are, hopelessly; but I think I rather like it.' Yes, it was his chivalry, Ursula realised, that made Tony dislike the idea of women being munitionists, just as it had made him dislike the idea of their being suffragettes. Only, in that case, he had not felt that the end justified the means; now he did. It was rather odd of him. Foolishly, perhaps, she put her thought into words; it was the first time the old, unhappy subject had come up between them. 'But never mind,' she broke off. 'Your views don't hurt me now for the Cause is won. Today everybody, even *The Times*, is a suffragette!'

'But, darling, doesn't that show that my views were right and that militant tactics were a mistake? You see, women will get the Vote now, not because they are making themselves a nuisance, but because they are throwing in their lot with the country and playing up so splendidly.'

'And abjuring militancy in munition factories?' Ursula suggested with a smile. 'But Tony, I don't believe that what women are doing now would have brought them the Vote without our previous militancy, simply because no one would have known that women wanted the Vote; they would not have known it themselves.'

'I think on that point we shall have to agree to differ. After all, it is over and done with, dearest. Don't let us argue on our last evening together.'

'No.' Ursula came still closer. 'How curious it will be,' she went on musingly after a moment's pause, 'if the greatest war in history ends in Women's Suffrage when the stock anti-argument was always that women could not have the suffrage because they took no part in war.'

'Very curious.' This remark, at least, was not debatable. There was another silence, a very long one. Of what was Ursula thinking, Tony wondered, as she sat there, so close to him – so far away. Was she living again in those old, miserable suffrage days? Or was she following some line of thought in connection with her present research? Or was she simply grieving that he must go tomorrow? The possibility made him bend his head and kiss her hair. Then, at last, she spoke; and he found that she was not thinking of any of these things, or perhaps, she was thinking of all of them. 'We poor little creatures work so hard, and do so little of what we intend. Perhaps, as you say, all my effort and desire counted for nothing in Women's Suffrage, and all your effort and desire will count for nothing in the war. It may be that the thing I shall do in life is to bring military success, and the thing that you will do with your war is to bring votes to women. What do we know, Tony, as we beat so desperately in the dark? We only know that we love each other.'

'Yes, we know that,' said Tony softly.

CHAPTER TWENTY-FOUR

The next day Tony had gone, and Ursula began to 'soak' herself in her work even more completely than before, if indeed such a thing were possible. It might almost be said that her work never stopped. For at all times, when she was chatting with her mother, when she was scanning the newspaper – now one long agony column – when she was writing to her lover, even when she was asleep, the problem lay at the back of her mind, taking shape and developing like some new entity with life of its own.

And then one day the solution came. It came in the most unlikely of places, when she was in her bath. For it was not so much a deliberate solution as a sudden light, a realisation that a door stood open, which up till then had been closed. Everything lay before her, simple and clear. The only surprising part was her not having seen it before. She felt so confident of the revelation that it seemed almost a waste of time to prove it. But, of course, it must be proved. And then would come the practical application, the use of this new principle in fighting liquid fire.

Up till now, although Ursula's unconscious work on her

research had never stopped, her hours of actual experimenting had been fairly reasonable. The illuminating flash could not be hurried, she had felt. But now it was a mere question of practical development. Apart from her keen scientific interest, there were her dreadful spectres to goad her on. So rest and recreation were cut down to a minimum. Could her meals be sent up to the laboratory? she asked. At this point, her mother protested. 'My dear child, you will save an hour and be in bed with brain fever for a month.'

Ursula scoffed at the brain fever, but there might be some truth in Mammykin's words. Indeed, they frightened her, for until her 'job' was done, a breakdown in health could not even be contemplated. To guard against such a disaster, the girl had serious thoughts of acquainting the War Office with her 'extinguisher' in its present imperfect form. But it would be a mistake, she reflected. The authorities, in their anxiety to save the soldiers, might insist on the immediate adoption of the invention, and she felt so certain that with a few more days or weeks of work, it would be immensely improved. The ultimate result of delay would be a gain and not a loss of life. No, she must just go on working – working hard, but not too hard. She would refuse to read the newspapers, which now increasingly contained unnerving references to liquid fire. By a supreme effort, she would banish the spectres from her mind. In order to help she must forget.

At last the day came when the 'extinguisher' was ready, and Ursula herself satisfied. Indeed, she was more than satisfied, she was amazed. Her experiments were certainly, to use the scientific phrase, 'very pretty'. It was almost miraculous to see the little artificial flares of liquid fire waver for an instant and then go out. Now for the War Office. She had long decided on the first step – a letter to Vernon Smee. It seemed almost providential that he should be on the Inventions Committee.

The letter did not take long, although she hesitated over the commencement. Ought she to say 'Vernon' or 'Professor Smee'? However, her news was too important to worry about such trifles. She would not have a beginning at all. So she wrote, plungingly, that she wanted to show him some important experiments. Would he come and see them the next day, in the morning if possible? A brief description of the new principle and its application followed. If he were satisfied when he saw the working of the extinguisher – and she was certain he would be satisfied – would he arrange for her to give a demonstration before the military bigwigs? Naturally the matter was very urgent, for she was positive that her extinguisher, used in sufficient numbers, would absolutely safeguard the men against this horrible liquid fire.

As she was closing the envelope, a maid came in with her tea. It reminded her that she could send the letter round to the College by hand; Vernon would probably not yet have left. Then she could get an immediate reply telling her the hour of his visit tomorrow. She supposed the official demonstration could not take place until the day after. Then there would have to be tests in the open and possibly further tests under service conditions in France. Still, a fortnight ought to see the manufacture of the extinguishers started. And they were so simple in construction; in three weeks, a few, at least, should be in use.

Alas! from the very first, the schedule went wrong. For the maid came back from the College with the statement that the Professor was lecturing, and so the letter could not be given to him. He would receive it immediately he had finished. It did not matter, Ursula said. He would doubtless send a 'phone message or a wire. All the evening she sat expecting it. Nothing came. Well, there would be a letter by the first post in the morning. There was no letter. Perhaps it had been delayed, she told herself; the post now was so frightfully slow. Or, perhaps, Vernon had not understood that she expected an answer. He had guessed that in any case she would be at home all day working, and he just meant to come. Yes, that was it. He did not come.

As Ursula was dressing for dinner another possibility suggested itself. How stupid she was! Of course what had happened was that Vernon had not got her letter. Probably the College porter was some queer old crock who was replacing the real man. A whole day lost! She pitchforked on her gown and rushed down to the 'phone. It was hardly likely that Vernon would still be at College; she had better ring up his private address – still Clarendon Road, she noticed. A maid answered her that Professor Smee was out. No, he was not expected home until late. Perhaps he was still at the College.

Desperately Ursula rang up the College. No, Professor Smee had left early in the afternoon. Perhaps he was at his private house. Oh, he wasn't there; then one couldn't say where he might be. Yes, the letter that came by hand yesterday afternoon had been delivered. Yes, there was no doubt about it. It was the porter who was speaking. He had given the letter to Professor Smee himself.

Well, it was unaccountable! Surely Vernon must realise what this delay meant. Why, every hour, every moment, a man might be dying whom her extinguisher might have saved. The only explanation was that Vernon disbelieved in her invention – but he had no right to disbelieve, at least not without seeing it. The matter was too horribly important for offhand scepticism. It was not as though she were a novice. Vernon knew her work; he knew that she would not be putting forward a wildcat scheme. Quite apart from her scientific status, she would have thought that their old friendship would have made him come when she asked him. A recollection crossed her mind of the ending of that friendship; of Mrs Todd's revelations. Was that the explanation? Was Vernon afraid of a renewal of their old intimacy, either for his own sake or for that of his wife? How petty and preposterous! As though people were justified in having private feelings at such a time. Why had she been such a fool in the past, Ursula reproached herself. If she had never permitted that indiscreet friendship, Vernon would not now be shunning her. Then there came an inspiration. She would ring up Mrs Smee and explain the position to her. After all, the woman could not be utterly devoid of sense and good-feeling. Why, Mum was forever lauding her marvellous management of the canteen.

The idea was at once put into practice. Mrs Smee herself answered the telephone. 'Who is speaking?' came the natural inquiry. Ursula had a moment of hesitation; would the crash of the dropped receiver follow the announcement of her name? Nothing of the sort occurred, though possibly there was a slight accent of surprise as Mrs Smee repeated 'Miss Winfield.' The new Charlotte led too busy and important a life to be tormented by the old jealousies, nor indeed was there any ground for them. For Vernon had always worshipped success, and his wife's triumph at the canteen had both astounded and impressed him. As he sometimes laughingly told her, all his 'fine lady friends' were now her scullery maids. So the new Charlotte, instead of going off into a tantrum, merely reflected as to what could be the reason of Miss Winfield's telephoning. But of course it must be for her mother – the difference in name had almost made her forget the relationship. 'Has Mrs Hibbert something to say about the canteen?'

'No, it is not Mother who wants to speak to you; it is I.' Ursula embarked upon her account. Even over the 'phone Mrs Smee's interest was apparent. Possibly the interest grew still more cordial – so much of the old Charlotte survived – when the real reason for the confidence was disclosed. 'You say you have not had any answer from my husband to your letter,' she repeated. 'Oh I am so sorry, Miss Winfield; he must have forgotten. You see, he's so taken up and bothered with his own work for the war. I often tell him he'll be forgetting his own name next! Yes, of course, the very minute he comes home I'll ask him about when he can see your experiments. He shall 'phone you first thing in the morning, if he is too late tonight.'

'And please tell Professor Smee that I shall only take up a few minutes of his time. I just want him to see my work so as to be able to give me introductions in the proper quarter. Thank you so much. Goodbye.' On this amiable note the conversation ended. This amiability had been due as much to the new Ursula as to the new Charlotte. For this Ursula could – sometimes – see things from another person's point of view, and so it had occurred to her that possibly Mrs Smee might not like her husband's scanty leisure being monopolised by another woman, even in the great cause.

In any case, Charlotte Smee would have kept her word, but Ursula's parting remark certainly made it easier. When Vernon came home and was comfortably discussing an excellent supper – Charlotte's catering talent did not exhaust itself in the canteen – he was dumbfounded by his wife suddenly bringing up Ursula's name. 'Miss Winfield telephoned and seemed a bit put about at your not having answered her letter.'

'Confound Miss Winfield!' Had any misgivings as to her husband's sentiments lingered in Charlotte's breast, this remark would have dispelled them. Indeed, Vernon's annoyance was so pronounced that his wife was amazed rather than relieved. What could have vexed him so? The poor girl only wanted to show him her experiments. Vernon used to be too fond of Miss Winfield, but now he seemed positively to dislike her.

Charlotte was not far from the truth. For if Professor Smee did not dislike, he certainly resented. Whenever his thoughts turned to Ursula, which, of late, was but seldom, it was to remember the way in which their friendship had ended. For over two years he had danced attendance on the girl; he had treated her as something sacred, had never breathed a word of love – why there weren't many men who could have done it – and then at a moment's notice she had turned him down like a drunken lackey. 'I can't be bothered with Miss Winfield and her letters,' he growled aloud. 'I'm too driven with my own work.'

'But, dearie,' his wife remonstrated, 'Miss Winfield says that she has invented something that will help the boys out there. If that's so, one must be bothered. Or don't you believe in her idea?'

'No, I don't!' Vernon's tone was even more annoyed than before. To Charlotte's amazement she found herself treated to a scientific disquisition. Presently her husband pulled himself up, presumably realising the futility of the proceeding. 'But all this is Greek to you, isn't it, old lady?' he said with a good-natured laugh. 'Anyway, you can take it from me that Miss Winfield's scheme is worthless, 'nappoo' as your Tommies say, don't they? It's a perfectly absurd idea. Oh yes, I'm certain. I happen to have gone into the question myself. I – ' Vernon again checked himself. Perhaps it would be as well not to tell Charlotte just now of his own 'liquid fire protector'. Certainly she would have to know about it some day. In a few weeks the thing would be in use, and then the papers would be sure to get hold of it. Besides, there would be the pleasant tangible results; why, very likely he'd get a knighthood for it. 'Sir Vernon and Lady Smee'; it sounded rather well. Of course, his own invention being along the same line had nothing whatever to do with his attitude towards Miss Winfield's. If he had thought that her 'extinguisher' had any practical value, naturally he would have helped her to bring it forward. He couldn't have done anything else. But Charlotte might not understand. Women were so queer. 'Well, old lady, it must be bedtime,' he yawned.

'Yes, I'm half asleep myself.' She hesitated. 'But I promised Miss Winfield you'd 'phone to her, anyway in the morning.'

'D – ' He cut short the expletive. 'Well, you 'phone for me to Miss Winfield in the morning; you're the early bird of this establishment. Apologise and all that; tell her I'm absolutely distracted with work or I'd have answered her sooner. Break it to her that in any case I can do nothing.'

'But can't you tell her of anyone she could write to, just to satisfy her mind?' Charlotte kindly urged.

'Oh, Pritchard's the proper person, General Sir Everett Pritchard, KCB – though it's not of the faintest use.'

'I am afraid she will be very disappointed.' Charlotte's own tone was disappointed. 'She thought her invention was going to do so much. You are quite certain it is no good your even seeing it?'

'Quite, absolutely certain. And now for goodness' sake do let's drop it and get to bed.' This time, although he did not swear, Vernon made no effort to conceal his vexation. Of course, he was certain, he was saying to himself. It was impossible that there could be anything in Ursula's idea. If there had been, was it likely that so simple a principle should have been overlooked up till now? No, her 'extinguisher' was absurd. All the same, he wished she had not told him about it. Her doing so was all part of her damnable selfishness.

CHAPTER TWENTY-FIVE

Astonishment is a mild word to express Ursula's feelings when she received the telephone message the next morning. She could hardly find breath with which to answer Mrs Smee. All these weeks she had refrained from any mention of her invention lest it should be prematurely wrested from her. And now that it was complete, Vernon, one of her oldest friends, would not even take the trouble to see it.

But it was no good sitting down under the rebuff. Rather, the two days' delay was a reason for increased activity. At any rate, she now knew the right person to approach; that much, at least, Vernon had done for her. A letter to Sir Everett Pritchard was written forthwith, and sent off, again by hand. Not that this time she really expected the messenger to bring back a reply. But in her letter, she begged that an answer might be sent not later than the following day. She would remain at home until it came, she said, and was prepared to go at once to the War Office, or any other specified place, and give her demonstration. As she dated her letter, she noticed it was June 20th; tomorrow would be the longest day.

It certainly was, Ursula thought, as she spent it waiting on the postman's knock or the telephone bell. No message came. The following day brought the same result. Well, she had better write again. This time, at the risk of appearing self-laudatory, she mentioned her scientific qualifications. It was true that she had not done much chemistry during the last five years, but her theory, which had been so scornfully treated at the Plymouth British Association, was now universally accepted, although it was usually coupled with Leveridge's name. However, on the Continent, she had received her fair recognition. Shortly before the war, there had come a bulky volume in German on the *Extraction of Atmospheric Nitrogen*, two whole chapters of which were devoted to her work, while references to the '*Winfieldische Formel*' fairly sprinkled its pages. But it was not much use quoting German appreciation, she reflected ruefully. She would just speak of the original BA paper in which she had put forward the theory and also of her other two papers given at the Royal Society.

Four more days went by, not quite idly, for she was still working on, and improving, her extinguisher. At last, on June 28th, the long-expected envelope arrived with its printed 'War Office Inventions Department.' She tore it open breathlessly. 'Your communication of the 20th instant has been received,' she read, 'and will be reported upon in the proper quarter.' It was signed Watkins, presumably a clerk. Her second letter did not seem to have penetrated far enough even for acknowledgment. Then silence again descended.

Now that her work was practically complete, Ursula was once more reading the newspapers. What did it matter, her being harrowed? Everyone ought to be harrowed at such a time. One evening, about a week later, she saw a paragraph about *'Flammenwerfer'*. The Germans were using them extensively in their present push. The capture of one of our salients was attributed to their use. They had caused many casualties. The loss of a salient seemed negligible to Ursula, but the mere mention of casualties maddened her. 'Casualties' – what hypocrites we were, hiding away tortured, writhing bodies under this bland word! And her extinguisher might have saved them. The thought was unbearable. In the early morning, after a sleepless night, a third letter, unwisely violent, was penned to Sir Everett Pritchard, enclosing the newspaper cutting. Before Mrs Hibbert started for the canteen, she was confronted by a demand for the name of the most influential War Office man of her acquaintance. To him also Ursula wrote, stating the whole case.

Further silence – absolute, baffling. The days passed, a week, two weeks. Finally, on July 19th, another letter arrived from the War Office. Miss Winfield's communications of June 20th, the 22nd, and July 3rd were to hand. The matter was under consideration, and she would receive a reply to them in due course. On the same day, by a curious coincidence, she had news of her mother's uncommunicative friend. The poor man had had a nervous breakdown. Complete change and rest were ordered; no correspondence was being forwarded.

Ursula set her teeth. Fortunately this one man did not exhaust the possibilities of the Hibbert circle; he had merely been the most promising. For the first time Ursula found satisfaction in her parents' military *milieu*. All her stepfather's cronies, all her mother's 'dear boys' who were still alive, were bombarded with letters; she even treated them to scientific details which they all alike found absolutely unintelligible. It was little good. Nearly all of them were abroad. What could they possibly do in the matter? they wrote. One or two of Colonel Hibbert's contemporaries had been given commands at home, but they were not stationed in London, and presumably they considered that leave should be consecrated to amusement. Certainly they never came near Ursula's laboratory.

July drew to an end; August, September. Ursula had written several times to the War Office. She might be a beggar asking for alms instead of a person offering them a valuable invention as a free gift, she reflected. Perhaps her mother was right, for that shrewd little lady had said from the beginning that Ursula ought to ask for a royalty; it would make the authorities think more of her work. But the girl had felt that she could not make money out of the war. It was impossible. Besides, she had been and still was absolutely confident of ultimate success. 'Only at this rate the war will be over before they take the extinguisher,' she wrote to Tony, 'and then it will not be of much use to our men! So I mean to go on worrying Pritchard's life out of him. I am case-hardened to being a nuisance. Too much depends on it for me to mind.'

In spite of her words, she did mind. And apart from the actual fatigue of her efforts was the strain of the ever-present accusing spectres. In the press now there were constant references to liquid fire. She did not think she could have borne it but for Tony's sympathy. 'I am trying hard to get leave, dearest,' he wrote in one of his daily letters. 'When I am at home, I may be able to help you. It might be a good plan, my bringing back an extinguisher here. Sometimes the "heaven-born" irrupt on us, and I could give them a show.'

At last, at the end of October, there came a definite reply, signed this time by Sir Everett Pritchard himself. Miss Winfield's extinguisher had been duly considered, but had been found to have no practical value. She was thanked for her kind offer.

Anger almost overpowered Ursula's distress. 'Fools! Fools! Fools! When they have never seen it!' she stormed. She decided furiously to take the idea elsewhere, to the French, to the Russians. But the first question she would be asked at the embassies was whether our own War Office had seen the extinguisher. When they heard that the British authorities had 'turned it down', they would certainly not consider it.

Well, if no one wanted her invention, she would take it to the enemy. They, at least, could appreciate science, and liquid fire was being used against, as well as by them. True, it was the German scientists who had perpetrated this horrible new method of warfare, but was that any reason why the German common soldiers – fellow human beings – should suffer unnecessarily this torture? Was it her fault if Germany was the only nation sufficiently scientific to accept the extinguisher? Returning sanity revealed the preposterous nature of her idea. Apart from any question of patriotism, she would be shot by the Allies as a traitor and by the Huns as a spy before she ever got to enemy headquarters.

Her woes were poured out in a desperate letter to Tony. 'All I am asking,' she wrote, 'is that my invention should be given a fair trial. Of course I don't want it used unless it is going to do its business. But I am certain it would. And to think that all these months our men are fighting without a weapon that would give them complete protection against this fiendish fire. I rage, but what is the use of that? I feel myself beating against a blank wall.'

It was through Tony that an opening in the wall at last appeared. One of the young man's many connections, a certain Mr Venning, was on the permanent staff of the War Office. Naturally, Tony had long ago written to this man asking him to go and see Miss Winfield's extinguisher, but the visit had not materialised. Mr Venning was old and excessively overworked. He really was not called upon, he felt, to wait upon every young lady who thought she had made some little invention. But now Tony wrote again, very urgently, and mentioned that he was engaged to Miss Winfield. Without doubt that altered the position. Tony was a dear fellow, the old gentleman told himself. The least he could do was to call upon his fiancée.

So one afternoon Mr Venning was announced. He was nearly an hour late – an appointment for three o'clock had been made on the 'phone – but he considered the use of taxis unpatriotic, and he never could get the right bus. Today he had found himself nearing Hampstead instead of Lowndes Square, he told Ursula plaintively; the numbers on the omnibuses only made it more confusing. The girl laughed; she had taken a liking to this kindly, courteous, white-bearded old man, although by no stretch of imagination could she picture him as a shining light in an important government post.

The liking was mutual. How nice-looking Tony's girl was, Mr Venning reflected. He regretted naively that he had not come before. Perhaps she was a little over-intense. She need not have suggested going up to the laboratory before giving him tea. He would have liked a chat and to hear all about Tony. And what a number of flights of stairs.

He subsided, gaspingly, on one of the laboratory stools. Dear, dear, the modern girl was delightful, but strenuous. What would have been said to such proceedings in his young days? Although breathless, he smiled upon Ursula with a paternal benevolence as she turned on a spray of minute jets of flame that issued from what looked like the rose of a watering-pot. Then the model extinguisher was set in action; it was a tiny apparatus in a box not more than a couple of inches square, which gave off a crackling sound, but produced no current of air of any kind. The flames wavered – Mr Venning's smile changed into a look of surprised interest – then they suddenly, magically, went out!

Another experiment followed. A toy balloon sailed in the room. From it began to drop small pieces of flaming phosphorus – the floor of this part of the laboratory was covered with a sheet of metal. An outer ring of the phosphorus lay on the floor blazing merrily. But all the pieces that came down in the vicinity of the little apparatus reached the ground as mere dark lumps, extinct and harmless.

Mr Venning appeared transfixed. 'Wonderful, wonderful,' he had kept murmuring like a man mesmerised. 'They must see it at the War Office,' he announced at the end. 'I will *make* them see it,' he said as he put on one of Colonel Hibbert's hats in his enthusiasm.

The old gentleman was as good as his word. The very next day he reappeared, accompanied by another War Office man, evidently someone of importance. The latter was not as childishly overwhelmed as Mr Venning, but he seemed impressed. 'You will certainly hear from us further in the matter,' he told Ursula.

A week passed, however, before the girl did hear, during which time her spirits had again dropped to zero. But the news, when it came, was satisfactory. She was asked to give an open-air demonstration of her extinguisher at Woolwich. The Commandant there would report on it, and, if this report were favourable, the manufacture of the extinguisher on a large scale would be put in hand.

A busy fortnight followed. It was both busy and happy, for at last Ursula could feel that the matter was moving. The Commandant was almost as enthusiastic as old Mr Venning. Ursula's energy probably infected him, for his report was completed with what the War Office must have considered indecent rapidity. He sent a copy of it to Ursula. It was all that she could have desired. 'At last, at last, my work is done,' she wrote to Tony in a triumphant Christmas letter. 'Glory. Hallelujah!'

She little knew. Far from the work of the launching of the extinguisher being done, it was barely begun. For, to her astonishment, the Commandant's report was not followed by any communication from the War Office. She did not doubt that the manufacture of the extinguishers was in hand; how could the War Office have stopped short after such a report from the man whom they had themselves appointed? No, what worried her was that the work was being carried on without her supervision. Could she be given the address of the factory where the extinguishers were being made, she wrote. No answer. Would they kindly send her a few sample extinguishers for her inspection? No answer. How many extinguishers had actually been despatched to France? No answer. A reply-paid telegram, 'Were any of the Winfield extinguishers in use at the front?' at last brought back a curt reply in the negative.

Probably the authorities would hardly have treated Ursula's invention with such indifference had not Vernon Smee's 'liquid fire protector' now been to the fore. The latter, although not entirely satisfactory, had at least diminished the casualties. But poor Ursula had not even the comfort of knowing of this rival invention. She could only feel that eight months had passed fruitlessly. So she wrote in a frenzy demanding what steps, if any, were being taken with regard to the extinguisher. The answer arrived fairly promptly on March Ist. It was almost a duplicate of the letter she had received the previous July. 'The matter of your extinguisher is under consideration,' she was told. 'So they have not even started on it,' she wrote to Tony in an unprecedented burst of despair. 'I want to curse God and die.'

It was again through Tony that help came. For he had carried out his suggestion, and on returning to Boulogne after his leave had taken with him a couple of the extinguishers. These he had assiduously been showing, but so far without result. But now a Brigadier with scientific tendencies appeared on the scene. He was not only interested in the extinguisher himself, but, unknown to Tony, he interested the Commander-in-Chief. One day the Brigadier returned accompanied by a Divisional-Commander with his entire staff and the Liquid Fire Expert of the First Army from GHQ. The entire battalion, Tony wrote, gasped at this blazing spectacle of the great and glorious.

When the letter arrived, Ursula was too ill to be either cheered or amused by it. For the strain of the last few months had ended in a series of her old giddy attacks. On the previous day, she had lost consciousness for a considerable period. The doctor, whom Mrs Hibbert distractedly summoned, vetoed all mental effort for several months. Nor did Ursula resent the decree. At first she felt physically incapable of any work. Afterwards, she told herself, that even were she allowed to work, there was no work for her to do. Nothing seemed to have resulted from Tony's demonstration to the 'heaven-born'. Silence had again descended on the War Office. So, to Mrs Hibbert's surprise, Ursula made no objection to the proposal that they should go away for a long holiday together, indeed the girl was thankful to leave London for a time, if only on account of the air raids. The Zepps had ceased their attentions during these last few months, only to be now replaced by aeroplanes. Ursula was not frightened by the raids, but she found them extraordinarily tiring. Her mother really seemed to mind them less than she did. Little Mrs Hibbert, who screamed at the sight of a spider and had hysterics at a mouse, listened to the booming crash of bombs and shrapnel with absolute composure. 'I can do nothing, so what is the use of agitating?' she wisely observed. Only for one thing did she stipulate – when they came at night, she was to be left in peace in her own comfortable bedroom and not worried to go into damp cellars – 'where there might be black beetles,' she shuddered. Ursula, who knew her mother's intense objection to being seen before she had received Célestine's morning ministration, forbore to press the point.

They did not go to Dumdrochie, for both Ursula and her mother felt that the long train journey to Scotland for pleasure was unjustifiable. Probably, in any case, Mrs Hibbert would not have gone. For she selected instead the very antithesis; a crowded, luxurious hotel at a large south coast resort. Such a place was Ursula's particular detestation, but her mother had urged plaintively that she, too, must have a holiday. She was tired to death of housekeeping and these appalling wartime domestics – why was it that only the good servants went as munitionists? In any case, the programme answered. At the end of three months, when they returned to town, Ursula was quite well.

They had been back about a week when, one afternoon, an unknown Colonel was announced. 'He asked to see *Mr* Winfield,' the servant giggled. The poor Colonel was obviously embarrassed at finding himself in a lady's presence. 'I have come about the Winfield extinguisher –' he began and blushed still deeper. 'I mean the Miss Winfield ex – your extinguisher, Miss Winfield. I am in charge of the manufacture, and I was told to come here for the pattern and instructions. Five thousand have been ordered urgently for the front.'

The letter that was sent to Tony that evening was quite unlike the letter he had received the previous Christmas. Now that there seemed real ground for triumph, Ursula was not triumphant. 'It sounds hopeful, but I am afraid to hope,' she wrote. 'I have lost all faith. And, in any case, it is fourteen months since I first submitted the extinguisher. If it was of no use then, it is of no use now. If, as they say, it is of use now, it would have been of use then. However many they make, it will not bring back the men who have suffered and died, the men whom my extinguisher would have saved.'

CHAPTER TWENTY-SIX

Although Ursula could not rejoice, as she would have done a year earlier, over the acceptance of her invention, yet it did make her feel that an enormous burden had been lifted from her shoulders. And not only was her extinguisher taken, but now, when women seemed no longer to care, they were going to get the Vote. The third reading of the women's enfranchisement clause had been carried without a division. She had been right when she had told Tony that the Cause was won. And although, like everyone else, Ursula had been too busy of late to think very much about suffrage, she could not but feel that this lifted a second burden. Now, if only this horrible, horrible war would end. But there were repeated rumours of peace in the air. Surely it could not go on very much longer.

Ursula was in this hopeful frame of mind when, one day in October, she got a wire from Tony announcing his immediate arrival. She felt quite tremulous with joy. What a heavenly ten days they would have together! The telegram only came late in the afternoon, and directly after dinner he followed it. She rushed into his arms, but even as he kissed her she felt that something was amiss. Was he very tired – hungry? He negatived both suggestions. He had arrived in London before lunch, he told her, rather to her amazement, but he had had to go to the War Office and also to call on someone. He was on special leave – only three days. But it was not counted as leave, he added as Ursula exclaimed in dismay. Doubtless he would get his proper leave later. And now what about the extinguisher?

Such a curious position, Ursula related. She would be boiling with rage if it were not so absurd. GHQ had asked that someone should be sent to the front to instruct the men in the use of the extinguisher. Naturally she had assumed that she, as the inventor, would be invited. On the contrary, they had told her that such a thing was absolutely out of the question. She did not like to delay matters by making a fuss, and also her old assistant, Mr Flecker, was providentially at hand. He had been given the temporary rank of captain, and was to start tomorrow. She did not think she could have acquiesced so tamely, but the doctor had said that the work would probably be too much for her. She might have another breakdown directly she got out. Besides being personally humiliating, such a thing would do actual harm to the women's cause. 'Well, I am deeply thankful to your doctor,' Tony observed. Then he relapsed again into a moody silence.

What could be the matter with him, Ursula wondered. It was so unlike Tony. 'You had better tell me about it,' she said presently with a smile.

'I think I had.' Tony did not smile. 'Only it is rotten. I am almost ashamed to tell you.' He paused. 'I mentioned in my last letter that a Brigadier-General was coming to inspect us.'

'Yes, and I wondered if it was the same one who had been so nice about the extinguisher.'

'No. I'd never seen this man before – and I never want to see him again.' Tony stopped short.

What had happened? Had the Brigadier fallen foul of Tony – or had Tony fallen foul of the Brigadier? Visions of court-martials passed before Ursula's mind. In any case. Tony had been in the right; she was certain of that. 'Wasn't this Brigadier agreeable?' she inquired.

'Agreeable! A perfect swine. Got reeling drunk at mess. But it wasn't his getting drunk that mattered to me, but what he said when he was drunk.' Again Tony stopped.

'But if he were drunk, how could you mind what he said? Of course, it wasn't true,' Ursula suggested.

'It was. It was damnably true. Oh, what a fool I've been – a despicable fool.'

'But Tony, *what* did he say?' Ursula was getting more and more puzzled. How was it possible for a stranger, a man whom Tony had never seen before, to upset him like this? 'What did the intoxicated Brigadier say?'

'He said – ' Tony broke off; his face was turned away. 'He said' – the words came slowly – 'that I had been kept at the base because a certain pretty lady had pulled the strings.'

'What do you mean?' An explanation presented itself. 'Do you mean Mother?'

'Good Lord, no!'

In the silence that followed the clock ticked loudly, but

Ursula felt as though her heart were standing still. What did Tony mean? What could he mean? Why had he said that he was ashamed to tell her, that he was a fool, a 'despicable fool'? He would not have said that if a 'pretty lady' had merely taken trouble about him, had even fallen in love with him. There must be something on his side. What was between him and this 'pretty lady'? Was it she whom he had been to see this afternoon? Never in her life had Ursula been so horribly frightened. She was afraid to ask anything. And her throat was so dry. She did not think she *could* speak even if she would.

Still the clock ticked on. Tony stared at the fire, and Ursula stared at him. How was she to go on living, she wondered dully, if such a thing were true? And Tony had said that it was true. No one but Tony himself could have made her believe it. 'Damnably true.' What but one thing could be damnably true?

At last Tony looked up. He saw Ursula's face, and his own changed, softened. 'It is awfully good of you to mind so much, darling,' he said unexpectedly, 'I didn't think you would, because, of course, I know that it must have been a relief for you.' He got up and sat on the arm of her chair, possessing himself of one of her hands. 'I might have guessed that you would understand how I feel about it.'

Understand! It was all utterly incomprehensible! But one thing was certain – her vile suspicion was false. In her relief, Ursula wanted to laugh, to cry. Had Tony been able to see her face now, he could hardly have thought that she 'minded so much'; fortunately, from his perch, her hair alone was visible. 'I don't think that I do quite understand, Tony,' she ventured at last when she felt her voice again under control. 'Who is the "pretty lady"?'

'Lady Diana Findon, my uncle's widow.' Ursula gave a nod of comprehension. Of course, the fair and foolish Diana, the great man's daughter, who had made the uneatable rock cakes. 'I saw a good deal of her when I was training,' Tony was explaining. His chambers had been let, and his brother's town house shut up, so Diana – he called his aunt, Diana – had told him to look upon her house as his London hotel. As it had been almost impossible to get a room elsewhere, he had been glad to do so. Besides, he had put himself out a lot for Diana three years before when his uncle had died – there had been a bother about money affairs and a scoundrelly solicitor – so he had thought there was no harm in letting her make a return. He could never have imagined that the little idiot – He broke off, either because he was speechless with anger, or because, even in his anger, he could not abuse a woman.

'But Tony – ' Ursula still did not quite understand. Why had he called himself a fool, she asked? What had he to be ashamed of? He had not known that Lady Diana was 'pulling strings' on his behalf.

'I ought to have known. I should have known if I had not been an utter fool.' Tony began striding up and down the room in his agitation. 'Of course, I realise now that I should never have been kept for such an eternity at the base unless someone behind the scenes had been working it. Yes, while other fellows were being killed, I was sheltering behind a wheedling woman! And then you say there is nothing to be ashamed of!'

'Tony, you are ridiculous and exaggerated.' Ursula checked herself. She was trying to live up to her lover's previous good opinion of her, trying not to feel too grateful to the 'wheedling woman' who had kept her Tony safe for two years. It was made a little easier by a realization that, however correct Tony's feelings had been, the fair Diana's interest was probably in excess of an aunt's. 'You know, Tony, you did ask to be sent to the front several times,' she reminded him comfortingly.

'Asked! I ought to have insisted.'

'You really are absurd, dear!' Ursula laughed.

'Theirs not to question why,
Theirs but to linger by,'

she misquoted gaily. 'As though a mere lieutenant can insist, Tony!'

'He can sometimes.' Tony was again sitting on the arm of her chair. He kissed her hand. 'When I go back on Friday, it is to the front. I have exchanged. You must have known.'

Yes, she had known. She had, not thought it would be as soon, but she had known. She had known that no power in the world would now keep Tony out of danger. But had not Tony, her Tony, been in danger that very evening? If the horrible thing that she had suspected had been true then, indeed, she would have lost Tony. She would have lost him not only in the future, but in the past. Her Tony would never have existed. So the misunderstood news that Tony had already brought made the real news that he now brought not harder to bear, but far,

far easier. By comparison it almost seemed a little thing. 'Darling,' Tony said at last, frightened by her silence. 'I ought not to have blurted it out like that. Speak to me.'

'I don't mind so very much.' Suddenly Ursula began to cry. She was still not very strong. 'I don't mind so very much,' she repeated, clinging to him. And she wondered if she were crying for sorrow or for joy.

Yet once more Tony was lucky – or unlucky. For the first letter that Ursula got was from a rest camp forty miles behind the lines. 'We are here for several weeks,' Tony wrote. 'Of course I am pretty sick not yet to be in the *tranchées* and able to wipe off the past. But this Company have had a fearfully hot time, and are in need of a rest. A lot of the officers are new – by the way, I've been given a temporary commission as Captain which they say will certainly be made permanent – and we all need to shake down a bit before we have dealings with Fritz. So, you see, you can feel there is no cause for anxiety for quite a long time.'

Tony did not refer to the trenches again. Indeed, although he wrote every day, his letters were the merest scribbles. He was desperately hard-worked, he said; it sounded ridiculous, but he thought he had never been so hard-worked in his life before. He was taking the rôle of a children's nurse plus a JP plus a 'varsity tutor, only he had to 'tute' subjects he knew nothing whatever about. He was thankful Ursula hadn't been there the day before to hear him lecture on range-finding – the howlers he must have made! Fortunately the men knew even less than he did. All the same, he particularly objected to a pretence of knowledge he didn't possess. The other officers were an awfully decent lot. His opinion of 'Tommy' had gone up even higher than before.

Ursula was nearly as busy as Tony, for she was devising a small improvement in the extinguisher. She sometimes wondered if she could have done it if Tony had gone to the trenches; would she have been too anxious for original work? But now, as he said, there was no need for anxiety. The rest-camp was as safe as Boulogne, and he was evidently far happier. Indeed, in some strange way, even anxiety for the future had largely left her. After all, there were men who had been all the time in the trenches and who had never had a scratch. As a scientist, Ursula would have told you that she did not believe in luck. Yet the fact that Tony had escaped all danger for years did make her feel that he would go on escaping it. Despite her science, like any ignorant work-girl, she had a secret conviction that her 'boy' bore a charmed life.

She was working in the laboratory one afternoon when the servant brought in a telegram. Yes, that would be the one she was expecting about her extinguisher. For the moment she could not take it as she was in the middle of an experiment, but she told the maid to put it down. The War Office was behaving quite decently, she reflected. She had only sent them the particulars of the improved extinguisher two days ago. What a pity she had not known a year ago that a reply-paid wire was the only way in which to get an answer out of a government department! Her stopwatch showed her that she could now take the voltmeter reading. She jotted it down and picked up the telegram: 'War Office reports Tony wounded. Am asking further details. Claude Balestier.'

It was not true. It could not be true. Tony could not be wounded. He was not in the trenches. She had heard from him that very morning. Or was it possible that he might be? His letters took a long time coming. But even so, he would not be wounded. One did not get wounded the moment one reached the trenches. It was impossible. Why was she trembling when it was not true? There had been some mistake. This man was another Balestier. Such things happened. They often happened. It was silly to feel like this when it was not true. Oh, why could not the War Office telegram have come straight to her? Why had they said they could only communicate with a wife or near relation? If she had had the original telegram, she would have seen the mistake. Tony's brother had misunderstood. She would telegraph to him at once. She would telegraph to the War Office, to Tony himself. Tony was still at the rest-camp. He was not hurt. It was not true.

She sent off her telegrams and waited. (It was not true. It was not true.) She knew that any reply that evening was improbable. Claude's would probably be the first, and his had to come from Exeter. (It was not true.) There was a possibility of Claude being sent to India. If he were, would the War Office still insist on communicating only with him? (It was not true.) How proud Tony was of his brother for going into the army! It certainly was rather fine, for Claude was delicate and at least ten years over military age. And what persistence he had shown. He had even dyed his hair, Tony said. But then Claude was neither married nor engaged. There was no one to whom he was of supreme importance. (It was not true. It was not true.) Despite her reiterated assurance, Ursula did not sleep that night.

About eleven o'clock the following morning there came, not one of the expected telegrams, but a letter from Tony. Ursula was seized with another fit of trembling; indeed she was trembling so much that it was difficult to tear open the envelope, to unfold the pencilled pages. The heading? Yes, it was the rest-camp! She had known it. The War Office telegram was not true. Tony was not wounded. He was safe at the rest-camp, forty miles from the trenches. She began to read her letter – it was longer than usual, but she found that she could hardly grasp it. How could she be so stupid? It was all about the gunnery course that Tony was giving to the men. Perhaps it was too scientific for her mind! She found it difficult even to follow the account of an afternoon's trip to the nearest French town – the excellent coffee, 'a divine omelette'. Oh dear, how her head was aching! She remembered that she had not slept. Well, she would go to her room now and have a sleep. But what was this? Something she had overlooked – a hardly legible postscript written along the side of one of the pages, and evidently added in desperate haste: 'We have received unexpected instructions to move up tonight. Will write again as soon as possible. Darling, don't be more anxious than you can help.'

Ursula was still staring at these scribbled words when the servant, by one of life's coincidences, brought in a telegram. 'Fear there is no mistake. War Office wires Tony's condition serious. Going out to him if can get leave. Claude Balestier.'

Then it was true. It was not a mistake. Tony was wounded – seriously wounded. At this very moment he might be mangled, crushed. He might have no arms – no legs. He might be blind – like that man in the hospital. If she saw him, perhaps she would not know him. And all in a few hours. This was what they had done to him, to her Tony. Her Tony, who was so beautiful, so strong, so well. Suddenly Ursula began to swear; never in her life had she done such a thing before. 'Oh, God, damn them, damn them, damn them. Damn our rulers. Damn all the governments; damn their war.'

The paroxysm of fury passed. She re-read the telegram. Claude spoke of going out to Tony. Yes, that was good; Tony was fond of his brother, he would be glad to see him. But, of course, she must go too. Indeed, she would not wait for Claude. It might be days before he got his leave. She would go by herself, at once. Why, Tony would be wanting her; even now he might be calling her. No, she must not think of Tony, she must think only of how to get to him. But where was he? In a hospital, of course, but where? Why had Claude not told her? Perhaps he did not know. Tony was very ill and they did not even know in what country to find him! But this would not do. She must pull herself together, be business-like and cold. What was the first step? To go to the War Office and ask for Mr Venning. And that other place at which people made inquiries – Cox, yes, that was the name. She must take money with her, a lot of money; she would cash a cheque on her way. And take her dressing case; then she could start off to Tony without first coming home. Mum? She must tell Mum. Oh, Mum would be out; this was a canteen morning. She had been out all yesterday too, so she knew nothing. As Ursula raced upstairs she decided to leave Claude's two telegrams for her mother to read. They would explain the position. It was not as though she herself were in any danger of forgetting their contents, she reflected grimly.

At eight o'clock in the evening, Ursula, still carrying her dressing case, returned home. Not only had she been unable to 'start off to Tony', she had not even found out where he was. After hours of waiting at the War Office, she had seen Mr Venning. He had been most kind, most sympathetic, but entirely unable to help her. Through his good offices she had interviewed various other busy officials with the same result. From the War Office Ursula had gone on to Cox's Bank, only to find it shut. With some delay, she had obtained the address of their special inquiry department, but that, too, was closing as she reached it. She made her way in, almost by force, and confronted two of the voluntary workers who were putting away papers preparatory to leaving. These ladies also were most kind and sympathetic. Indeed, although they were used to tragic applicants, Ursula's white, set face frightened them. When they heard that money need not be considered, they wrote and sent off telegrams to agents at various possible places in France and Belgium. They were almost sure, these ladies said, that they would be able to give Miss Winfield news some time the next day. Meanwhile there was nothing more that could be done that evening – absolutely nothing. One of them fetched a taxi for Ursula to go home.

When Mrs Hibbert saw her daughter, she was even more horrified by her appearance than Cox's ladies had been. She did not, however, make any comment; nor beyond a brief 'Any news?' did she refer to the subject of the telegrams that had been left for her to read. When her daughter was miserable, Mrs Hibbert knew by experience that sympathy was the one thing she could not stand. So the little lady chatted brightly, perfectly aware that her auditor was not taking in a single word. If only Ursula could cry, she was thinking; it would be much less terrible for her than this silent, stony calm. She herself had been crying; indeed, it was apparent from a certain streakiness of complexion irreparable on Célestine's evening out. 'You'll have one of those nice little cutlets in aspic, won't you, darling?' she now said, as she served the dainty cold supper. 'I had them in from Flercey. Our woman's cooking is so appalling that one is driven to seek outdoor relief.'

Ursula obediently cut off a mouthful. Then she laid down her knife and fork. 'I can't, Mother.' Mrs Hibbert was wise enough not to press the point; she realised that eating was probably a physical impossibility for her daughter. Instead, she went away and presently reappeared with a cup of liquid meat essence. In it she had dissolved a sleeping draught. 'Drink then, my dear child.' This Ursula managed. Afterwards, by her mother's advice, she went off to bed. Half an hour later, when Mrs Hibbert looked in, she was sleeping heavily.

This day was for Ursula a mere forerunner of many similar days, similar, at least, in not getting any nearer to Tony. She certainly did have news of him. Although the War Office still seemed in ignorance, Cox's ladies were as good as their word, and within twenty-four hours were able to give her the name of the hospital. Two days later they sent quite a budget of information. Their agent had seen Captain Balestier. His condition was very serious, but not hopeless. He was suffering from a shrapnel wound: the piece of shell had penetrated the body and had, it was feared, touched the spine. Captain Balestier was unconscious; he had been unconscious ever since it had occurred. He was to be transferred at once to a base hospital, and there he would be operated upon.

Ursula's feeling was one of relief. Tony's condition was not hopeless. He was in no pain, either physical or mental. He was not disfigured or terribly mutilated. And she had been picturing such horrors. Yes, she was thankful – thankful, above all, for his unconsciousness. What a thing for which to have to be thankful crossed her mind with a quick return of her first rage. But she was almost too worn out for rage. Moreover, she was too busy. For she would not slacken her efforts to get out to him. If Cox's man could see Tony, why could not she? It did not matter very much while Tony was unconscious, but at any moment he might regain consciousness. Then he would want her. She must be there.

She was not there! One day she heard at Cox's that Captain Balestier had been operated upon and was now conscious. They did not know if the operation was considered successful; they knew nothing further. Five days later a service letter arrived in an unknown, feminine hand. Captain Balestier was going on as well as could be expected; he was considered practically out of danger. The doctor had given strict orders that he was not to exert his mind in any way, so he could neither dictate nor receive letters. The writer did not know whether she was justified even in sending a message, but Captain Balestier was so anxious that it should go. The message was: 'Say I want her. I love her.'

Ursula burst into a passion of tears. She had not cried before, but the very childishness of Tony's message overwhelmed her. 'Tony, Tony,' she whispered, half crying and half laughing, 'Tony, beloved, and I love *you*. I want *you*.' She was happy at hearing from her lover; she was happy at the nurse's assurance of his being practically out of danger. But, presently, beneath her happiness, she grew afraid. Tony was so reserved. How unlike him to send such a message through a stranger. How still more unlike him to say he wanted her, when he must have known she would be there if they would let her come. He must still be very, very ill, she told herself. But this decided it. Somehow or other she would get to him. Wild thoughts raced through her brain of taking the first train to some south coast village and there bribing a fisherman to sail her across. Surely if she paid enough it could be done. But, landed in France, how should she manage? She would have no passport, no papers of any sort; she could not even speak French. Suppose, by a miracle, she got to Tony's hospital, then they would not let her in. No, the only way was to go on hammering at the War Office and the Foreign Office – hammering with redoubled energy. But first she would write to Tony's nurse.

Among the many outpourings that the kindly little nurse had received, in answer to letters written for the 'boys', she had rarely had one that touched her more than Ursula's;

indeed, she cried over it almost as much as Ursula had cried over hers. 'But I don't believe they'll ever let Miss Winfield come over to see him, particularly now that he is out of danger,' she reflected judiciously. 'If she were coming, I suppose I ought to tell her about him – only it seems so dreadful. He must have been such a fine-looking fellow. I don't think he has guessed it himself. It seems so dreadful for both of them that he should be paralysed.'

CHAPTER TWENTY-SEVEN

The little nurse was wrong. Tony had guessed it! But it was true that he had not done so during those first days of recovered consciousness. When he had only just come back to life, it did not seem to him strange that part of his frame should still remain inert. All he knew was that he wanted Ursula. He wanted her quiet, tender strength. She would make him well again. But now his mind seemed more active. He was daily growing stronger. His arms, although wasted and feeble, were under his control. He could hold his medicine glass, pick up his handkerchief. And yet – the little nurse was telling him of her letter from Ursula, 'such a sweet letter,' she said. 'Why are my legs always numb, Nurse?' he demanded suddenly.

The little nurse's rosy face grew rosier. She was not good at lying; the question, unexpected at the moment, had taken her aback. 'Well, you are still weak, you see,' she stammered.

It was enough. Now he knew. The next day he attacked the doctor; he, too, was inclined to prevaricate. 'You may as well say it straight out,' Tony observed. 'I am paralysed from the waist down.'

Yes, it was unfortunately true. But when they had operated, they had not found as much mischief as had been expected. The piece of shell had grazed the posterior process of a lower vertebra, but it did not seem to have damaged it. No, Röntgen rays were of not much use in such a case; there was too much thickness and the processes overlapped. Of course, if the vertebra had been touched, a minute splinter of bone might now be lodged in the vertebral canal, or possibly a clot of blood had been formed there. But in the doctor's opinion, the paralysis was due to shell-shock rather than to actual physical injury. If he were correct, another sudden shock might bring back the use of the limbs; such recoveries had occurred quite frequently in this war. In any case, he was very hopeful that massage and electric treatment would give a good result.

'How long will the good result be in coming, if it does come?' Tony interrupted.

Such a question was impossible to answer. A doctor was not omniscient! In a month they could probably hope for some signs of improvement. Meanwhile – the doctor turned to the little nurse – the patient was still to be kept absolutely quiet. No, no letters of any kind. He was to have a complete mental rest.

Tony made no further remark. When the doctor had gone, he asked the little nurse to write and explain the position to Ursula. 'I want you to tell her exactly what they say, both about the paralysis and the chance of improvement,' he insisted.

The letter was a second bombshell. Still, Ursula felt, it was not as bad as the original news of Tony being wounded. For her temperament was fundamentally sanguine; she seized upon the doctor's suggestion of recovery. Of course Tony would recover. How could he help recovering when he was so strong? In a few months he would be walking about again. Why was she not there to tell him so, to give him confidence? Belief in getting well was halfway towards getting well. Besides, while he was paralysed, she would be able to do so much for him. If he were a long time in recovering, if he did not recover – she would hardly admit the thought – well, that was all the more reason why she should be with him. They must be married directly – while he was still in hospital. Then, at any moment if he were discharged, she could take care of him. But first she must get over there. Her efforts and importunity were redoubled. Five weeks later, almost to her own surprise, she found herself in France.

She had first to go to Paris, for the pretext upon which Mr Venning had finally procured her a permit was that her presence in that city was necessary in connection with the extinguisher. In any case, further authorities had to be interviewed there in order to get the authorisation to visit the base hospital. Well, it gave her time to wire to Tony's nurse and ask her to prepare his mind. He must not be startled by her sudden arrival. The next day a telegram came in reply: 'Sorry Captain Balestier transferred to England yesterday do not know where.'

It was too much! After all these weeks of ceaseless effort in order to reach Tony, she found herself as far away from him as before. She was, indeed, worse off. For again she had been plunged into the uncertainty of those first few days, only now he was 'somewhere in England', while she was in France! To think that they actually must have crossed on the journey. Why had not some instinct warned her? It was maddening! Well, the only thing to be done was to return home immediately.

It was more easily said than done. If it had been hard to get over, it seemed equally hard to get back. Red tape enmeshed her in Paris as in London. Her permit had been made out for six weeks. The most she could do was to curtail it by two. Thus over a month had passed before she found herself once more at home.

Of course during this time she had not been without news of Tony. He was in London, at a private house near Regent's Park, transformed for the time being into a military hospital. Someone, she presumed it was a nurse, wrote to her every two or three days. This person was the worst correspondent whom Ursula had ever come across. The letters consisted, for the most part, of two phrases, 'Captain Balestier has passed a good night and his general condition is unchanged,' or else 'Captain Balestier's general condition is unchanged and he has passed a good night.'

It was while Ursula was in Paris that the Representation of the People Bill received the King's assent and became law. So now women, or at any rate women over thirty, would be able to vote. It left Ursula almost indifferent. How curious it was when once it had seemed to her the most important question on earth. But what did the Vote or anything else matter in a mad world? There was only one thing that mattered – Tony.

Ursula was not entirely dependent on the nurse's monotonous bulletins. Her mother went to the hospital two or three times, and, of course, described her visits. But these letters, although long, really did not add much to Ursula's knowledge. Tony was not so very changed in appearance, Mrs Hibbert wrote, though he was frightfully thin. But he was so awfully silent; she couldn't get a word out of him. She supposed he was feeling too blue. Oh, why wasn't she there to comfort him? poor Ursula reflected miserably.

At last the day came when she *was* there. Her heart was beating chokingly as she walked up the short drive to the rather imposing stone house. The garden, a fair-sized one for London, held sheets of yellow daffodils; they looked like sunshine on the ground, but the wind was biting. Ursula rang the bell and was asked to wait in the lounge-hall; this was evidently almost unchanged from its private days, although crutches and an invalid carrying-chair jostled curiously with the Renaissance cabinet and a pair of great Nankin vases. Presently she was shown into a drawing room – what a curious stiff preface to meeting Tony! Two groups were already there – an officer with one leg talking to an elderly man, perhaps his father; and a boy – he looked absurdly young – with a bandaged head and one arm in a sling, who was carrying on a gay conversation with two girls, quite evidently not his sisters. But when was she going to be taken in to Tony? Ursula wondered impatiently. Then a door opened on the other side of the room, and a wheelchair was pushed in by a nurse. Ursula looked up carelessly. Perhaps this nurse would, at last, take her to Tony's room. It *was* Tony!

Ursula went forward. She had imagined Tony certainly in bed, and to see him up was almost a shock. But how splendid that he should be well enough! They shook hands like strangers – of course, there was nothing else to be done with all these people about. But his hand-clasp was unsatisfyingly short and unresponsive; perhaps it was because he was still so weak. She sat down beside the wheelchair and the nurse left them. At last she could look at Tony, really look at him. She found that he was looking at her, but he turned his eyes away at once. Again, it struck her, that it was like a stranger. 'Tony,' she said softly, almost appealingly.

He paid no attention. 'So, you've got the Vote at last?' he said instead with rather a high laugh.

'What?' Then Ursula realised his words. 'Yes, we have got the Vote,' she repeated dully.

'Aren't you frightfully elated? I thought you'd come waving flags and banners!' He laughed again.

Surely this gaiety was unnatural. And this quick, excited way of speaking was so unlike Tony. Still, it was his voice. 'I should be elated if – Let us talk about something else,' Ursula broke off.

'Well, how about the extinguisher then? Is it booming?'

The extinguisher seemed to Ursula hardly more attractive as a topic of conversation than suffrage. For the first time in her life it needed an effort to switch her mind on to her work. Oh, yes, they were using the extinguisher in large numbers now, she told him; she quoted the latest figures.

Tony was obviously interested, and he had grown serious; that was a relief. 'Well, it's a pity they didn't start using it a trifle sooner,' he remarked. 'When we were rushed up to the front, it was because Fritz had broken through; they'd captured a bit of front-line trench, and it had been done by liquid fire – so the chaps said whom we relieved. Our men had panicked when they saw the whole show blazing – small blame to 'em. I asked the CO if they had any extinguishers, but he'd never even heard of such a thing.'

'So if the War Office had taken up the extinguisher when I first offered it, the Germans would not have broken through, and you –' Ursula stopped. Such a thing did not bear saying; above all, it did not bear saying to Tony. 'But I don't want to talk about the extinguisher, either. I want to talk about you.'

'I am afraid I am not a very interesting topic of conversation.'

How difficult it was! What was amiss? Ursula felt almost as though a physical barrier were dividing them. It was horrible these other people being there. If she could have put her arms around Tony, have pressed her lips to his – 'Isn't there anywhere where we could be alone?' she murmured.

'No, it is one of the drawbacks here. If one can go into the garden it is not so bad, but they won't let me out today; besides, it would be too cold for you. We could go into my ward, but there would be just as many people there.'

'Well, I don't think we can be heard in this noise.' The bandaged boy and the two girls were indeed laughing to such an extent that other conversation was largely screened. 'What do the London doctors say about you, Tony? You know I have heard nothing.'

'They say that what the man in France told me about the possibility of shell-shock was all rot. They say that I am not likely to sprout a new vertebra, so there can't be a recovery.'

'Tony, it isn't true.' She braced herself from the blow, and even tried to laugh feebly. 'I am quite sure they don't talk of vertebræ 'sprouting'.

'Not in so many words, but that is what they mean. Or rather they think it is a new vertebral column I need. And the proof of it is that all this electric treatment and massage has not done me the least good. If anything, I am worse.' He sank his voice still lower. 'I shall never be fit for anything again. I have got both feet in the grave – and both legs too for that matter! I didn't mean to hurt you. It is better to tell you the truth.'

'Much better.' It was a horrible moment. She wanted more than ever to touch him, to hold him. In what way could she comfort him? The one-legged officer and his friend had got up and were going out of the room. Ursula almost prayed that the other group might follow them. They did stand, but resettled themselves, with an air of permanence, on a couch. However, they were now farther off and making even more noise. 'But, darling,' Ursula whispered under cover of the laughter, 'you can still think and feel – that is the most important part. And you have still got the use of your arms; why, there are lots of things you will be able to do.' Then she remembered the doctor's embargo. 'For surely you will soon be allowed to read and write again.'

'Oh, I am allowed to read and write now as much as I like,' Tony said carelessly.

Ursula stared. She could not have heard him properly. One might easily make a mistake when they were both talking so quietly. Because if Tony were allowed to write, of course he would have written to her. She had often wondered, indeed, that he was not allowed correspondence, when he seemed to be allowed visitors. 'You didn't say that you were allowed to write?'

Tony nodded. 'Yes, ever since I came here. These medicos think that cutting it off was folly on the part of the doctor in France.'

'But, Tony, you are allowed to write and you never wrote to me?' It was with difficulty that she kept her incredulity *sotto voce*.

'I did not write because I did not know what to say.'

'You did not know what to say?' She seemed unable to do anything but repeat his words in an imbecile way like a parrot.

'I was still hoping up till quite lately that what the man in France said was true – that there was no real physical damage and that some day I should get back the use of my legs.'

'But, Tony, what has that got to do with writing to me? You don't write with your legs.' Her whisper was rather desperate because she suddenly knew the answer to her question. 'Anyway, you won't have to write to me now,' she went on with a forced gaiety, 'because I shall always be with you.'

'No, you won't.' Tony also was speaking beneath his breath. 'I knew you would say that, but I won't accept the sacrifice.'

'Tony, don't be utterly ridiculous – after all these years – the only sacrifice would be not to be with you – ' How difficult it was to carry on a conversation of supreme importance beneath one's breath! 'Of course we are going to get married at once.'

'We are not going to get married at all. I will not be married out of pity.'

'Pity! If there is any pity about it, it is pity for myself.' (This whispering was maddening!)

'You would be more to be pitied if you were tied to a log. You saw how I was wheeled in just now?' (Tony's bass tones fortunately for him carried less easily.) 'A refreshing spectacle, wasn't it?'

'Tony!' Ursula's voice failed her.

'I wouldn't have minded your marrying me,' Tony went on more gently, 'if there were any hope of my eventually recovering, but there isn't.'

'Yes, there is.' Ursula had indiscreetly raised her voice, but she remembered in time. 'And if there isn't, it is all the more reason for my being your wife.'

'You would not be my wife.' Tony also was finding such a conversation in whispers rather trying; perhaps otherwise he might have expressed himself less bluntly. 'You would only be my nurse.'

'I would sooner be your nurse than nothing at all.' Ursula stopped and began pulling down her veil. She felt as though she were going to cry, and whatever might happen, she could not cry before a room full of strangers. Suddenly another idea occurred to her, an idea which turned her cold and stopped her tears from flowing. She had heard of illness changing people's feelings. Perhaps Tony's feelings had changed.

Perhaps his reluctance to marry her was not for her sake but for his own. But there was the message he had sent her from France. 'What you said, after the operation, that you wanted me, that you loved me, it was true?' she stammered, though still in a low tone.

He had seen the tears in her eyes despite the veil. 'Yes, of course it was true, darl – ' the doubly indiscreet word was cut short. 'But I ought never to have sent such a message. I didn't know then, I didn't realise. And when I did know, that fool of a doctor told me – ' Even louder peals of girlish laughter rang through the room. The bandaged boy must have been a wit. 'We can't discuss the question in this beargarden,' Tony muttered ungallantly.

'No, we can't.' Ursula got up. 'Though it is not of the least use discussing it anywhere. Whatever you say, you won't make me accept my dismissal.' They again shook hands as strangers.

CHAPTER TWENTY-EIGHT

When Ursula said goodbye to Tony at the hospital, she made up her mind not to visit him there again; the position was too impossibly difficult. But she might not have had the strength of mind really to carry out her decision if the choice had been left in her hands. The authorities, however, perhaps on account of the air-raids, suddenly transferred Captain Balestier to a hospital near Cheltenham.

Now that Ursula knew that the embargo on letter-writing was raised, she began again, unabashed, the old, daily lover-like correspondence. At least on her side it was begun again. Tony wrote at much less frequent intervals, odd, stiff notes with no beginning, and no ending except his name. From them Ursula learnt that the weather was beautiful; that he was sitting in the garden most of the day; that his condition was unchanged; that he was shortly to be discharged from the army; that he was then returning to his old chambers at the Temple; that he supposed it was useless telling her not to write, but that when he came to London the matter must be settled in a final interview. After some years, he concluded, if he were still alive and she wished it, they could meet again as friends.

Poor Ursula hardly knew whether to laugh or to cry. Imagine not seeing Tony for years and then meeting him as a friend! But it was impossible to discuss their relations in a letter. On the other point, however, she did write to him. Tony's chambers on the top floor in the Temple seemed to her wildly unsuitable. How was he to get up and down stairs? The fact that at the hospital he was sitting out all day showed the importance that was attached to fresh air. Then his food? Catering was difficult enough now under any circumstances with the rationing and queues; who would undertake it for him at the Temple? Besides, Fleet Street was a perfect magnet for enemy aircraft. Apart from the actual danger, the noise of the bombs and the excitement must be bad for anyone in Tony's state. All this was vehemently pointed out by return of post.

One day, soon after, a visiting card was brought up to Ursula – 'Mr Claude Balestier'. She hurried to the drawing room, for she liked Tony's grave, quiet half-brother, in spite of finding his excessive conventionality somewhat irritating. He had just paid a flying visit to Tony at the hospital, he said, and so had come to report. A further reason for his call was soon apparent; he wanted to find out the real state of affairs between Ursula and his brother. 'You must excuse me if I appear intrusive, Miss Winfield,' he said with a gentle politeness that reminded Ursula of Tony, 'but I may be sent off to India at any time – yes, definite orders have come through at last – and I feel so anxious about leaving the poor dear old fellow in his present state. He told me, or rather he implied, that his engagement to you is at an end.'

'It may be at an end on his side, but it is not at an end on mine. And it takes two to break an engagement!'

'Ah!' Mr Balestier looked relieved; he seemed to think it would be indiscreet to inquire further. 'And this preposterous Temple scheme – I suppose Tony has told you about it? Have you tried to persuade him to give it up?'

'Oh, yes, I have written to him. I told him it was absolute folly with all those stairs and the raids; he has not answered yet. But you have seen him, Mr Balestier; could you not bring him to reason?'

'I dwelt on all the disadvantages at immense length! But Tony is an obstinate beggar, as you are probably aware, Miss Winfield. He said that there was nothing he could do out of doors, so he would not want to go up and down stairs. As for the air-raids, they seemed a positive attraction! The fact is, that the poor dear chap is so down on his luck, he does not care where he goes or what becomes of him. And his chambers will be empty on the tenth – the tenants are leaving in any case – so that occupying them himself is the plan that seems to call for the least effort.'

'But there is no one to look after him there! How will he get proper food?'

'I went into that too, for I know the Temple kitchen is shut. But Tony only treated me to a long tirade to the effect that no man who is not actively serving the country ought to have food – I presume he meant beyond the barest minimum. He apparently applies the same rule to attendance, for I found he actually proposed living in his chambers alone and merely having a nurse in for certain hours of the day – ' Ursula gave a little exclamation of horror. 'Yes, imagine it, a man in his condition! However, I did get him to consent to my finding him a male attendant. He was very reluctant; he said that it was iniquitous he should take up the time of an able-bodied man, and that he would loathe having a stranger always fussing around.'

'Yes, he would loathe that.' Ursula's tone was curiously absent.

Although Ursula continued to write to Tony every day, she made no further reference to the Temple plan – much to his surprise! And when the plan had become an actuality, when he had finally left the hospital, a private citizen once more, and was established in his chambers with the attendant whom Claude had found, then he was still more surprised; for Ursula's letters suddenly stopped. Here he had been in London five whole days and not a word from her, not a sign. Of course, it was a mere foretaste of his whole future life. He himself had said that they were only to meet for a final interview, but he could not understand why she should stop writing before they had had that interview. Perhaps she thought it would be better not to have it; that it would be better simply, without a word, to part. And perhaps she was right. If only he had not counted so much upon seeing her once more, upon seeing her alone. Not that he had meant to go back to their old relations even during the farewell hour; that would not be playing the game. He had meant to treat her as a stranger. Only he had been unable to keep from thinking that perhaps Ursula would refuse to be treated as a stranger. Suppose he were to feel her arms around his neck, her lips on his cheek. Her recent letters had made it seem more than a possibility. Never, not even in that first long ago year of their engagement, not in these last years of service in France, had she written to him with such tenderness, such passion. And he had had nothing else to do all day but to read these letters of hers, to re-read them; to think of them and to think of her; to think of their meeting and forget that it was to be final. If only she had never started writing to him again! Although he had so much appreciated her letters, he had thought all the time that they were a mistake; now he was sure of it. For in the French hospital, and afterwards in London, when correspondence was debarred to him – or Ursula thought it was – he had grown accustomed to her silence; or perhaps he had felt too ill to mind about it. But now she had made him want her letters; she had made him want her, want her horribly. And it was at this moment that she had stopped writing.

He could have stood it better, he felt, if he had had other friends. But all the men he knew, who had not been killed, were serving abroad. Old Claude had sailed two days ago; if only the U-boats kept off the ship! He felt frightfully anxious. And things were going desperately badly at the front, although, of course, he knew our men would pull it off in the end. Life in these chambers was rotten; yes, Ursula and Claude had been right. He had told Claude that his surroundings did not affect him, but he had found out his mistake. He had found that he did mind never getting out; he minded it immensely. The small rooms penned him in, suffocated him – of course it was absurd; what did it matter when, in any case, he could not walk about? He minded the other things too, the inadequate cleaning of his frowsy 'laundress', the general disorder, the absence of beauty – surely it had not been so bad when he had lived there before? He minded – although it humiliated him to mind – the unpalatable food, the rough way in which it was served – certainly he had no temptation to exceed his ration!

What he minded most of all, however, was the attendant whom his brother had, with so much difficulty, secured for him. Even in this class one suffered from 'dug-outs', Tony reflected humorously. For the man was an absolute fool, with no method or punctuality. This was his evening out; it was now ten o'clock. He ought to be back, but probably he would stroll in nearer eleven! Twice the idiot had forgotten his key and had left it inside when he went out. It would have been precious awkward, Tony reflected, if he had not had this spring arrangement fixed up by his chair which enabled him to open the front door. This morning, too, when he had spoken to the fellow about something, he had been downright impertinent. He ought to have been sacked on the spot, Tony told himself. He would have sacked him, but it would probably be impossible to replace him, and there was the promise to Claude. If he had only known before that he might hope some day to get on to crutches, he would never have made such a promise. It was odd; the doctor at Cheltenham, who told him about the crutches, seemed to think that he had got better there. But it wasn't true. He had tried several times, and he had no more use in his legs than he had had before.

Anyway, he would write to Claude and tell him that if he ever were able to get about on crutches, he should consider himself absolved from his promise. Yes, the first thing he would do would be to sack this fool of a man – chuck the crutches at his head! But how in the world was he going to stand him until that happy day arrived? How was he going to stand everything? He was sick and tired of it all. Life – this could not be called life. If only he could hear from Ursula it would be more bearable. If only he could see her!

He did not know it, but Ursula was not very far away. At that very moment she was coming up the stairs. As she passed quickly up the many deserted flights, she thought of the only other time she had come here to visit Tony – that summer evening so many years ago. How shocked he had been; he had not let her come farther than the entrance. Well, now he was going to be shocked again!

She remembered the door, and this time again 'the oak was not sported' – Tony had told her once that this was the proper expression. She knocked; in spite of herself it seemed rather a timid sound. Would it be heard? However, the door opened at once, apparently by itself. Ursula was not surprised, for Claude Balestier, during his farewell call the day before he sailed, had told her of Tony's spring arrangement. Neither was she surprised at the non-appearance of Tony's attendant, for Claude had also mentioned that the man had an evening out once a week – this evening. How worried poor Claude had been about it; and she had been worried too – then.

She had by now walked into the hallway, the front door closing behind her. What was she to do next? One of the four doors that gave on to the little hall stood slightly ajar, showing a line of light. Dared she push it open? She did so. Yes, it was all right; it was Tony's study. And there in an armchair, almost facing her, sat Tony. But he did not look up. He was reading. Yet, surely he must have heard the creak of the room door as it swung open; he must have heard the knock on the outer door – besides, who had worked the spring to open it if it were not he? But she was sure he was looking better than that afternoon at the hospital – less thin, less nervous. How lovely!

'I suppose you have forgotten your key again?' The tone was exasperated. He still did not look up.

'I have not got a key yet.'

'Ursula!' He had looked up now. He was staring as though he saw an apparition; perhaps he thought he did. Ursula did look rather wonderful in that dusty, untidy little room, as she stood there in her blue cloak of some soft, shining material and her white felt hat with its long blue feather. Her cheeks were flushed and her dark-lashed eyes looked very big.

'But I dare say I often shall forget the key,' she went on. 'You know I am not very good at remembering things.'

'Ursula!' He ignored her jesting words. He was still staring, and his breath came quickly. 'What are you doing here?'

'Isn't it obvious?' She was pulling out her hatpins as she spoke, and now she neatly laid down both her hat and cloak, revealing a white summer gown. 'I suppose I may sit down, although you do not offer me a chair.' Her tone was quite unemotional. She meant to be unemotional. Tony must not be excited more than she could help.

He watched her as though he were hypnotised. 'Why have you come?' he said at last. His voice was hoarse.

She had settled herself in the other armchair opposite to him. 'You suggested having a final interview yourself,' she remarked.

'But not at this hour, at ten o'clock at night. You must go home at once.'

'I am a little later than I meant to be, but they are not expecting me at home. I have said good night to Mother and to my stepfather – he is on leave, by the way. So they think I am in my own room. I shall not be missed until tomorrow morning, and then they will find a note of the stereotyped kind to explain matters.'

'To explain matters! Ursula, have you gone out of your mind? You are to go home at once. My man may be back at any minute. He can't find you here!'

'I should think he would hardly be able to help finding me here, for I shall be here all night, and the place does not seem very large.' Ursula's tone was still quite calm. 'Now, Tony, it is no use getting agitated. I know I shall be compromised – hopelessly compromised. Probably Colonel Hibbert will forbid me to return to Lowndes Square; you know how conventional his views are about women – almost worse than yours! He will say that his door is closed to me, as he did when I was a suffragette. But it will not matter in the very least, because we are going to be married at eleven o'clock tomorrow morning. I have got a licence. Perhaps you would like to see it?' She began feeling for the pocket of her cloak.

'Ursula!' Tony had appeared almost dazed. 'I will not have it,' he now exclaimed violently. 'I tell you I will not have you sacrificed by marrying me.'

'And I tell you that I will not be sacrificed by *not* marrying you.' She resumed her soothing tone. 'So we are really of one accord.'

'I will not have it! I will not marry you!'

'Well, what are you going to do about it then?' Ursula was playing carelessly with the long string of blue beads that she wore. 'You can hardly tell your man to turn me out by force when he comes, can you, Tony? And by tomorrow I shall be hopelessly compromised.' She seemed to enjoy the words.

'Ursula, you are to go at once. You are to go; do you hear me?'

She looked up and was going to make some light retort, but the words died on her lips. She seemed to stop breathing. For Tony was standing – standing alone! They gazed at each other for perhaps ten seconds; then he sank heavily back in his chair. But now Ursula was beside him, kneeling beside him, with her arms around him. She could feel his heart beating like a hammer. 'Isn't there anything you should take – brandy?' She glanced around the room.

'No – I shall be all right – in a minute.' The words came in gasps. They remained there in silence, Tony in his chair and Ursula kneeling by him. Time passed; it might have been three minutes, it might have been thirty. She could feel his heart-beats growing more regular, less pounding. At last he spoke. 'Well, that was rather unexpected.' He laughed, but the laugh was shaky. It is unnerving suddenly to pull both feet out of the grave. 'So that old josser in France was right after all!'

'Yes, he was right.' Ursula was still keeping herself in hand, although it was difficult. 'And tomorrow, dear, we will go to another doctor, the best specialist I can find in London. We will go on our way back from the registry office.'

'The registry office? You meant it about the licence?'

'Of course I meant it. I have even asked Mother to our wedding in the note I have left for her. And we must cable to Claude.'

'Yes, old Claude will be pleased. About the last thing he said to me in his quiet way was that he would not mind leaving me if it were in Miss Winfield's charge. Why did you not write to me all these days, Ursula?'

'I suppose I was like you – I did not know what to say. It seemed mean to write and not mention the bombshell I was preparing!' He did not speak, and she went on. 'You are not still thinking sillinesses about my being sacrificed? You can't think them now that you are going to get well?' For the first time there was a shade of anxiety in her voice. 'Tony, you don't mind marrying me?'

'I can put up with it.' This time Tony's laugh was more steady. He turned slightly and put his arms around Ursula as she knelt beside him. He kissed her lips. There was another long silence.

It was Ursula who broke it. 'In a few days, when you are quite rested after all this, we will go into the country, won't we? Oh, Tony, we shall have the whole lovely summer before us. And I feel so certain that I can make you well again, quite well and strong. I shall teach you to stand, little by little, and to walk. It will be like having a husband and child in one.'

'But it will not always be in one, darling, I hope,' Tony interrupted softly.

Perhaps Ursula did not understand the full significance of his words, or perhaps she only pretended not to do so. 'Of course not, Tony,' she said gaily. 'By the end of the summer you will not be a child at all. Why, I expect you will be as strong as I am – stronger. Probably you will be scolding me for jumping stone walls without your help.'

'And certainly you will be continuing to jump them in spite of my scolding.'

He was not referring to the actual stone wall incident, Ursula realised, but to their suffrage estrangement. It turned her thoughts into another direction. 'Dearest, I had to fight in the woman's Cause. It seemed a sort of – Call, and I nearly died for it. And you had to fight in the war, that was a Call, too, and you nearly died for it. And now, I suppose, we are called to each other, not to die, but to live. Is it not wonderful, after all we have gone through? Yes, after it all we have got each other. At last we have got each other. We have got each other at last and forever.'

If you have enjoyed this Persephone book why not telephone or write to us for a free copy of the Persephone Catalogue and the current Persephone Biannually? All Persephone books ordered from us cost £13 or three for £33 plus £2.50 postage per book.

PERSEPHONE BOOKS LTD
59 Lamb's Conduit Street
London WC1N 3NB

Telephone: 020 7242 9292
sales@persephonebooks.co.uk
www.persephonebooks.co.uk